Rise of the Gorgon
Myths of Stone
Book II

Galen Surlak-Ramsey

TinyFox
PRESS

A Tiny Fox Press Book

© 2019 Galen Surlak-Ramsey

All rights reserved. No part of this book may be reproduced, stored in a retrieval system, or transmitted in any form or by any means, electronic, mechanical, photocopying, recording, or otherwise, without the prior written permission of the publisher, except as provided by U.S.A. copyright law. For information address: Tiny Fox Press, North Port, FL.

This is a work of fiction: Names, places, characters, and events are a product of the author's imagination or used fictitiously. Any resemblance to actual persons, living or dead, locales, or events is purely coincidental.

Cover art by Eddy Shinjuku

Library of Congress Catalog Card Number: 2019943548

Print ISBN: 978-1-946501-16-5

Tiny Fox Press and the book fox logo are all registered trademarks of Tiny Fox Press LLC

Tiny Fox Press LLC
North Port, FL

For Granny, whose power dwarfs even the gods'

Chapter Monster Hunt

Euryale had never been a fan of violence, despite being a gorgon. Never mind the propaganda about her and her sisters, Medusa especially. Sure, a few people here and there had been turned to stone over the centuries. Maybe a few others had been shot with arrows or stabbed with spears, but to be fair, they had all deserved it.

Thus when Euryale was presented with an opportunity to avenge her sister's murder, she happily seized the moment.

The gorgon raced through the forest on a pair of supple legs. Her golden eyes darkened, and her claws lengthened as she closed the distance between herself and Perseus. The man, so intent on tracking the chimera which had eluded the heroes of Elysium for the past two weeks, never saw her coming. She kept a grip on her bow with her left hand and used her right to grab him by his curly hair and ram his head into a nearby tree. His bearded face made a satisfying crunch as it hit nose first, and for a split second, wood and skull had a competition to see who was the strongest.

The wood won.

Perseus moaned incoherently as he slumped to the ground and drifted out of consciousness.

"I should cut your head off for Medusa's sake," Euryale spat. Long-dormant fires of revenge lit in her soul, and the vipers that slithered around her head hissed with anger.

The gorgon had to spend a few seconds steadying herself to keep from morphing into her monstrous serpentine form. As she stared at the fallen hero, she wondered how long it would take the others to notice his disappearance if she threw his body into a pit and had her way with him over the next few centuries. As much as she wanted to, she knew she couldn't, and that furthered her frustrations and rage. "You're lucky Athena likes you," she growled.

"Euryale! Where did you go?"

The sound of Alex, her husband, calling out to her extinguished her flames of hate, and by the time he cleared the brush and stumbled onto her handiwork, she had reverted to the sweet, loving woman he'd fallen in love with almost a year ago.

"Please tell me you didn't do what I think you did," Alex said, coming to a stop and driving his spear into the forest floor with his muscular arm.

"Do you think I came running over here moments ago when I heard him trip and fall?" she asked as she strolled over and draped her arms around his neck.

"That's what you're going with?"

"Depends," she said before leaning in close and kissing him softly on the lips. "I can't possibly imagine what else would have happened."

Alex tilted his head so he looked over her shoulder. "That had to be one hell of a trip."

"He was probably running too fast," she replied, placing a hand on his cheek and redirecting his face toward her.

Alex looked at his wife, and then at Perseus, and then back to her again. He played with his beard for a few seconds before glancing left and right. "It's a good thing we aren't hunting while it's dark," he finally said. "There's no telling what pit he might have fallen in since he's so careless."

"Exactly. On that note, maybe we should suggest one at night?" she said.

"Now I think you're pushing it."

"Am I?" she asked, raising an eyebrow.

Alex chuckled. "Next thing you know, you'll have all the other heroes getting lost in a labyrinth, pitted against one another."

Euryale furrowed her brow, and her green skin hardened as the faint outline of scales appeared. "You mean as Aphrodite did to us?"

"Well, yeah," Alex stammered, immediately regretting the comparison. "Bad example, I know."

Euryale's voice darkened. "Don't ever liken me to that vile goddess."

"That wasn't my intention, honest," he said, wrapping his arms around the small of her back and drawing her close. "I didn't mean for this to be such a big ordeal. Can we get back to the hunt? I want to bag this one before the others do. I haven't made a kill in, well, ever. I think the guys are feeling like I'm not earning my keep."

"You, not earn your keep?" Euryale said with a light laugh. "I don't remember any of them fighting Ares on their own. If anyone has nothing left to prove, my love, it's you."

"Thanks," Alex said.

Euryale ran her fingers through his hair and then trailed her fingertips across his cheek and down his bare chest. The act further helped to center her on what was important. "Maybe tonight you could show me what sort of hero you really are."

"When are the kids coming back?" Alex asked, grinning like a teenager who had just been told his parents were going to leave for the weekend.

"Not till tomorrow," she answered. "Dad wants to build sandcastles with them one more time."

The wind changed, and with it, Euryale picked up a new scent. Her vipers tasted the air as she tried to place what exactly it was. It only took a second. It was the scent of chimera blood, faint but there.

"Come," she said, scooping up her bow. "It's close. And try and stay quiet this time. You're still about as stealthy as a minotaur in a china shop."

Euryale took off running, making less noise than a gentle breeze. She darted around thick scrub and between countless oak trees before working her way up a small rise. Near the top, she crossed a small, babbling stream as she continued to follow the coppery scent for another ten or fifteen minutes. Finally, she slowed at the sounds of heavy breathing and tracked them to the bottom of a large overhang.

Underneath that overhang lay a giant chimera on its side. Dark blood caked the rocks around the creature, and a grievous wound to the ribs looked both painful and crippling. Its large wings were sprawled across the ground, while its lion head panted, resting on a small rock. A second head, this one of a goat, lay twisted to the side with its eyes closed, mouth open, and tongue hanging out. Only the monster's third head, that of a snake that happened to be at the end of the creature's serpentine tail, took note of the gorgon's arrival. When it did, the chimera staggered to his feet like a prize fighter on the verge of a knockout.

The lion bared his teeth, and the goat lowered its head to point its horns at Euryale. Though it took a crouched stance that was an obvious prelude to a pounce, the gorgon could tell the last thing the beast wanted was a fight.

"I'm not here to hurt you," she said, outstretching her right hand and slowly lowering her bow to the ground with the other. "This doesn't have to end like this."

The monster inched backward.

"Easy...easy," she said, her voice as soothing as any divine balm. "We monsters have to stick together. I promise I'm only here to help."

The chimera lowered its guard and let out a soft grunt.

Euryale stepped forward cautiously, and when the beast didn't run or strike, she relaxed and smiled.

The chimera jerked its heads to the side and growled at the sounds of approaching heroes arguing and laughing with each other about whose turn it was to kill what and where.

"No! Please!" Euryale begged.

A heartbeat later, the chimera attacked.

Chapter Petty Heroes

"This is getting ridiculous," Perseus said with a scowl on his bloodied and bruised face. He wore the usual attire for heroes on the island this time of year, nakedness, and he wore it well. Thousands of years of constant exercise had shaped his body into a sight that would make any man or woman swoon. His skin had bronzed to perfection, and even though his cheek was cut and his right eye swollen shut, he lost none of his rugged handsomeness. "This is the seventh one we've lost."

"What do you propose we do?" asked Heracles. The hero's hero stood a pace to Perseus's side and was everything Perseus was twice again. He had biceps that were the size of a small country and whose chief export was pain. His abs looked like they could double as emergency stops for runaway rocket engines, and his legs probably had to deadlift Jupiter just to get warmed up. The only thing the man didn't have twice as much as Perseus did was hate. Instead of the anger and frustration so plainly showing on Perseus's face, Heracles had eyes that smiled and a grin ten times as bright.

"What we do is, we lay some ground rules. She can't keep stealing kills like this."

Heracles chuckled and looked to Euryale who was casually leaning on a stone chimera. "Would you like to weigh in?"

"It's not my fault the rest of you are so slow," Euryale said with a shrug. "I think the lack of true challenge has made you soft."

"If you're offering to be that challenge, then count me in," Perseus replied, narrowing his dark eyes at the gorgon. "I'll take your head the same as I took your sister's."

"While I'm sleeping?" Euryale growled. "Truly a courageous act to brag about. Or will you come back and lie as you did before? Perhaps tell a story where we fought to the death, and it was only by your sheer strength and cunning that you bested me?"

Heracles stepped between the warring pair and clamped a giant-crushing hand on Perseus's meaty shoulder. "Enough," he said. "She's wed to one of our own and has the favor of more than one Olympian. Such infighting will only bring us trouble."

"And who am I?" Perseus asked with a snort of disbelief. He shook his head and shrugged Heracles off before wiping the dirt from his brow. "Tell me, hero's hero, do I not carry Athena's favor as well? Do I not carry it more than she?"

"You do."

"Then stop protecting her," Perseus said. "And why are you when her husband does not?"

"Because she doesn't need me to," Alex said, breaking free of the tree line and coming to his wife's side. He panted a few times to catch his breath before continuing. "Sorry, I'm late. What did I miss?"

"That," Perseus said, pointing to the petrified chimera. "I'm getting sick of your wife's gaze. She's ruining the sport. I say if she's not going to hunt with bow, spear, or sword, she doesn't get to come. It's only fair."

"You wouldn't know the first thing about fairness," Euryale said. "You think you're so grand running around here, slaughtering creatures for the fun of it, as if that makes you somehow a better person. Tell me, who are you saving? What towns do you keep from ruin or what widows and orphans are not made thanks to your hand?"

"That's a fine lecture coming from someone who petrified a monster moments ago," Perseus said. "Again."

"I spared it from torment, nothing more," she said.

"You know, if I didn't know better, I'd say you're protecting them," Perseus said. "Once a monster, always a monster, right? That's the reason your sister had to die. We couldn't risk her leaving that island of yours or hope she'd ever be worth saving."

Euryale glanced out of the corner of her eyes to where her bow lay—her sister's bow. She wondered if she was fast enough to scoop it up and get off a shot before any of them could react. How fitting would it be if she drove an arrow through his heart with her sister's weapon? Not that it would kill the hero. No, he, like everyone else, enjoyed immortality here in Elysium, but it would feel damn good to make him suffer.

Alex took Euryale by the hand and intertwined his fingers with hers. "I think we're getting too heated here," he said. "We'll sit the next one out till we can figure out what to do. How's that?"

"No, Alex. We won't."

"Listen to your husband, gorgon. It's for your own good," Perseus said. "He might be one of us, but you are not, and you never will be. I don't care how much of a god your father is."

"I don't need him to fight you," she replied.

Perseus smirked. "If you want a war, you can have one, gorgon."

Before Euryale could offer a retort, it was Alex's turn to jump in the middle. He put himself between his bride and her attacker with his sword up and ready. "Ares said the same thing to me," he said. "We both know how that turned out."

Perseus didn't back down. His brow dropped, and he shook his head. "You disappoint me, Alex," he said. "I'll bite my tongue for your sake until you give me a reason not to, but I will say this: you would be wise to rein in your wife. Her favor with the Olympians is threadbare at best, and yours is only two strands better. If the two of you strike at me, you'll quickly see who the gods support on this island."

With that, he waved to Heracles to follow, and the two disappeared into the forest.

Several tense moments passed in silence before Euryale spoke. "Thank you," she said softly. "For coming to my defense."

"Part of my job," Alex said. He then laughed. "But it's not like you need it. I've fought you when you're angry. You've got the strength of a titan and enough venom in those snakes to drop a thousand legions of elephants. They wouldn't stand a chance."

"I know," she said, her voice going soft and trailing. "I wish…I wish it weren't like this."

"Like what?"

"This," she said, sweeping the area with her hand. "I hate being around them. I hate seeing what they do to 'monsters.' I hate how they'll never treat me as an equal, or worse, our children. Do you honestly think they will ever look at them as anything but hideous creations fit only to hunt for fun?"

Alex dropped his gaze. "I hadn't thought about that, but would they really? Surely they know we'd both defend them to the ends of the earth, and that's not even counting what The Old Man would do if he lost his newest grandkids. I dare say he'd unleash the leviathan so it could feast on their bodies for a thousand years."

The tiniest of grins formed on the gorgon's otherwise downcast face. "That would only be the start. But still, Alex, even if they didn't openly attack them, do you want our children to grow up in such an awful place?"

"Where would they grow up? The real world?"

"I don't know," Euryale said, clearing her eyes after a couple of sniffs. "I don't like that place either. The people there are so cruel."

"Well, that cuts down on our options," Alex said. "I don't think there are any vacancies in Olympus."

"No," she said with a laugh. "Not for us at least."

"For what it's worth, no neighborhood is perfect, and this has to be better than living in exile."

"It is," she said. "And I'm grateful for that. I couldn't handle having to live alone again."

Alex took a few steps toward his bride and embraced her. She snuggled into his chest and spent the next few moments listening to his heartbeat. She would've fallen asleep had he not tapped her on the shoulder and said, "Can I ask you something?"

"Of course," she replied, looking up. "What's wrong?"

"Nothing's wrong, per se," he said. "But when are you going to stop the charade?"

The corners of her mouth drew back as she glanced at the stone chimera. "Never?"

"Isn't Hades going to want his gloves back?"

"No," she said. "He said I could keep them for as long as I want."

"And what are you going to do when one of them catches you shaping stone into supposed victims of yours?"

"Alex," she said, kissing him lightly before holding up a pair of leather gloves she had tucked in her belt behind her back. "These gloves work a moment slower than the speed of thought. They will never, ever, ever, catch me making copies of the monsters I've saved."

"Until they catch you smuggling one out," he said.

"You worry too much."

"And you don't worry enough," he said. "Perseus obviously has it out for you. But the rest of the guys, Heracles, Achilles, Odysseus, I think they're trying to give you the benefit of the doubt."

"You give them too much credit," she said. "I hear their whispers and see the looks they give me when you're not around.

All of them would rather me not be here. Perseus only happens to be the most vocal."

"All the more reason you need to be careful. Maybe saving every monster on the island isn't the best way to live around here."

Euryale pulled back, but she kept a hold of both of his hands in the process. "Do you think I'm doing the right thing? Be honest."

"I think you're saving creatures that want to kill people," he said. "Sending them off to our old home on that remote island doesn't change what they are."

Euryale nodded and tried to hide the hurt in her eyes. "Thank you for not lying."

"Look, I know this means a lot to you, but have you ever thought that you're not doing it for them, but for you? I mean, I think you're projecting yourself onto what's going on."

"No, Alex. I'm not," she said, shaking her head, but as the words left her mouth, she had reservations about their sincerity. Maybe he was right. Maybe she was trying to save them because she needed to save herself still. Deep down, she knew she was a raging monster who would eventually break free of its cage and destroy anything and everything in her way, and that scared the hell out of her.

"Are you okay?" Alex asked.

"No, stupid," she said with a pained laugh. "I'm definitely not okay, but you always make it better."

"Well, I'm glad to hear that, at least. Not that I want you to be not okay, but, you know what I mean."

"Yes, Alex. I know what you mean." Euryale smiled and sighed. She loved how clumsy he got when trying to soothe her pains, but she also knew she couldn't wallow in pity all day, either. She had a lot to do before the day was up, and there was one incredibly pressing matter that she needed to attend to, a pressing matter that in one sense was far more important than saving monsters. "Did you get the eclairs? I promised Hephaestus we'd have some for him."

"I did."

"They're his favorite, you know."

"I know."

"And you got the custard-filled ones, right?" Euryale asked with a nervous tone. "After all he did for us last year, I want to make sure we get his dessert perfect."

Alex smiled. "There's a dozen custard ones in the fridge as we speak. Well, eleven. One didn't make it."

"How's that?"

"Casualty of transport," he said, grinning and patting his tummy.

"Make sure that's the only one," she said with a sigh. "What about all the invitations? Did you get those out?"

"Yeah, of course, I did," he said. "Hermes picked them up this morning. He said he'd make deliveries first thing tomorrow, just as you asked."

"He got all of them?"

"Yes, he got all of them. You think I'd only hand him half?"

"No," she said, shaking her head. "But it's incredibly important that everyone gets one. Our first anniversary is coming up, and if we leave anyone out, things could get ugly fast."

"How ugly?"

"Ugly enough to turn me to stone."

Alex chuckled and began to lead his bride back to their home. "Relax, sweetie. I promise I filled them all out, checked the list three times, and personally gave them all to Hermes himself. The only way someone's not getting invited is if he gets caught in traffic, which I'm pretty sure has never happened in the entire history of the universe."

"Okay." Euryale blew out a puff of air before wrapping her arm around his. "There's one last thing you can do for me, then."

"Anything."

"When we get home, I still want to see you be the hero," she said with a seductive grin.

CHAPTER HOOK UPS

That email/password combination is not recognized.

Zeus furrowed his brow as he stared at his phone. It was no ordinary phone, but an Olympi-phone, one of a few dozen artifacts that had been made and distributed by Hermes (in an effort to modernize his place in Olympus as the Messenger of the Gods). It could do everything a mortal smartphone could do and more, and even better, it wasn't tied to silly things like reception or clear Wi-Fi signals.

But to use online apps, however, it still needed the correct user-password to be entered, especially after logging out of everything and clearing all browsing history (thank a nosy wife for that one).

With a huff, Zeus tried logging in again.

That email/password combination is not recognized.

Zeus grunted and tried a third time. On this attempt, he carefully pressed the keys on the tiny screen, being sure that his oversized fingers weren't inadvertently hitting the wrong ones.

That email/password combination is not recognized. This account has been locked.

"Sons of Cerberus," Zeus growled. Arcs of lightning shot from his fingertips and singed the leather chair he was in. Though he was seated in the lobby of a grand hotel, he was tucked in a corner, and no one noticed. Or if they did, they didn't say anything out of the need for self-preservation.

Zeus muttered some curses and hit the reset password button on the screen. A few seconds later, he opened his email, clicked the recovery link and went to work restoring his access to his Divineder account—a dating app owned by Aphrodite, Goddess of Love, that let mortals find their perfect match. It was, of course, a direct rip-off of everything else out there, but none of the others could claim they had the endorsement of an actual goddess. Correction: it was a direct rip-off of everything else that used to be out there. Aphrodite had cornered the market three months ago thanks to skillful negotiations on her part, which may or may not have included a curse or two. Or twenty.

"There we go," Zeus said as it accepted his email. He drummed his fingers as he tried to think about what he wanted his new password to be. It had to be one easily remembered, but not one that Hera, his wife, would guess. She'd been snooping around more so than usual lately. When it came to him, he grinned and punched it in.

Password must have at least 8 characters.

Zeus added an extra 's' at the end.

Password must contain at least one number, one lowercase letter, and one uppercase letter.

Zeus growled as he remembered why he hated signing up for this thing in the first place. The women he'd ravish, he quickly reminded himself, made it worth it. He tried again.

New password cannot be the same as your previous password.

"By the everlasting Fates!" he roared as he sent a bolt of lightning streaking through the air. It hit the far wall, blasting out a decent chunk of brick. Unlike before, this time everyone noticed. However, as before, no one said anything since every onlooker valued staying alive over touring the afterlife.

With his brow furrowed, Zeus grumbled to himself and tried one last time. Thankfully, for both his sanity and the structural integrity of the hotel, it worked.

"Finally," he said, standing up. He walked across the lobby to the elevators and checked his messages. He had twelve, but only one interested him, the one from the woman he'd swiped right last night. They'd hit it off right away, and after concocting the perfect plan to ditch breakfast with Hera, he'd agreed to meet her for a seven-day romp.

Zeus opened the message, and his eyes lit up:

Room 2452. Door is unlocked. Let yourself in.
Xoxoxoxo

With renewed vigor, he pushed the button for the twenty-fourth floor. The elevator sped upward, but not nearly as fast as he wanted. Couldn't it go any faster? He shouldn't have to suffer any delays. He was a god, damn it, and not simply any god at that. He was the King of Olympus, the ruler of the world, the only being to defeat not only Typhon, Father of Monsters, but Cronus as well, a titan who could control time like Zeus could control lightning.

The elevator came to a rest. Once the doors started to part, Zeus gave them a mighty shove out of impatience that not only pushed them open but also mangled metal and machinery in the process.

Zeus hurried down the corridor, took the bend, and found the room near the end of the hall. He felt his heart quicken as he tried the handle. It turned, and butterflies of excitement fluttered in his stomach. As he slipped in the room, he heard the sounds of a shower running in the back.

"Exactly what I need," Zeus said to himself as he shed his robe before briefly checking out his chiseled physique in a nearby mirror. "Mighty as always."

Zeus took two steps into the suite's main room and froze. His stomach tightened. His genitals withdrew.

Sitting on the couch with her legs crossed and toying with an Olympi-phone was his wife, Hera.

Chapter Bye Bye, Divineder

Aphrodite, Goddess of Love, leaned back in her cozy pink office chair and kicked her feet on top of her mahogany desk. With an air of accomplishment about her, she raised a glass of red wine and gave a silent toast to her computer screen. Today marked exactly a hundred days since Divineder, the dating app she'd created all on her own, had blasted onto the market, and by every measure, it was a wild success.

No, it wasn't merely a wild success. It was her baby, her love, her everything that she'd poured herself into, and now that it was out there, she relished the praise it received time and again for how easily people could find their perfect match, unlike those other dating apps that had once been.

There was, however, one thing that was missing from the celebration, one thing that made her feel incomplete. She knew exactly what that was, or rather who. Thus, she sighed heavily and picked up her Olympi-phone, dreading the call that she was about to make.

Aphrodite's fingers hesitated. Should she call Ares? Could she? What if he didn't answer? What if he flat out turned her down? She wasn't sure she could handle hearing those words. They hadn't spoken for nearly a year, not since she'd stormed out of the Great Hall when the God of War had abstained from a vote that ultimately saw Alex become a hero and Athena win a love contest between her and Aphrodite.

Surely he'd gotten over her being mad at him, right? After all, they'd fought plenty of times before and made up.

Aphrodite bit her lower lip, put the phone down and stared at it. Then she picked it up. Then she put it down. She stuffed it into her robes and then took it out. She repeated this loop of indecision so many times that even a housecat wanting to be both in and outside would've become frustrated.

"This is so stupid," she finally said, huffing. Before she could think herself out of it, Aphrodite sent a quick text.

Come over?

Aphrodite bit on a knuckle before plopping her phone on the desk, face down. He couldn't reject her if she didn't see. Seconds ticked by. Nothing.

She checked the time, which was a convenient excuse to make sure the text was sent. It was seven o'clock, and indeed, the text had gone out less than a minute ago. With no reply, she finished her glass of wine to pass the time.

Then she had another.

Then she had another.

Then she had another.

(And another and another and another.)

Now she was drunk, and it was only five after seven.

If there was a saving grace to this embarrassment (aside from being tipsy in the morning), it was that Aphrodite had a feeling this would make excellent standup material, if only she were witty enough to go on stage and talk about everything ranging from phone calls to the gods to public bathrooms to cats in heat.

But alas, she wasn't.

Her shoulders fell. She was about to pick up her phone and text again when Ares warily entered the room. Though he was now here, and despite the history that existed between them, one filled with passion that put all other couples to shame, he looked at her with so much indifference she wondered when his heart had completely frozen.

"You texted?" he asked.

"I did, and you came," she said, jumping out of her chair in an ungainly manner. Her wine glass went one direction, and her phone flew in another. Trying to save both, she ended up nearly toppling over her seat and saving neither.

"Is something the matter?" asked Ares as he rushed to his former lover's side and kept her steady by placing his hands on her elbows.

Aphrodite looked into his big brown eyes and sighed. She ran a hand up his cheek and went to kiss him, but he pulled away. "What?" she asked.

"You know what," he said, backing away. "I'm not a dog you can kick over and over and expect to come running back whenever you want."

Aphrodite's gut tightened. That wasn't what she wanted to hear, but it wasn't the worst she feared he'd say. "I know," she said softly.

"Do you?"

"Yes, and I'm sorry."

Ares straightened. "Did you—"

Aphrodite laughed, which was good, because between her intoxication and a year's worth of regret on how she treated him, she was about to work herself into an ugly cry. "Yes, I said I'm sorry," she said. "I was in a bad place then. I've…I've worked a lot on that, and I miss you."

Ares' mouth hung open for a moment, but then his eyes found the empty wine bottle—from Dionysus' special reserves—and he shook his head with a sigh. "You're drunk."

"I am," she said, nearly tipping over as she made her approach. "But it's not the wine talking. It's my heart."

"Or your loneliness," he said, pointing to the bottle.

Aphrodite playfully scoffed at him. "No, silly. The wine was a celebration, a celebration I wanted you here for."

"Finally getting divorced?"

Aphrodite frowned. "If only. You'd be the first to know, my love. I swear."

"Then for what?"

Aphrodite directed his attention to her computer screen. "That. My app. My site."

Ares leaned in for a better view. "You made this? I'm impressed. I hear these computers are ornery beasts infested with bugs that can drive any man insane."

Aphrodite smiled. She had wondered if her brute—a term she used affectionately—had bothered catching up to the modern world yet, and apparently he had. More importantly, he understood the pains she'd had to go through to make her app. "I did, and those bugs will drive you mad."

"How did you do all this?"

The goddess pointed across the room to where four giant bookcases stood against the far wall, completely laden with books on programming, database design, and theory on user interfaces.

Ares cracked a half grin. "You? Read?"

"Yes, thank you," she said, taking the tease in stride. She made a quick dive into her desk drawer and pulled out a pair of thin-rimmed glasses. "I have these."

"But your eyes are perfect and beautiful already," he said.

"I know," she said, blushing slightly, a reaction that always occurred no matter how many genuine compliments he paid her. "They make me feel smarter."

For the next couple of hours, Aphrodite showed him her creation, from how to create a user profile to all the little niceties she'd added to the near unending praise she'd received by media outlets. "I'm even being invited to a talk show to speak on it," she boasted at the end. "Isn't that fun?"

Ares nodded. "I don't know what to say."

"Say you'll stay the night."

Ares frowned and his hands curled. She knew that look all too well. It was the look of inner conflict. "I don't want things to be how they once were," he finally said, taking a step back. "I don't like only being with you in the shadows."

"Neither do I," Aphrodite said. "If you can convince Dad to grant me a divorce, I'm all yours."

Ares shook his head. "We both know that will never happen."

"Then stay the night anyway," she said, practically pleading. "Some time together is better than none."

Ares shook his head again, but before he could say a word, Aphrodite's phone rang. She didn't answer, so it went to her voice mail, but then it rang again, and again, and since Ares was using the interruption as a convenient way not to speak on matters between them, she groaned and snatched the phone off the floor. When she saw who was calling, she wished she'd ignored it.

"Hello, Hera," she said, taking the call.

The Queen of Olympus appeared on screen, standing inside her temple and wearing her usual garb of crown and white robes. Zeus could also be seen in the background, but he sat on a chair, eyes downcast as he muttered to himself. "Aphrodite," she said, her words dripping with disdain. "We need to talk."

At this point, although Aphrodite had no idea what this was about, she decided that the last thing she wanted to do was talk with Hera. Still, she knew she had to, or she'd face Hera's wrath. "Is something the matter?"

"Yes, something's the matter," she replied, tone full of venom. "Your 'service' has led my husband astray."

"I don't understand."

"Zeus, your father, my husband, has an account on Divineder," she said, slowly enunciating every syllable. "You, as the sole creator, owner, and operator, are responsible as such."

Aphrodite's eyes widened. "Me?" she said, sticking a finger in her chest. "This isn't my fault."

"I don't see how it isn't."

"I didn't even know he had an account."

"And that's my responsibility?"

"No, but what was I supposed to do?"

"You were supposed to keep my husband from having an affair," Hera said. "You are the Goddess of Love, are you not? It's time you started acting like it."

"You have to be kidding," Aphrodite said, throwing up her hands. "Even if I did know he had an account, I can't control him. You know that."

Hera's eyes narrowed. "This isn't up for discussion. Perhaps if you ever bothered to think a tenth as much as you lust, you'd have realized you were never capable of adequately making and overseeing such a business."

"But—"

"Was I done talking?" Hera bellowed. "By all means, your Most High, don't let me keep you from opening that whorish mouth of yours."

Aphrodite shrank. She tried to keep a flat affect, but she could feel her eyes glistening under the onslaught, not so much for what had been said, but for what soon would. Hera's vindictive nature, everyone knew, never stopped at mere words.

"Now then," Hera went on as she took off her crown and began buffing it with a cloth. "Until I'm convinced he'll never be able to use it again, I'm turning full control of your little pet project over to Athena. Under her tutelage, maybe you'll glean a little bit of wisdom when it comes to the best way of running things."

Aphrodite's heart skipped. "No!" she said, clutching the phone. "You can't do that to me!"

"I can't?" Hera said, face marred with shock and outrage. "Do you want to see what I can and can't do?"

"She'll tear the whole thing down just to spite me," Aphrodite said, her voice cracking and her eyes watering. "And if she doesn't, she'll turn it against me, lord it over my head for all eternity."

"Perhaps you should have thought of that before you neglected your duties," Hera replied.

Before Aphrodite could say another word, Hera ended the call. The Goddess of Love, trembling, slumped to the floor. "It's not fair," she said weakly. "I poured my soul into that for a year, tortured myself writing and rewriting everything so it would be perfect and something everyone would love. And now she's taking it all away. She didn't even listen. She never listens."

Ares knelt at her side and wrapped his huge arms around her shoulders and squeezed. She sank into the embrace and cried until she covered his skin in a salty mix of tears and snot. "I'm sorry," she said, wiping her face.

"Don't be." His voice was rough and angered.

Aphrodite looked up and saw he had his phone in hand. "What are you doing?"

"Fixing things," he said as he dialed.

"She won't listen to you," Aphrodite said.

"I know. I'm not calling her."

"Then who?"

Ares held up a finger right as his call was answered. She couldn't hear what was being said on the other end as he stood and walked off a little. "Athena. Yes, it's me," he said. Annoyance crossed his face. "No, I don't want to play your silly mind games. I don't care if I can play white. What I want is something else."

There was a pause on his end as Athena prattled on about something. Finally, Ares simply cut into whatever spiel she was giving him. "I want you to leave Aphrodite's dating site alone."

Another pause.

Aphrodite tensed, then her heart sank even lower when she heard Athena burst out in laughter.

"This is not amusing," Ares growled into the phone. "I will make your life miserable for the next thousand years if you don't stay out of this." The God of War straightened as if he'd suddenly been slapped. "You think you can say that to me? No, I will not hush, and no, we're not having an affair again...I don't care what you think! I swear, Athena, if you don't bow out of this fight, I'll make sure you regret it."

The line went dead. Or at least, Aphrodite assumed it did because Ares launched his phone at the wall with such speed it nearly broke the sound barrier. Thankfully, Hermes had made them incredibly tough, so when it hit stone, the granite cracked and not the phone.

"She said no?"

Ares snorted like a bull. "Don't fret, my love, before I'm done, she'll change her mind."

Aphrodite's eyes lit up. "Love?"

"I...it..." Ares stammered. He spent a few extra seconds trying to come up with some words, but they all seemed to get tangled in his mouth before making it out. Finally, he threw up his hands. "Bah. You know I can't stay mad at you," he said, scooping her up. He kissed her hard on the lips, and when they finally broke, they each smiled brightly. "See you tonight?"

Aphrodite kissed him again. "I'll wear something special."

"Good. I have one thing to attend to first, but after that, I will make Athena pay."

With that, Ares bounded out the door with the glint of war in his eye.

Chapter The NFL

Athena, Goddess of Wisdom (and stuff), walked out of her private bathhouse feeling ten thousand years younger. Around her body she wore an elegant, white bathrobe with a fluffy shawl collar and extra-deep pockets. She'd procured the bathrobe during her last trip out among the mortals where she had run into a young businessman who had been praying for wisdom when it came to balancing his newly formed company with the needs of his newly formed marriage.

The man, Jonathan was his name, had been exceedingly polite and gracious when they had met, something that Athena appreciated to no end. Furthermore, when he had realized who he was talking to, Jonathan insisted that she take the last robe he had in stock as an offering for taking up her valuable time, regardless of the fact that he would not be able to manufacture more for some time due to a lack of finances and unforeseen issues at the textile factory. Though she had taken the robe out of amusement, never once thinking it would ever live up to his claims about how soft and comfortable it was, now that she had it on she had to admit she would be hard-pressed to find one better. As such, she decided that after she finished reading her latest book, *Jessica, The Monster Slayer*, she would drop by Jonathan's home and bless him with a stock tip or two.

That thought, however, vanished faster than Aphrodite's faithfulness to her husband, Hephaestus, when Athena crossed her inner courtyard and entered her library to find out that her home had been burgled. Whoever the thief was, he'd left her golden chalices, her tomes and scrolls of ancient, priceless literature and teachings across the ages, and had even ignored her helm and spear—both of which had been imbued with considerable power. The only thing missing from the room was her aegis.

True, the highly polished, round shield was technically her father Zeus's, but for all practical purposes it was hers, and she lent it to him when he wanted it, not vice versa. Furthermore, the fact that Zeus had at least partial claim to the shield narrowed down the list of suspects considerably. As Athena stood in her library, arms crossed over her chest, brow furrowed and jaw set, she knew she was looking for somebody who had a grudge to settle with her and who was either incredibly brave or incredibly stupid. Probably both. Only one god fit that description.

"By the Fates, Ares," she said to herself while shaking her head. "Do you ever get tired of starting wars you can't win?"

"Sweets?"

"Yes?" Euryale said, turning to face her husband who stood nearby, looking both worried and amused.

"I don't think that's going to work very well."

Euryale looked back at what she was doing and frowned in confusion. The chimera she'd saved—now happy and healthy—sat on his haunches, staring at her, and didn't seem to care in the least about the harness she was holding. "Why? It should fit. And I promise the leash is long enough."

"Yeah, but that's not a dog," Alex said.

"I never said it was."

Alex chuckled. "He looks more like a big cat. He's a big, mutated cat, what with the wings and all, but still a cat. In my experience, cats don't like being put on a leash."

"Do you have a better idea on how to get him out of here?"

Alex leaned against the cavern wall. "No. But you could always let him be. No one's found him here yet."

"They will eventually," Euryale said. "You're overthinking this. It'll be fine."

It was not fine.

The moment Euryale slipped the harness around the chimera and snapped the leash in place, the monster went berserk. He roared and jumped back, wiggled and squirmed in a blurry, spastic display. Euryale tried to hold on to the leash, and she did for a few seconds. But when the chimera jerked hard one last time, the leash flew from her grasp. Immediately, the creature bolted past her, frantically snapping his head from side to side, yowling and jumping around.

"Don't let him get outside!" Euryale shouted as she scrambled after him.

"I got him!" Alex said. He made a diving tackle for the escaping monster and was quickly reminded why he'd become a pianist in life and not an NFL player. Though he struck the chimera with his shoulder, the beast weighed five times as much as he did, if not ten, and easily overpowered him.

Euryale leaped over her husband and gave chase. By the time she got to the mouth of the cave, the chimera was gone. "Great," she said after muttering to herself. "There's no telling where he'll run off to."

"All the more reason for us to go home and finish getting ready for the party," Alex said as he joined his wife at her side.

Euryale's shoulders fell. She knew he was right, but then she heard a horn blow off in the distance—a horn that signaled the start of a new hunt. "Damn it," Euryale said. "What are they going after now?"

Alex shrugged. "I have no idea. The guys never mentioned getting together. In fact, Heracles and Odysseus went freediving today."

The horn blasted again, and Euryale cocked her head. "That's Perseus's horn. He must be out on his own."

"Probably looking to get something before you ruin it again."

Euryale growled and set her jaw. "Well, he's not getting anything if I have a say about it."

"You're going after the chimera, aren't you?"

Euryale leaned over and pecked him on the cheek. "Yes. I'll get him off this island and be home before you know it."

As she trotted off, she caught Alex giving a not-so-quiet quip. "Famous last words."

"Hush," she said, sticking out her tongue. "You'll see."

"You're right about that," Alex said with a grin. "We'll definitely see."

"Ares, buddy, my man. How about a drink? Ambrosia, right?"

The God of War opened his eyes and shifted in his cramped seat inside the stretch limo. Due to his sheer size, the tiny act caused the vehicle to rock back and forth and made the man across from him laugh nervously. "What is that?" the god asked, eyeing the tall, chilled glass being offered to him.

"Ambrosia," said Derek McIntosh, exclusive sports agent of the Olympians. Well, to be honest, that self-appointed title was still a work in progress. But in the last half hour, it had been made especially clear to Ares that making such a title a reality was of prime importance to the man. What exactly that entailed, Ares had no idea, but he was promised fame, glory, and combat with giants and titans unlike any other, which is precisely why Ares tolerated the skinny mortal and his shifty blue eyes that seemed always to be looking for something they shouldn't.

"Ambrosia?" Ares repeated skeptically as he took the glass. He gave the concoction a whiff before tasting it. It was sweet with hints of alcohol, but by no stretch of the imagination was it anything close to ambrosia. As such, the god snorted and flung the drink toward the driver. It bounced off of the dividing window before splashing all over the leather seats and Derek's department-store black suit and Rockport boat shoes.

"Hey!" Derek exclaimed as he did a little bunny hop away from the spill. "That was practically top-shelf rum! And it took me forever to find some decent grenadine!"

"You promised me ambrosia," Ares said, leaning forward. He raised a massive hand and stuck a finger in Derek's face. "I do not like it when mortals make promises they are unable to uphold."

Derek laughed nervously, and a little bit of color drained from his freckled face. "Okay, okay," he said with his hands up. "I get it. You want the top shelf. No worries, my man. When we get you signed, we're going to have so much stinking money, you can buy and throw as much ambrosia as you want."

"I want to know when we're getting to the fields of glory," Ares said as he settled back into his seat.

"Soon. I promise."

"You said that an hour ago."

"Traffic. Can't be helped."

"I bet if I threw some cars down the highway, that would speed things up."

"Probably," Derek replied with a grimace. "However, that might complicate things a tad, so let's save that plan for last."

Despite the exchange, Ares didn't mind the delay. He was using the extra time to develop his strategy he'd employ against Athena. No doubt, things would be heating up shortly, and he wanted to be prepared. Normally, he'd have done this at home or while boxing polar bears for fun, but as this was an appointment that had been made prior, one that interested him greatly, he figured he could flex his tactical might on the road as well as anywhere else.

Right as he was perfecting a strategy to see Athena tarred and feathered, Derek reached over and held down a switch, lowering the window that divided their section of the limo from the driver's.

"Mark," said Derek. "How much longer?"

"About ten seconds, sir," the man replied in a distinct old English accent.

"Outstanding!" Derek exclaimed with renewed enthusiasm. "See, Ares? I told you we'd get there soon. Mark, go ahead and pull us up right to the front. No need to park."

"Very good, sir."

Ares crossed his arms over his chest and waited patiently for the limo to slow and eventually stop. Though the windows were up, he could hear the faint sounds of men clad in armor hitting each other along with the yells and screams of glorious combat.

Simply hearing that little bit making its way into his ears brought a smile to Ares' face. For the last several months, he'd been looking for a new war to join, one where combatants still fought honorably and didn't hide behind their rifles and tanks and planes. He'd grown weary of running around third-world countries, smashing their armies to pieces. And the bigger nations were cowards, much to his dismay, and never joined the fun. None of them wanted to fight with one another, which he found incredibly strange and disheartening, especially since they had missiles that could wipe out entire islands and continents. Why any being, mortal or deity alike, wouldn't want to throw those around to pass the time was beyond him.

That's where Derek came in. The man had contacted Ares a few weeks ago, promising him a place where he could test his battle prowess in hand-to-hand combat while at the same time being adored across the globe for his efforts. Derek was light on the details, or at least the details didn't make sense to Ares, but Derek assured him that everything would be clear enough once they reached the titans. And if he was going to go to war with Athena again, Ares figured having a team of titans at his command could only be of benefit.

"This way, sir," the driver said once he opened the door and motioned for Ares to get out. The man wore a typical ensemble for his profession—a well-pressed and immaculate dark suit with a crisp, white, long-sleeve shirt, dark-red tie, black gloves, and a matching cap. He looked at the god with brown eyes set in a wrinkled face which held no expression.

Ares pushed out of the vehicle with Derek following right on his heels and surveyed the surroundings. He stood in front of a massive stadium made from concrete with trims of red and blue all across. The word "NISSAN" was splashed across the front in large, bold letters that Ares approved of. It was good that this titan, Nissan, projected himself as a mighty adversary, and Ares felt that this was a promising start.

"Nice, isn't it?" Derek asked.

"Adequate," Ares replied. "I'll be more impressed if these combatants measure up to your claims."

"They will. They will," Derek said. "Come on. Let's go meet them."

Ares followed the man into the stadium. They went through a set of glass doors before winding their way through an interior that held a number of concession stands and shops where one could buy trinkets and offerings to the titan who called this arena home. Ares scoffed at all of it since none seemed to be made of gold or even silver, but there were scores of uniforms that could be purchased as well, so he had to admit that somehow the titan had gathered a large following of mortals. As such, perhaps he would be met with Ares' approval after all.

"Here we are," Derek said as they reached the field.

Ares furrowed his brow as he took it all in. The designated combat area was rectangular with a well-manicured grass field.

Numbers and lines had been painted at regular intervals across it, and Ares surmised they were used to help with ranging, but for what? Javelins and bows, maybe? He wasn't sure. Possibly catapults.

Also on the field were almost two dozen men of considerable bulk. They wore modern, colorful armor that was clearly dedicated to the titan, Nissan, and they were repeatedly smashing into each other at high speed before wrestling one another to the ground. As this went on, other men, clearly brothers in arms, and what looked like a captain of the entire group, either shouted words of encouragement or yelled jeers of condemnation, depending on how the mock combat was going.

This, Ares also approved of. That said, they were still only men. He saw no titan, let alone giants, he'd be pitted against.

"So, what do you think?" Derek asked as they started walking again.

"These men have heart. I will grant you that," he said. "But this does not seem to be what you promised."

One of the men near the sidelines turned and took note of Ares and Derek as they approached. He handed a clipboard to his subordinate as he took off his headphones and put them around his neck. When he reached the God of War, he extended an open hand. Ares shook it, as he'd been taught was customary for this time and part of the world, and squeezed, hard. The man didn't flinch, and Ares gave an internal nod of respect.

"Victor Hammond, offensive coordinator," the man said with a gravelly voice. "Coach couldn't be here and extends his apologies. His daughter is having her appendix out. But he wanted to let you know he's thrilled you're going to be on the team. We'll be absolutely unstoppable."

"Daughters are a precious thing, and I appreciate his fondness of what I can do," Ares said. He then sized the man up. He wore dark-blue athletic pants along with a matching ballcap and a white sweatshirt. Though the clothes were hardly fitted, the god could tell there was strength to the man's frame. Not nearly as much as his, or even equal with the men on the field, but a respectable amount. "I wonder, little mortal, if you've assumed too much. At the moment, I have no intentions of joining anyone."

"I'm sorry, Mr. Ares, is it?" Victor asked as he looked at Derek with no small degree of annoyance. "We were under the impression that this was a sealed deal."

Ares shot Derek his own scowl, and the weaselly man inched back with a nervous chuckle. "I am looking for a place to challenge myself and find untold amounts of glory," Ares said. "But looking at your men, I wonder what challenge I would find on this field. I see no famed heroes among them, nor do I see titans to crush or giants to disembowel."

"Trust me, Ares, these guys are some of the toughest in the world," Victor said. "And the men they will be playing against are the same. You don't get to play pro ball by being a weakling."

"Play?" Ares scoffed. "I'm not looking to play a silly game."

Derek shot his hands up. "Hang on a moment. This isn't a silly game. I promise."

"My sister plays silly games," Ares said. "I do not like them. She promises me bloodied combat and delivers pointless board games where kings are at the mercy of pathetic footmen and heroes are no stronger than feeble priests. I want battles with sword and spear. I want wars where armies struggle for decades, where spears break over shields and swords cleave flesh and bone."

"Holy Jesus," Victor exclaimed, shaking his head. As quick as his exclamation came, however, he recomposed himself just as fast. "Look, we don't do wars like that anymore."

"I've noticed."

"But that's a good thing," Victor added.

"I don't see how."

"Wars in the civilized world are frowned upon," he said. "There's no glory to it anymore."

Ares folded his arms over his chest and nodded. "Yes, I know there is no glory to it anymore, not the way you fight now."

"But the world considers football to be one of the most glorious games—no, combats—ever," he said. "Millions, if not billions watch these highly trained, elite micro-armies struggle against one another to claim a championship each year. Unimaginable sums of money are spent in pursuit of it, and for the victors, well...you can only imagine."

"I can imagine quite a lot."

"Money. Women. Endorsements. You name it. You'll get it. Especially with who you are. There's no doubt in my mind with you on the team, we would pound everyone into the ground."

"I like pounding men into the ground, but you still make bold claims for your offerings."

Victor laughed. "They're not bold claims. If you want, come to my office, and I'll show you how absurd the offerings are we can shower you with."

"And where are the titans and giants we are to fight?" Ares asked. "I am not so easily fooled into believing your men could ever wrestle one, let alone many, to the ground. And if they can't do that, what good are they when it comes to fighting my sister?"

"Giants?" the coach repeated. A spark of understanding then gleamed in his eye. "Ah, yes. There are no giants, per se. Those are team names."

It was at that point in the conversation that a new voice joined in. A refined, female voice that grated on Ares' nerves like no other. It was the voice of his sister, Athena. "Ares, what in Hades' name are you doing here?"

"None of your business," he said, not bothering to turn to face her.

The Goddess of Wisdom came to their side. "You're right," she said. "It's not any of my business, and frankly, I don't care, even if this place is too stupid for even you."

"Then leave," he growled.

"Not until you've given me back my aegis."

"Your aegis?" he asked, turning to face her. His head cocked before his jaw dropped, and shock, mixed with equal amounts of dread, splashed over his face. "You lost father's aegis?"

Athena didn't respond in under a half second, which meant, of course, that she had lost it. To that, Ares cracked a grin. Even if it was a serious matter, he couldn't wait to see Zeus tear her a new one when he found out. The shield was one of the most powerful artifacts in all of Olympus, and her being his favored daughter would not spare her his anger.

True to her form, however, Athena admitted nothing and tried to save face. "I know it was you," she said. "You're the only one dumb enough to take it from me out of my very own home."

"I've never wanted that shield," he said. "And I never will. I don't need to hide behind it to cleave mortals' heads from their shoulders. You do."

"Then it was your lover," Athena said.

"Aphrodite wants nothing to do with it either," Ares said. "Besides, she's spent the last few days preparing for her interview."

"Interview? What interview?"

"For some late-night show," he said. "Now begone. I tire of your presence."

Athena folded her arms and pressed her lips together as she stared at him, not giving the slightest hint to what she was thinking. After a few seconds, she nodded and left, but not before giving Victor a bit of advice. "If I were looking to run my team wisely and wanted to ensure that professional football survived another month, I wouldn't sign my brother. But what do I know?"

Once she had gone, Victor and Derek exchanged nervous glances. Victor was the first to speak out of the three. "Maybe we should think this through. I mean, with all due respect, Ares, I do get the feeling you're looking for something…a little more violent than what we're offering."

Ares made a fist and started cracking his knuckles one at a time. He thought about his sister's words, or more accurately, his sister's words burned in his mind and tormented him. She had always been one to play games when it came to getting him to do things that she wanted, and he had a nagging feeling this was one of those times.

Thus, Ares stewed. Was she trying to get him to play this game, football, or not? She was certainly trying to elicit a reaction out of him, and either way, Ares knew she intended on humiliating him. Again.

Ares frowned as his sister's motivations eluded him. Then a thought struck the god. It was clear Athena either wanted him to play or didn't, but it also dawned on him that if he wanted to thwart her plans, he would have to do something unexpected. "I've come to my decision," he said, turning to face Victor with determination in his eyes. "I do not desire to play this football game of yours."

"Oh, good," the coach said with relief.

"No, I intend to take control of all the teams and shape the sport into a contest worthy of my approval."

Chapter New Pets

Aphrodite casually strolled down the hall in a little black dress that contrasted sharply against her fair skin. Her red, full lips held a slight smile that brightened every time her eyes captured the gaze of a stagehand and sent him stumbling for balance and word. Her golden hair bounced playfully as she went, and her hips swayed to and fro, hypnotizing all around. Though she walked in two-inch stilettos on the hard floor, she made not a sound, but did trail a sweet, enticing fragrance the entire way that would capture any man's heart as quickly as her unparalleled beauty could—a beauty that reminded everyone everywhere that perfection was attainable, but only by one. Only by her.

Ahead, Aphrodite could hear the talk-show host stall for time by making bad jokes about some sort of protest going on somewhere or other—not that that mattered any to her. In fact, hearing about it only annoyed the goddess. Mortals were always protesting something, and they could never seem to be happy for more than a second with the fact that they even existed. But she didn't want to dwell on that. She was there to have a marvelous time and to talk to adoring fans.

Aphrodite had been slated for the interview ten minutes prior, but she wasn't late, at least not to her mind. She was, after all, the goddess. She could come and go as she pleased, and if her own obsessive, oppressive husband couldn't tell her otherwise, certainly no man would be able to either.

Her gut tightened at the thought of Hephaestus, and she had to exhale slowly and steadily to push thoughts of him away. Now was not the time to ruin her upbeat mood by dwelling on him, or rather, her arranged marriage to him. Though she did have an inkling to air all of the dirty laundry about the whole affair on worldwide television to set the record straight. Some people, apparently, had caught wind of her infidelity and thus whispered behind her back while at the same time ignoring the fact that she'd been forced to wed.

As much as she wanted to do that, it wouldn't do any good. Hephaestus would grow even more insecure and controlling, and her father, Zeus, who'd arranged it all, wouldn't lift a finger to change it. Why? Who knew? She figured that since he was miserable in his own marriage to Hera, he probably didn't care how miserable she was in hers.

When Aphrodite was a couple of dozen paces away from reaching the stage, she paused near a closed door that led into a makeup room. There was a conversation going on, one that she couldn't quite catch the words to, but there were two distinct voices. One male. One female. The male was doing most of the talking. And although she didn't know precisely what he was saying, she knew the tone, and she knew it well. It belonged to a man trying to get something that wasn't his, or rather, someone.

The stagehand at the end of the hall caught her eye and waved anxiously at her to keep coming so the interview could begin. "One moment, dear," she said, holding up a finger.

She then quietly tried the door, but the handle refused to turn. Aphrodite whispered an old cantrip, and a heartbeat later, she had the room unlocked. Carefully, she opened the door and looked in to see a man standing behind a woman who was seated at an ornate vanity. He had his hands on her shoulders and was massaging them with as much tact as a boar rooting around a garden. He wore a gray suit and highly polished shoes, as well as half a head of hair and a bulging gut. Given the woman's distress on her freckled face and how her once-fixed makeup was smeared and had run down her cheeks, Aphrodite could easily tell each one's station before another second passed.

"Look," the man said, giving the woman an extra squeeze. "If you're going to succeed, you've got to network. Everyone knows that. And if you're going to network, you've got to be able to offer something that others want."

"I know, but..." Her voice sounded weak, and her eyes never looked up from the floor.

"Think of it as a business transaction, if you must. Where two consenting adults spend some hours after work together to get what each one wants."

"More like what you want," she mumbled.

The man tightened his grip, and she yelped. At that point, the Goddess of Love went to work. Her eyes narrowed, but only for a moment, because as she slipped into the room and shut the door behind her, she hid her desire for justice under the perfect guise of lust and wonderment.

"There you are," she said with a breathy voice. "Do you always make the girls have to try so hard to find you?"

"Who the hell—" The rest of the man's objection stuck in his throat when he spun around and saw Aphrodite strutting up to him. His round face turned crimson, and sweat beaded on his forehead.

"You can stay there, dear," Aphrodite replied as she glanced at the woman. "This will only be a second."

"I'm sorry, but did you say you were looking for me?" the man finally asked, sounding every bit as flustered as he looked.

"Absolutely," Aphrodite replied as she stopped less than a half pace away. She leaned in so close that a finger was all that separated her lips from the man's cheeks, and she spoke softly, but slowly, so that he hung on her every word. "I'd love to take you home and grant your every desire."

"My every desire?"

"More than you know."

"I can't wait," he stammered. "My place then, after the show?"

"No, I think the pound for you," Aphrodite said, voice growing sharp. "And in heat."

The man cocked his head. "What?"

Aphrodite snapped her fingers, and the man disappeared. Or at least, his human body did. His clothes collapsed in a heap on the floor, and from beneath them, out came a mutt with floppy ears, adorable puppy eyes, and a short-hair coat of black and brown. Aphrodite knelt and smiled as she lifted the dog's chin so the two were staring at each other. "You want to be a dog? Well here's your chance."

The dog whined and tucked her tail between her legs. Aphrodite grinned and snapped her fingers again, and the mutt disappeared.

The Goddess of Love then stood with an air of satisfaction before smoothing out her little black dress and checking her hair in the mirror. It only needed a minor correction, and it was a correction that only she'd have ever noticed.

"Th-thank you," the woman said, popping out of her shock.

"Anytime, love," Aphrodite replied. "And before I go, if anyone else tries that with you, just tell them what happened with…well, whoever the hell he was."

"He was the CEO."

Aphrodite shrugged. "I guess someone's getting a promotion. Might want to short the stock while you can."

Few things in life smelled better than a cake baking in the oven, especially when that cake was going to be big enough to satisfy the appetites of twelve Olympians. That, however, assumed one's nostrils weren't being assaulted by the smell of mud fresh from a bog mixed with a hefty dose of chimera slobber.

Euryale made a diving tackle in her spacious living room and managed to wrap her arms around the waist of the chimera. As the monster turned and playfully wetted her face with a pair of scratchy tongues, she called out to her husband who was in the kitchen. "Honey! Get the basement door!"

"What?" Alex called back over a commotion of his own he was dealing with. Twenty obols said the twins, Aison and Cassandra, were getting the better of their father. They truly were in their savage sixes, but thankfully—or maybe not so much, depending on how one viewed the next stage—they'd look and act like pre-teens in six months, thanks to their divine blood. At least at that point, Euryale and Alex would only need to watch them for another year until they fully matured into adult demigods.

"I'm back with Tickles!" Euryale shouted, fighting to keep ahold of the squirming monster. "He's covered in mud, and I can't get him in the basement!"

Alex appeared in the kitchen doorway. He wore a pair of red-and-black athletic shorts that Euryale had snagged when she'd made a trip to the realm of the living along with a blue Doctor Who T-shirt. Over all of that he had on a white apron that was covered in cake batter and powdered sugar. Written across said apron, barely visible underneath all of the baking gore, were the words, "Kiss me, I'm a hero."

"Did you just call that thing Tickles?"

Euryale, who had now worked her way up the beast's torso and had gotten a firm lock around its chest as it thrashed her into their leather couch, froze. "Um...no?"

"You did! I heard you!"

"Well, I couldn't go around calling him 'chimera' all day."

"I can't believe you named it!"

"Hephaestus named his big monster dog," Euryale objected. "I don't see you getting all up in arms about Cerberus."

"Yeah, and he's a god—"

"And our good friend—"

"Which has nothing to do with the fact you named a chimera!" Alex exclaimed. "Now the kids—"

Alex hadn't even finished his sentence when their twins bolted out of the kitchen, covered head to toe in flour to such a degree that the snakes on their heads had not a single green scale in sight. Vipers for hair aside, they appeared as any other set of six-year-old brother and sister, having the brown eyes of their father, the determined look of their mother, and the hearts of them both.

"We got a chimera?" they asked. When they saw the beast in the living room, a happy dance ensued. "We got a chimera! We got a chimera!"

"We did not get a chimera!" Alex said, trying to sound as stern as possible but failing worse than Pandora trying to close a forbidden box.

Aison frowned and stuck his lip out. "Mommy said we did!"

"And she named it!" Cassandra added, sticking her lip out as well.

"No, she didn't," Alex said. "You misheard."

Tickles wiggled and tried kicking off of Euryale's stomach to get away. It nearly managed to slip free from her grasp, but the gorgon locked her arms around its waist before pulling it back in toward her. "Would someone please get the basement door? I have to put Tickles up before he wrecks the place."

"See! See! She named it!" the twins said, hugging each other and jumping up and down.

Alex buried his face in his palm and shook his head. "Why did you bring it back here?" he asked as he went for the door. "I thought you were going to take it to our old island."

"I forgot the beef jerky for Cerberus," she said. "You know he'll never let me by with a monster if I don't bribe him."

"Okay, wait here," he said. "I'll grab the jerky, and then you get rid of Tick—the chimera."

"Daddy said it, too!" Cassandra said. She bolted across the living room, leaped on the couch and used it as a springboard to launch herself into her father's arms (who barely caught her in time). She wrapped her tiny arms around his neck while she and her vipers assaulted his cheeks with kisses. "Oh, thank you! Thank you! Thank you! This is the bestestest present ever!"

Aison, following his sister's lead, attached himself to Alex's leg. "Can we ride him like Leviathan?"

"Honey?" Alex said with a pleading look to his wife.

"We can talk about this later."

"If by later you mean you getting rid of it right now, perfect."

Euryale groaned and readjusted her grip on the playful monster. "Alex, we don't have time to run him out now," she said. "We've got to finish getting ready. The party has to be perfect."

"Perfect might be a little hard with that thing running around."

"Don't you think I know that?"

"Then let it go!"

"No!" she snapped. "I'll not let him get hunted down again!"

"It's going to be worse than that when the whole island finds out about him, not to mention the gods. You're the one saying how you have to get on their good side."

"I know, Alex."

"Then why are you risking being thrown into exile over a big cat with extra heads?"

Euryale groaned in frustration and cleared her watering eyes. The stress of the party was already enough to break her, and now that Tickles had been tossed into the mix, she was one spilled drink away from a psychotic break. Every second the chimera wasn't put away, pressure mounted in her head and threatened to cripple her for a week. "Please, Alex. I can't handle arguing with you right now."

A knock at the door halted everything.

Alex froze, and Euryale's eyes went wide with fear. Whoever was there knocked again, and Euryale sprang into action. The gorgon jumped to her feet and manhandled Tickles into the basement, drawing strength from her frustrations. Along the way, she gave stern orders to both her children and spouse. "Alex, get the door," she said. "Kids, if you even breathe a word about Tickles, you'll both be petrified for a month, so help me gods."

Alex snickered at the threat and went to attend to their new guest. As he did, Euryale pulled Tickles down into the basement, and the kids closed the heavy door behind her. As she descended, she held her breath and tried to figure out who would've come calling. Persephone, maybe? She was her only friend in the Underworld, Alex aside. They had had to take a rain check on their last ladies' night out. Hermes? If so, hopefully he would be carrying nothing but a message. Gods, how she hoped it wasn't more evangelists. How they ever managed to find their home here in Elysium was beyond her, and why they insisted on preaching the Good News to a gorgon of all beings was equally baffling.

Halfway down the stairs, she stumbled. Tickles was being far from cooperative. Even when she reached the basement floor, he kept playfully wrestling in her grip, and no less than three times he nearly knocked over a wine locker. Eventually, she led him into the very back of the basement where she had previously built a large cage to temporarily house creatures she'd adopted into foster care.

Like any chimera, Tickles wanted nothing to do with said cage. He fought her tooth and nail as she tried to push, drag, coerce, and beg him to enter. It was only when she grabbed a keychain hanging on a nearby post and used the laser pointer attached to it, that she got the big guy to chase the dot inside.

"Okay, that was pretty rude of me," she said when Tickles spun around and realized he was caught. "If you're good, I'll stay here until it's over."

Tickles cocked his heads and let loose a meow-growl-baa. Euryale shot her hands forward with open palms. "Shh! You're going to get us both in a world of trouble."

She then scooted inside the cage and partially closed the door behind her. This seemed to calm the chimera, and she spent the next several moments slowly stroking the tops of the lion and goat heads.

The basement door opened with a creak, and Euryale froze. Alex's voice called down to her. "Euryale, dear," he said, his voice unsettlingly calm. "Someone's here to see you. Says it's important."

"Can I get a rain check?"

"No."

"Take one anyway."

"Not going to happen. Too important."

Euryale buried her face in her hands and muttered. Why did today of all days have to be so difficult? "Okay," she said quickly recomposing herself. "Who is it? I'll be right up."

"It's Perseus, and he's insisting on seeing you."

Chapter Humiliation

"What a filthy pig hole," Perseus sneered as he stood in the entryway. "I always knew you gorgons were disgusting, but I never realized how much you loved to wallow in the mud."

Euryale stood a couple of feet away and kept her eyes fixated on the hero. She knew the house was a total disaster and had no intentions on defending its current state. "It's called having kids."

"Monsters, you mean," he said. "I have seven sons and two daughters. None of them would have ever dreamed of tracking in a tenth of the mud your home is covered in, but, like mother like children, I suppose."

Euryale took a half step forward, feeling her anger start to burn. "Few are stupid enough to insult a gorgon in her own home. Did you have a point to your unwelcomed visit?"

With an underhand flip of the wrist, Perseus tossed a couple of decapitated snakes at her. "Consider this your de-invitation to any of our activities."

Euryale's soul recoiled in shame and horror, but she managed to keep a flat affect regardless. She would not give the hero the satisfaction of seeing her break down. Instead, she issued a single word for a reply. "Because?"

"Because your kind does not deserve our comradery. I may have to put up with your existence, but I don't have to put up with your company."

"Why do I get the feeling the others didn't agree to this?" she asked.

Perseus laughed. "Who? Odysseus? Heracles? Do you honestly think they care that much about you?"

Euryale felt her throat tighten. She'd thought at least those two had taken a liking to her, at the very least for Alex's sake. Had she been that foolish to think that even one person other than Alex would ever enjoy her company? No, she couldn't believe that. Wouldn't believe that. "You're lying."

"Ask them yourself," he said, not missing a beat. "I made it clear that if you were going to be around, I would not. Guess whose company they value more."

Euryale tried to come up with a retort, but before she could, a tremendous crash came from below and was quickly followed by a roar. She stiffened, and fear showed on her face. "Speaking of children," she said with a nervous chuckle. "I should see what they're destroying now. We can argue about this later. So if you'll excuse me, I have things to attend to."

"That didn't sound like children. It sounded like—"

"I'm not interested in your opinions," she said, pushing him toward the door. "Go on your own, or I'll drag you out with hooks through your groin."

Another crash came from the basement followed by a second roar. At this point, Perseus shook her off and stiff-armed his way inside. "The Fates can strike me down if that came from your children."

It took a second for Euryale to snap out of it and give chase. She caught up with him in the middle of the living room and grabbed him by the shoulder. "Get out of my house right now!"

Perseus didn't. He pulled free, bolted through the basement door, and ran down the stairs with his sword drawn.

"Alex!" Euryale shouted as she went after the hero. By the time she reached him, he was already at the bottom, face to face with Tickles. The chimera stood next to a toppled wine locker with paws stained a deep purple.

"What's he doing here?" he asked, his face reflecting the shock in his voice. Tickles growled, and Perseus grinned broadly. "You'll not escape me a second time, beast."

At that point, he charged, sword ready to strike. Tickles leaped back as the hero's blade flashed through the air. He quickly reversed the attack at the end of its sweep and brought it down in an overhead arc. The follow-up sent Tickles scampering back in a corner where the chimera entered a low, desperate crouch.

Euryale rushed to the aid of her newly adopted family member. "Leave him alone!"

"Unless you want to be my next trophy, stand aside," he sneered.

Perseus lunged with a feint, and when Tickles dodged left, he ended up dodging right into Perseus's follow-up attack. The hero's blade cut through the air and the chimera's shoulder, sending a spray of dark blood across the room.

The sight of Tickles being cut open sent Euryale over the top. She launched herself onto Perseus's back, screaming obscenities the entire time. Though she managed to wrap an arm around his neck, she didn't hold onto him for long. Perseus, veteran of a thousand battles, easily threw her over his shoulder so she landed flat on her back.

"That was the last mistake you'll ever make," he said. He stepped on her right arm before making a jab with his sword to keep Tickles away. "After I've slain this beast, I'll make sure Athena casts you into exile forever."

"Stop, please!" Euryale said, holding up her free hand. "I can explain."

Perseus snorted. "Too late for that. And you know what? I'm going to enjoy the look on your face when you realize you'll never see your children again."

While pain ripped through her heart at first, unbridled anger quickly took its place. Euryale growled, and her pupils turned to slits. In a flash, she rolled to her side and sank her fangs into his calf. The vipers on her head followed suit, and together, they injected enough venom to kill a thousand elephants.

Perseus screamed in agony. He stumbled away, and before either he or Tickles could do anything, Euryale was on her feet, attacking.

Her nails had elongated into razor-sharp claws. With them, she turned his flesh to ribbons. Despite the grievous wounds he suffered, the hero was far from finished. He batted away her arms with one hand before delivering a vicious elbow across her cheek. As her head snapped to the side, he made a thrust with the tip of his sword. The blade dug into her thigh and cut deep, but the attack fell short when Tickles joined the fray.

The chimera slammed into Perseus's chest, knocking him over and Euryale to the side.

"Euryale!" Alex yelled as he came running down the stairs. "What are you doing?"

The gorgon, clutching her leg with one hand, limped over to Perseus, who was now pinned by the chimera. "He threatened me, Alex," she spat. "He threatened all of us and stabbed me in the leg!"

"Oh my god, are you okay?" he asked, hurrying over.

"I'm stabbed in the leg! I'm certainly not okay!"

Perseus coughed, sending flecks of blood in all direction. "You were never okay."

Euryale glared at the fallen hero. "Shut up."

"Control your wife, Alex," he said with a pained laugh. "Unless you want Athena's wrath to spill onto you and your children as well."

"Shut up!" Euryale screamed.

"You're only heaping more coals upon your head, monster," Perseus replied. "Your children's heads, too."

Euryale snarled and kicked him as hard as she could under the chin. The hero's head jerked back, and his body went limp. "I told you to shut up," she growled. "I should toss you in a volcano."

Alex muttered a slew of curses as he ran his fingers through his hair. "This isn't good."

"I know, Alex."

"This is really, really not good."

"For Fate's sake, could you stop saying that?"

Alex took a deep breath and huffed. "What are we going to do?"

"I don't know," she admitted as the weight of the situation bore down on her. What had she done? Perseus carried the favor of most of the gods, if not all. He was one of Athena's favorites. When she found out what had happened, exile might turn out to be a luxury she'd beg for. Her hands trembled, and her voice wavered as she spoke. "We'll have to hide the body."

"But he's not dead."

"You know what I mean!" she said, tears now flowing. "Please, Alex, stop arguing with me. I'm freaking out enough."

"Sorry."

Euryale took a few more deep, calming breaths and nodded. "Right then. Grab the arms. I'll get the legs. Once the party is over, we'll figure out how to handle his release."

Danny Johnson, host of "Some Late Show," leaned across his wooden desk with a glowing look on his spirited, clean-shaven face. As he did, he slid his black mug to the side before folding his hands together and looking Aphrodite right in the eyes. Their interview had gone on for nearly thirty minutes and had no signs of slowing, even if the show was technically in its final segment. "So apparently you tried one of these dating apps before creating your own, Divineder," he said. "How'd that go?"

Aphrodite hid the pain of losing her app to Athena with a well-practiced laugh. She scooched forward to the edge of the gray loveseat she was on and flipped her hair over her shoulder. "Oh, I tried, all right," she said, smiling brighter than the lights that illuminated the stage. "It was nothing more than idle curiosity."

"So this wasn't a jealousy thing?" he asked. "I only throw that out there because it seems some rumors had floated that maybe it was."

"No," she replied as innocent as a first true love's kiss. "Don't be silly. Me? The jealous type? Of course not. I'm here to make people happy and find bliss with one another. There's nothing to be jealous of when that's what you live and breathe for."

"I imagine an app's track record of success is a lot worse than yours," Danny said, laughing.

"Exactly!"

"So what happened?"

"Well, I started by making a profile on Divini-Match, naturally—"

"—Of course! Match made in heaven, or so they say—"

"Mhmm," Aphrodite said, not minding the interjection at all. "As you know, each profile is reviewed and approved before it's allowed to go live. Supposedly this keeps the—how do you say it—creep factor down to a minimum."

Danny grinned. "Supposedly."

"I don't have a baseline to measure against, but I will say the experience hardly wooed me," she said as she put her hand over her chest. "Anyway, after I filled out my profile, I sat around the house and waited for my first match. I wasn't looking, obviously, but as I said, I was insanely curious as to what you mortals had come up with."

"Let me guess; it paired you with the polar opposite of who you would've been looking for?"

"No," Aphrodite said with a giggle. "It didn't pair me at all. Can you believe it? I sat there as the minutes ticked by and no one messaged me. Five. Then ten. Then thirty. Then an hour. And still nothing. At first, you know, I was little impressed. I thought, hey, you mortals must have really come up with something good since it's taking this long to search for someone who might appeal to me."

"But?"

"But then, I'll admit, I started to get a little panicky. What if the app was trying, but no one was interested? What if I was getting rejected by billions? That might sound silly, but that's what was going through my head, and I ended up flopping back on the couch trying to keep from spiraling into a panic attack."

Danny grinned. "You're right. I do have a hard time believing that. If I may, you're beyond gorgeous. Did you think maybe everyone was simply too intimidated to approach you?"

"Nope, I went straight to nobody loves me," she said. "So do you know what I did?"

"No. What?"

"I did what any sensible woman would do. I broke into the wine stash, and after my third bottle of Dionysus's finest, I was getting mad. How dare no one message me! I'm the damn Goddess of Love! They should be cramming my inbox so full of messages it would take a thousand years to read them all! Who the hell do these mortals think they are ignoring me like that?"

"Oh geez," Danny said. "I hope you didn't sling a few curses around in that rage."

Aphrodite raised her shoulders while giving a sheepish look. "None that were too severe...I don't think."

Danny turned away for a moment to stare into one of the studio cameras. "If you or a loved one has recently been turned into a frog and kisses aren't working, give us a call before the hour is up. I'm sure she'll make things right."

"I will. I will," Aphrodite said with a melodic laugh. "So anyway, right when I was about to lose my mind, my phone beeped, and lo and behold, I got a message. An actual message! I was so excited I squealed like a little girl. But when I opened it up, it wasn't from a suitor, but rather it was a statement saying my profile had been removed due to fraud."

Danny grinned and bit down on a knuckle. "Fraud?"

"Well it seems that the terms of service are very explicit about providing correct user information."

"Oooooh..."

"Yeah, and so I even called to protest," Aphrodite said. "And the man I spoke to was very nice. He calmly explained that because I had lied about my age, he couldn't allow my profile to go through."

"You lied about your age?"

"You're surprised?" she asked, laughing. "The funny thing is, he wasn't surprised. And he said to me, and I quote, 'Ma'am, I know for a fact you're not four thousand years old.'"

Danny's smile grew to one that spanned ear to ear, but he said nothing and let his guest finish the tale.

"And because, you know, I was a little intoxicated, I broke down crying," Aphrodite said. "It was a really ugly cry, too. Somewhere in all those tears, I managed to blubber out, 'Okay, okay. I'm not four thousand years old. But I've worked really, really hard to stay looking that young. Can you please let it slide?'"

"And?"

"And he still didn't believe me! So, I, Aphrodite, Goddess of Love, was perma-banned from a dating app for lying about her age."

"That's hysterical," Danny said. He was about to say something else when he put his hand over his ear for a moment before returning to the conversation. "Aphrodite, we can't wait to hear all about your app, Divineder, but before we dive into that topic, I'd like to ask about one little thing, namely a wedding you arranged between a gorgon and a man named Alexander Weiss."

"Oh, that?" Aphrodite said, keeping a pleasant affect for all to see despite the knots that formed in her stomach. "It was nothing, really. I'm happy it all worked out."

"Yes, well, if you don't mind, we would like to bring on another guest and talk to you both."

Aphrodite's smile faded, and she tried not to show her angst at being potentially upstaged by another. "Who?"

"It seems that your sister, Athena, was in the area and has dropped on by." Aphrodite caught herself from scowling too much, but it was enough that Danny made an uncomfortable clearing of his throat. "Everyone in the audience, please give a warm welcome to the marvelous Athena, Goddess of Wisdom!"

Aphrodite twisted in her chair to see her sister stroll out on stage to a thunderous applause. She wore a white chiton with emerald clasps, and her brown hair had been pulled back and fixed with a simple brooch. The look was certainly several steps above her common apparel of bronze helm and spear, but it still left a lot to be desired for such a public appearance among men. If Athena was going to crash her interview on worldwide TV, as far as Aphrodite was concerned, the least she could've done was dress a little nicer.

"Pallas Athena," Danny said, jumping up and ushering her to a seat next to Aphrodite. "Such a pleasant surprise. To what do we owe the honor of you being here?"

Athena sat and put a gentle hand on Aphrodite's forearm. "Well, I happened to be nearby and wanted to talk to my sister about a few things before the party."

Aphrodite tilted her head as her mind tried to wrap itself around Athena's words. "Party? What party?"

"Euryale and Alex's first anniversary?" Athena said, staring at her sister as if her words were obvious to all. When Aphrodite could only offer an open mouth and tied tongue as a response, Athena added, "Everyone else in Olympus is going. Didn't you get the invitation?"

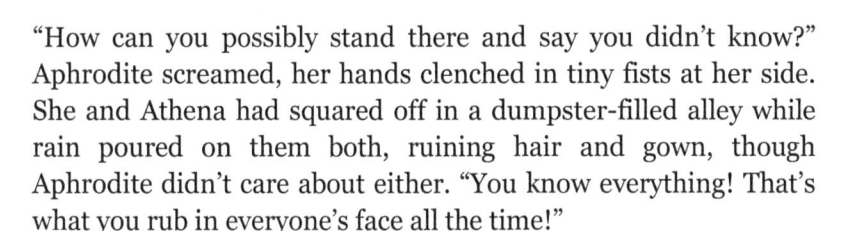

"How can you possibly stand there and say you didn't know?" Aphrodite screamed, her hands clenched in tiny fists at her side. She and Athena had squared off in a dumpster-filled alley while rain poured on them both, ruining hair and gown, though Aphrodite didn't care about either. "You know everything! That's what you rub in everyone's face all the time!"

"Sister, I honestly thought you knew," Athena said, taking a half step toward her. "I only came because I thought you might have...borrowed my aegis."

"Don't give me that!" Aphrodite said. "I saw the look on your face when you mentioned your precious pet's party. You came to humiliate me like you always do! I guess stealing my business wasn't enough, was it? I can only imagine the thoughts running through your head: Oh, how can I trick my dumb sister today? What's that? She's going to be in front of the entire planet, and I can turn her into a fool? That could be fun!"

Athena growled, clearly not liking the challenge. "If I wanted to embarrass you, you'd know it."

"As if I don't already?" Aphrodite sniffed hard and tried to clear her eyes, but they kept producing tears and stayed puffy. "It's no wonder no one wants to be with you. You're such a vindictive bitch."

"Don't you dare turn this on me," Athena said, pointing an accusing finger at her sister. "It wasn't even a year ago when you tried to ruin Alex and Euryale's life together due to petty revenge."

"And why was that? Did it have anything to do with you trying to take away the only thing that made me special? You never saw me trying to be you, trying to steal your title as Goddess of Wisdom just for the fun of it."

Athena laughed with a biting, mocking tone and shook her head. "You could never be like me. Now, where's my aegis?"

"You're right," Aphrodite said, swallowing hard and finding her backbone in the midst of her humiliation. "I could never be like you because I want to feel connected to the one I love. I want to relish his touch. I want to be the reason he smiles, and the one who infects his every thought. All that you want to do is judge and belittle everyone from your ivory tower so you can show the world how clever you are."

"You're one to talk about judging," Athena countered.

Aphrodite shook her head again. "I never, ever made you feel stupid. I never made you feel worthless, and that's all you've ever done to me. And why? Because I like to feel pretty? Because Dad might love another daughter of his? Is that it? Are you that damn insecure?"

Athena's mouth hung open, and for the first time since Aphrodite could remember, the Goddess of Wisdom had nothing to say.

"You know what? I don't even care," Aphrodite said before turning to leave.

Athena took a few quick steps to catch up to her sister. "If you didn't take it, help me find who did."

"I'll never help you, ever," Aphrodite said, quickening her pace. "I hope whoever stole your precious shield melts it down because that's the only thing you care about."

CHAPTER ARACHNE AND JESSICA

Arachne, dressed in flowing green-and-gold robes and wearing snug sandals, casually strolled up the cobblestone driveway that led to Jessica Turner's mansion. It had been built to mirror the style and feel of some of the most exceptional chalets around the world. With its gorgeous wood construction, alongside a hefty mix of stone, Arachne appreciated how well it blended in with the surrounding landscape. Being one with nature, after all, was of prime importance to The Spider Queen.

Arachne smiled to herself. She liked the sound of that, The Spider Queen. Funny it took her so long to claim the title, but then again maybe it wasn't. After all, for over two thousand years she'd been cursed to be an insignificant arachnid, but now that said curse had been broken, now that she had been blessed with powers beyond her wildest dreams, it was time to take her self-image to the next level. After all, one couldn't rule the world feeling trivial compared to everyone else, and one certainly couldn't take down the Olympians with such an attitude, either. And though most mortals didn't know a lick of her story, that would change in the very near future. She'd see to that.

When Arachne was within a couple of dozen paces of the front door, she wiped her lips one last time and was surprised, and also amused, at the slight bit of blood that she'd picked up. Apparently, she hadn't fully cleaned up after she had snacked on the guard who'd been manning the gates. Wouldn't that have been embarrassing? She could picture the conversation with Jessica now:

"You've got something on your lips."

"I do?"

"Yes. It looks almost like blood?"

"That's because it is blood."

And then the woman would undoubtedly flip out like most mortals did; either that or she'd beg to be turned into a...What was it some people worshiped now? Vampires, that was it. Why that was the case, she had no idea. But if Jessica happened to be one of them, perhaps she wouldn't mind being drained when Arachne wanted a midday snack.

With that thought, Arachne quickened her steps and came to the front door. Before she announced her presence, she looked herself over one last time and made a slight comfort adjustment to her silk robes.

Satisfied with everything, Arachne rang the doorbell. Time passed, and nothing happened, so Arachne rang again, and again. Finally, a woman in her mid-thirties answered the door wearing a hefty layer of sweat along with a white summer sport top and hot pink shorts. Her sandy-brown hair was pulled back in a ponytail, and freckles ran across the bridge of her nose from one sun-kissed cheek to the other.

"Oh," the woman said, sounding caught off guard. "You're not FedEx."

"Afraid not," Arachne replied.

"Can I help you?" she asked as she took a half step out of the door and looked around. "Are you sure you're in the right place?"

"I'm here to see Jessica Turner, so I believe that puts me in the right place," Arachne replied.

"Did my agent set up an appointment or something that I forgot?"

"No."

"Did we meet somewhere?"

"No."

Jessica took in a slow, deep breath and crossed her arms over her chest. Her brow furrowed and the look on her face was not fear or worry as Arachne would have predicted, but irritation with no small amount of I'm-going-to-kick-your-ass thrown in as well. "Who are you? You better not be some stalker, or I swear to god you'll regret ever coming here."

"Is that so?" Arachne said, approving of Jessica's attitude. She liked the idea that this woman wasn't one who would simply run away from adversity.

"Ask the last one, although now that I think about it, it might be hard to get an answer."

"Why's that?"

Jessica laughed and shook her head. "You really don't know?"

"No, I don't."

"Well, then you sure as hell aren't a stalker," Jessica said. "Because it was all over the news when I broke the guy's jaw in four places."

"Well, I assure you, I'm here strictly on business," Arachne said. "More specifically, I'm here about Alexander Weiss."

Jessica put her hands on her hips and sighed. "You'll have to do better than that. What's your name?"

"Arachne."

"As in the woman who Athena cursed?"

Arachne let the pain of the memory show on her face before nodding. "The same."

"Well, you get points for being original," Jessica said. "But I have no way of knowing she's you, especially with all the loonies around claiming this, that, and the other."

"I imagine this will suffice," Arachne said, pulling out a sealed envelope and handing it to her.

Jessica took the envelope and read the inscription. "This is to Aphrodite?"

"It is, but that's your Alex's handwriting, is it not?"

Jessica wrinkled her forehead as she stared at the letter. "Where did you get this? He better be okay."

"It's a bit of a story."

"I've got time."

"So you do. Let's say a friend of mine got it from him," she explained. "He's quite the exceptional thief. Puts even Hermes to shame. That said, I assure you, Jessica, for the moment, Alex is quite safe. May I come in?"

"What do you mean 'for the moment'?"

"The future is about to bring change, and honestly, this is a conversation better had in privacy."

Jessica hesitated, and for a few seconds, Arachne wondered if her request wouldn't be granted. But the woman nodded, much to The Spider Queen's pleasant surprise, and ushered her inside. Jessica led her through an extravagant welcoming hall and brought her into a spacious, cozy living room. Two blue couches had been set up in an L-formation around a wrought-iron coffee table, all of which was in front of a giant stone hearth. The wall at the far end had a number of full-length windows which gave a fantastic view of a rapidly flowing mountain river and bright blue skies. A baby grand piano sat in one corner, while in the other was a massive terrarium that looked like it held a miniature rainforest.

"What's in here?" Arachne asked, instantly drawn over to it.

"Mr. Peepers," Jessica replied. "Hope you don't mind tarantulas."

"Mind? Surely you jest," Arachne said with a warm smile. She leaned in close to the terrarium's glass walls and scoured the place for the spider. It didn't take her long to find him. He was a gorgeous rose hair tarantula with a reddish hue and glistening fangs that Arachne adored. She beckoned it over with a finger while calling to him softly, and the spider ran out from under its hollow log and stopped right in front of her. "You are a beautiful thing, aren't you?"

"He's a keeper, in my book," Jessica said, watching from the middle of the room.

"And does she take good care of you?"

"Of course I take good care of him," Jessica said, sounding put-off.

Arachne glanced over her shoulder. "He says you do. Don't worry."

"Right..."

Arachne turned back around and found herself a place to sit on one of the couches. As she dropped down, she had a slight change of heart in terms of what she was going to do. "May I ask you something?"

"I think you already did," Jessica said playfully as she sat on the other couch.

"Indeed," Arachne replied. "I was curious as to how you felt about Athena and Aphrodite."

"What about them?"

"Well, from what I understand, they nearly got you killed over a bet," Arachne said. "Some people might have a problem with that. You might even say some people would hold a grudge, or at least want some sort of cosmic justice for them both."

Jessica leaned forward and clasped her hands together while resting her elbows on her knees. "That's one hell of a question," she finally said.

"It is."

"Why are you asking?"

"Because I'd like to know what you would like," Arachne said. Judging by Jessica's reaction to this conversation, she was reasonably sure the woman wouldn't go along with what she was planning, but at the same time, she wanted to give her a chance. Anyone who cared for spiders as much as Jessica deserved at least that much, especially when there was a decent possibility that she, too, had a grudge to settle.

"I think, and I'm only thinking at this point," Jessica slowly said, "that it doesn't matter. She's a goddess, and I'm not. It's that simple. And even if I feel like she was completely wrong in all that she did, not even counting Aphrodite, if I don't forgive and move on, I might as well poison myself with hemlock, because going to war with an Olympian will promise a lot more suffering than that."

Arachne's lips slowly drew back. "What if I could promise you a different future down that path?"

"I'd say that's one hell of a promise."

"Humor me," she said.

Jessica eyed her suspiciously. "You know, more than one Olympian has shape-shifted to keep their identity a secret."

"You think I might be doing that?"

"I'll tell you what," Jessica said as she locked her eyes with Arachne's. "Swear by the River Styx you're not deceiving me in any manner, and I'll indulge you in this conversation."

Arachne cocked her head to the side. "You know your oaths."

"I do," she said. "So are you willing to make one? Or are you afraid of what the Fates will deal you if you break it?"

"I'm afraid of no such thing, but such oaths are not to be demanded lightly."

"This is hardly a light request."

Arachne stood and placed her hand over her heart. "Very well. I swear by the River Styx I'm in no way, shape or form, lying to you about the promise I can and would like to make you."

Jessica leaned back on her couch. "Okay. I'm listening."

"I think you can take off the rag now," Euryale said, referring to the drug-laced cloth that covered Perseus's face. She had created the cocktail to help soothe rescued monsters for their trip out of Elysium as they weren't always agreeable to transport. Or to touching. Or anything else other than biting, and Euryale was not a fan of biting unless it was with Alex.

"Let me check the chains first," Alex said as he walked behind the unconscious hero. He leaned down, inspected the shackles, and then gave the chains a solid tug. Both the links and the anchor point on the dungeon wall held fast. "I think we're good. Well, relatively speaking. I mean, if Athena finds out we're holding him prisoner…"

"I know, Alex," Euryale said, exhaling sharply. "At least it has to all be downhill from here, right?"

"Yeah, well," Alex stammered.

"Well what?"

"Maybe I should bring it up later."

Euryale playfully rolled her eyes. "Too late now."

"Right," Alex said. "It's nothing. Well, not nothing, nothing, but I mean nothing compared to all of this. Your dad sent a letter earlier. He said he couldn't make the party. Something about the sirens preparing for war with Charybdis and a fissure in the sea cracking open."

"That figures," she said. "I wish he'd get with the times and use a phone like the rest of us. At least that way he'd speak with the kids more often. Not to mention, I might be able to find him every now and again."

Perseus stirred. He groaned and tried to rub his head, but quickly discovered the shackles keeping his hands behind his back. "Let me go!"

"Soon," Euryale said.

"Now!" The hero thrashed around but was rewarded with nothing but sweat for his efforts.

Once he'd calmed, relatively speaking, that is, Euryale squatted near him. "I want you to know you'll be treated well," she said. "I'm not a monster."

"Reality says otherwise."

"We'll feed you twice a day," she went on, trying her best not to let his remark dig under her skin. "And once we can all agree to live in peace, you'll be set free."

"The only thing I agree to is stepping aside when Athena comes to flay you herself," he said with hate-filled eyes.

Euryale sighed. With a nod of her head, she bid Alex to follow, and the two left the dungeon, shutting and barring the door behind them. Neither spoke a word as they climbed the mossy spiral staircase. But when they finally reached the surface, where sunlight peeked through large holes in the ruins that surrounded them, a few words were exchanged.

"Think anyone will find him here?"

Euryale shook her head. "Not for a while."

"Think you can get him to come around?"

The gorgon's shoulders fell. "No, but I'm going to pretend otherwise."

Chapter Athena and the Lighthouse

Athena, having followed a long trail of clues to this particular location, picked her way along the shoreline. Though she was hot on the trail of whoever Aphrodite or Ares had hired to steal her aegis, she let her eyes dart to the nearby tide pools on occasion to admire the crabs and small fish in them. Aquatic life had always found a special spot in her heart, as their creativity and diversity gave her so much to think and learn about.

Dolphins, for example, slept with only half their brains at a time, which, if truth be told, had always made the Goddess of Wisdom jealous in that she would love to be able to spend the extra time catching up on her reading list.

Then there was the fascinating colossal squid. She had no idea why Poseidon, God of the Sea, had made it so that it literally ate its food with its brain before the food actually got to the stomach (food that was swallowed went down the esophagus, through the hole in its doughnut-shaped brain where nutrients were pulled out, and then into the stomach), but she had to admit that it was an exceptionally clever way of designing the digestive system so that the brain was properly fed. And a properly fed brain meant a healthy brain, which Athena had always considered to be of paramount importance.

Athena paused near one of the wider pools as an eastern wind tossed her hair. Her eyes scanned the area before she ended up kneeling to examine the tracks. There was something familiar about them. Where she had seen them before, she couldn't say, but she knew she'd seen them sometime in the last year or so. They belonged to a mortal, perhaps five foot six and weighing around a hundred and forty pounds, give or take a few ounces. It was hard to be precise given the composition of this particular sand.

A low rumbling drew her attention out over the ocean to where thunderheads gathered. Though they were far on the horizon, she could tell that they were spreading quickly, and the rain that fell from their blackened bottoms would quickly destroy the trail she was following.

Athena drove forward with greater speed than before. She soon found herself headed for an old lighthouse up ahead. As she went, the air dropped in temperature and the wind increased. While both brought a biting cold, the latter brought a swell of waves that would soon threaten anyone still caught on the sandy shore.

A sinewy creature with six legs, a misshapen head, and a gaping maw filled with jagged teeth burst from the water. The Goddess of Wisdom (and the occasional war) was more annoyed at the poor ambush than anything. If someone or something were going to attack her, the least they could do was treat her with at least a modicum of respect for her abilities.

Athena whipped her spear in line with the now-flying-and-soon-to-be-dead creature. Before it had time to blink, the monster impaled itself with a sickening crunch on her spearpoint. Keeping with the monster's momentum, Athena spun the weapon sideways and slung it away.

Athena hurried over to where it hit the beach. It twitched a few times before going still, at which point she squatted and examined the thing. It didn't appear to be part of any one particular species, but then again, most monsters weren't. Though the return of the Olympians the prior year meant that all sorts of creatures had come back or awoken as well, she doubted its presence here was coincidental.

"Who made you?" she asked.

The monster, being dead, didn't reply, which was all the same to the goddess, as even she would've thought that unsettling.

With no further answers, Athena returned to following the trail that had led her this far in the first place. When she was within a quarter mile of the lighthouse, the clouds had gathered overhead, and the first drops of rain fell on her face. She didn't mind the shower, but she frowned at the thought of the tracks she was following being washed away. They still looked as if they were headed straight for the lighthouse, but one didn't become the Goddess of Wisdom by blindly following the most obvious clues to the most obvious of conclusions. Even if there weren't trickery involved, the trail could always make a turn west to where a sleepy nearby town stood. Who stole an aegis from a goddess and hid out in a rundown lighthouse, anyway?

Less than a minute later, the droplets of rain turned to a torrential downpour. Lightning streaked through the skies and thunder crashed so loud that Athena had trouble hearing herself think. Her prediction also held true, and the trail vanished under the deluge of water. Thankfully by now, she had followed it to within a couple of hundred yards of the lighthouse, and as such, she did not doubt that that was where her shield would be. Or at least, that was where whoever had stolen it would be.

Athena slowed as she started down the narrow path. Up ahead and lying off to the side were the remains of not one hideous, deformed creature made of lobster claws, scorpion tails, and dragon hide, but three. Each one had multiple wounds across its body, as well as gaping holes in its sides where spear had pierced flesh and bone.

Who had done such a thing remained a mystery for only a few moments. Past the bodies, nearly to the lighthouse keeper's home, a shadowy figure crouched against a nearby boulder, its back at the goddess and a long spear clutched in its hands.

Athena adjusted the grip on her weapon and continued forward. At first, she was going to challenge whoever it turned out to be, but that all went straight to Hades when she recognized the woman. "Jessica?"

Startled, Jessica popped up and spun around. The look of terror on her face flashed away as relief took its place. "Oh, thank the gods, it's you," she said with a sigh of relief. "I thought for a second I'd left one of those things alive."

"What are you doing here?"

"Me? I'm trying to get back the pendant The Old Man gave me," she said. "Some a-hole cyclops stole it, and I followed him here."

Athena tilted her head. "A pendant? What kind of pendant?"

"One that protects against all things gorgon," she replied. "Or so I'm told. I haven't tried it yet. What are you doing here?"

"Apparently, tracking the same thieving cyclops," Athena said, narrowing her eyes and setting her jaw. What the damned thing was going to do with her shield and Jessica's pendant, she had yet to figure out, but given that the race of one-eyed giants had been known to work a forge on occasion, she had the sneaking suspicion that this cyclops intended to repurpose both pendant and shield for the creation of something new.

"I've been sitting here trying to figure out how to get in there without him getting the drop on me," Jessica said. "I thought I could probably sneak in with the storm."

"Nice work on those monsters back there, by the way."

"Yeah, thanks," Jessica said with pride. "I guess I've taken to the title 'Jessica, the Monster Slayer' fairly well. Maybe when I can get back to Elysium, Odysseus and Heracles will invite me on another hunt. I'd love to show them what I can do now seeing how last time I almost got eaten by a harpy."

"The three of those look much more dangerous than a harpy," Athena said, glancing back toward the monsters.

"Exactly. But a cyclops has to be as dangerous as fifty of them, hence me thinking," she replied. "But now that you're here, we can go in together."

"No," Athena said. "I'll handle it. You wait here. If he slips out somehow without me noticing, I want you to scream your head off. Think you can do that?"

Jessica smiled. "I've been known to scream on occasion. But if he gets mad at me and charges, do me a favor and don't be long? I'm not ready to meet Kharon on my way to the afterlife."

Athena dropped a hand on Jessica's shoulder and squeezed. "The only one that should be worried is that cyclops."

With that, the Goddess of Wisdom swiftly moved up to the keeper's house and flattened herself against one of its walls. She then inched forward until she reached one of the windows and peered inside. She couldn't see much other than a quaint kitchen that had a small electric stove in one corner that had been placed by a worn, white refrigerator which was probably only a few birthdays shy of being as old as she was. Nearby was an open doorway that led into a dining room, but what was in that particular room other than tables and chairs, she couldn't tell due to her angle.

Athena ducked her head and moved beneath the windowsill, making sure she was well clear of the area before popping up. She rounded the far corner right as a particularly large wave broke on the rocks below, sending a massive, salty spray all over her rain-soaked body. She didn't mind. The extra noise the storm brought would mask any sound she might inadvertently make.

When she reached the front door, she waited for a clap of thunder before quickly opening it and slipping inside. The front hall she found herself in had gray tile on the floor and chipped paint on the walls. Ahead, a dilapidated staircase ran to the second floor. Each step seemed barely fit to hold a small child and would probably give any OSHA inspector a heart attack, or a cause to celebrate depending on his personality and how far along he was in his monthly quota of violation citations.

She turned left and was presented with a fairly ordinary living room. A couch sat against one wall. Opposite that stood a TV on a wooden stand. In between those, however, stood a coffee table with her shield placed directly in the center. Sitting on her shield, to her shock, was a large fox with a gorgeous coat of red fur, bright green eyes, and a what-a-tasty-snack-I've-discovered smile upon his face.

"Teumessian Fox?" Athena asked, trying to wrap her mind around who she was looking at.

The Fox grinned broadly and bowed his head. "The one and only."

"How?" she asked.

"How did I steal your shield?" he asked, sounding offended. "As if I could ever be caught."

"No, how did you escape imprisonment?" she clarified. "Father turned you to stone."

At that point, Athena realized the house had dulled her senses, and the spell that muted her powers had been hidden by the storm's presence long enough for the trap she'd walked into to be sprung.

Athena turned as she was hit with a long, heavy silver chain. It wrapped around her body, pinning her wrists to her waist and then her legs together. All of this was more than enough to send her off balance and have her topple to the floor.

A foot peeking out of a gold-and-green robe appeared next to Athena's head. Though she hadn't seen it in eons, she knew exactly who it belonged to. "I should have squashed you long ago," Athena said.

"Yes, I suppose you should have," Arachne replied. She smiled as her tongue flicked over her fangs. "As long as we're confessing,

I'm surprised this was so easy. It's nice to know even goddesses get overconfident and sloppy from time to time."

"Using Jessica was a nice touch."

"Wasn't it?" Arachne said, beaming with pride.

Athena struggled against the bindings, but they held fast. One might even say as she worked against them, they grew stronger, and she grew weaker.

"They've been enchanted for precisely this occasion," Arachne said. "But I'm sure you've figured that out by now."

Athena nodded, and her gray eyes narrowed. She might be in a predicament that was a few battles short of ideal, but she wasn't about to capitulate whatsoever. She needed information if she were going to gain the upper hand. "What do you want from me? Or is this all about revenge?"

"It's about revenge. There's no grand scheme here," Arachne said. "How long this all takes, however, will be up to you. I only need to know one thing."

Athena laughed. "If it's information you seek, you'll never get it from me. My mind is a fortress, and it's more secure than Olympus itself."

"We'll see," Arachne replied, not missing a beat. "And for the record, if I were you, I wouldn't consider Olympus all that secure."

Chapter Calm Before the Storm

Euryale, after changing the bandage to her leg again, found her husband at the end of their wooden pier with his feet dangling in the cool, clear water. Beneath the glass-like surface, an array of bright coral decorated the underwater landscape, and tiny fish darted in and out of the safe harbor they provided.

The gorgon took a seat next to Alex and leaned her head against his shoulder. As stressful as this day had been, as stressful as she'd found living in Elysium to be, she relished this little end-of-the-day ritual they'd done for the past year. Sitting out on the dock as the light waned helped her to unwind, to cope, and to focus on what was important: her family.

"One more sleep until the party," Alex said. "Then you can relax, right? What else is there left to do?"

"At this point, I don't care," she said. "I need a break from the planning. Besides, if we're not ready now, we'll never be."

"You sure?" Alex said, leaning to the side so he could get a better look at his wife. "I don't mind finishing up. Just tell me what to do."

"All I want at this point is for you to spend time with your adoring wife who loves you very much," she said.

"And?"

"And that's it."

Alex nodded and kissed her on the cheek. "I can do that. But..."

Euryale arched an eyebrow. "But what?"

"Perseus?"

Euryale groaned. "I can't think about him now."

"I know, but we're like in kidnapping territory now. Or hostage taking, right?"

"It'll be fine, Alex," she said, though she had a nagging feeling it would be anything but. "Heroes used to capture each other all the time, for years even. Besides, that old dungeon we tossed him in is cozy enough."

"Not sure I'd call it cozy."

"Compared to a lava pit, it is."

"True," Alex replied. He then wrapped his arm around her and squeezed. "Sorry. This is still new to me. I'll let it go."

"Thanks," she said. She sighed heavily. "I wish I didn't look like this."

"All the planning you've done, I think anyone would look frazzled."

"No, silly. Like this," she said, sweeping her hand over her body. "Life would be so much easier."

"Oh." The two sat silently for a few beats before Alex spoke with hesitation. "There's nothing we can do, though, right? I mean, I love you as you are, but I want you to be happy, too."

Euryale shook her head and then rested her chin on her hands. "No. Athena could reverse it, or maybe one of the other gods like Hera. But they don't like me enough for that."

"Maybe I could ask."

"Sweet, Alex, but even all the heroes on this island couldn't sway Athena's mind," she said. "She's definitely the no-chance-at-parole type of goddess."

Alex grimaced. "How much longer do you have to serve on your sentence? I guess I never asked."

"Eternity."

"Well...hell..." Alex said.

"Exactly. So unless you can reverse time, I'm stuck."

Silence reigned once again, and eventually the subject was changed when Alex gave her another squeeze. "Don't suppose you know what you want to do after the party, do you?"

"Hadn't thought about it." Euryale shrugged. "What do you want to do tomorrow?"

"Odysseus wants to try and get that new hydra," he replied. "I think I'll pass, though. Thought we could slip out and see your dad. It's been a bit."

"He'd like that." Euryale snuggled into him further. "I would, too."

"Still have some jerky for Cerberus? We'll need to bribe him, as usual."

Euryale laughed. She put a hand over her mouth and tried to stop, but she was unsuccessful.

"What?"

"Nothing."

Alex turned to his wife. "What? C'mon, tell me."

"Heroes can leave whenever they want," she said. "It's just sort of a joke played on the newcomers, see how long it takes them to figure it out."

"No..."

"Yes."

"But Heracles, Achilles, Perseus—"

"Are never around when you go looking for them, are they?" Euryale interjected with a smile.

"Well, it's a big island..." Alex shook his head before he laughed and hit the pier with the bottom of his fist. "Son of a bitch. We can really go whenever we like?"

"Pretty much, as long as we keep things low-key."

"Well, I'm really, really glad to hear that," said a familiar voice from behind.

Alex twisted in place to see Jessica standing a few paces away. Her hair, pulled back in a ponytail, looked like it hadn't been washed in a week. Dirt clung to portions of her skin, and a few bruises showed as well. Her tank top, khaki shorts, and hiking boots had all seen better days, too. Despite all this, Alex leaped to his feet and ran over to her. "Jessica! It's so great to see you! How have you been?"

"Never better," she said. "Got home last year and became rich and famous with all those pictures I'd taken. People are still trying to wrap their heads around the gods showing up, but getting in on the action from the start has been lucrative, to say the least. A wee bit dangerous, too, I might add."

Alex's shoulders fell, and he cursed. "Oh, damn. You're dead, aren't you?"

"No," she said, laughing. "I'm not quite dead yet. Got a little spell of protection from all things gorgon cast on me courtesy of The Old Man. That said, I need help from the both of you—if you're up to it."

Alex glanced back at his smiling wife, who gave an encouraging nod. "I hope this doesn't involve us going to war with Ares."

"Nope. But by the time this is over, you might wish we were."

Alex's eyes widened. "Worse than going to war with Ares? What could be worse than that?"

"Going to war with Zeus, for one," Euryale said while holding up a finger. While she continued her list, she continued using the rest of her digits to illustrate her point. "Or going to war with Hades. Or going to war with Poseidon. Or going to war with all three. Or fighting an army of titans. Or fighting an army of titans led by Ares. Or pretty much being anywhere should Cronus awake from his slumber and escape the Cave of Nyx. If that ever happens, everyone and everything would be destroyed."

"Is that all?" Alex asked with a nervous laugh.

"No," Jessica said as she held up a finger of her own. "There's at least one more."

"Which would be?"

"You explaining why I didn't get an invite to your anniversary party."

A knowing smile slowly spread across Euryale's face. She couldn't wait to see how her husband would wiggle out of this one, especially since the two had argued for quite some time on whether or not they should send her an invitation. "Yes, dear," Euryale said. "Tell her."

"Well, I didn't think you could come," Alex said, stammering over the explanation. No doubt in his mind he had thought it would be a good one, but his delivery and tone were far from convincing.

"Didn't think I would come? Me? After all we'd been through involving Athena and Aphrodite? And don't even get me started on plowing through the Underworld together and nearly getting pulverized by a cyclops. Oh, and then there was that little bit where your wife tried to kill me—no offense, Euryale, I know that wasn't your fault."

Euryale nodded. Over the last year, she'd come to appreciate Jessica's place in Alex's life, and any jealousy she had had for the woman was now long gone. "It's okay," the gorgon said. "Not my proudest of moments, but I'm glad you can forgive me, at least."

"I can, but what I can't forgive is Alex thinking I would miss this party for anything in the world," Jessica replied, putting her hands on her hips. "I mean, really, you didn't think I would come?"

"I didn't say I didn't think you would want to come. I said I didn't think you could come, as in I didn't think you'd be able to," Alex said, this time sounding a little stronger than before. "We had to sneak you in and out of the Underworld every time before, remember? Apollo and Persephone were both adamant about the fact that Hades would lose his mind if he knew mortals were coming and going out of his realm like it was an amusement park."

"I think I'm a little more than an everyday mortal," Jessica replied. "Besides, I did his pictures, remember? And he loves them. I'm sure you could've pulled some strings and gotten me in and out if you wanted. At the very least, Alex, you could've sent me a letter explaining what was going on in your mind."

"Well, Euryale had suggested that but—" Alex sighed and shook his head. "Okay. You're right. I should've sent you an invitation, or at least let you know I was going to try to sneak you in somehow. I'm sorry. I didn't want you to get hurt, is all, but now that you're here…"

"Yes?" Jessica replied with an amused smile.

"If you're free tomorrow, how'd you like to come to a fantastic party? You and Euryale could talk girl talk, too. That's still a thing, isn't it?"

"It is," Jessica said. "In fact, unless you two love birds have something I'm intruding on at the moment, I'd love some girl talk with her right now."

"For the record, Jessica, I was going to send you an invitation later this evening," Euryale said. "I was hoping to talk Alex into sending one himself, but then you showed up."

"Thanks," she said. "So how about that chat?"

"Sure," Euryale said, warily taking to her feet. There was something in Jessica's voice that told her that the woman had more in her heart than idle gossip. Then again, maybe stress from planning the party was causing her to read more into it than there actually was. "Hope this doesn't take too long. I'd love for you to meet the kids before they sack out for the night."

"You have kids? Oh my goodness, I bet they are the most adorable little things ever!"

"They are, but the games they play can turn into matters of life and death in a flash."

Jessica laughed. "My sister has kids. She says the same about them."

"I wasn't being figurative."

"Right. Point taken," Jessica said, stuffing her hands into her pockets. "Maybe I'll just wave at them from afar."

The two walked until Euryale's house and pier were well out of sight. They ended up at the shore of a small lake which was dotted with orchids, daffodils, and hyacinths that gave off pleasing aromas, and the colors offered up by them were a welcomed sight for Euryale. Hostile heroes aside, the beauty of Elysium made for much different living than the barren island she'd had to live on before. This scene, as far as she was concerned, was what the afterlife should be. Not a place filled with monsters hunted for sport or so-called men who longed to torment her at every opportunity.

Euryale pushed those thoughts away. Now was not the time to indulge in them with Jessica here. "So, what's on your mind?" she asked.

Jessica fidgeted with her hands for a few moments before replying. "Do you ever think about what happened?"

"When?"

"Last year, in the labyrinth."

"Yes, and with complete regret," Euryale said. She felt her heart shrink as anger and embarrassment at her actions surfaced. Even though Aphrodite had manipulated her into losing her sanity, ultimately Euryale knew that she was the one who had turned into the monster. She was the one who had nearly killed Jessica, and she was the one who had forced her husband to die—again—to stop her rampage. "If you're looking for an apology, I'll certainly give you one."

"No, I'm not," Jessica said. She laughed and fixed her ponytail, which didn't need fixing. "I guess what I was asking is, do you ever wish you could do something about it?"

"I try not to dwell on the past."

"Try?"

Euryale nodded. "Yes, but I'm not always successful. Besides, what's done is done and there's no undoing it. I have Alex, and you're still alive. What else could I ask for?"

Jessica's eyes darted left and right, and she bit on her lower lip before answering. "Is this area secluded?"

"This is Elysium. It doesn't get any more secluded. Well, maybe my old home was more so, but not by much."

"No, I mean, is there any chance anyone will be listening?"

"Like who?"

"Like the gods," Jessica said, her voice barely a whisper.

Euryale tilted her head, and her brow dropped. She didn't know what the woman had to say, but no doubt it was of great importance. "There's always that chance, Jessica. But here, not as much as, say, smack dab in the middle of Zeus's temple."

"What about them?" Jessica said as she bobbed her head toward a pair of peacocks who were watching them from across the water.

"They look like birds to me," Euryale said. "Nothing out of the ordinary. But if you're this uncomfortable, perhaps you should keep those thoughts for another time."

"No. We need to talk…I need to talk."

Euryale nodded but kept quiet.

Jessica let out a nervous laugh and kept her voice low. "Do you ever wish you could have justice for what happened?"

Euryale straightened. "Oh," she said. "Oh…"

"Yeah."

The gorgon, of course, like any being with a heart and even the smallest sense of right and wrong, had certainly thought about how poorly Aphrodite had treated her, how the goddess had abused her to try and settle a score with her sister Athena, and how the goddess had nearly succeeded in tearing Euryale away from the only man who'd shown her any sort of love since before she'd been cursed. "What are you getting at?"

"You have, haven't you?" Jessica asked, this time her voice strong and full of energy.

"I have. You know I'd be lying if I said otherwise."

"Then I'm offering you a way to help set things right, to ensure that that bitch never does anything like that again."

Euryale quickly closed the distance between the two and took the woman's hands. They were softer than she had expected, and while long ago she had had no small amount of jealousy for the woman, now she only had compassion and worry. "Jessica, I tell you this as someone who knows the gods. You can't ever talk of such things. You will only make things worse—and they can always get worse. Always."

"Are you sure about that?" Jessica asked, staying strong.

"Very."

"You don't even want to hear what I have to say? Do you honestly not want Aphrodite to have to answer for her crimes against you?"

Euryale shook her head. "It's not that I don't want to listen, but what you're hinting at will never happen."

Jessica went on, seemingly not hearing a word that the gorgon was saying. "And what about Athena? What about the one who cursed you and your sisters? What about the one who sent Perseus to slay Medusa? What about the one who banished you into exile for how long again? She hasn't given any of that a second thought, and as far as I know, she's not even the least bit remorseful. Proud, even. Tell me you don't want to hear at least how she could be made to answer for what she's done as well."

Euryale took in a slow, deep breath. She'd always been polite around the Goddess of Wisdom, more out of necessity than genuine respect and affection, and Athena had shown a little favor to Alex, so there was that. And, of course, Athena had come to his defense in the end, thereby allowing Euryale and Alex to be reunited and live in Elysium.

That said, the thought of all that Athena had done to her and her sisters, as Jessica had so pointed out, made Euryale's blood boil. The gorgon could feel her eyes darken and her nails grow. As much as she wanted to give in to that rage, her rational side was still in enough control that she reminded herself of the futility of such desires.

"Aphrodite might not be the smartest of Olympians, but she's still a goddess," Euryale said. "I admire your determination, Jessica, but she will still tear you to pieces, and that's not even counting all of the other Olympians who would come to her defense—like Ares. On top of that, you want to go after Athena as well? The favored daughter of Zeus? The Goddess of Wisdom *and* War?"

Jessica didn't bat an eye. "Yes."

Euryale laughed. "You mortals are full of so much hubris. It really is a wonder you've lasted this long. Athena will not be tricked like Ares was. She knows anything and everything you could throw at her, and she will use each one of those things to bring you lower than you ever thought possible."

"You don't want to hear me out at all?"

"No," Euryale said as she shook her head, her face full of remorse. "Because I want you to understand how destructive this path will be for you, I'm not going to indulge this conversation whatsoever. Look at me. Look what she made me. She turned me into a monster to suffer until the end of time, and she wasn't even that mad. Now think what she'll do to you and anyone else you love if you face her true fury."

"Do you want your family living under such fear?" she asked. "If the Olympians aren't ever held accountable, it's only a matter of time before either you or Alex runs afoul of them again. Or your children, for that matter, and it wouldn't even have to be their fault."

"I know how fickle they can be," Euryale replied. "But you're asking me to risk more than my life. Aison and Cassandra would be held accountable as well. I can't put them in that sort of danger."

Euryale was about to suggest that they return home and enjoy the party and forget this entire conversation when Jessica blurted out the most unexpected of things.

"It's not just me," Jessica said, now sounding a little more desperate. "Athena, and all the Olympians in fact, have a long list of enemies, and that list is about to catch up to them."

"Who did you meet?" Euryale said, tilting her head.

"Arachne."

Euryale grabbed Jessica by the shoulders, perhaps a little too forcefully as the woman jumped back but didn't get far due to the gorgon's viselike grip. "Jessica, do you know who she is?"

"Of course I do. She's the woman Athena turned into a spider."

"What did she say?"

"She said she's going to bring them all down," the woman replied. "She said she's been planning this for thousands of years."

Euryale shook her head as she let Jessica go. "Did she say how?"

"She said she'd tell me the specifics later," she replied. "She wanted me to recruit you and Alex first. I guess as a test of faith?"

Euryale nodded. A nervous flutter formed in her stomach, and she wondered if her eyes reflected the fear that she was trying to suppress. "Listen to me, Jessica," she said, locking her eyes with the woman's so that she didn't miss a single word that was being spoken. "Arachne can't be trusted."

"Why would you say that?" Jessica asked, straightening. "She was nice."

"Of course she was. The web of lies she spins requires nothing less."

"You're saying she's tricking me?"

"I'm saying she's getting you into a total disaster," Euryale said. "She's a clever woman, and since I'm assuming she's no longer a tiny spider, she's grown tremendously in power as well."

"I'm sure she has," Jessica said. "But if you're worried that she's trying to hide that, don't. She's been very upfront."

"Did she tell you who she's working with? Or rather, who's pulling her strings?"

Jessica rubbed the back of her neck as she thought. "She only said she was working with an exceptional thief. Hang on a sec. What do you mean someone's pulling her strings?"

"I mean even if she did find a way to break Athena's curse on her own, there's no possible way she's orchestrating a war against any of the Olympians without someone far more powerful backing her."

"Isn't that good for us?" Jessica said, stammering. "You're the one who said you didn't want to seek justice against Athena or Aphrodite because it would only end badly. And now, apparently, Arachne has an ace in the hole."

"A what?"

"An ace in the hole," Jessica repeated. "It means she's got a secret play that will win the game."

"She's got a secret, no doubt," Euryale said. "But it can't be good."

"I don't see how, especially if it means those two godawful sisters answer for torturing us."

"There are two options here," Euryale said, holding up a pair of fingers. "One, she's working with others who she believes are strong enough to bring down the Olympians but aren't, in which case their utter and eternal torment is guaranteed. Or two, she's working with those who might pull it off, but the war that they will bring will be so terrible, nothing left will be alive by the time the dust settles on the battlefield. Do you want the death of countless billions of people weighing against your soul? Surely your thirst for vengeance doesn't run that deep."

Jessica folded her arms, and her gaze drifted to the grass at her feet. She spent a few moments in quiet contemplation, which was something Euryale was grateful for as she didn't like the idea of Jessica making such rash decisions. "There's nothing that will change your mind, then?"

"No," Euryale said. "And even though I loathe those two goddesses, not all the Olympians are bad."

"How can you say that?" Jessica said, shaking her head as tears glistened in her eyes. "None of them helped you. None of them stood up for you. They let Athena and Aphrodite have their way with you and Alex while they went about their own business."

"How can I say that? How can you say that?" Euryale countered. "Zeus is the one who gave Alex a chance at life, and Apollo let you tour the stars with him. And that's not even counting Hephaestus who came to Alex's aid multiple times."

"I know, but I'm not talking about them."

"If you join a war, all of them will come to Athena and Aphrodite's defense. You can count on that," Euryale said. She then cocked her head and eyed the woman with suspicion. "In fact..."

"In fact what?"

"You're not the Jessica I know, nor the one I've heard so much about."

"If I'm not, it's only because the more I think about how unfair things are, the more I want to do something about them," Jessica said, her voice taking a razor's edge. "I'd hoped you would be the same, or at least understand."

Euryale, however, took no offense at the woman's sudden change in affect. "I understand. Believe me, I do. But I also know starting a fight you can never win is not the answer."

"So you're not interested."

"No, and for your sake, I'd distance myself from Arachne immediately. You can stay here if you like until this resolves, or—"

"Or what?"

"Or if you wanted to win favors from the gods, you could always become a spy. We both could. Fates know I could use some of their gratitude."

Jessica sighed and kicked a rock that was near her foot so that it sailed a few dozen yards before splashing into the lake. "You really mucked up my plans. You know that?"

Euryale shrugged with a slight grin, feeling as if the situation had defused and Jessica was coming around to seeing the insanity of her idea. "Sorry. When we get back, we'll have some wine. I'm sure a few glasses will help you feel better."

Chapter The Party

Compared to any other party Euryale had had over the last few thousand years, this one was a smashing success. After all, it was being held on the beautiful island of Elysium under a gorgeous morning sky as opposed to a barren rock cropping out of the sea where she'd once been banished. Also, this party had a massive table with plenty of delicious food for guests to dine on, ranging from various types of cheese to meats to loaves of bread. Then, of course, there were the guests. Whereas Euryale had once had to celebrate occasions with only her monstrous sisters and whatever stone statues they felt like dragging into place for company, this party had actual, living attendees. However, those who had come numbered exactly two, which was far less than the number she'd expected. Far, far less.

The first to arrive was, of course, Jessica.

The second was one Euryale would've never dared guessed would be the only other attendee, and that guest was Ares.

The God of War sat at one end of the table, feasting on a giant leg of turkey while helping himself to large quantities of wine as he talked to Alex. Euryale had been nervous when they'd first met, seeing how they hadn't interacted whatsoever since the two had been pitted against each other in war a year ago. Judging from Alex's initial apprehension at seeing the god, he shared similar concerns, but as it stood now, the two were seemingly enjoying a good conversation.

At the very least, they weren't throwing spears and grenades at each other. Hopefully, it would stay that way, but knowing the God of War's temper, that could change in a flash. Thus, she decided to eavesdrop on their conversation.

"I can't believe you took over professional football," Alex said, shaking his head before popping some grapes into his mouth.

"Believe it, little mortal. I have great plans for the sport," Ares replied, beaming.

"Why do I get the feeling that your plans are not the same as the league owners'?"

"Because your feelings are right," Ares said. "The warriors on the field have strong hearts, but their owners are weak and hold them back. They say their men will not appreciate having bones snapped and blood spilled on the field of battle."

Alex cringed. "Yeah, I don't think the fans are going to appreciate that either."

"So I've heard," Ares said with a frown. "But that is only because they are too used to watching a boring game where a ball is chased up and down the field with little else. What they need is something new. Something exciting. Something never been done before."

"You know we've tried the whole gladiator thing, right?" Alex asked. "That didn't work out for humanity, and we ditched it like two thousand years ago."

"I know," Ares said. He leaned over to Alex and held up a finger as he grinned from ear to ear. "But I have grand ideas, Alex. Grand ideas you gave me."

"Me?"

"Yes, you. Remember when you threw that grenade, and it exploded in my face?"

"Yes, but that was out of necessity, not sport."

"But it could be sport!" Ares said raising his fists in excitement. "Think about it! What if the ball they threw exploded? How thrilling would that be?"

"I don't think anybody is going to want to catch that ball," Alex replied. "And you can't blow up players."

"Of course I can," Ares said. "You dare think I can't?"

"What? No," Alex said, holding up his hands defensively. "I'm saying, if you want to take over football and have it be popular, blowing people up is exactly the opposite of what the fans want. Also, it's bad for morale, and cleaning up the field after each game…I mean, is that something you want to invest in? Plus, if the Marines are right, all that blood is going to make the grass grow, a lot, so your bill for lawn mowing is going to go through the roof."

"I have watched these TV shows of yours. You mortals love wanton violence. They will like it, or I will crush them."

"If you crush the fans, who will watch the game?"

"The ones that like the violence and don't get crushed," Ares replied.

Alex sighed and rubbed his temples. "Let's put this whole blowing up players in the maybe category, okay? I'm not saying it's a definite no, but perhaps you've got some other ideas that could work?"

"I do have a few more," Ares said, leaning back and smiling. "My next idea will be the first I implement. Nothing drastic, mind you, but one to get things moving in the right direction."

"So you're going to warm up the crowd to your all-out war on the pitch?"

"Precisely. Now envision this: the football, instead of being an inflated piece of leather, is a hunk of wood."

"Wood? Why wood?"

"So it can hold the spikes, of course!" Ares said, giving a fist pump. "Picture every detail I'm about to tell you. The center snaps the ball. The quarterback settles into the pocket. He looks for an open receiver. Suddenly one of the defensive linemen breaks through. The quarterback has nowhere to scramble. So instead of taking the tackle, he drills that ball right into his attacker's face! Now that's a game I can get into!"

"Oh, Jesus," Alex muttered.

"Yes, Jesus! A man who can appreciate wood and nails! I would think all of his followers would get behind the idea as well!"

Alex cringed and buried his face in his palms. "I think we need to put that one in the maybe pile, too. At the very least, we need to refine these before your first season."

Surprisingly, Ares nodded. "That is why I ultimately decided to come to this party. I wanted your input, little mortal, as you are one who has shown yourself worthy of fighting me to a draw."

"Right, a draw," Alex repeated, figuring it wasn't a good idea to correct the god whatsoever.

"Something is still missing in all of this. I don't know what. Equipment, perhaps?"

"I hope you don't mean weapons."

"No," Ares said. "I had already thought of that."

At this point, Jessica put a hand on the gorgon's forearm and drew her attention. "Is there anything I can do? Maybe get some more wine or something?"

Euryale smiled as much as she could. Jessica had practically been attached to the gorgon for the past hour. She didn't know if the woman was offering to help so much and keep her entertained because she felt bad for Euryale, or if she was behaving in such a manner because of the conversation they had had about Arachne. Truth be told, Euryale didn't care. She needed the distraction as she was on the verge of tears.

"No," Euryale said. "You've done enough already. Thanks."

"Surely I can do something," Jessica replied. "You look positively miserable."

"You would be, too, if this happened to you," Euryale lamented as she gestured at the table full of empty seats.

"At least you'll have plenty of leftovers, right?" Jessica said, putting her goblet of wine on the table and giving the gorgon a one-armed hug. "I mean, better you have too much food than too little."

"I don't understand," Euryale said. "We've always been on good terms with at least a few of the Olympians, like Apollo and Zeus. Not to mention Athena."

"Maybe...maybe they're busy."

"I can't believe they ignored us like this," Euryale said, feeling her throat tighten. "And Hephaestus, too! Why would he ever refuse our invitation? He made Alex swear to visit him often and has always loved our company, and he was thrilled when Alex stuck it to Ares and Aphrodite."

"I'm sure there's a good reason."

Euryale slumped. "Maybe I've been lying to myself for the past year, and I'm still just a monster no one can stand. I mean, not even the heroes we share the island with came."

The conversation was interrupted by the screeching of a tiny voice. "Mom! Mom!"

Euryale whipped around as Aison came barging out of the house, his little face completely flustered. "What?" she asked. "You better be missing a leg with that noise!"

"Cassandra's trying to turn me to stone!"

"It's not like it would last!" Cassandra shouted as she came flying out of the house. "He said he was going to chop my head off!"

"I did not, liar!"

"You're the liar!"

"No, you are!"

"Shut up, hydra butt!"

"Siren sucker!"

In a flash, the twins grappled each other and ended up on the ground in a messy fight. Tiny fists and feet struck each other as vipers from both of their heads sank miniature fangs into flesh.

"That's enough!" Euryale bellowed, jumping to her feet. Jessica and Alex shrank under the blast, and even Ares grimaced.

Foliage for a hundred yards in each direction withered to nothing, and her children froze. "You two will go upstairs and play nice, or I'll feed you to Charybdis myself!"

The twins stopped their wrestling match and disengaged. As they slowly came to their feet, they shared unspoken words between them, apparently trying to gauge how serious their mother's threat was. As far as Euryale was concerned, she wasn't threatening a thing. It was a full-on promise.

"If that's how you talk to your children in public, I can only imagine what they suffer when no one is around," said a sickeningly sweet voice from behind. "I suppose that's why everyone wanted to come to my party instead of yours."

Euryale pivoted to find Aphrodite slowly approaching. An elegant yellow dress with a scoop neck clung to her figure, and her gorgeous hair seemed as if it had somehow been made even more perfect—because, of course, it would be. "Your party? What do you mean, your party?"

"Oh," she said, lightly touching her fingers to her lips while blushing at the same time. "I guess I forgot to send you an invitation. I'm sorry."

"You stole my guests?" Euryale asked. She could scarcely believe the words coming out of Aphrodite's mouth, even though deep down she knew such a thing was not beyond her. "Why?"

Aphrodite folded her arms and sneered. "I didn't steal them," she said. "I merely offered them a social gathering that I thought they'd enjoy. If I had known you were trying to play hostess, I would've at least told you of my plans so you could perhaps pick another date for your own quaint celebration. After all, that is a lot of food you've wasted."

Euryale blinked and then shook her head. "This is low, even for you. I sent you an invitation, so don't pretend otherwise. This was deliberate."

In a flash, Aphrodite closed the distance between herself and the gorgon. "You snubbing me was deliberate," she said as she poked Euryale in the middle of her chest with two fingers. She narrowed her eyes and leaned in close, her voice dropping in volume but doubling in anger and spite. "You think you were an outcast before? Take a long look around you, Euryale. This is the most company you'll ever see for the next ten thousand years. Mark my words. Athena won't intervene for Alex's sake, and from the looks of things, she doesn't want to be here, anyway."

"I'll—" Euryale stammered, but she never finished the statement.

Aphrodite, smelling blood, pressed the attack. "You'll what? Cry to your father? The one who loves you so much he left you on an island to rot? Or maybe your beloved, Alex? Go ahead. There's not an Olympian alive who will hear your case."

Euryale shrank, though she wished she hadn't. She quickly found her backbone and squared off with the goddess. "I sent you an invitation, but now I wish I hadn't. The only reason anyone else tolerates you is on account of your looks. Strip that away, and you're a useless, ugly thing who—"

Aphrodite slapped the gorgon. Hard. Not the sort of slap that might leave a red mark, or even fine lines across the skin where nails tear through flesh. No, this was a divine slap, one filled with ancient power that sounded like a freight train running full speed into a concrete wall.

The blow sent Euryale spinning to the ground, but in less than a second, Euryale shot up with fangs bared, arms outstretched, and razor claws leading the way. She did not, however, propel herself on feminine legs. Behind her trailed a serpentine tail longer than a fully grown anaconda.

"I'm going to rip that pretty face of yours to shreds," Euryale said as the two interlocked.

Dread washed over Aphrodite's face. She fended off Euryale's initial attacks, but it was clear she was on the losing end of the fight. The two wrestled for a few heartbeats, and then Alex and Ares joined the fray. Both the God of War and the newest hero of man ended up taking a number of blows as they struggled to separate the pair, but Euryale wasn't about to let either one of them stop her.

The gorgon wrapped her tail around Aphrodite's waist before coiling the rest on Alex's chest. This not only kept her anchored in place, but thanks to her legendary strength, not even Ares could pry her off his lover.

"How much will they love you when I peel your skin from your body?" Euryale asked. She ducked a fist from Ares and then blocked another strike from Aphrodite with her arms before laughing. "You'll never get away."

The four of them continued to fight for what felt like an eternity. They knocked over chairs, stumbled into the table multiple times, and sent food and wine flying on each occasion.

Euryale managed to get a hold of Aphrodite's wrist and was about to sink her fangs into it when Alex suddenly relinquished his grip. "Who the hell is that?"

Alex's voice was surprised and genuine enough to bring the entire melee to a temporary truce. Euryale whipped her head to the left. Running out of her home was a red-haired man in a cheap tan suit, clutching a pair of swords in his hands—swords that had been given to Euryale and Alex as a wedding present.

A split second later, flames burst from every window and doorway to Euryale's home.

Jessica's face soured like she'd taken a sip from a milk carton that'd been left in the sun for a week. "Damnit. I thought you four would've been fighting for longer than that."

Chapter Cake and Scorpions

Fearing more for her children than the his-and-her swords that were currently being stolen, Euryale uncoiled and dashed forward. Her assault was stopped when Jessica outstretched her hands, and from all ten fingertips, a mass of thick webs shot forth. Euryale managed to twist out of the way, but Jessica followed up by slinging a long chain that caught the gorgon's forearm and then entangled itself around Aphrodite's wrist.

In less than a second, a three-way contest was held between Euryale's momentum, her balance, and the strength of the metal chain. The chain won. Her arm yanked backward, thus causing her to fall to the ground in a heap while at the same time, dragging Aphrodite down as well.

"You dare attack my love?" Ares roared, vaulting over Euryale and Aphrodite with a single leap and spear in hand.

Jessica backtracked and pulled a crystal vial from one of her pockets. It held a thick, dark-red liquid inside. She threw it at the ground at Ares' feet, who leaped back and shielded his face—no doubt having flashbacks of a certain duel with a mortal that ended with him getting up close and personal with a hand grenade.

The vial didn't explode, but it did shatter into a thousand pieces, sending the dark liquid spattering across the ground. The earth rumbled within a few heartbeats before heaving into the air. Rock and debris rained for a hundred yards in each direction as a giant scorpion burst forth. The thing stood at least ten feet tall, not counting its arched stinger, and it sported claws that looked like they could peel the armor from battleships.

"Ha! Now this is a party!" Ares yelled, charging headlong, spear tip leading the way.

With the giant monstrosity busy with the God of War, Euryale tried to make for her burning home, but as she was still tethered to Aphrodite, moving anywhere was next to impossible, especially since the goddess had yet to take to her feet.

"Get up, damn you!" she hissed.

"I would if you'd stop dragging me everywhere!" Aphrodite shot back.

"I'll get the kids!" Alex yelled as he bolted by.

He didn't get far. A second eruption sent him scrambling backward as another enormous scorpion came out of the ground. It drove a stinger at his head, and Alex was forced to leap to the side to avoid being impaled. The monster didn't follow up with another attack, however. Instead it turned to the side to face Euryale and Aphrodite and charged.

Euryale crouched as her tail coiled beneath her and she let slip a deep growl. As far as she was concerned, this monster had made one fatal mistake, and that was getting between her and her children. It might have had size on its side, but she was the daughter of a god, and her father, Phorcys, hadn't raised a girl who cowered to mindless beasts.

The scorpion drove its right claw at her, and she tried to leap forward, using her tail to propel herself. To her dismay, however, Aphrodite backpedaled in the other direction, the net result being the two of them collapsing forward as Euryale's strength ultimately won but Aphrodite's action trumped the gorgon's balance.

"Look out!" Alex yelled.

Flat on her back, Euryale looked up in time to see the scorpion raise its left claw and drop it down like a massive hammer. The gorgon bear-hugged the Goddess of Love and rolled to the side, narrowly avoiding a crushing blow.

The scorpion turned with the pair and tried stabbing them with its tail, but Euryale rolled once more, and now that Aphrodite was no longer thwarting her, she used her tail to drive them out of harm's way. Before the creature had a chance to launch yet another attack, Alex appeared on top of its head and began punching the ever living mythological crap out of one of its eyes.

"Crashed the wrong party, didn't you?" Alex shouted as he rained blow after blow. The scorpion reeled and shrieked under the onslaught, giving Euryale and Aphrodite a brief respite from the fighting.

"Get off me, you disgusting thing!" Aphrodite yelled as she hit Euryale with her tiny fists.

"Gladly," she said, shoving her off.

As the scorpion staggered backward, blackened goo dripping out of one of its eyes, Alex caught his bride's attention. "I've got this one," he said. "Get the kids!"

Euryale, practically dragging Aphrodite along, slithered toward her burning home faster than a dragon divebombing a wayward knight.

The fires of her home were at least twice as tall as the structure itself at this point. The blaze gave off such a heat that she was sure Hephaestus could have used it as a forge if he pleased. Any mortal would have long succumbed to the blaze, even one a dozen yards away. Her only hope for her children's survival, her only prayer to the Fates, lay with the fact that they had divine blood running through their veins. Hopefully, it would be enough. The entire structure collapsed a second later, sending a huge plume of smoke and a shower of sparks high into the air.

"No!" Euryale screamed.

She was about to dive into the inferno when Aphrodite dug her heels into the ground and brought the two of them to a halt.

"Stop it! I have to save them!" Euryale screeched, now tugging at the goddess like any mother succumbed to total panic.

"I'm not burning for anyone!" she said.

Euryale pulled, and then twisted and grabbed Aphrodite's wrist to try and yank her forward, but Aphrodite stayed rooted in place. "Please," the gorgon said, tears now glistening in the light of the fire. "We have to go in. They could be in the basement where it's safe."

"I don't have to do anything!" Aphrodite shot back.

The gorgon pulled time and again, each one more frantic than the last. Breathing was practically impossible, and her heart beat so fast it was a miracle it hadn't exploded already.

"Mommy!"

Euryale spun in a half circle at her name.

Tickles charged around the back of the inferno with Aison and Cassandra holding on to his back for dear life, all three covered in soot and ash. The chimera collapsed a moment later, panting, and the twins jumped off and ran full tilt toward their mother's outstretched arms.

"My babies," she cried, snatching them up with one arm and squeezing them tight. "Are you hurt?"

The two shook their heads at the same time and replied as such. "No."

"Little help!"

Euryale turned to see Alex in a losing battle with the scorpion he was tangling with. Though he was still on its back, the thing was bucking so hard and fast, the number of seconds he had left on it before being thrown could be counted on two fingers.

"Stay here," Euryale said, putting her children down.

"What are you—?"

But that's all Aphrodite got out before the gorgon charged into the fray, dragging the Goddess of Love along. She was about halfway down the hill to the battle when the scorpion threw Alex off. He hit the ground and rolled, no doubt intent on dodging whatever follow-up attack the creature had. The scorpion, however, lashed out with its stinger and stabbed him in the side of the hip.

"Alex!" Euryale shouted.

Ares, who had both of his scorpion's claws in his hands and was currently wrestling it into submission, glanced over. He looked to his feet where his spear had fallen, and with a quick kick, he sent it sailing toward Euryale. "Catch!"

Euryale reached for the weapon, but so did Aphrodite. And thus neither one caught it, and instead it bounced off their forearms and fell to the side.

"He was throwing it to me," Aphrodite growled as they scrambled for the weapon.

"You? You've been useless this entire time," Euryale countered. "Shut up and look pretty. That's all you're good for."

Euryale's words were enough to sting Aphrodite into temporary shock, thus giving the gorgon enough time to snatch up the spear. Once the weapon was in hand, she charged forward to save her Alex, who was now firmly in the grasp of one of the scorpion's claws.

"Die, damn you!" Euryale screamed as she drove the spear into the scorpion's abdomen. To her shock and dismay, the spearpoint bounced off of the creature's exoskeleton.

"In the eye!" Ares called out right as he flipped his monster over and jumped on top of it.

Euryale darted forward. As the scorpion brought Alex to its mouth, she positioned herself for the perfect strike and drove her spear into its left eye. The head of the spear sank deep into flesh, driving all the way through until it sank into the monster's brain.

The scorpion staggered sideways, releasing Alex in the process. Euryale, even with Aphrodite attached to her arm and being dragged along, did not relinquish her grip on the spear. She twisted the weapon, and when the monster's legs gave out, she pulled it free before stabbing it four more times. The fifth stab was to be sure that it was dead, and the sixth and seventh were simply because she wanted to.

Covered with gore and scorpion blood, Euryale looked to Ares to see if he needed help. The answer was a resounding no. In fact, by the look on his face, one might correctly assume that he had been toying with the monster the entire time. He stood on its head and repeatedly bashed it with a chunk of its exoskeleton, sending flesh and chitin in all directions until the creature's head was an unrecognizable pulp.

Alex rolled over on the ground. Foam poured out of his mouth and blood flowed from his hip and seeped into the ground. Euryale was at his side in a flash, and when he saw her face looming above him, he smiled, reached out his hand, and stroked the side of her face. "The kids?"

"They're okay," Euryale said, forcing a smile and choking back her tears.

"Oh, good," he said with labored breaths. "Does that mean we won?"

"We did."

Alex held up a finger. "Good, because I think I'm about to throw up."

"Great, I'm bruised," Aphrodite said as she stared at her forearm where the chain had repeatedly pulled against her.

"Oh, the horror," Euryale said, rolling her eyes.

The two, still connected by seemingly unbreakable chains, sat at the party table with their backs facing each other and scowls resting upon their faces. While the Goddess of Love had managed to clean most of the dirt and blood off of her, thereby returning to her usual state of immaculate beauty, Euryale had yet to return to her mostly human form. From the waist down, she still bore her serpentine tail, and she still sported both claws and fangs that could tear flesh with little difficulty, but they had grown smaller since the battle had ended.

"What I don't get, and she really is a nice girl, for the record," Alex said, seated across from the pair, barely staying upright and slurring his words as if he'd had three bottles too many to drink. "Is why Jessica would torch the house?"

"She didn't torch the house, Alex," Euryale said. "Whoever she was with did."

"Yeah, well, details…Details…" He fumbled for a pitcher of water and ended up spilling most of it when he knocked it over, but he was fast enough in his scramble to save a few gulps, which he quickly took down. "I'm a little fuzzy…on the specifics…And I can't feel my legs…or my hips…Which is probably a good thing since I can cram all of my fingers into the hole on my side."

"It wasn't Jessica, either," Aphrodite said. "You of all people should know that."

"Her shooting webs out of her fingers clue you in?" Euryale scoffed.

"No, thank you. Some of us realized that it wasn't her before she pulled that stunt."

"Sure you did."

Aphrodite turned and glared. "Are you saying I'm a liar?"

"I'm saying even in your wildest dreams, you could never be half as clever as Athena," the gorgon replied. "There's no way you knew it was someone else before she attacked."

"It's too bad you'll never have to eat those words because you have no idea how wrong you are. I knew the moment I saw her. I could see it in her eyes."

"See what?"

"The way she looked at Alex," Aphrodite said as she tended to her hair. "There was no love there, not even a mild fondness that acquaintances might have."

Euryale's mouth opened to try and form some sort of retort, but nothing came out.

Aphrodite smirked. "Exactly."

Alex was about to say something else when he suddenly flopped to the side and puked. Once he finished, he stayed there and groaned. "Oh, man, I don't feel good."

"Next time don't get stung by a gargantuan scorpion," Aphrodite said.

Euryale glared at the goddess. "That's rich, coming from you. You were useless the entire time."

"Useless?" she scoffed. "I'm the one who kept you from burning up like kindling. You should be thanking me on your knees that you didn't become even more hideous than you already are."

Ares suddenly appeared behind Euryale and Aphrodite with a large axe in hand. "Here, we can try this."

Aphrodite yanked her arm to the side so that the chain that connected them was pulled taught. "Hurry, and don't you dare miss."

Ares nodded, and after he made a few slow practice swings, he brought the axe high overhead and swung it down with enough force to cleave a boulder in two. The weapon bounced harmlessly off the chain, and he barely redirected the blow in time so that the axe head bit into the table instead of his lover's arm.

"I said be careful!" Aphrodite said, jumping back.

"You said not to miss, and I didn't," Ares replied, dropping his brow.

Aphrodite groaned. "It's the same thing. Now try again and make sure it works this time."

The God of War took three more chops at the chain, but all he succeeded in doing was cracking the axe against the stone table on the last attempt. With a grunt, he tossed the broken weapon to the side. "You're going to need to go elsewhere to get this done."

"Elsewhere?" Aphrodite repeated, shaking her head. "I can't go elsewhere."

"I don't think you have a choice."

"Are you kidding me? You want me to travel around and be seen with this...this...*thing*?"

Ares grinned. "We could always take advantage of this bondage in private, if that would help your mood."

"Take advantage of what, exactly?"

"I believe the modern term is ménage à trois," he said, his grin brightening further.

"You can't be serious," Aphrodite said.

"She has great strength and is full of vigor," Ares replied. "Her passion would be...interesting to test."

"*She* is not interested in either one of you," Euryale growled, deciding to put an end to this stupid conversation once and for all. She would've been annoyed at Alex for not jumping in immediately, but with the scorpion venom still ravaging his body, he was currently emptying his stomach for the umpteenth time. So, she could give him a pass.

"Well that's one thing we can agree on," Aphrodite said. "*She* won't be with us. Ever."

"I suggest the two of you see Hephaestus," Ares said. "No doubt between his forge and the tools he owns, he will be able to break these bonds."

"No," Aphrodite quickly said, her voice edging on panic. "There has to be another way."

"I wish there were, my love, but these chains are beyond my strength."

"No, Ares, I can't."

Euryale yanked on the chain to get the goddess's attention. "You're the one thinking being tethered to me is worse than life itself. Stop the dramatics. Let's just go see your husband and get this over with so we can both go on our way."

Alex pushed himself up and wiped his mouth off with the back of his hand. He struggled for a few moments to keep his balance before speaking his mind. "Okay, answer me this. Since we all agree that wasn't Jessica who attacked us, who was it?"

"Arachne," Euryale replied.

"Ara...Arak..."

"A-rack-knee," Aphrodite said with an exasperated sigh. "It's not that hard."

Alex held up a finger, took a deep breath, and conquered the pronunciation. "Arachne. There. I did it. Who's that?"

"A woman who was cursed by Athena when she proved to be the better weaver," Euryale explained. "For that terrible crime, Athena turned her into a spider."

"That was the biggest, most Jessica-looking spider I've ever seen," Alex said.

"She's obviously found a way out of that curse," Aphrodite said.

"Right," Alex said. He closed his eyes and took a deep breath, and for a moment, it looked as if he'd empty his stomach once more. But he didn't, and he continued his questions. "Why did she come after us?"

"I'm guessing it has something to do with those swords Hephaestus made us," Euryale said.

"Our wedding presents?" Alex asked looking and sounding thoroughly confused. "Why?"

Up until now, Euryale hadn't devoted any time to thinking things through, but it only took a few seconds to put the pieces together. At least, she put the pieces together enough for a general idea of what was going on. "She's looking to take over Olympus, and somehow those swords play a part in it."

"Oh she is, is she?" Aphrodite said with a chuckle. "Is she going to storm the gates with a pair of his-and-her swords and defeat all the gods?"

A low growl came from deep within Ares' chest. "She has Athena's shield, too, I suspect."

Euryale perked. "She does?"

Ares nodded. "It was recently stolen from her, and she tried to blame me for it."

Hope and excitement filled Euryale's soul, not to mention a little bit of regret at having those emotions given the circumstances. If Arachne had stolen Athena's shield, and if Euryale could return that shield to her, surely the goddess would be appreciative of such a gesture—perhaps even enough to undo her curse. She'd have to. Surely, or at least insist that others treated her better.

"Now I'm still not completely up on my Greek mythology, but that sounds bad," Alex said.

"It's problematic," Ares replied.

"Even more so when you realize she's not acting alone," Euryale added. "And I don't mean her little thief, either."

"You know she's not acting alone because...?"

"Because first of all, she's not good enough to steal from the gods," Euryale said. "And second, when she was faking being Jessica, she tried to recruit me to her little scheme and said there were others."

"Others? What others?" Aphrodite demanded.

"She didn't say."

"It doesn't matter," Aphrodite said. "Dad will strike her down with a thousand bolts of lightning before the day is done. Now let's get to my party, grab Heph, and get free of each other before you make me throw up."

The goddess took to her feet and yanked Euryale along. She'd barely gotten a step away from the table when Alex stood and cleared his throat. "Wait, what about Jessica?"

"That wasn't her," Aphrodite said.

"I know, but, Arachne must've seen her, right? I mean, she said a lot of stuff at the party that only Jessica would know."

Euryale held fast despite the goddess's continued tugs. "I'll stop by her house once I'm free."

Alex shook his head, which ended up causing him to fight for balance again. "No, she's in trouble, and we might not have that long. You need to go there first."

"We are *not* going there first," Aphrodite said.

"I'll go. You don't have to."

"No, Alex," Euryale said forcefully. She nodded toward Aison and Cassandra who were currently playing with Tickles. Or maybe Tickles was playing with them. It was hard to tell since the chimera had Aison pinned to the ground while Cassandra swung playfully from the chimera's horns. "Stay and watch the twins."

"But—"

"No buts, Alex! After what happened, they can't be left alone. Besides, you're in no shape to go anywhere."

Alex flopped back on the chair. "Fine. I'll stay with the kids."

She then leveled her gaze at Ares. "And you, don't leave his side."

"You think you can order me around?" Ares laughed.

"No, but I do remember the oath you made," Euryale said. "You swore by the River Styx you'd not let Alex come to harm. Or have you already forgotten?"

"That was not my oath."

"Are you sure about that?" Euryale asked. "Because this seems like an awfully dumb way to lose your immortality if you're wrong."

Ares knitted his brow, which was precisely the reaction the gorgon was aiming for. Truth be told, she had no idea what sort of oath Ares had made to Alex on the banks of Acheron last year, but she did know it was enough to get Ares to cease his war against the two of them. She could only hope that it would still be considered binding to this day or that the god couldn't remember the specifics. "Fine," he said. "I shall stay with your husband until his mind is clear and his body heals. After that, his fate is in his own hands."

Chapter A Goddess Snubbed

Alex patiently waited for his bride and Aphrodite to step into the goddess's swan-drawn chariot and fly off before doing anything but sit quietly like a good boy. The twins in the meantime were gorging themselves on cake while Ares sat across from him, deep in thought. But after a few moments in quiet contemplation, the corners of Ares' mouth drew back into a massive smile.

"What's that about?" Alex asked.

"This battle has made me realize what's missing."

"You mean with Arachne?"

"No, little mortal," Ares said, shaking his head. "That matter will be resolved shortly, I'm certain. What I mean is I have finally figured out what's missing from football for it to be a truly magnificent sport."

"I hope it doesn't have anything to do with trading the pigskin for artillery shells."

"No, but I like how you think," he said. "What the game needs are monsters. Lots and lots of monsters."

"Monsters? Really? That's what you're going with?"

Ares nodded with enthusiasm. "Yes! I took great joy when I pounded my scorpion to death. No doubt, fans will want to see that as well, especially if there's a scoreboard attached to it all."

"Let me see if I understand where you're going with this," Alex said as he rubbed his temples in a vain effort to soothe his venom-induced headache. "You're going to put monsters on a football field and have teams of men fight them? That still seems an awful lot like gladiator sports."

"It will be much better than that. They won't just fight them. They'll play with them and against them. They will be part of the team! They will help drive the ball to the end zone while others make spectacular tackles and rip ball carriers to shreds. It will be the best of both worlds, the modern and ancient—well, ancient according to your kind."

"I'm really not—"

"It will be the best of both worlds," Ares repeated, slowly and with finality.

Alex decided it was in his best interests not to argue, especially since Euryale had indeed been mistaken about Ares' oath. The god had only sworn to end the war that he had been in with Alex and Euryale. Technically, there was nothing in that oath that compelled him for continued protection, and certainly nothing that prevented Ares from entering a new war against him. That said, the two had gotten along amicably over the last hour. Perhaps fighting giant scorpions together had a lot to do with that, male bonding over shared adversity and whatnot.

Though Alex wasn't sure about that last point, there was something he was quite certain of. He wasn't about to sit around Elysium while his friend, Jessica, might be in danger. "Ares," he said. "How would you like to go find a new fight?"

Ares half laughed, half snorted. "How does a spear like to pierce a man's heart? How does the catapult like to tear down walls?"

"Right," Alex said, smirking at himself for asking such a stupid question. "Let me rephrase. Let's go check on Jessica."

"I will gladly go, little Alex, but do you know the wrath you risk?"

"With Euryale?"

Ares nodded. "Most think I'm a dumb brute, only knowing or caring about war, but they are wrong. I know a lover's wish and fear, and you should know this, if you leave your children here alone, you will break your lover's wish and risk her deepest fears coming to life."

"Way ahead of you," Alex said. "We'll swing by Hades' fortress and see if Aunt Persephone will watch them for a few. Not to mention, she ought to have some stuff I can patch myself up with."

Ares eyed Alex with eagerness and wariness. "Are you sure you know what you're doing?"

"Yes...well, I think," he said. "But what safer place can there be around here than the lair of Hades, God of the Underworld?"

As much as Euryale hated to admit it, Aphrodite's party would have been a thousand times better than the one she'd tried to host. The location—a gorgeous spot tucked away near Mount Parnitha—offered a breathtaking view of the area. Countless tables had been carefully arranged with colorful umbrellas and settings, all surrounding a crystal-clear pool with giant, blue-and-purple floats that partygoers could sit on. The pool was fed by a waterfall in the back and was connected to eight hot tubs all around. In the center of the pool stood a wet bar, with three other bars strategically placed around the pool's edge. The party would've been a thousand times better, that is, if it weren't for the fact that all of the guests attending lay strewn about as if they'd all been simultaneously hit with tranquilizers, heroes and Olympians included.

"What in the Fates' mess happened?" Euryale asked, taking it all in.

The question snapped Aphrodite out of her shock. "My party..."

In a panic, she ran to the nearest Olympian, Dionysus. He was face down in a lounge chair with his butt in the air. The god looked peaceful, albeit awkward and uncomfortable, like a two-year-old child who'd collapsed in the evening when his batteries finally ran out. Aphrodite tried to rouse him with several hard shakes, but she was not successful.

"They're all sleeping," Euryale said, surveying the area. "Even Zeus."

"This has to be Arachne's doing," Aphrodite growled. "She'll rue the day she ever dreamed of crossing me."

"I can't imagine what it's like to have your party ruined."

Aphrodite narrowed her eyes, and she yanked the chains that bound them. "Keep running your mouth, gorgon," she said. "I can still make an example of you yet."

Euryale squared off with the goddess. "Ares isn't here to protect you. I'm not the one who should be careful."

A groan captured the attention of them both and stopped the fight. A few yards away, Hera stirred near the pool's edge. Groggily, she pushed herself up and adjusted the crown atop her head. "For the love of Chaos," she said.

Euryale and Aphrodite rushed to her side. The gorgon offered a hand up, but Hera refused it with a look of disgust. "I'd sooner smear myself with manure."

"Are you hurt?" asked Aphrodite.

"No, but no thanks to that godawful wine you served," she said. She shut her eyes and rubbed her temples. "I barely had time to cast a counterspell. What did you put in it?"

"Nothing, I swear!" Aphrodite said. "Arachne must have drugged it."

"Arachne?"

"She had a hand in ruining my party, too," Euryale replied. "But at least she dared to do it to my face, unlike one coward I know."

"I did you a favor, gorgon," Aphrodite said with disdain. "Your food was atrocious and your table settings were pathetic. It's not my fault everyone would rather be around beauty and grace than...well, look at you."

Euryale snapped her arm to her side, jerking Aphrodite off balance. She caught the goddess by the wrist with her other hand and glared as her snakes hissed and her tail rattled. Before things could escalate, Hera took over.

"Shut it, both of you," she snapped. The moment she spoke, she grimaced and rubbed her head again. "You, gorgon, will never speak to an Olympian that way again. I don't care who your father is," she said. "And you, Aphrodite, find a way to free yourself from this revolting creature so I don't have to be around her."

"I've tried," Aphrodite lamented. "Ares can't break the chains. I was hoping Hephaestus would be here to help."

"He's not," Hera replied.

"He's not?"

"No, he's not," she repeated, sounding as if she were about to cross the hairline that separated irritation from infuriation. "Why am I telling you things twice? He never came."

Aphrodite clenched her fists and muttered some curses. "I can't believe he'd snub me!" she said. "Me! His own wife! I sent him the sweetest invitation of them all!"

"You sure about that?" Euryale asked with a smirk.

Aphrodite swung an open palm at Euryale's cheek, intent on knocking said smirk off her face. The gorgon, however, was quick to bat it away and in turn, she smacked Aphrodite's side with her tail.

The two ended up in a tussle that went to the ground. Aphrodite landed several blows on Euryale's face, each packing a considerable punch. Euryale, likewise, fought back with a vengeance and quickly coiled around the goddess, squeezing her tight.

"Enough!" Hera screamed. She stumbled back and grit her teeth. "By Gaia, I need some aspirin. If I have to listen to you two squabble any further, I'll cast you both in Tartarus. I don't care who starts it. Now get out of my face."

Chapter Heph's Place

With a peace treaty formed only out of necessity, Euryale and Aphrodite flew to the home of Hephaestus, which was a lonely volcanic island in the middle of nowhere. As they flew over the sea, Aphrodite practiced her pitch while Euryale clung to the sides of the chariot since she hated flying with a passion.

"Heph? Sweetie? The funniest thing happened today, and I could really use the help of my kind, understanding, and adoring husband," she said before dropping her head, pouting her lip, and folding her hands at her waist.

This last gesture made things incredibly awkward for Euryale as the chains pulled her hand down, practically forcing her to grab the goddess's crotch to stay upright.

"Well, what do you think?" Aphrodite asked, going back to guiding her swan-drawn chariot with the reins. "Too much lip this time?"

Euryale shrugged as she shifted yet again in the cramped chariot. The thing barely had enough room for two, and with her elongated tail, half of her spilled out of the sides and trailed behind as they flew, making the entire experience extremely nerve-wracking.

"Are you going to answer me?"

"Can we wait till we're on the ground? I don't like heights."

Aphrodite snickered. "You? I don't believe it."

"Alex always flew his chariot low, and anytime we went to Olympus, I kept my eyes shut the entire time."

"You're a mess, gorgon," Aphrodite said with a laugh. She then ordered her swans into a shallow dive, and soon they skimmed the water. "There. Now answer me. Did I give too much lip? Or maybe I should try rubbing his shoulders at that point. That always makes him pliable. What do you think? Or better, what would you do?"

"I wouldn't manipulate my husband, for starters," she said.

Aphrodite snorted. "We can't all have fantasy marriages."

"Why can't you?"

Aphrodite pressed her lips together, and for a moment, Euryale thought she wasn't going to answer. "I guess Ares and I are hardly a secret," she said. "I might have skipped out on Hephaestus last year to go see Victoria Falls. He's still cross with me for that."

"Let me guess. You went with Ares?"

Aphrodite looked wistfully out to the horizon before sighing heavily. "Yes." One side of her mouth drew back. "And we didn't see a whole lot of falls. But they sounded lovely."

"I can't believe you're like that," Euryale said as she felt her stomach churn. How and why the goddess had been ordained by the Fates to be the Goddess of Love was beyond her. Goddess of Lust, maybe, but there wasn't a devoted strand in her entire body as far as Euryale could tell.

What friendly demeanor Aphrodite had had up until this point vanished in an instant. Her face grew hard and frightening, uncharacteristic of the goddess but not completely unheard of. "What do you know?" she spat. "You have no right to judge me."

"At least I'm loyal to my husband," Euryale countered.

"As if you have any other options," Aphrodite replied. "Or as if he had other options, for that matter."

Euryale didn't give a second thought to her first statement. She'd always known she was hideous and had adjusted to her cursed looks for thousands of years now. The other part of what she said, the insinuation that Alex was only with her out of necessity, however, stabbed her through the heart. Although it had been a year since he'd devoted himself to her, even when she had been at her worst, she still had doubts—no, fears—that as long as she was a monster, she would never be good enough, and Alex continued to be with her only out of some sense of duty. Despite those fears, however, a thought dawned on her, a thought that needed addressing. "Is that why you hate me?"

Aphrodite straightened, clearly caught off guard by the question. "There are so many reasons why I hate you," she finally said as she pulled the reins to her swans and brought them to a stop at the shore of the island. With a jerk, she yanked Euryale off the chariot and stepped onto Hephaestus's island where the volcano stretched high into a starry night sky. "But yes, forcing someone you supposedly love to marry you is one of the reasons why I detest the sight of you. If your father weren't The Old Man, I'd have buried you under more curses than any wife had leveled at her wayward husband."

"I didn't force him," Euryale said, feeling small. It was a rare feeling for her, but one that usually took hold when she thought about her arrangement with Alex in the beginning as well as a few other life events. But as she mulled over the goddess's words, another thought came to her, one that was both true and redeemed her in her own eyes. "Even if you're right, I would let Alex go if he wanted. I'm not forcing him to stay with me."

"If you say so."

The two began to trudge up the rocky terrain to where one of many caves led to Hephaestus's forge at the heart of the volcano. It was a rough climb, one that demanded a great deal of effort, even if they hadn't been tethered to another. But since both Euryale and Aphrodite were joined at the wrists, it was even more difficult.

More than once, one or the other lost their balance and sent them both sliding down the mountain a few feet.

"I hate this place," Aphrodite said after the sixth time they slipped. "Would it kill Hephaestus to build some stairs? I mean, really, it's no wonder no one wants to visit him."

Euryale didn't pay much attention to the goddess's words. She was still dwelling on the previous conversation. "Why else do you hate me?"

Aphrodite looked over her shoulder, again surprised. "Why does it matter?"

"I want to know," she said. "If I knew why you did, then perhaps..."

Her voice trailed, and Aphrodite tilted her head and chuckled mockingly. "Perhaps what? We'd be best friends?"

Euryale shook her head. "No. But if I knew why you hated me, maybe I'd understand why Athena does as well, and I could do something about it."

"And that," Aphrodite said, pointing an accusing finger at the gorgon, "is also why I hate you."

"Why? Because I want Athena to return me to normal? Because after she cursed my sister for committing the unforgivable act of being raped by Poseidon in her own temple, Stheno and I came to Medusa's defense and ended up sharing her fate?"

"No, because all you can think of is how to please Athena," Aphrodite said, showing no empathy to Euryale's story. "You never once asked for my blessings when you were going to get married to Alex. You never once came to me to find love or listen to my protests against Athena's involvement. In fact, you didn't listen to me at all. All you did was cry to your father, who forced Athena's hand. Alex, I'll forgive eventually, because he simply didn't know any better. You, however, have known since you were born who I am and where my domain is. You knew all of that and still you chose to spit in my face and ask Athena to find you a husband."

"I never went to her."

Aphrodite's eyes narrowed. "Don't get cute with me. You could've come to me at any time, and you didn't. You knew exactly what you were doing."

Euryale didn't have anything to say, because ultimately, the goddess was right, even though she hated to admit it. She hadn't gone to Aphrodite, and she knew she should have. Why? That answer was simple. Euryale didn't have to do a lot of soul-searching to find that one. She wanted more than anything to get back into Athena's good graces, or at least, enough so that she would be forgiven and have her curse lifted, which was the same reason why she needed to get Athena's aegis from Arachne right now.

"For Cronus's sake, Heph needs to plant some flowers," Aphrodite said as they reached the mouth of the cave and a strong sulfur smell washed over the two of them. They entered the cave and then the dark tunnel that led into the heart of the volcano. "And some stupid torches, too. By all that is sacred, how does anyone move around in here?"

Euryale laughed quietly as she heard the goddess smash a set of toes on a rocky outcropping in the tunnel. As she was part viper and could sense even the slightest changes in heat, navigating the dark was second nature to her, and since she now moved on a serpentine tail, rocks on the ground were of no concern to her either. That said, Aphrodite was far from helpless, even if she had recently nailed a couple of piggies. The goddess conjured a simple ball of blue light that served to illuminate their way.

While ultimately Euryale appreciated being spared the shadows, part of her was disappointed that she wouldn't be able to accidentally steer the goddess into another obstacle or footfall as she led the way. Juvenile, Euryale knew, but she didn't care in the least. She might not be in a position to get total revenge on the goddess, let alone seek any sort of justice, but petty revenge? There was always the opportunity for that. She simply had to keep her eyes open.

When Euryale and Aphrodite broke free of the tunnel and entered Hephaestus's workspace, they were welcomed with a large chamber that had its walls covered in weapons and armor of all sorts. Across the way sat a forge that could swallow the Scylla whole, and off to the left sat a small side room with a single bedroll at the far end along with a scattering of knickknacks lying on the rocky floor.

"Hephie, I'm home," Aphrodite called out. "Hephie?"

Euryale looked around and saw no sign of him. "I don't think he's here. Maybe he's wandering the island?"

"Him? Go outside and appreciate beauty?" Aphrodite said with a snort. "No. All he's interested in is bending things to his will. Making what he wants."

"So where is he, then?"

Aphrodite shook her head and scoffed. "As if I keep his social calendar. Probably caught wind of my party being ruined and is off celebrating."

"Must be dreadful to have someone bathe in your misery," Euryale said.

"Bite your tongue and help me find something to cut these chains with."

The two began an arduous search of the area, which under normal circumstances would have taken two people a short amount of time, even if the forge was large enough to outfit a titan. However, these were not normal circumstances, and the two continuously yanked each other into opposite directions as they fought over which way was best to go, and which tool may or may not be the right one. They tried saws. They tried hammers. They even tried a few hand axes, much to Aphrodite's terror, but none of them managed to break the bonds that held them together.

"We should try heating the links in the forge," Euryale said.

"And get burned in the process? No, thank you."

"Would you rather be attached to me for the rest of eternity?"

Aphrodite sucked in a breath and frowned. It was clear that the goddess was genuinely weighing the two options against each other, and Euryale didn't know if she should feel insulted by that or not. The goddess's eyes drifted to the side, and her frown disappeared as her mouth opened a few inches in surprise. "We can't."

"Can't what?" Euryale asked, turning.

"We can't heat the chain," she said, pointing to the forge. "The fires are nothing but coals and the billows are missing."

"Why would the billows be gone?" Euryale asked.

Aphrodite slowly approached where they had once been. Nearby was an anvil and an empty table made from iron and obsidian. "His hammer and chisels aren't here either."

"This seems bad," Euryale said as she quickly connected Arachne's actions to what they had discovered here. But what did that mean for Hephaestus? Euryale's stomach soured. Whereas before, she was upset with the god for snubbing her at her party, now she was worried something terrible might have befallen him.

"Why would Arachne take the tools but not the weapons?" Aphrodite asked. "That doesn't make sense."

"Unless she's going to use what she took to make new weapons," Euryale said, thinking such a point was obvious.

"Hardly. Even with my husband's tools, she wouldn't have his skill. Also—"

Aphrodite stopped when her eyes fell on a shaft that had been tossed into a nearby corner. She approached it with worry splashed on her face and picked it up. It had been made of dark wood with gold bands at both ends and a leather wrap toward the bottom. "This is one of Artemis's javelins," Aphrodite said, her eyes never leaving the shaft.

"Are you sure?"

"Seeing how I used one to get Alex in trouble with Ares, yes I'm sure," Aphrodite replied. "But the head is missing."

"Was Hephaestus working on it?"

"Possibly. Do you see it lying around?"

Euryale glanced left and right, but it was nowhere to be found. Aphrodite's search yielded similar results. The two scoured the area for the next ten minutes, looking on every shelf, in every chest, under every fold of Hephaestus's bedroll, and in every shadow that clung to the corners and walls, but still they came up empty. They did, however, find a small flask in a drawer that held a semi-clear, sticky residue.

"What is that?" Aphrodite asked.

Euryale took a whiff, wrinkled her nose, and then lifted a small bit of the substance with her finger. Her skin warmed immediately, and within seconds, her hand felt numb. "An anesthetic. A potent one at that."

"Probably for when he smashes his thumb with his hammer," Aphrodite said with a half grin.

"This doesn't sit well with me," Euryale said, setting the flask aside and focusing on the current situation at hand. "Arachne has something devious in mind."

"But what?" Aphrodite asked. She folded her arms over her chest and drummed her fingers. "Think. Think. Think," she said to herself. "What would Athena do?"

Euryale almost made a jab at the goddess but caught herself as she realized her energy was better spent elsewhere. "Do you know what that javelin head was made out of?"

"Adamantine, I'm sure," Aphrodite said. "He always used the best when he made his gifts for us."

Euryale took another look at the weapons and armor that hung on the walls. They all looked deadly and superbly made, but she doubted any of them were made from the precious metal. They didn't have that subtle glow about them. Still, she needed to be sure. "What about these?" she asked, sweeping her hand toward the collection.

"Those are his play projects, nothing more. Made from copper, bronze, and steel, depending on his mood," Aphrodite said. Her face suddenly brightened. "What if Arachne is stealing only things made from adamantine?"

"That's what I'm thinking."

"I told you I wasn't just a pretty face," she said with a bright smile. "But that still doesn't answer what she wants them for."

Euryale said the first thing that came to mind. It felt frighteningly accurate, and she prayed to the Fates she was wrong. "She must be melting everything down to forge something bigger, more powerful."

"No, that's stupid," Aphrodite said, clearly more out of denial than anything else. "She's not skilled enough. Besides, this is the only forge in existence with fires hot enough to accomplish such a thing."

Euryale, irritated that her plausible theory had been tossed so quickly, tutted. "What else is it, then?"

"Oh, look who it is, boys," said a low, rough voice from behind. "She said you two might come here."

Euryale twisted around, which ended up being a fight for balance as she pulled Aphrodite to the side and saw a trio of grotesque giants lumber into the forge. They each wore a pathetic array of patchwork for pants and had enormous bellies that sagged over them. Numerous copper rings pierced their ears, noses, and lips, and their weathered hands with gnarled fingers gripped barbed spears and large, rough sacks.

The one in the lead gave a smile that was more rotten gums than it was teeth and leveled his spear at Aphrodite. "Try not to scuff that one up too badly," he said. "She'll be a fun one to have."

The three giants came forward, and Aphrodite narrowed her eyes. "You dare threaten an Olympian? You'll be struck down before you take another step."

The giant chuckled, sending ripples through his belly. "Your husband said the same thing," he said. "Put him down before he could swing that hammer of his a second time."

Euryale snatched a nearby labrys off its mount on the wall. The double-bitted axe was not a weapon she was familiar with, having only practiced with her sister's bow and spear, but it felt balanced in her hands. Moreover, it felt good to have something to defend herself with, especially when she noticed that the tips of the giants' spearheads were coated with a moss-green substance.

Chapter A Powerful Surprise

"When do I get to drive?" Aison asked.

"When you're sixteen and pass your driver's test," Alex said as he brought the chariot to a halt outside of Hades' fortress.

"Aw, but Cassandra got to drive last week!"

"Cassandra stole the chariot last week," Alex said. "Difference. But if you want, you can steal it, too, and see what happens when mommy finds out."

Aison eyed the leather straps before hopping off the chariot. "I think I'll wait."

"Smart move."

"Daddy," Cassandra said, still in the chariot but pointing a finger at the steps that led to Hades' abode. "Shouldn't those doors be closed?"

Alex looked up to see that the pair of gargantuan double doors that led inside had indeed been left open. Now, Alex was far from an expert when it came to Hades and how he ran his home, but from what interactions Alex had had with the god, Hades had always struck him as the type who didn't like people simply wandering in unannounced.

"You told him we were coming, didn't you?" Alex said, clinging to a new theory that was much more palatable. "You sent him a little Hermes telegram while I wasn't looking? I mean, that dude is fast. I could've blinked, and you two would've sent War and Peace back to each other line by line."

"I do not do peace," Ares said.

"Well, I did include the war part," Alex said. "Let's say he wrote the peace."

Ares kept his focus on the open entryway and grabbed his spear from the chariot. "I did not speak to my uncle, Alex."

"Great," Alex said with a heavy sigh. "I thought you'd say that."

"You should wait here. I will go inside and let you know if it's safe."

At first, Alex was going to agree, but for whatever reason, perhaps simply his nerves, as he had never gotten used to the sight of the Underworld or of the shadows surrounding Hades' looming stone fortress that seemed tenfold more sinister than the last time he was here, he didn't. And seeing how the last time he'd come he ended up being chained to a wheel of fire, that was saying a lot. "You know what? We're coming inside as well," Alex said. "I think the safest place is going to be next to you."

"Perhaps the safest place is at home," Ares said. "Your wife would no doubt agree."

"Our home burned to the ground," Alex pointed out. "I wouldn't exactly call Elysium a sanctuary anymore. Besides, Persephone might also need help. And if she doesn't, I still need her to watch the kids so we can check on Jessica."

"I admire your bravery, Alex," Ares said with a grin. "Come, let us hope we find an adversary worthy of our time."

With that, the God of War trotted up the stairs. In the meantime, Alex knelt by his kids and gave instructions. "Stay close, okay? And if I tell you to run, you run. You get back to this chariot, and you fly it all the way home. You don't wait for me. You don't wait for Tickles. You just go. Understand?"

The twins nodded and became like second and third shadows to Alex as he caught up to Ares. Once he was at the doors, he unsheathed his sword and peered inside. Gloom, as it had been before, was the decoration of choice, the runners-up being a three-way tie between emptiness, depression, and biting cold. The red carpet, which ran all the way from the front doors to the throne room, was the only thing that offered any bit of color to the area, aside from the occasional brazier that flickered with the barest of flames.

"Hades? Persephone?" Alex called as he took one of the giant knockers on the doors and announced their presence. All he received for replies were echoes.

Tickles, who had been off rubbing his head against nearby statues outside, plodded over. His hair bristled, and his tail went straight before he let out a hushed growl.

Ares tilted his nose up in the air and sniffed a few times. "I smell the sweat of recent battle."

The God of War then entered the fortress with Alex, the twins, and Tickles right behind. He marched with purpose to the throne room, never once deviating down any of the side halls or throwing any of them more than a glance. Part of Alex felt that this was a little too foolhardy for his likes, but another part of him appreciated the fact that this meant Ares was keeping a strong pace. And if there was a strong pace, that meant Alex had little time to think about what had happened.

They were about halfway to the throne room when Alex spied something on the floor and immediately wished he hadn't. But now that his brain wouldn't let go of the dark spattering, he decided to bring Ares' attention to it. "I think that's blood," he said, nudging the god with an elbow and pointing to the floor.

Ares knelt, and with two fingers he picked some of it up and rubbed it between his thumb and pointer before bringing it up to his nose. "I know whose this is," he said.

Without another word, the god took to his feet and ran down the hall, leaving Alex no choice but to follow with twins in tow. "Hades? Hades!" the god bellowed. "Hades, answer me, uncle!"

A deep, mournful howl blasted from the direction they were headed. Ares surged forward, leaving Alex without a second thought. Alex tried to keep up, but pain surged through his side. When he finally caught up to Ares, he was not prepared for what he saw.

Ares had stopped right inside the threshold of the throne room and looked stunned. Hades, God of the Underworld, had fallen at the far end, covered in wounds and blood, with barely a hint of life about him. Smashed columns and rubble lined most of the floor, except for a small portion in the center. There, Persephone lay curled in a fetal position, her royal white gown stained crimson and her arm draped over her face. Cerberus stood directly over her, covered in so many gashes that his wounds had wounds. On both flanks, as well as in front and behind, lay hunks of flesh and partial limbs of...of what? Alex couldn't tell. They looked leathery, but also looked like they might have bits of an exoskeleton, too. Whatever they came from, they must have been large and nightmarish.

The hellhound wagged its three tails upon seeing Alex and Ares. Two of the dog's heads dropped with flattened ears and whined while the third hung limply to the side.

Ares cleared the distance between himself and Cerberus in two strides. The god dropped to his knees in front of the beast and after quickly lowering his ear to Persephone's face he straightened. "She lives."

Alex exhaled the breath he didn't realize he was holding. "What the hell happened here?"

Cerberus nuzzled his heads into Ares, and when the god scratched each one behind the ears, he bathed the Olympian in hellhound slobber.

Once the assault was over and Ares' face and neck glistened, the god began inspecting the hellhound's wounds. With each one he saw, his face reddened more and more. "Who did this to you?"

Cerberus flattened all of his ears and growled.

Both Alex and Ares turned right as a minotaur came up a set of stairs and entered the throne room. In one hand he held a large sack slung over his shoulder, and with the other, he dangled a three-tailed chain whip at his side. The beast stood nearly as tall as Ares, and his arms and legs were nearly as thick as the god's as well.

Once the minotaur took note of the two, he dropped his sack. It hit the ground with a metallic clank, and countless gold coins and precious gems spilled out. "Looks like the pooch won," he said, glancing at the bodies on the floor. "Didn't expect that. Or for him to bring friends."

"You're going to tell me what happened to my uncle," Ares said. "And if you don't, I'll tie a millstone around your neck and toss you into the River Acheron where you'll have a new understanding of eternal torment."

The minotaur grinned. "I think not."

Four creatures came up the stairs a moment later and fanned out to either side of the beast. Three looked like cursed souls who'd come up from the bottom of the sea, with bloated bodies and large chunks of skin covered in shell. Their arms no longer ended in five-fingered hands, but rather grotesque clubs or blades made of bone. Their heads, too, were misshapen, as if made from balls of clay that had been hit with a mallet a few times before being put through the kiln. One had a broken jaw that hung loosely to the side, while the other two had one eye swollen shut. Hair fell from each of their scalps in ragged clumps, and blood oozed from their mouths. The fourth, however, was simply a one-eyed giant sporting a thick club.

"You will curse this day for all eternity," Ares said, bringing up his spear. "I promise you that."

"I've heard that before," the minotaur said, not losing a bit of his smile. "Today, in fact, from your uncle."

Cerberus growled again, and Ares held out a hand. "You've fought well. We'll handle it from here."

Alex put himself between the monsters and his kids, and Tickles joined him at his side. Though he never took his eyes off the four who had come in the room, he reached back with one hand, squeezed Cassandra's shoulder, and spoke to the twins as calmly as he could. "Remember what I said before we came in here?"

"Yes, Daddy," they answered softly.

"Get ready to do it."

The words had barely left his mouth when the minotaur charged along with the other monsters behind him. Ares gave a bloodcurdling war cry and met them all head on. He deflected an overhead chop from one of the monsters and drove his spear straight through its chest. His powerful legs kept driving him forward, and as they went, he lifted the creature off the ground and used it as a battering ram against the minotaur.

The minotaur, however, deftly moved to the side and struck out with his three-tailed whip. The chains raked across Ares' back, and the embedded hooks in the links gleefully tore through flesh and muscle. Ares' legs buckled, and he roared in defiance before he went crashing into the wall. Though weakened and in obvious, excruciating pain, he twisted around and used the creature he had impaled as a meat shield, which the monster served well for the next two strikes the minotaur gave.

The other two humanoid monsters didn't press the attack on Ares. Instead, they split to each side and began advancing on Alex and the twins, while the last, the cyclops, ended up squaring off with Tickles.

"Go, now!" Alex yelled to his kids as he lunged at the creature nearest the exit, his sword leading the way.

The creature snarled and used its club-like arm to bat the strike to the side. It hit Alex's sword with such force that he nearly lost the weapon and the shockwave that ran up his arm no doubt would've turned concrete to jelly.

"Jesus!" Alex yelled as he jumped back as the creature counterattacked, forcing him to dive left when the other tried to impale him.

The blows from both creatures came hard and fast, and Alex had to scoot faster than he thought possible on his heels to keep any of them from landing. The one with the club abandoned all pretenses of defense and ran straight at him, weapon high overhead, and drove it down in an effort to shatter Alex's skull.

Alex caught the blow with his sword by using one hand on the hilt and the other pressed against the flat of the blade to reinforce it. The shock was heavy as before, but manageable since Alex had been expecting it. Before the monster could recover, he made a snap kick that caught it square in the chest and sent it stumbling back away. Alex's eyes watered as his wound from the scorpion stretched, but he did not let it slow him down. Operating on pure instinct that had been born from a year's worth of training on Elysium hunting monsters with the other heroes, Alex took advantage of the situation and skewered the nightmarish thing straight through the chest.

Thick, dark blood oozed out of the monster like boiling tar, and when Alex yanked his weapon free, it felt just as sticky. Despite the stab that would've felled any other, the monster did not fall. It only staggered before swinging again with his club.

The attack caught Alex off guard, and he wasn't fast enough to avoid it thanks to his gimpy leg. The strike glanced off his shoulder and brushed under his chin. His arm went limp, but thankfully it was not his sword arm.

Alex hobbled to the side and behind one of the columns, which absorbed the next blow. In that moment of brief respite, he saw Ares locked in a draw with the minotaur. The god fended off strikes of the whip with his spear but failed to land any blows of his own. Where the other monster had gone, he couldn't see.

"Oh, crap." Alex ducked just in time to keep his head attached to his shoulders.

The club smashed into the column, sending chunks of marble in all directions. Alex spun into his attacker and drove the point of his sword through the monster's exposed armpit and deep into its torso. Again, the creature staggered back, but this time Alex did not relent. As soon as he withdrew his sword, he brought it around in a tight, fast arc that neatly lopped off the creature's head.

The decapitated monster dropped to its knees before falling back onto the stone floor to move no more.

"Daddy!"

Alex spun at the sound of his son's panicked voice. The other creature had the twins cornered on the other side of the throne room. Aison was pressed against the wall, clutching his knee, while Cassandra stood in front of him with the same determination and ferocity as Cerberus stood over Persephone.

Alex limped over as fast as he could. Time slowed as the monster brought its arm back to issue a killing blow. Out of desperation, Alex drew his arm back to throw his sword but never did. Cassandra's eyes turned black, and she bellowed with so much force that had Alex not seen it himself, he'd have sworn Euryale had been in the room. The blast staggered everyone, Alex included, but that was not the end of what surprises his children had.

When the monster lost its balance and tripped, Aison was on top of it, vipers hissing and fangs bared. He grabbed the sides of its face, and then his eyes flared a brilliant green. The monster screamed, but its cry of agony was cut short in less than a second when its body went rigid. A crackling sound filled the air as the color in its body vanished, and stone replaced flesh.

The fierceness in both of his children's faces disappeared along with any semblance of life their attacker had, and they looked at their father, eyes wide and hands trembling.

"You've got powers?" Alex said, staring at them in disbelief.

The sounds of continued battle pulled Alex back to more pressing matters. He pivoted on his heels. Tickles ducked under a clumsy swing by the cyclops and drove his horns into the cyclops's ribs. The one-eyed giant reeled back, blood gushing from the wound. Tickles did not relent. He dodged another strike and pounced. His lion jaws closed around the giant's throat as he pulled his adversary down. Claws from all four legs shredded flesh, while the serpent at the end of the tail struck time and again.

Sensing this battle was almost over, Alex turned his attention to Ares. Like the chimera, the God of War seemed to have the fight nearly finished. The god's spear drove forward with blinding speed. Though the minotaur managed to keep it from hitting anything vital, the wounds he suffered on his legs, shoulders, and arms, would soon catch up to him. Ares might not beat him with a single strike to the heart, but death by a thousand cuts was still a death.

"Even with your cursed weapons you are no match for me," Ares chided. He feigned a jab at the minotaur's neck, and when the beast dodged to the side, he ended up right where Ares had predicted. The god changed the line of attack and drove the tip of the spear through the minotaur's knee. The blade completely pierced the joint, and down the minotaur went, howling in pain.

"What have you to say now, beast?" Ares growled.

The minotaur snorted. His arm went back to issue another attack—albeit a pathetic one—but Alex had caught up to the battle at this point. With a quick slice, Alex cut the minotaur across the inside of his wrist, causing the monster to drop the whip.

Ares grabbed the minotaur by its horns and flipped it onto its back. The throw, while rough on its own, was made all the worse because his spear was still embedded through the beast's knee, although when it was over, the lower leg hung on by a couple of tendons.

"Why did you come?" Ares demanded.

"You'll find out soon enough," the minotaur replied with a snort. "You'll never stop what she's put in motion. Enjoy what days you have left, Olympian."

"Tell me!" Ares shouted. When the minotaur didn't answer, Ares cracked open the beast's skull with a single hammer strike of his fist.

The minotaur's head rolled to the side before his eyes managed to find Ares' face and focus. "No."

The minotaur stiffened, and Ares let go in shock. The beast hit the ground, and Ares quickly rolled him over with his foot. Sticking out from the middle of the monster's chest was a small dagger.

"Coward," Ares muttered, kicking him in the face and then three more times for fun.

Alex ran back to his kids and scooped them up in his arms. He sank into the tiny hugs, ever grateful that he could still feel their embrace. His eyes leaked right up until Cassandra spoke.

"Daddy?" she asked

"Yes?"

"That...was amazing!" Cassandra shouted, her arms shooting into the air.

"No, it—" Alex started, but his twins went off like a pair of machine guns.

"—the way you clobbered that nasty—" Cassandra said.

"—and how Cassandra was all screamy like mom—" Aison tossed in.

"—and they went all stumbling around—"

"—and I jumped on that one—"

"—and your eyes got all scary—"

"—and I turned him right to stone!" Aison finished. "Did you see that part? Did you, Dad? That was the best ever!"

Alex, stupefied at his children's reactions, didn't know what to say or do. On the one hand, he was thrilled that not only had they not been scarred for life by the attack, but they had also unleashed powers that clearly came from their mother's side. On the other, however, he still knew he had to play parent, and his instincts told him that encouraging such behavior wasn't especially wise. "Yeah, that was pretty cool," he said, proud as ever but still trying to look as serious as possible. "It was still dangerous, though. Let's not forget that."

"Only for them!" Aison said.

Cassandra bunched her hands into little fists and brought them under her chin as she tried to contain her budding excitement. "Let's find more monsters to kill! Can we, Dad? Can we? Can we? Can we?"

"No!"

Tickles came over, and Aison jumped in the chimera's face before playfully wrestling with the monster's goat horns. "We could even take Tickles! He'd love that!"

"I said no, and I meant it."

Cassandra crossed her arms and stuck out her lower lip. "Aw, you never let us do anything fun."

"All the other hero kids get to kill monsters," Aison added.

Before Alex could get sucked in further, Ares spoke from across the throne room. "Alex, we will find a battle to train your children with later," he said before motioning to Persephone. "Tend her wounds. I will make sure no one else is lurking about."

"You don't want bandages for yourself first? Your back looks dreadful."

Ares twisted as he looked over his shoulder. "I've had worse."

Alex almost let it go. Almost. Fear of what the minotaur was wielding, however, outweighed his fear for how Ares might take his follow-up. "Are you sure? I don't think that whip was normal," he said. "Who knows what weapons anyone else might have."

To Alex's surprise and relief, Ares took no offense. He nodded and pointed to the fallen whip. "It's been coated and imbued with powerful magic," he said. "Arachne is far from the simple spider she once was."

"Coated? With what?"

Ares shook his head. "I know not. But the curse that weapon wields is not one I wish to face again. I'll be honest, little mortal, a more skilled opponent would have caused me a great deal of trouble with such a thing. Now see to Persephone and then to Hades. I need to search this place before speaking with Aphrodite. She must be warned."

Chapter Giant Fun

"Think you could grab a weapon before they beat us into a pulp?" Euryale softly hissed.

Aphrodite hesitated, and the momentary helpless look on her face disappeared under a stoic guise. "You want me to take up arms?" she replied with a snort. "I am an Olympian. I am the Goddess of Love. Armies of heroes flock to my defense. The gods worship at my feet. If anything, you should be begging me for the honor to defend my well-being on your own and win my favor."

Euryale turned to face the goddess with her jaw hung open. "Look around, your most gorgeousness. No one is coming to our defense."

The giant in the middle chuckled. "You've got that part right."

"My husband and my father will both skin you for a thousand years if you even breathe on me," Euryale said. She crouched slightly but was unsure what the proper stance would be for someone using an axe. She assumed it would be similar to one using a sword, but the uncertainty in her mind only added to her worry. This wasn't a fight she was ready for, or ever would be in her mind, and any doubt only furthered her fears that this was going to end badly.

"I've heard enough from you, ugly," the giant said, pointing his spear at Euryale's chest. "In fact, no more talking. I wants my ravaging."

The giant charged, and Euryale reflexively pulled backward, yanking Aphrodite in the process. She swung her labrys and managed to deflect the point of his spear, but she was not accustomed to its heavy head, and thus wasn't able to bring it back around in time to issue a counterattack of her own. In fact, given how Aphrodite kept her off balance, it was no small favor of the Fates that kept her from getting skewered when the giant quickly recovered and stabbed again.

As before, Euryale managed to knock the blow aside, and she retreated even faster when the other two giants came lumbering forward to join the fray. Dragging the Goddess of Love with her, Euryale set up a few feet inside Hephaestus's bedroom in order to use the entryway as a bottleneck. She knew she had very little odds one-on-one against a giant, especially with a hopeless goddess tethered to her arm and slowing her every move, but her odds of defeating three were probably only slightly better than her marching up to the Fates and successfully lopping off their heads.

"You could help anytime you want," Euryale said. A third and fourth attack came, but now she was getting used to the axe's weight, so much so that when the fifth was made, Euryale deflected it again and lunged forward in time to successfully bring the axe down. It bit deep into the giant's forearm before he could pull away, yet despite this small victory, Aphrodite was far from pleased.

"Stop jerking me all over the place," she said. "I'm not your plaything."

"Stop being so worthless," Euryale countered. "I'd have better odds being tied to a bedpost."

Aphrodite snickered. "Dear, no one's tying you to a bedpost. Besides, I am helping. I'm giving you a worthwhile reason to fight. Now kill them already before I lose my temper."

A guttural cry ended the juvenile quarrel between them. The wounded giant charged forward, spearpoint leading the way. The attack caught Euryale by surprise, though in hindsight she should have seen it coming as there was no realistic way she would be able to defend against it. As such, it was only a matter of time before the giants realized that.

The gorgon sprang to the side, and once again thanks to the bonds that held her and Aphrodite together, the two crashed into a heap against the bedroom wall. Before she could fully recover and get upright, a trio of spear points were inches away from the two of them.

"Easy, boys," the lead giant said. "I don't want the good one damaged before I've had my fun."

"Best not let Nug go first, then," the one on the right said, chuckling. "You know how he is."

"How I is?" Nug replied. "You're one to talk! You broke that cow when you tried to pet it!"

"Did not!"

"I was there, Pid! Broke its back, you did!"

Pid frowned. "That's cause its cuteness got to me, it did."

"Its cuteness?"

"Yeah, I loved it so much I got a little excited and gave it a hard pet. Is that alright with you?"

"Not if you break her, it isn't. I'll be mad, I will. And so will Bemus."

Bemus, the leader, hardened his face. "Quiet, you two. I'll get her first, and that's that."

"Why should you get her first?" they asked in unison.

"Because I'm the good-looking one," Bemus replied. "You two can have ugly while you wait. She might even make you look handsome."

Pid faced Bemus. His nostrils flared, and his face turned three shades of red. "I'm the ugly one? You're the one bleeding all over the place. That makes you the ugly one. A fine woman like that doesn't want your gross blood."

"And I've got three teeth," Bemus countered. "She don't want no slobber mouth from a one rotten toother like you."

Nug smiled broadly, showing off a crooked array of four not-so-pearly whites. They were more of a putrid green, really, with hints of moldy black along the edges. "Ha! Guess that means she's mine," he beamed. "You two get ugly."

Bemus turned and backhanded Nug. His face snapped sideways with a spray of blood. When the giant recovered, he wasn't smiling anymore. He also wasn't the handsomest either, going by the current scoring method. Bemus had him beaten by one point.

In a flash, the three began arguing with one another, loudly, and predictably that argument turned into punches, elbows, and bites. At least, it turned into that right up until the point when Euryale and Aphrodite, having thrown glances at each other and having the same unspoken idea, took to their feet. Before they could leave, the giants made an instantaneous truce and glared at their cornered prey.

"Where do you think you're going?" Bemus growled. "We're just sorting this out."

Before Euryale could think of anything to say, Aphrodite took the lead. Her eyes lost what fear she'd been trying to hide, and instead she gazed on the giants with wonderment. She began to pant, and her skin flushed. She spoke with a flirty voice. "Don't stop," she said. "I want to see who will fight over me the hardest."

Nug's and Pid's eyes widened like adolescent boys who'd caught sight of nymphs bathing in a secluded pool.

"Tell me who to clobber!" Pid said.

"No, I clobber better!" Nug said. "Tell me!"

Bemus leveled a glare at the two. "Don't be stupid," he said. "She's trying to trick us."

"No, I'm not," Aphrodite said. She coyly reached out and traced the wound on his forearm with her finger before shutting her eyes and sucking in a deep breath as if she had touched pure ecstasy. "I really, really like it rough," she whispered in such an over-the-top breathy voice, Euryale couldn't help but roll her eyes. "Ask Ares."

Though her charms had no effect on the gorgon, the same could not be said for the giants. The three looked at Aphrodite with more lust than Euryale thought possible, and she found herself envious of her, though she hated herself for being that way. Not even Alex, who could barely keep his hands off her, had ever gawked at her the way these three gawked at Aphrodite.

"So," Aphrodite said, breaking the mini-silence that had settled between them. "Who wants to satisfy my needs?"

Pid socked Bemus in the side of the head. The giant stumbled, and that was all the catalyst that was needed before the room became the epicenter of a three-way brawl.

Euryale and Aphrodite bolted out of the room, never looking back.

Alex scooped one hand under Persephone's neck and snaked the other under her knees before lifting her off the ground. The Queen of the Underworld stirred with a whimper, and Cerberus let slip a tiny growl.

"Easy, boy," Alex said. "I'm doing my best."

Ares, who was almost out of the throne room and in search of a basin for water, paused and shot Alex a devious smile. "There's a reason why I'm having you tend to her."

"And what would that be?"

Ares nodded toward the three-headed hellhound. "Cerberus does not take kindly to those who would hurt Persephone."

"But I'm trying to take care of her," Alex said. His gaze dropped to Cerberus, whose six ears lay flattened against his heads.

"Come on, Cerb, I thought we were friends. Remember all that jerky I gave you?"

"That jerky is probably the only thing keeping you from having your throat torn out."

"Fat good that'll do. It's not like it won't grow back," Alex said before he'd had a chance to really think things through.

Ares' grin broadened as if he'd single-handedly outwitted Athena. "Do you think that makes things better or worse?"

Alex, having flashbacks of how a year ago he'd been eaten over and over by a lion thanks to his regenerating body, cringed. "Point taken." He looked back to Cerberus and tried to convince the dog how much of a good guy he was. "I'm only helping, buddy. Please don't eat the help."

The hell hound kept his intense stare, but didn't growl any further, which was a welcome relief to Alex. He took Persephone out of the throne room and headed for one of the guest suites that he had seen earlier. He didn't know where her room was, as he had never been given a full tour of the fortress, but somehow he didn't think she would mind. If anything, she might later thank him for not staining the bed she slept on.

Alex was about halfway to the room, limping through one of the ill-lit halls, when Persephone's eyes fluttered open. She squinted for a moment, as if trying to focus, before a confused look splashed across her face. "Alex?"

"It's me," he said. "Don't talk."

"Why?"

"Because, well..." Alex's voice trailed. "I don't know. That's what they always say. So it can't be all wrong."

"Who's they?"

"You know, the characters on TV shows and movies and what not." As soon as the words left his mouth, Alex shook his head. "Never mind. You probably don't know."

The tiniest of grins formed on her face, but it didn't last. Her icy-blue eyes squeezed shut, and her brow wrinkled as she grimaced. Her body trembled, and a few tears fell to the ground. Thankfully, though Cerberus growled softly, he didn't opt to take a chunk out of Alex's backside.

"By the Fates," she whispered. "Birthing an elephant would be less painful."

"I believe it. You're a mess."

"Do you always speak such sweet words to royalty?"

Alex stopped right outside the door to the guest room, unsure if she was trying to stay lighthearted to keep her mind off of her battered body or if she was taking genuine offense to his off-the-cuff comment. "I didn't mean anything by it," he said, opting to smooth over any potential transgressions. He had learned long ago that inadvertent insults and intentionally uttering blaspheme could both land him sans liver equally as fast. "I hope you know that."

"I know, Alex," she said. "I'm glad you're here."

Alex nudged the door open with his hip and carried her through the threshold. The room, unlike the barren corridor he had come from, had a lot of decoration to it. Four braziers, one in each corner, provided ample lighting. A large oak bed stood on the opposite wall, flanked on both sides by a pair of exquisite nightstands. In the corner to his right, a full-length mirror provided guests a place to prepare for the day, or it acted as a basic alarm against vampires. (But did the Greeks even have vampires? Alex wasn't sure. They probably had something like them, though, in which case the mirror would still be handy.) And like any good guest room, the opposite corner held a sizable set of drawers along with a single stick of incense that offered up a sweet, pleasing aroma.

"I'm not sure what to do," Alex said as he carefully placed Persephone down on the bed. Her back stuck to his arms, as did her knees, thanks to the blood coating them both.

"Gods, that hurts," Persephone said, cringing again.

In a flash, Alex had his hands a hair away from her skin as he desperately tried to think of something, anything he could do to alleviate her pain. "I'm sorry," he said. "Forgot about your back. I could roll you."

Persephone shook her head. "No, that whip had its way with me on my front as well. Just let me be. You've done nothing wrong."

Alex blew out a tense puff of air. "Thanks. That means a lot. It's not like I know what I'm doing. Hell, I'm a pianist, not a doctor, and to be honest, I'm glad I got you here without spilling your guts all over the place."

"Anything you could do to ease the pain is all that I'd ask," she said, her eyes still closed and voice shaky.

Cerberus jumped on the bed from the opposite side and inched his way up to her before whining and licking her cheek.

"I don't suppose you have any morphine floating around?" Alex asked, looking left and right. "As I said, I'm not an anesthesiologist, but I do have some experience using that. Seems like it's good stuff. Maybe I could stick you with a syrette or two."

"There should be some balm in the storeroom near the throne," she said. "Get that, if you will. It'll ease the pain and heal the wounds."

"Okay, I'll be right back," Alex said. He threw a glance at Cerberus before he left and added, "Don't let her go anywhere."

Cerberus growled low, but a fair hand on top of one of his heads calmed the beast.

With that, Alex hurried out of the room. It only took him a few minutes to find the storeroom and even less than that to find the balm. It was sitting in a clay jar on a shelf to his right, squished between several rolls of cotton bandages, two of which Alex grabbed, thinking they would be useful given his impromptu status as a field doctor. He also grabbed a nearby knife before hurrying back to the queen.

She had barely moved when he returned, having shifted only a few inches in the bed. The white sheets that she lay on, however, were quite different. While previously some fibers had been stained crimson, now it seemed that more than not had been soaked in blood. Her skin, too, though always light in tone, looked paler, almost deathly. Had she not been an immortal and wife of one of the most powerful Olympians, Alex would've been sure she'd have only seconds to live. To be honest, his worries still weren't far from that.

Alex quickly popped the top of the clay jar. The balm inside was thick and crème-colored, and it smelled like cotton candy. Once it was open, he set the jar to the side and looked her over, trying to make a quick assessment of where to begin. Though her peplos kept her modesty intact, there were more than enough bloody tears in it to make him wonder if the jar he had would be enough. If not, was there more? He couldn't remember. Surely there would be.

"Please, Alex," she whispered, almost begging in tone. "Why are you waiting?"

"I don't know," he said. "I don't want to mess this up, I guess."

Persephone giggled and then cringed. Despite the tears that ran out the corners of her eyes, she held her smile. "Oh, Alex, you won't mess anything up. Don't fret."

With a shrug, Alex dipped his pointer finger into the jar. The moment the dab he pulled touched his skin, a euphoric feeling washed over him. Goosebumps raised across his body, and his mind was instantly transported back to carefree days long gone where his biggest concern had been whether or not he would indulge himself in practicing twelve or fourteen hours on his piano with his latest Chopin endeavor.

First, and because it was the easiest, he stuck a dab on his hip. The burning ache that had been radiating through his body lessened considerably, and he sighed with relief. Then, he gently applied the balm to the wounds on Persephone's forearms, and within seconds, the same euphoric look that washed over his face struck hers. At that point, he wrapped the wounds as best he could with the cotton bandages before looking her over and trying to decide his next step.

"Don't stop," she said, eyes shut.

"I'm not sure where to go next," Alex said.

Persephone managed a weak chuckle. "If the skin is broken, that's where you go next."

"Yeah, but—" Alex stammered. It wasn't that he didn't know where he could apply the balm, it was more of a question of should he. Or at least, how he should. As far as the untended wounds to her front went, he could see a few on her chest that needed treatment. A glance downward also revealed there were several more on her abdomen and upper thighs. To get to them, however, he knew her clothes would have to come off.

Alex balked and balked some more. After another balking, he decided he needed to grow up. This was stupid, after all. He wasn't copping a feel. He was tending to his patient, and anyone or any god was going to have to accept that fact, Hades included. "Right, here goes," he said. "I'm going to have to remove your dress. Is that okay?"

Persephone murmured something, but she had drifted into the land of semiconsciousness. Alex tried to wake her enough to let her know what was about to happen, but she did not rouse. Thus Alex was forced to proceed without expressed consent and simply hoped for the best.

He carefully reached over and undid the clasps on her shoulders that held her peplos up. He'd barely pulled the dress down an inch when Cerberus snapped at him with all three heads. Alex reflexively jumped back with a startled cry and quickly counted the fingers on his right hand. Five. Exactly five untouched fingers remained on his hand. Alex sighed with relief before meeting the dog's intense stare.

"Look, doggo. Doggos. Doggii? Whatever. I have to treat her," Alex said, trying to sound as strong as he possibly could. "Do you want her to suffer? Because that's all you're ensuring."

Cerberus growled with two heads and whined with the third. "Exactly," he said. "Now let me work."

Alex tried again, and this time, thankfully, Cerberus kept his growls to a minimum and didn't try to make a snack out of Alex's fingers. The first wounds Alex tended to were right below the collarbone, three of them, maybe two inches long, but shallow. As he had with the arms, he also put a bandage on each one, which ended up being more of a covering than anything as he had no way of securing them in place.

With those finished, Alex carefully cut and peeled the peplos down further exposing her breasts and midsection. At this point, Alex was in full-on performance mode, going through the routine of applying the balm, bandaging, and moving on to the next area without a single thought as to who he was tending to and where.

"What in Hades' name are you doing?" Ares boomed.

Alex snapped his head to the right to see the god standing in the doorway, holding a pitcher in one hand and a shallow basin with the other. The twins waited patiently a few feet behind. "I'm tending to her wounds," Alex said. "Like you told me to, remember?"

"You have the Queen of the Underworld naked for all to see!" At that moment, Ares straightened and averted his gaze. "You should have her covered at all times!"

"I can't see what I'm doing if I do that," Alex replied. "Besides, no one else is here, and she asked me to put the balm on her in the first place."

"Did she ask you to strip her bare as well?"

"Well, no," Alex said. "Not in those precise words. But she did say to treat her completely. So that's what I'm doing. If you don't like it, you can take it up with her. And for the record, Cerberus here has already made it clear what is and isn't appropriate. So you're a little late to the let's-attack-Doctor-Alex party."

Ares shook his head while still avoiding looking at Persephone. "I won't have to take it up with anyone, Alex. You're going to be the one to have to answer to her, and then again to Hades. So for your sake, you had best pray you're right."

"I know, but at the same time, I'm going to have to answer to both for not taking care of her as well," Alex said. "Did you get a hold of Aphrodite? How's Euryale? They didn't kill each other yet, did they?"

"The call went to voicemail," he said. "I'll try again soon."

Alex nodded and went back to work. A few minutes later, he finished. Alex looked Persephone over from top to bottom, his eyes tracing over every inch of her naked flesh, trying to make sure he hadn't missed anything. It would be hard not to, given how much of her skin was still caked in blood. "That pitcher," he said. "Is there water in it?"

"There is," Ares replied.

"Can you bring it over? I should clean her up before I roll her over and get her something new to wear."

Ares muttered something about continuing to touch the naked skin of Hades' wife, but it was quiet and short-lived. He handed Alex the pitcher, at which point Alex cut some more bandages, dabbed them in water, and cleaned her body with more precision and care than a conservator would use to restore something by Leonardo da Vinci.

Twenty minutes came and went, and during that time Alex managed to carefully roll Persephone over without causing her too much pain before tending and cleaning her back. Once that was finished, he cut the bedsheets right up the middle, separating the non-soiled linen from the parts which were ruined, and then used that as a makeshift peplos to replace the one she'd had on previously.

"Thank you, Alex," Persephone said unexpectedly once he'd moved her to the other side of the bed.

"Don't mention it," he replied. "Hope you don't mind, but I had to give you a change of clothes."

Persephone shook her head. "Of course not. Despite what others might say, I'd rather not be in pain than not expose my skin."

"Good. I mean, not that this was good, but...well, you know what I mean."

"I do."

"Can you tell me what happened? And who was that minotaur?" Alex asked.

Persephone closed her eyes and shuddered. "Athena came," she said. "Only it wasn't her. It was someone else disguised as her. She had dark braided hair and eyes as black as the abyss. I don't know her name."

"Arachne," Ares growled.

"Arachne?" Persephone echoed, confused. "The woman Athena cursed so long ago? How?"

"We don't know," Alex said. "What did she want here?"

"To rob us," Persephone said, her voice strangled as she tried to fight her emotions long enough to get her story out. "She poisoned my husband, but thankfully, he realized the deception before he drank his entire goblet. Though it weakened him, he was still strong enough to rip her illusion away and try to fight her off. But she had Athena's aegis, and then hordes of monsters came as well. They...they beat him mercilessly. I...tried..."

Persephone stopped, and she shook her head. Alex gently touched her shoulder and gave it a soft squeeze. "What else? Please, it's important."

Persephone cleared her eyes. "I tried to defend my home. I picked up Hades' bident, and—" she stopped, laughed, and gestured to her broken body. "You can see what happened. They tore me to pieces and took the weapon. Arachne left right before Cerberus barged in. A few minutes later, you arrived."

"So Arachne now has Athena's shield and Hades' bident, along with the swords Hephaestus gave us for a wedding present and whatever else she's stolen that we don't know about," Alex said.

"I think they also got his helm of invisibility," she added. "Arachne was saying something about having it before she left. But at least she didn't get his scepter."

"Even so, that sounds really, really bad," Alex replied. "Like 'telling Athena she doesn't know what she's talking about' bad. Like 'starting a fight with my man Ares' bad."

Ares grinned as he clasped his hands together. "No, Alex, it is much worse than that."

"Then why are you smiling?"

Ares didn't answer, at least verbally. He simply let his face brighten until it outshone the sun.

"Oh, hell," Alex said. "We're going to war, aren't we?"

"We are," he said beaming. "Now excuse me while I call our lovers again and tell them the glorious news."

Chapter A Meeting With Hera

The fight went something like this: Aphrodite took a call from Ares. Then Euryale called Alex when she insisted she should. At that point, Alex filled her in on what had happened, and Euryale listened, spoke, listened some more, and ended the conversation screaming with rage and chucking her Olympi-phone as hard as she could. It sailed through the air and plopped into the ocean. And that was just fine with Euryale. Just fine, indeed.

"You seem upset," said Aphrodite.

Euryale groaned as she dragged her claws down the sides of her face before reaching up and grabbing a pair of vipers and tugging on them. "He brought our kids into battle! Actual battle! How could he ever think that was a good idea? Here I am trying to get Athena's shield back and he's putting our children in danger! I swear by the River Styx if he doesn't—"

"You might not want to finish that," Aphrodite said, holding up a finger. "Oaths made in anger are as binding as any other."

Euryale pressed her lips together as she seethed. All she wanted to do was sink her fangs into Alex for ever risking their children in such a way. She didn't care what excuses he'd come up with, and certainly at the first signs of danger, he should've left with the twins and gone home. "Why doesn't he listen? Am I asking him to put the world on his shoulders or wrestle Cronus into submission?"

Aphrodite didn't reply, though the gorgon had fully expected her to come back with some insult as she always had. "Be glad his offense is so small," Aphrodite finally said.

"Small? You call that small?"

The goddess, who had previously had her back to the gorgon, turned to face her. Where life had once radiated from her eyes, now there was nothing but emptiness. The corners of her mouth were turned down, and even her golden hair seemed as if it had wilted. She still had an unparalleled beauty, but it was a beauty steeped in mourning. "It's small in the sense that he was doing what he thought was best, and he loves you. I could see it in his eyes as you talked, as he took in every word you said. I'm certain he won't do it again." Aphrodite's shoulders fell, and before the gorgon knew it, the goddess was leaning her small frame against hers. "But me? They never listen and never will."

Euryale tried to form words for a reply, but none came to her. Her mind went blank as it attempted to process what was going on. "What do you mean?" she managed to ask. "Everyone listens to you, even giants wanting to maul us."

"They only listen to what they want," she explained. "So I've learned to turn that against them. They don't actually listen to me. Not my husband who will never grant me a divorce. Not my father who refuses to annul what he made in the first place—after all, can't have his precious, beautiful daughter running around, available. Fates know what sort of war that would start as I tempt all the boys into one bloody contest after another to win my hand."

"But...But I thought the only one you wanted was Ares," Euryale said. "He's the one you always run off with."

"That's my point. If anyone listened, they'd know I wouldn't lead anyone else on. Ares would be mine, and I would be his," she lamented. "But that will never be. I'll always be ignored. All I am is the weak, pretty one, who only has a seat in the throne room on account of my body. If I didn't have that, I'd have nothing."

Euryale reached her hand over, took Aphrodite's hand in hers, and squeezed. "I never would've thought someone so gorgeous could be so sad, but here you are," she said. She then straightened and jerked away awkwardly. "Sorry. That came out wrong."

"It's okay," Aphrodite said. She sniffed and cleared her eyes before giving a half grin. "I never thought anyone so ugly would ever be happy, but here you are."

Euryale gave her a friendly bump with her shoulder. "May I ask you something? It's nothing offensive, I don't think."

"Oh, I think with a qualifier like that, it almost certainly is," Aphrodite said, leaning away playfully.

"Is that why you didn't fight?"

"When?"

"Back at the forge," Euryale explained, slowly picking her words so she didn't inadvertently shatter what little connection the two had unexpectedly made. "You refused to fight. I was wondering why."

"You think anyone ever bothered to teach me how?" Aphrodite said. "Of course not."

"Not even Ares?"

Color returned to Aphrodite's cheeks, and she bit on her lower lip before replying. "The lessons never lasted."

"Due to him or you?" Euryale asked.

"Both."

"I see," the gorgon replied. "We'll have to change that."

Aphrodite erupted in laughter. "You're kidding, right?"

"No, I meant about you not getting lessons," she said. "Not about you and Ares acting like lovestruck teens. I'm hardly the weapon master, but once we're free, if you like, I could help you develop those skills. I mean, fighting, training, and fighting some more is pretty much all that happens on Elysium. I could even show you how to use a gun. Alex taught me a while ago. It's a lot more fun than swinging a sword around."

"Train...with you?" Aphrodite said. Her eyes sparkled and a wry grin formed, but it only lasted a moment. An unspoken thought struck her, and her face went blank before she ended up staring off into the distance. "Thanks, but I can shoot already."

"You can?"

"Something I learned a few months ago, personal growth and all," she said.

"What did you shoot? People?"

Aphrodite laughed with shock. "Heavens, no. Trap. Skeet. You know those clay pigeons that fly off and you blast with a shotgun?"

"When did humans learn to make birds from clay?" Euryale asked with surprise.

"No, they're discs made of clay. They call them pigeons," Aphrodite explained. "It was a lot of fun, but it made my hands smell terrible. So I gave it up."

"Oh, I see. Well, we could still train with sword and spear," the gorgon offered.

Aphrodite blew out a slow puff of air, one that seemed to deflate her completely. "No. Thank you. I can't be..."

Euryale swallowed hard as her voice trailed off. She didn't need the goddess to finish the statement, and she felt foolish thinking things had changed between her and Aphrodite to any meaningful degree, or any of the Olympians for that matter. "You can't be seen with me. Appearances and all."

Aphrodite straightened. She breathed deep before adjusting her dress and fixing her hair. "Exactly," she said. "But your kindness here will be remembered, provided you speak of this to no one."

"Don't worry. I've never been one to gossip," Euryale said. "So what now?"

"We tell Ares and Hera what's going on," she replied. "After that, we find Hephaestus, get cut free, and go our separate ways."

Aphrodite whipped out her phone and dialed. The line picked up, but it wasn't Hera who answered. It was her assistant, Patricia, an uptight, ill-mannered woman who thought too highly of herself and enjoyed way more protection from the Queen of Olympus than any mortal ever should.

"I need to talk to Hera," Aphrodite said. "Put her on."

"She's busy scrying."

"It's urgent."

"And scrying isn't?"

Aphrodite groaned. "When will she be done?"

"I have no idea," she said. "If you feel the need to talk to her is that urgent, you're welcome to come here and interrupt her, but I'd be remiss in my duties if I didn't tell you she expressly stated she did not want to be disturbed under any circumstances."

"But—"

"*ANY* circumstances."

The call ended, and Aphrodite's face soured. "I hate that insufferable bitch," she said.

"Hera or her little pet?"

Aphrodite laughed. Hard. "Both."

Euryale and Aphrodite soon made it to Argos, a Greek city that had always held a special place in Hera's heart. It was a lovely city with a rich history and plenty of trees and mountains surrounding it. Where the two were headed inside the city limits was the Peacock Tower, a corporate monolith that Hera had built last spring. It dwarfed not only everything in sight, but it was also three times as tall as the previous world-record holder when it came to the tallest building in the world.

The stupid would say Hera was compensating, even if it was in a figurative sense. Everyone else, however, knew she was declaring, no, daring the world to challenge her. No one did.

Aphrodite landed her swan-drawn chariot on the skyscraper's helipad, which sat below a three-hundred-foot spire. Ares was there waiting, having been called prior to their arrival. At that point, the trio hurried into the elevator and took it down to Hera's office.

Not long after, they stood in Hera's boardroom as she sat at the head of the meeting table, wearing her white peplos and crown as always. She folded her fingers together, and her large, cowlike eyes narrowed with sparks of anger. While her features had always been sharp, now they had such an edge that even Euryale thought they might split diamond. The only feature about her that wasn't threatening everyone with unspeakable horrors was the tiny amount of glitter in her hair. Apparently, before this meeting, Hera's scrying had also included a little bit of a rave.

When it came to the other Olympians who were present, they numbered exactly three: Poseidon, God of the Sea; Artemis, Goddess of the Hunt; and Ares, still God of War and now possibly football, too. The first two gods, as it turned out, had not been present at Aphrodite's party, and thus had never been drugged. On a similar note, Demeter would have been there as well, as she'd left Aphrodite's party early, but when she'd heard what had happened to her daughter, Persephone, she'd rushed back to the Underworld to be at her side, along with two dozen satyrs who would help take care of not only Persephone, but the fallen Hades, too.

"You have no idea where Athena is?" Hera finally asked after stewing over the news Aphrodite and Euryale shared.

"I assume Arachne has her," Aphrodite said.

"I'm not assuming anything!" Hera roared, taking to her feet as her thunderous voice echoed off the marble walls. "I want answers. I want that insolent woman found and brought to me before this day is over. I want her on her knees, begging me to end her miserable existence after I've heaped more curses upon her than there are stars in the sky! If she wants to bring war to this house, then by the Fates, she will have it."

Silence reigned for a few moments, and Euryale was the one who dared to speak first. "It might not be that easy."

"Did someone ask you for your opinion, gorgon?" Hera asked. "Or did Zeus make you our equal without my knowledge?"

Had Hera not ended with a question, Euryale would've stayed quiet, but since she had, the gorgon used it as an opportunity to speak her mind. "I would never presume Zeus did such a thing," she said, "but if Arachne melts the artifacts she's taken to create something new, there's no telling what power she could have."

"Ridiculous. Hephaestus's forge is the only place with fires hot enough to melt adamantine," Hera said. "And even if she could accomplish such a thing, even she is not dumb enough to go there."

"She must have another place in mind," Poseidon said as his weathered fingers toyed with his white beard. "As you said, even she is not dumb enough to return to Hephaestus's island."

"Or she doesn't intend to melt them down at all," Hera countered. "We'll keep watch on Hephaestus's forge, but we can't go on a wild goose chase since most of us still sleep. We simply do not have the resources."

"How long until you can awaken them?"

Hera sighed. "That's what I've been working on nonstop since I got back. I'll break her spell. That is not in question. But progress is slow."

Artemis, smallest of them all, adjusted the circlet with a crescent moon on her head. "Arachne has proven herself a proficient huntress, even if it is momentary," she said. "But since she's answering to someone else, our true foe is even stronger, craftier."

Hera's lips pressed together as she turned the goddess's words over in her mind. "We need to know who that is."

"A mortal?" Aphrodite offered. "They've come a long way since we've been gone."

"No mortal is powerful enough to undo Athena's curse on Arachne, and none are strong enough to put us all to sleep, either,"

Hera replied, shaking her head. "I don't care what inventions they've made."

"A titan, then," offered Ares. "They are mighty foes, some with long lists of grudges against us."

"Let's hope it's not Cronus," Poseidon replied. "If Nyx is led away and he escapes her cave..."

Hera's anger washed away under a deluge of worry, and rightly so. Though the God of the Sea hadn't finished his statement, he didn't need to. Everyone knew what Cronus was capable of. He was the King of the Titans, God of Time, and former ruler of the entire cosmos. His reign came to an end when Zeus, with help from his mother, Rhea, led a ten-year war and barely defeated him. At that point, Zeus imprisoned the titan in the only place strong enough to contain him: the Cave of Nyx. There, Cronus slept, but if he were ever to awaken and return, he could—and likely would—devour all of creation to satisfy his need for revenge, especially since he hated Zeus with a passion.

"Arachne wouldn't dare wake him, would she?" asked Hera.

"A woman who suffered at the hands of Athena for thousands of years? Who knows how twisted that mind has become and how many of us she blames," Artemis said. "If releasing Cronus was the only means to catch her quarry, I'd not put it past her."

"She did say she had a way to topple Olympus," Euryale said, thinking back to the conversation she'd had with the woman when she'd posed as Jessica.

Hera's anger resurfaced. "The insanity of it all," she spat. She spent a few moments stewing while tapping a finger on the table. "Nyx must be warned, first and foremost. Ares will go along with Aphrodite and the gorgon. There you will stand guard until further instructed."

"Nyx does not take kindly to visitors," Poseidon said. "Even Zeus fears her, and rightly so."

"Then they'd better be polite," Hera replied. "You and Artemis, in the meantime, will scour the land and sea until you find Arachne and whatever forge she might have made. While you do that, I'll see what I can do about breaking this spell that has put everyone else to sleep."

"I should go to the mortals," Aphrodite said. "The media love me. They could be of use to us."

"No," Hera said. "We've barely been among them a year, and I'll not have them think we can't take care of our own house. What sort of fools will they take us for then?"

"But Arachne could be up to something other than waking Cronus, and we—"

"I'm sorry, Athena, is that you?" Hera interrupted. "I didn't recognize you with that aura of 'look at me, I'm so pretty' hanging about. I must say, you play the role of a clueless tart quite well. Tell me, why should we leave only one to guard Nyx's cave again?"

Aphrodite shrank under Hera's beratement. Euryale, however, did not. Her muscles tensed, and her tail slowly coiled beneath her. "Listen to her, for once," the gorgon said. "A single error threatens us all."

"Again you tax my patience," Hera said. "Forget your place again, and I'll see that curse you bear increases tenfold." She then turned her attention back to Aphrodite and continued scolding her. "Since you want to argue, pay close attention so you'll understand why once again your short-sightedness could cost us everything," she said. "Cronus is our greatest threat and would love nothing more than to see Zeus and the rest of us be destroyed. We can deal with anyone else. So until I'm completely certain he's not going to be released, that is where our focus will be. Do you understand?"

Aphrodite started to protest, but she never got beyond opening her mouth. With a broken posture and an equally broken spirit, all she could do was nod.

"Good," Hera said, easing her tone. "Before you go, I need you to open your father's vault and fetch me his bolts. We'll need his lightning if Cronus wakes."

Aphrodite didn't respond at first, but then to Euryale's utter amazement, the Goddess of Love stood tall and locked her eyes with Hera's. "No," she said. "That's one thing I will not do."

Chapter Cursed

"My ears must be deceiving me," Hera said as her eyes narrowed. "I could have sworn by the River Styx I heard you disobey me."

Everyone pulled away from Aphrodite, even the mighty Poseidon. Everyone pulled away, that is, except for Euryale. And it wasn't because they were joined by the chain. The gorgon hadn't budged at all, something that both surprised and relieved Aphrodite. The goddess was glad at least someone was standing with her, even if it was someone as hideous as Euryale.

A twinge ran through Aphrodite's gut at that last thought. She was being overly harsh on the gorgon, that she realized. Before she could turn the thought over any further, Hera spoke again.

"Forget where you put your mirror?" Hera mocked. "Get your mind out of the clouds and fetch me those bolts."

"No," Aphrodite said as evenly as she could. Her voice fluttered, and her hands trembled. She could only hope Hera would listen, even if she hardly had ever before. "I won't. I can't. He strictly forbade it."

"He is not part of this equation anymore!" Hera sharply replied. "He would tell you himself to give them to me if he could! You think his need to be the only one who touches them trumps his need to keep all of Olympus safe?"

Aphrodite shook her head and tried to mentally prepare herself for the battle she was getting herself into. "He made me promise never to fetch them for anyone but himself."

"Cronus will be marching on our door, and now you develop some sort of unwavering loyalty? Tell me, goddess of morals, where does your virtue go when you run off with Ares time and again? Or does it only matter when our very existence is at stake and not your pathetic need for instant pleasure and gratification?"

Aphrodite's chest tightened, and she fought hard to keep her eyes from watering. Zeus had always been explicit with her on when she could ever open the vault and retrieve his lightning, and as concerning as this situation with Arachne was turning out to be, she still felt in her heart of hearts that Zeus would want to keep his weapons safe.

"We still don't know Arachne is working with Cronus," Aphrodite protested.

"I will not wait until that titan wakes and devours half the world before acting!"

"If the need is so great, then I will carry them, especially if I'm to guard Nyx's cave," Aphrodite said.

Hera snickered, as did Poseidon and Artemis. "As if you're capable of putting up a fight, lightning or not. You can't even run a dating site without it leading to disaster."

"That's not true," Aphrodite said, her voice cracking and her self-esteem crumbling. How she hated how little everyone thought she was capable of. How she hated thinking the same. Who was she, after all, to claim she could ever do such a thing?

"I can see it in your face. Even you don't believe it. Remind me again: how fast did you run away during the Trojan War when that mortal nicked your wrist? Now hand them over."

Aphrodite glanced around the room. None of the other Olympians offered any support. Even Ares, her lover, held an apprehensive expression which told her she should capitulate to Hera's demands.

Euryale, remaining silent, once again defied the goddess's expectations. The gorgon slipped her hand into Aphrodite's and gave a gentle squeeze. That simple act was more than enough to break the emotional wall Aphrodite had erected to save face in front of the other gods. Though tears ran down her cheeks, her spirit drew strength that would let her set the world on her shoulders for a thousand years without complaint. "No," she said. "His lightning is not yours to command. The bolts will stay in the vault, or in my hands, until I hear Dad say otherwise."

Hera growled, and she took a few steps back. She opened her right hand and raised it in front of her face. A dark ball of flame appeared, a few inches above the palm, and the Queen of Olympus began to dance it around her hand like a street magician might with a ball made of sponge. But she was no mere street magician, and the ball she toyed with was not soft and harmless. This ball held a curse, or two, or ten.

"I will not ask again," Hera said.

"I will not change my mind," Aphrodite answered as her throat constricted. She could barely see due to the water clouding her eyes, though part of her was glad that was now the case. If she could see Hera clearly in her full anger, her nerve would likely fail. At least this way, she could show she was not the weak goddess, even if that trait was being artificially created.

"Then you will suffer Euryale's fate a dozen times over."

With a sidearm flick, Hera sent the dark fire hurling toward Aphrodite. The goddess, knowing she had nowhere to go, especially being tethered to a gorgon, didn't react. In the end, however, she didn't have to.

Euryale jumped in front and bore the full brunt of the curse as it hit her directly.

"Are you sure those chains will hold?"

Arachne paused with a key in her hand. "They're the same that bind Euryale and Aphrodite together. They'll hold," she replied to The Fox. "Don't let her trick you into thinking otherwise."

"If they fail, Athena won't be tricking either of us," he rightly pointed out. "She'll be our end."

Arachne smiled. "They'll hold."

"What if she doesn't talk?"

"If she doesn't, we can manipulate her sister with a little extra work." Arachne then inserted the key into the jail door they stood in front of and unlocked it. The door swung open, and they stepped into Athena's cell, a cozy little place carved out of rough stone and decorated with mold, mildew, and a powerless goddess.

"Ready to talk?" Arachne asked.

Athena looked up from her chained position on the floor. "Only if we're negotiating your surrender."

Arachne laughed, but The Fox didn't. How she hated that about him. For someone so sly, he showed a lot of fear coming into this cell. Not that she could blame him too much, she supposed. After all, they were dealing with Athena, Goddess of Wisdom—the one who was renowned to be a thousand steps ahead of any opponent. As such, they could only hope their mysterious benefactor had thought things out a thousand and one. So far, Arachne reminded herself, that had proven true. "I still have a few things on my shopping list I'd like to take care of the easy way."

"That doesn't sound like your surrender."

Arachne smiled and shook her head. "It's not. Fox, show her what we've brought."

The Fox, in his human form, carefully placed a metal bucket on the ground next to Athena. He then pulled out a canteen, carefully unscrewed the top, and poured water into said bucket. When he finished, he backed away as if he'd armed a nuclear bomb.

"Know what's in there?"

Athena tilted her nose up a half degree. "Water from the River Acheron."

"You are clever," Arachne replied. "So you know how unbearably painful a drop is, even for the gods."

"Everyone knows," Athena said without a hint of fear in her gray eyes. "Do you honestly think you can torture my secrets out of me?"

Arachne shrugged with indifference. "I don't know, but it'll be fun to try."

Using a spoon, Arachne took a small bit of water and poured it on Athena's leg. It sizzled the moment it struck her skin, and the goddess jerked back and grimaced, but she didn't cry out.

"Impressive," Arachne said. "We can get more, you know. This bucket won't be the last. We could even flood your cell so the agony is never-ending."

"Here's what I know," Athena replied after taking a few steadying breaths. "Time is my ally. Not yours. If I were you, I'd think long and hard about how much you want to anger me."

"Are you threatening me?"

"These chains won't sap my strength forever," Athena said evenly.

"You're right about that," Arachne replied. "They'll come off, but only after you've been devoured."

Chapter Pizza

"Extra babies."

Arachne, now on a break from interrogating Athena in order to tend to other matters, cocked her head as she looked at The Fox. "Say again?"

"I want extra babies," he said as he swished his bushy tail back and forth with eagerness. "It says right here in the advertisement I can have any toppings I want for a dollar."

"We are not getting babies on our pizza," she said, settling into the leather couch in Jessica's living room.

"We can at least get babies on half," he replied. "You don't have to eat any."

Arachne felt the blood in her body rush to her face. She may have been cursed, and there were certainly some out there who would disagree with her morals and actions as of late, but there was a lot more than a fine line that separated an arachnid-human hybrid from a wanton devourer of infants. Maybe if she'd been born in Sparta, where infanticide had been a national pastime, she would've had a different outlook on the request. "Neither one of us are eating babies," she said with finality.

The Fox sat on his haunches and, using one of his front paws, gave himself a tongue bath. "You want my help? Then ask for extra babies. I'm tired of running around and not getting what you promised."

Arachne groaned. "Fine, I'll ask." She returned to the teen who was patiently waiting on the phone to complete her order. "Can we get extra babies in lieu of cheese?"

"Extra...babies? Is that what you said?"

"Yes. But only on half the pizza."

"Babies as in baby carrots?"

"No. As in tiny humans."

The teen gave a nervous chuckle before clearing his throat. "Um, we don't offer that."

Arachne lowered the phone for a second and smiled. "They don't have babies, sorry."

The Fox let out a huff. "Fine. I'll steal my own. Where's the nearest nursery?"

"Nowhere. We're on a tight schedule." Before The Fox could reply, Arachne held up a finger and finished ordering. Two cheese pizzas. One with extra cheese. One with extra anchovies. No babies. She repeated that last part twice just in case someone at the shop was indeed from Sparta and had a gimpy little brother or sister they wanted to get rid of. She didn't think that was the case as times had changed, but people, she knew, could always end up being a surprise when it came to tastes. She had, after all, heard some sort of screeching on the radio that supposedly passed for music. It assaulted her ear so badly, she was sure eating babies would have been ten times more pleasurable. So, who knew what toppings might be out there?

"Do you think he'll show?" The Fox asked.

"Alex? Of course. He has to check on his old sweetheart," Arachne said.

The Fox huffed again, apparently not satisfied with her prediction but at the same time not convinced otherwise enough to challenge her on it either. With nothing being said, Arachne went back to flipping through the channels on the television, mindlessly trying to find something interesting to watch.

Ten minutes after she'd been absorbed into a cartoon involving a secret agent mouse, his hamster sidekick, and their adventures in England, the front door burst open, and Alex came barging through, sword in hand.

At least, Arachne imagined him bursting through with sword in hand as she couldn't see him directly. After all, what sort of hero charged into the dragon's lair without his trusty weapon drawn? Or in this case, the arachnid's lair. Or really when you got right down to it, his ex-girlfriend's lair who, when this was all said and done, might end up donating the mansion to Arachne post-mortem anyway as the place had grown on her over the last hour. Arachne would, of course, need to tend to a few minor details before moving in completely or making it a secondary residence.

First, she would need to add some tapestries of her own so the place felt like hers and she wasn't intruding in another's home. Second, and almost as important, she would want to keep security up, which meant she would have to find a few more guards to hire, especially since she had snacked on the one from before. The biggest concern around that was should she find guards who were tasty or not? To the former, it would always mean she could have a bite to eat when the mood suited her. The latter, however, had the advantage of having a slower turnover rate when it came to employees. Not to mention, it would cut down on the questions.

"Jessica? Jessica! Where are you?" Alex yelled, his voice booming through the mansion and pulling Arachne out of her post-victory plans.

"Over here," Arachne called back. When she saw the fur on The Fox's back bristle, she held out her hand and shushed. "Don't be rude."

"I'm hungry," he said.

"We have pizza coming."

"Without babies."

Alex slid to a stop, right outside of the room, sword in hand and ready. His eyes narrowed when he spotted Arachne on the couch. "You better not have hurt her."

"Alex, dear, may I call you dear?" Arachne replied, casually looking at him with as much worry as a tarantula watching a cricket wander on by. "Please, have a seat."

"I'll have your head if you don't tell me where she is."

"I think you'll want to sit. Especially for pizza. You do like pizza, don't you? Maybe I should've asked what you like for toppings before ordering."

"I don't want your stupid pizza."

Arachne frowned. "Are you sure? I'm trying to make this time we have together pleasant. I even got one with extra cheese."

"At least you got what you wanted on it," The Fox tacked on.

Alex's eyes glanced to the giant fox who was now on his back near Mr. Peeper's terrarium, all four legs up and splayed to the sides. Upon spying the animal, Alex jumped back, but the startled look vanished a second later as the hero inside took over. Alex pointed the tip of his sword at Arachne's head. "I'm not asking again. Where is Jessica?"

"Easy, Alex. Easy. You're going to get yourself hurt rushing around like that," she said. "Didn't your mother ever teach you not to run with sharp, pointy things?"

"Didn't your mother ever teach you not to pick a fight with those who beat the gods?"

"Yes, your triumph over Ares and Aphrodite," Arachne said before she leaned forward and took the glass of wine off the coffee table and had a sip. "It's a very impressive tale, Alex. But before you come at me, I need you to know four things."

"What would those be?"

The Spider Queen enumerated each point with her fingers as she answered. "First, I am much more careful in my planning than Ares. Second, unlike Aphrodite, I don't mind getting my hands dirty. Third, and this might be most important right now, *you* are a guest in *my* house."

Alex scoffed before she had a chance to finish. "This will never be your house."

"Alex, Alex, Alex," Arachne said, shaking her head. "You're witty, and you're wise. And I doubt not the bravery in your eyes. But always remember this: as surely as The Fox is sly, I am the spider in this parlor, and you are nothing but a fly."

"Cute," Alex said. "Think of that all on your own?"

Arachne grinned, sipped her wine once more, and set it down. "I might've adapted something else for it."

"Enough. What's your fourth point?"

Arachne gestured to the ceiling. Unable to see due to his vantage point, Alex had to take a few steps inside. There, where she'd directed his attention, wrapped and glued above with a thick network of webs, was a very Jessica-sized cocoon.

"I'll kill you!" Alex said, charging. He didn't get but two steps before Arachne let loose a spray of webs that pinned him to the wall by his arm.

"I guess you'll have to stand for this," Arachne said with a shrug. "Pity. This couch is so much more comfortable."

"I'm going to rip your head off if you don't let us go this instant," Alex said.

"Keep talking like that, and I'm going to web that obnoxious little mouth of yours shut once and for all."

Alex's muscles bulged as he pulled against the webs, but they held fast.

"Seriously, Alex. Stop this. Regular spider silk is five times stronger than steel," Arachne said with an exasperated sigh. "I promise you what I weave is even more so."

Alex relaxed, and Arachne smiled knowingly. "Depends," Alex said, looking at his trapped arm before taking his sword with his off hand. "I might not pull free, but I can always cut free."

Arachne folded her arms and chuckled. "You think you can cut those bindings?"

"I think I can cut through my arm."

"You wouldn't."

"I've had worse," Alex said evenly.

"Then what are you going to do, bleed on me?"

"I'm invincible," Alex growled.

"You're a looney."

Alex narrowed his eyes. "Come on, then. Draw close."

For the first time since the encounter, Arachne felt a twinge of doubt run through her. She had carefully laid out her plan in an intricate web that saw every strand placed with the utmost care and purpose. Yet despite all that, she hadn't prepared herself for the sheer determination in her adversary's eye. "Well, before you make yourself an amputee, you might want to consider the fact that if you do that, I'll be forced to wrap you up as I have her. Then you'll simply be a gimpy hero in a cocoon who bled all over this lovely room, and no one wants that." When a beat passed and Alex didn't commit either way, she tacked on. "Alex, if I wanted to hurt you, we wouldn't be having a conversation right now."

That seemed to placate Jessica's hero. Alex breathed slow and deep for a few seconds before relaxing ever so slightly. "Fine," he said. "What do you want, and who's the pet wolf."

"Fox," The Fox growled as he rolled off his back and came to his feet.

"Fox. Wolf. Same thing. You're a big dog who talks."

"We're not the same thing," The Fox snarled. "Wolves get caught. I never do."

"Never? Not even once? After all, I caught you with my eye when I came in. Does that count?"

"Shut it."

"Looks like I've caught your anger, too." Alex grinned. "Oh! And twenty says whatever scheme the two of you have cooked up, before that, Arachne definitely caught your attention."

The doorbell rang, and a new voice joined in. "Hello? Everything all right here?" someone called out. "I've got your pizza, and the door was open. I promise."

Arachne held a finger to her lips before pointing to Jessica. "Let's keep this between us, yes? For her sake if no one else's."

"Hello?" the man called again.

"Better get your pizza," Alex growled.

Arachne nodded her head toward The Fox, and the giant animal rolled his eyes before changing into the form of a red-haired man who was dressed in a tan suit that looked like it had been marked down five times in the bargain bin before finally being tossed and written off as a loss.

"Fine," The Fox said, adjusting his shirt collar. "I'll get it."

Arachne waited for The Fox to leave before speaking again. "I don't suppose the two of you have ever been properly introduced, have you?"

"You'd suppose right."

"He's the Teumessian Fox."

Alex shrugged, or at least as much as the web allowed him to. "Sorry. That doesn't mean anything to me."

"I figured as much. I'll give you the short, short version. He terrorized the city of Thebes and was destined never to be caught in all that he did. Eventually, Laelaps, a dog who could catch any quarry, was brought to chase him down. The two entered a paradoxical contest due to their mutually excluding abilities which nearly tore all of creation apart. But before that could happen, Zeus turned them both to stone."

"That sounds like getting caught to me," Alex said.

"Paused," Arachne clarified. "It's a subtle, important difference."

"I guess. Let's skip the history lesson and get right to business. What do you want?"

Arachne took the bottle of wine that had been sitting nearby on an end table and used it to pour Alex a glass. "Would you care for some?"

"No."

"Suit yourself," Arachne said, sipping what she'd poured. "I want one of two things, Alex. I would prefer it if you took a deep, long look at what has happened in your life the last year and what will continue to happen to all of humanity and join my cause—you and your wife."

"You can save your breath," Alex said. "I'm not going to war with the Olympians. There's nothing you can say to make me change my mind."

"Alex, I'm not going to war with all of the Olympians," she said. "Only a select few. In fact, I'm hoping to avoid war altogether."

"Seeing how you stole a number of their artifacts, and as best I can tell, you've kidnapped Athena and Hephaestus, I don't think the rest of them are in the mood to offer a peace treaty."

"I'm also the one who stole Aphrodite's invitation," Arachne said. "Well, The Fox stole it, at my request."

"I knew it!" Alex said, pulling on the webbing. "Well, I didn't know that. But I knew I didn't forget to send her one...wait, why on earth did you do that?"

"Oh, you know," she said, toying with her hair. "Spinning webs of distrust among the Olympians is a delicate matter, but surprisingly easy once you get the knack. I dare say I could manipulate any of them given enough time."

At this point, The Fox came strolling in the room with two giant pizza boxes in his hands and an elated look upon his face. He set the boxes down on the coffee table in front of Arachne and held up a yellow box with red lettering. "And here you said they didn't have babies," he said, beaming.

Arachne tilted her head to the side before two things crossed her mind. First, The Fox was holding a box of candy, and second, he hadn't a clue what was inside. "You do realize that box is a normal one, right? It's smaller on the inside."

"Of course I know that."

"Then you also realize that a real baby can't fit inside, correct?"

Using a finger, he popped the lid and dug out a piece of chocolate. "Obviously," he said. "But they've clearly harvested the sweetest, chewiest parts for consumption, which is good enough for me."

"Okay, as long as we're clear on that," Arachne said with amusement before turning back to Alex. "So, where were we?"

"You were monologuing."

"Is that a reference joke?" she asked. "I saw that movie not too long ago. Quite funny. I guess you think I'm the bad guy in all this."

"The thought had crossed my mind. After all, you do have me and Jessica tied up."

"But unharmed," Arachne added. "If I wanted to hurt either of you, I could have long ago. Think of this as a temporary restraint for your own good."

"Sounds like something the bad guy would say," Alex replied.

"Fair enough," she replied. "But would your enemy let either of you go? Because that's what I'm going to do after we've had our chat."

Alex tutted. "I'll believe that when I see it."

"Then get ready to be a believer," she said. "Here's the…how do you say it, now? Deal? Yes. Here's the deal, Alex. Fox and I are working with others. All we want to do is change who sits on the throne of Olympus. No more. No less. When we do—and I assure you that change is about to happen—those who've escaped justice no longer will."

"Those like Athena, you mean."

"Precisely," Arachne said, beaming. "No one else has to get hurt, including you. Including Jessica, and especially including Euryale."

Alex eased forward. "You're crazy. You'll never succeed in taking down the Olympians."

"Never? Are you sure about that?"

"If I'm wrong, then tell me who else you're working with."

Arachne laughed. "Alex, you're not tricking me into giving up secret information. If you want to be on the right side of history when this is all said and done, you can do one of two things: You can either convince Euryale to side with me so she can live in a world where she's accepted for who she is, or you can say you have a lead somewhere, anywhere, and go chase it with her for a day. I don't care where that is as long as it's…let's say…somewhere in the Americas."

"You want me to lie," Alex said.

"If it makes you feel better, I'll give you a lead, and you can chase that. Ever been to Vegas? I hear there's plenty to see there."

"You want me to disappear for a day. One day."

"Yes," Arachne said with a nod. "One little day."

Alex smirked. "I might not be Athena when it comes to understanding the intricacies of war and espionage, but I have learned a thing or two since she and I first met."

"I hope it's not how to avoid a trap, Alex, because she's a horrible teacher for that one," Arachne said as she pulled a slice of pizza and ate. "Oh, this is good. This is really, really good."

"No," Alex said with a glare. "What she taught me was how to spot a bluff."

It started out as a deep, soft chuckle, but grew into a sinister laugh right before The Fox changed back into his canine form. Even when that was complete, there was an amused smile on his face and a look of pity in his eyes. "I told you he'd be like this."

"I never disagreed," Arachne remarked. "This isn't a bluff, Alex. This is a peace offering. I like Jessica. I do. She's witty. She's gracious as a hostess, and she takes wonderful care of Xavier, The Ever Watchful Devourer of Hearts and Scourge of Crickets."

"Who the what, what?"

Arachne motioned to the terrarium at her side where Jessica's tarantula was watching all this unfold. "Xavier, The Ever Watchful Devourer of Hearts and Scourge of Crickets, or as you might know him by his informal, mortal-assigned name, Mr. Peepers."

"I suppose he told you that," Alex said.

"Of course. Do you think I'd make that up? Pshhh." Arachne paused to indulge herself in another bite of pizza before washing it down with her wine. "But let's not lose focus, shall we? Not only do I like Jessica, but by default, I like you as well. You've kept your sanity and your humanity despite Athena's horrible trials she threw at you. And I like your wife, Euryale, and I can empathize with her greatly. If anyone knows what it's like to be cast aside, it's me. And to top it off, the one who I'm working with is very, very, *very* fond of her."

"That's a lot of verys. Are you insinuating her father is involved? Because honestly, I can't imagine who else you'd be referring to with that last bit. I love my wife, but I'm not delusional. She's not the most popular person. You saying your mystery backer is incredibly fond of her weeds out a lot of options."

Arachne sipped her wine one last time before crossing her legs and leaning back on the couch, arms outstretched. "Now, this is the part of the conversation where I'm afraid I'm not going to tell you any more."

"So it is him."

Arachne neither moved nor replied, not because she cared too much about what he did or did not know, or rather thought he knew, but for the last bit of her plan to come together smoothly, she needed him still in the dark, even if she ultimately hoped he'd join her. Otherwise, she'd have to run with Plan B. And she hated Plan B. It was so messy and would cause her a headache as she'd need to scramble to tie up loose ends.

"It is him," Alex repeated, but this time sounding about as sure of himself as if he'd taken a stab at answering a riddle from the Sphinx. "Isn't it?"

Chapter Clever Girls

Euryale dropped to her knees as the curse spread through her body. She cried out in agony and was convinced molten lead coursing through her veins would have felt better.

Her head swam, and her vision darkened and distorted as if she were peering through a dark glass. Hera and the rest of the Olympians melted into shadows. Their forms warped into demons, and their voices thundered in her ears. Her heart hammered against her chest, and no matter how quickly or deeply she breathed, it was never enough. The air scorched her throat, and unseen assailants tore at her arms, neck, and face.

"Get away from me!" Euryale shouted as she slashed at the air with her claws but connected with nothing.

The demons closed in, jabbing at her with forked tails and the butts of spears. One struck her on the back of the head, causing her to stumble forward, while another wrapped heavy chains around her arm and pulled so hard that it was nearly ripped from its socket.

A deep pressure built behind her eyes as she made eye contact with one of the demons, and suddenly the world flared a brilliant green.

When her vision returned, she found herself back in Hera's boardroom. The Queen of Olympus had her arms raised defensively, and her face was turned to the side. Shock was etched into her stone face, but that surprise paled in comparison to the disbelief Euryale bore when she realized that not only had Hera been petrified, but the rest of the Olympians as well—all of them, that is, save Aphrodite.

"What have you done?" she said, voice cracking as her eyes fixated on the statue that was once her lover, Ares.

At first, Euryale had no answer. A few seconds later, when the stone started to fade away from each of the Olympians as their flesh returned, Euryale still had no answer, but she did have a burning desire to escape while she still could. This desire was further reinforced when most of Hera, who was still petrified from the waist down, started to scream.

"I want the two of them cast into the deepest hole in Tartarus you can find!"

There was probably a lot more to her rants, but Euryale didn't wait to see what they were. She half pulled, half dragged Aphrodite along. They burst out of the boardroom and ran right into Hera's assistant, Patricia, who had a telephone in hand. The wiry secretary looked every bit as unpleasant as she always had, only this time her usual scowl contorted into equal parts shock and fright when Euryale's gaze fell upon her, and she turned to stone.

Unseen claws tore at Euryale's mind and drove her further into a frenzy of fight or flight. She twisted to try and free herself of the bonds that held her and Aphrodite together, as the goddess was not nearly as fast on her feet as she would've liked.

Aphrodite half laughing, half shouting, turned away and kept her hands up. "Don't look at me! Just get us out of here!"

Fire raged through the gorgon's body, and the world of shadows and demons faded back into existence. "No, no, no," she said, gripping the side of her face. "It won't stop."

A nightmarish creature jumped on her back and wrapped its arms around her neck. She thrashed about, trying to fight it off, but in a world of shadowy chaos where she couldn't even tell up from down, it was hard to do anything.

Something cool pressed against her cheek, and amid the constant pounding of noise against her ears and acrid smoke in her nose, a soft voice called out to her. "Stop fighting me," it said. "Go straight and don't look around."

Euryale obeyed, not knowing what else to do. She struck something hard with her hip, and the pain helped her concentrate. Though the world was still a swirl of blacks and deep reds, it took on a bit of focus. In the haze, she could make out a hall with doors on the sides.

"Keep going," the voice commanded. "Almost to the stairs."

"I can barely see," she said, hitting something else.

"That'll be the least of our worries if Hera catches up with us. Now move."

Mostly blind, still in pain, and barely able to function, Euryale went as fast as she could. Her flight seemed to take hours, and given the number of things she rammed along the way and people she heard shriek, there was no telling how many bones she broke or others she petrified.

When it was all over, Euryale ended up pressed against an outside wall as cool rain fell from the sky and splattered on her face. The drops helped her to relax, and she relished the feel as the water poured down her skin. Though her vision was still far from perfect, she could make out tall shadows of buildings on both sides, and there was the sound of traffic nearby.

"I can't believe you did that," Aphrodite said, laughing. Her melodic voice gave Euryale something concrete to latch on to and further brought her back to the real world. "Serves her right for giving away my dating site to Athena. Stupid cow deserved all that and more."

"What's happening to me?" Euryale asked.

"I'm guessing the curse Hera hit you with amplified the one you already had."

Euryale's pulse quickened and her mouth dried. "I'm worse than I was before?"

Aphrodite shrieked as the gorgon turned toward her. Her hands quickly found Euryale's cheeks and the goddess kept the gorgon from inadvertently turning her to stone. "I don't know how potent you are," Aphrodite said. "But until we figure that out, please don't look at me."

"You never wanted me to look at you to begin with."

"I know," she said. "But things are different now."

Euryale slumped against the wall, eyes closed. All she could think about was what this new curse meant for her in the long run. If she could petrify the gods, even if it were only temporary, what did that mean for Alex? Would she never be able to look at him again? And that was nothing to say of what this all meant for Aison and Cassandra. Could she trust herself around her children?

The more she thought about this, the more her sorrow turned to anger. Her body warmed, and her brow knitted. Claws grew from her fingertips, and she could feel her teeth sharpen into fangs capable of ripping anyone apart in seconds. "I'm going to kill her," she said softly.

"Who? Hera?" Aphrodite said with a disbelieving laugh.

Euryale dug her claws into the ground beside her. "You think I won't?"

"I think you're foolish to try."

"I don't care what you think," she said. "All I've ever done is try to make people happy, to get along, to please the gods. And what thanks do I get? I'm cursed time and again. As the Fates are my witnesses, I'm done being tread upon."

"Well, good luck with that," Aphrodite said. "But before you go on your grand crusade, I'd suggest we leave this place first."

"I don't even know where this place is."

"Me either," Aphrodite said with a lighthearted laugh. "An alleyway somewhere. Maybe a mile from where we left Hera."

"What do you think she's doing now?"

"Looking for us as much as she can," Aphrodite said.

"Then the first thing we need to do is get where she can't find us," Euryale said. "That way I'll have time to plot my next move."

Aphrodite chuckled. "No, the first thing we do is put a blindfold on you."

"And trust you explicitly?"

"I know I've given you every reason not to," Aphrodite said. "But on my life and everything I hold dear, I'd love to see you take Hera down. That said, even if you don't believe me, turning me to stone will only make things worse."

"How's that?"

"You'll be chained to a statue, for starters."

Euryale pressed her lips together and breathed heavily out of her nose. "Point taken."

"Glad you agree. Now sit tight a second," she said. There was the sound of tearing fabric, and then Euryale felt a long strip cover her eyes and get tied around her head.

"There we go," Aphrodite said. "Now we can go to the bar and lay low."

"A bar? You mean like a place the mortals go for drinks?"

"Exactly. There's a special little place nearby that Ares and I would go to from time to time when we wanted to keep things low-key. It'll be a good spot to hide and figure out what to do because I'm pretty sure once my elation over you turning Hera to stone fades, I'm going to lose my mind at being cast out of Olympus."

"If we stop Arachne, that should secure your place."

"That's what I'm hoping," Aphrodite said as she adjusted the blindfold. "I know this might surprise you, but I've genuinely befriended the owner. He's a good guy and he'll make sure we're snuck into one of the back rooms. Just don't ask about his peg leg."

"What about it?"

Aphrodite bopped Euryale on the top of the head. "I told you not to ask about it."

"Like I could being half blind, anyway."

"Point noted," Aphrodite said. "Can you see anything now?"

Euryale shook her head. "No. And I hate it."

"I hate being turned to stone more," Aphrodite said. "Until we sort this out, I'll be your eyes."

Euryale sucked in a breath, collected herself, and stood tall. Her pity party had to be set aside as well as her need for immediate revenge, she knew, but she still feared losing control. The spell Hera had cast still burned in her body, and that heat built more and more. With it came pain. With pain, came panic. And when she panicked, no one would be safe.

"I don't know how long I can last," she admitted. "That might be a problem."

Aphrodite put a hand on her forehead. "It won't last forever," she said. "The pain, I mean. Residual effects of the new curse."

"Can you do anything about it?"

"Perhaps," she said.

The Goddess of Love gently placed both of her hands on each of Euryale's cheeks. The anger brewing inside of her faded, and the gorgon sighed with relief. "Oh, that feels good."

"At least that's one thing I can do, make others feel good," she said with a melancholy tone.

"And keep my sanity intact."

"You sure about that?"

"Well, at the moment you are," Euryale replied with a half grin. Her hands then went for Aphrodite's, but in her blindness, she ended up grabbing the goddess's forearms instead. They were wet and sticky, and now that Euryale was paying attention, she could taste the blood in the air. "You're injured?"

"Courtesy of you," Aphrodite said.

"I'm sorry."

"I think you should say it again," the goddess replied. "Because if these wounds scar, I might have to rethink how much I enjoyed seeing you turn Hera to stone."

"I'm really, really sorry."

Aphrodite laughed. "I was kidding. Don't get me wrong, I'd rather be flawless, but all things considered, they aren't that bad. Besides, Ares will probably get turned on by them."

Euryale sighed with relief. She reached forward and gently took Aphrodite by the shoulder. "Thank you," she said before giving the goddess a gentle squeeze.

Aphrodite cleared her throat. "That's not my shoulder."

"It's not?" Euryale asked. She briefly felt the goddess some more before realizing what she had in hand was far rounder, softer, and sexier than any shoulder should have been. "Oh...Oh..."

"I suppose we're even then," Aphrodite said. "I probably ended up groping you a few times, too, trying to stay on your back. So let's never speak of this again and get out of here."

The corners of Euryale's mouth drew back as she chuckled. "Speak of what?"

"Exactly."

Peg-leg Pete's.

That was the name of the bar. At least, that's what Euryale had been told was the name of it, not that she had any reason to believe otherwise. Though she was far from a connoisseur of watering holes, she felt that the establishment Aphrodite had taken her to was both dark and seedy, the former having nothing to do with the blindfold on her head, which did add to the darkness. The air tasted like cheap tobacco, which drove the vipers atop her head crazy. She could feel them writhing about, using their forked tongues to try and find the source of their discomfort, which to both her and their dismay was everywhere.

The bench Euryale sat on was old leather. The gorgon could feel the cracks with her fingers, and she could hear it crunch under her weight when she'd first sat down. A table stood in front of her, and she coiled her tail beneath it. On said table was a mug of cold beer. It had a name she wasn't familiar with as wine was usually the gorgon's preferred drink. That said, the beer had a frosty head and a pleasing, sweet taste to it that she happened to like. So, if she couldn't indulge in some wine from her own cellar, this drink would suffice.

On the other side of the door she could hear the muffled sounds of karaoke being played in the main room. At least, she assumed it was the main room. She'd been led blindfolded to where she was now, and per Aphrodite's previous comments, they had skipped the bar area thanks to a side door and were now seated in a back room.

She heard a knock at the door, and Aphrodite answered it. "Come in. She still has her eyes covered."

The door swung open and the now-familiar clomp, clomp, clomp of a wooden leg striking hard floors filled the air.

"I'm a little wary coming in, if ye lasses haven't noticed," a man said with a rough, strained, and overly theatric voice. "I forget me stealthiness sometimes and didn't want to be sneaking up on ye. I'd rather not catch the gaze of the gorgon. Savvy?"

Aphrodite sighed heavily, and Euryale giggled. Despite everything they had gone through thus far, Pete's dedication to his character brought a smile to her face. "Savvy, but I heard you coming," Euryale said. "You know, the—"

She caught herself before finishing the sentence, but it was too late. She could practically hear Pete's grin on his face. "Me what?"

"Nothing."

"Me peg leg?"

"Yes, your peg leg."

"You had to ask, didn't you?" Aphrodite said.

"Technically, I made a comment. I didn't ask anything."

"Let me tell ye how I got this peg leg," he said. "I was upon my man-of-war, sails at full, with all hands on deck, about to plunder us a plundering greater than any plunderer had ever plundered. All of a sudden this bilge-sucking kraken burst from the sea, its monstrous tentacles coming at us from all sides trying to scuttle me ship. So what did I do? I sailed us straight into that leviathan's maw and had me crew light the powder kegs. The explosion took me ship, me crew, and me leg. But I'll be a scalawag three sheets to the wind if I didn't send that leviathan to the bottom of the depths."

"That's quite impressive," Euryale said.

"And that's only half of it—"

"Enough, Pete," Aphrodite cut in. "We don't have time for this right now. Besides, she's never going to believe you're a pirate, let alone that story."

"Sink me to Davey Jones's locker! Why wouldn't she?"

"Because her father happens to be the primeval god of the sea. And if their leviathan, sea serpent, or any other ship-eating creature happened to catch a face full of lit gunpowder, they'd know all the details," Aphrodite said. "Oh, and do you want to be the guy who killed their family pet?"

"Um, no," Pete said, adopting a much more normal tone. "But I could be a pirate, you know."

Aphrodite laughed. "You, my dear Pete, are far too kind."

"Hey now, I've got a mean streak a mile wide. I busted open a bank once. Took all of its money. Know what I did with it?"

"You bought chocolate," Aphrodite said. "You told me that story, remember? It was your piggy bank, and you were seven."

"Okay, okay. I yield," he said. "I only came back here to see if you two wanted anything else to eat or drink."

"I'm a little hungry," Euryale said. "If you could spare something, I would appreciate it to no end."

"How about some pizza and wings?" Aphrodite asked.

"Can do. I'll let you know if any of your friends pop on in, too, but at this point, I think it's safe to say no one knows you're here."

"Perfect," Aphrodite replied. "I'd like to keep it that way."

Pete left, and Euryale outstretched an open hand. "Can I borrow your phone? I need to check on Alex and the kids."

Aphrodite, who had recently begun brushing out her hair for the twentieth time, hesitated. "Can't you use yours?"

"Remember the beach?"

"Oh, right. You chucked it." Aphrodite sighed. "Well, you can't use it blindfolded like that, that's for sure. Tell me the number and I'll call and put us on speaker phone."

Euryale did, and Aphrodite dialed. Together they waited as it rang, but the call soon went to voicemail. So Aphrodite hung up and tried again, and again, and again.

Before the sixth try, Euryale offered a new tact. "Try a facetime call? He might answer that instead."

So Aphrodite did, and on that attempt, Alex picked up. "Hello?" Though she couldn't see thanks to her blindfold, she could hear the surprise in his voice. "Euryale? Oh gods, tell me you're not being held hostage."

"No, I'm not," she said.

"Then why are you wearing a blindfold?"

"Because I've been cursed, Alex," Euryale answered.

"I know that," Alex said. "Does this mean you're out in the real world trying not to petrify half of humanity?"

"No, Alex, I meant I've been cursed again."

"Cursed again? By who? Or by what? When? Where? How?" Alex said, stumbling along. "And most important, why?"

Euryale gave him a brief rundown of all that had happened with Hera and the other Olympians. As she recounted, her emotion grew more and more intense, and the burning desire for revenge nearly overcame her. When she finished, there was a long, awkward silence, one that she hadn't felt since Alex first put together who she really was and what curse she bore when they first met. "You can say something now," Euryale said.

"I don't know what to say," he said. "You turned them all to stone?"

"Yes, but it was only temporary, sadly."

"Sadly?"

"I would've liked that bitch to be a permanent fixture for what she did to me," she replied.

"Does this mean you can petrify me now?"

Sorrow extinguished the fires of hate she had, and Euryale fought back tears. "I think so."

"Maybe we should get a cauldron," Alex said. "Don't those help with making spells or removing them or whatever?"

"That's not going to help, Alex."

Despite her words, Alex kept going. "And we'll probably need some eye of newt, right? Where do you even get that stuff? I wonder if I can find some on eBay."

"Alex!" Euryale said with a sharp, demanding voice. "You're not listening. None of that's going to do anything. Short of Hera lifting it on her own, which she won't, the only way I'm getting this removed is Cronus reversing time."

"That doesn't sound too bad," Alex replied. "Why don't you go see him?"

"If by not too bad you mean waking the most powerful titan to have ever existed and watching him devour all of creation, sure," Euryale said.

"Which is why Hera is adamant about making certain he stays sleeping in the Cave of Nyx and keeping Arachne away from him," Aphrodite added.

"Precisely," Euryale said.

"Damn," Alex said. "Are you okay, at least?"

"Do I sound okay?"

"No, sorry. Dumb question."

Euryale buried her face in her hands and sobbed. "No, Alex. I'm sorry. I shouldn't have snapped at you. I know you're only trying to help. Where are the kids?"

"They're with Persephone and Demeter, probably playing with Tickles as we speak," Alex replied.

"Then where are you?"

"Jessica's," he replied. "You're never going to believe what happened, or maybe you will. I don't know. I'm still trying to wrap my head around it all." For the next five minutes, Alex gave Euryale a full account of what had happened once he had reached Jessica's mansion and ran into Arachne and The Fox, ending with the freeing of Jessica, true to Arachne's word.

"So you're telling me Arachne simply walked away?" Euryale asked, dumbfounded as to why.

"Yeah."

"And Jessica's unharmed?"

"She's shaken up, for sure," he said. "Right now, she's gorging on some French vanilla ice cream. Comfort food and all. I guess being cocooned for that long is enough to break anyone's diet."

Euryale tapped her fingers on her side as she thought things through. "Did Jessica happen to say anything about Arachne's plans or who else she was working with? Or maybe some random detail that stuck with her about the encounter?"

"No, and believe me, I asked," Alex said. "Apparently, after Jessica heard Arachne's limited sales pitch and rejected the offer, Arachne stuck her in a web, left, and then showed up at our place, looking like her."

"What do you make of it?"

"Beats the hell out of me," he said. "If I had to bet, though, I'd wager your dad is the one she's working with."

"Why?"

"Because she said whoever she was working with was very fond of you," he said. "I can't imagine who else that would be."

"It's not Dad," Euryale said, sinking into the couch. "He would've told me, and he certainly wouldn't have let anyone attack my husband, my children, or burn down my home."

"That's true," Alex said.

"What about her offer? Do you want to help her?"

The question clearly caught Alex off guard as he stammered through his reply. "What? No. I don't trust her at all. Do you?"

"As much as I hate Hera, no. I don't trust Arachne one bit," Euryale replied. She paused, thinking for a moment as she tried to come up with an idea of what to do next. Alex's story gave her a lot to consider. After turning it all over in her head for several moments, she didn't have a plan, per se, but she did realize she would likely need a few things down the road, things Alex was in the perfect position to obtain. "Alex, I need you to go back and get Hades' scepter."

"You mean, his scepter, scepter? Like the one I used to raise the dead last year? That scepter?"

"Yes," she said. "Arachne must have an army somewhere. If she's going to storm Olympus, we might need one, too, and in a hurry. Do you think you can still use it?"

"Of course I can use it," Alex replied. "Little wave of the hands, little music in my head. Bam! You've got your troops."

Euryale smiled, grateful that at least something was going their way. "Perfect. I'm hoping Persephone won't mind lending it to you."

"Given Ares and I saved her, and we'd be using it to bring down the eight-legged bitch responsible for sacking her home, I'm going to say she'll insist on giving it to me."

"Wonderful. I'll call you later," she said. The conversation ended, and Euryale turned to Aphrodite. "That's that. Any suggestions on what we do next?"

"Same as it's always been. Find Arachne," Aphrodite said as she put down her hairbrush. "But where do we start looking? Hera will be watching our only lead, Nyx's Cave."

Euryale hummed, but then ended up grinning and chuckling at herself for missing the obvious. "Not our only lead."

"What do you mean?"

"Hera was the one who wanted us to guard the cave, not you," she explained. "You had another idea. What was it?"

Aphrodite shook her head before grabbing a drink off the table and downing what was left of it in one go. "All I said was there had to be another forge somewhere. But there isn't."

"Yes, there is," Euryale said. "If she's melting down those artifacts, there has to be another forge."

"That's only a guess."

"It's a damn good one," Euryale said. "You're the one that noticed the head was missing from that javelin. Why take only the head if you had a completed weapon at your fingertips?"

"Maybe you're right."

Euryale shook her head and grinned. "No, maybe you're right."

"Look, even if there is another forge, I'm not smart enough to find it," the goddess said. "I wish I were, but I'm not Athena. She'd know, but by the time we went and read through her entire library to find the answer, we might as well have exiled ourselves for ten thousand years."

Euryale stood and slithered in front of Aphrodite. She was careful not to headbutt the goddess as she rested her forehead on Aphrodite's. She could feel the goddess tense, and the vipers on her head slither nervously around, but nothing came from either's anxiety. "You're not Athena, and you don't have to be," Euryale said. "Trust me on this. I know what it's like to constantly be compared to a sister—or two in my case. You have something Athena will never have."

Aphrodite chuckled. "Yes, I'm gorgeous, and she's...not completely vile."

"You are also married to the God of Smiths and Fire," Euryale said. "In all those years, Hephaestus never once mentioned anywhere else where he could go to forge his items? Never talked about a spot even remotely equal to his? Surely he must have."

"I—I don't know."

"Yes, you do," Euryale said, trying to sound as encouraging as she could but fearing that it was coming across as her being impatient. "You're smarter than you believe. And if it wasn't Hephaestus who said something, maybe it was Zeus? Surely you father told you tales of times long past, back when the Olympians went to war with the titans."

Aphrodite laughed, her voice bright with memory. "You might say he's recounted such tales a few times. His favorite was—"

The goddess sucked in a breath, and Euryale perked. "What?"

"I can't believe I didn't think of it before."

"Out with it already," Euryale said with a laugh.

"Typhon," Aphrodite said. "He's buried under Mount Etna. His defeat is Dad's favorite story, especially when he's feeling down after catching a berating from Hera."

Euryale beamed. Typhon—Father of all Monsters; son to Gaea, mother of the titans; and to Tartarus, god of the netherworld—was the only other being who had almost conquered the Olympians. Like the story with Cronus, Zeus had barely won a long, bloody war against the hundred-headed monstrosity. When it was over, Zeus chained Typhon under Mount Etna, and though the elder monster had no hope of escape, he would often thrash about in rage, causing earthquakes and volcanic eruptions that would shake the earth.

"Are you sure the fires Typhon creates can melt adamantine?" Euryale asked. "Because chained or not, I'm not sure I want to go anywhere near him unless I absolutely must."

"Neither do I, but Dad did boast once that the heart of Hephaestus's forge would be like a cool breeze compared to the fires that Typhon spewed."

Euryale swallowed, hating every word she was about to say. "Then that's where we go."

"We should tell the others," Aphrodite said. "We might need their help."

"That assumes Hera won't smite us first and ask questions later," Euryale said. "Besides, I fear it might be too late if we hold another council meeting."

"Are you sure?"

Euryale shook her head. "No, but if we stop Arachne and get everyone's artifacts back on our own, I'm sure they'll treat us differently."

"If they don't?"

"Then we'll be the ones with the power, and they'll have no choice."

Chapter Airports

Though Euryale had been married to Alex for barely a year, during that time she had always listened with enthusiasm to his stories of how the world now operated. She loved to hear about his travels for piano concerts, the grand cities he performed in as well as their world-famous landmarks, not to mention the more common but equally enjoyable experiences he partook in that ranged from visiting microbreweries to catching movies at his nearby IMAX theater. She loved listening to them because he painted such fantastic pictures of the mortal world that included dazzling lights, an array of music and sounds she had never heard before, and when appropriate to the story, how pleasing aromas would tantalize his nose and delectable food would delight his taste buds.

That said, however, amid all the stories told, never once did he talk about how fun it was to go to an airport, how relaxing he found it to pass through, or how beautiful the overall design was. Now that she was in one, she quickly understood why. People bustled by in a sea of noise in what she hoped was organized chaos, but it grated against her usual relaxed attitude and desires. After all, one doesn't live for thousands of years on a desolate island and not get used to or even come to love quietness.

If that weren't enough on its own, the repugnant smells that assaulted her senses caused her vipers to retreat under the hood she wore. Not that she could blame them. The mother in her abhorred the faint smell of two-week-old vomit lingering in the air. Would it kill someone to clean up the place? Evidently it would, because how hard would it be to track down the offending odor and deal with it?

"Hurry, our flight leaves soon," Aphrodite said, leading the way.

"I would if I could see anything. We should've just gone with the sunglasses and ditched the blindfold," Euryale said as she accidentally shouldered into somebody. "The sunglasses worked before."

"That was before Hera cursed you."

Euryale tutted. "And this is ridiculous, too. It's not like people aren't staring at my tail coming out the back of this trench coat."

"They aren't staring…much," the goddess replied. "It only has to keep us from being spotted from far away."

"This isn't going to work. A coat won't fool Hera's spies. We should've taken a private charter."

"There are none," Aphrodite said. "I checked. Now come on. We'll miss the flight."

Euryale picked up the pace as much as she could. They soon had to slow to push through a crowd, but right as she felt a gap form, Aphrodite surged forward with enthusiasm, and a few seconds later, they were at the check-in booth.

"May I help you?" asked a bubbly, young female voice.

"Two tickets for the ten o'clock flight to Catania," Aphrodite replied.

Euryale heard the click, click, click of fingers assaulting a keyboard and then a tiny intake of air. "That might be a problem," said the check-in girl. "Flight leaves in twenty-five minutes. Boarding closes in ten."

"Then hold it," Aphrodite said.

"I'd like to but—"

"No buts!" Aphrodite snapped. "Do you know who I am?"

"Oh, yes! Who doesn't? I saw your interview on TV. It was great. I loved how you guys came up with that bit with Athena. Won me twenty off it, I did."

"Say again?"

"Boyfriend and all," the girl replied. She then launched into a rant at warp speed with immense enthusiasm. "Noah said those shows were never scripted, and I bet him twenty they were. When Athena just happened to pop up and talk about a party you supposedly didn't know about, he had to pay up. Clearly written for the drama. No way you're a girl not invited to every bash there is, you know? Between you and me, though, might want to tone down your reaction next time. Came across as over the top. Remember, when acting, you want to be the person you're trying to be, not a caricature of them."

Aphrodite growled, and Euryale tensed. "I appreciate you were watching the show, but we need to make that flight."

"Can't, sorry."

"Kick someone off if you have to."

"It's not that. The flight doesn't have room for your pet."

"Her pet?" Euryale said. "I'm not her pet."

"All hazardous mythological creatures have to be checked, company policy," she said. "And space on that flight is extremely limited already. You'll have to wait for the next flight. I'm sorry."

"I can't check her in cargo. She's my..." Aphrodite hesitated before taking in a deep breath and continuing. "She's my emotional support gorgon."

"She is? Well, I'll need to see your doctor's note," the woman replied.

"A doctor's note? A doctor's note!" Aphrodite repeated as she worked herself up. "Now I need to justify the hardships I suffer? What kind of airline are you running here? I should curse you a thousand times for even thinking such a thing! This gorgon is my lifeblood! Without her I'd barely survive the day. Do you have any idea how stressful it is to be responsible for the love of everyone in the entire world?"

The woman at the counter stammered, and for a moment Euryale thought she was going to let them on, but that came to an end a heartbeat later. "You almost had me, really," the girl said with a nervous laugh. "You're filming for a show, aren't you? Emotional support gorgon. That's a proper bit right there, yeah? Love it. But again, the acting. Tone it down a couple of notches, and you'll kill it in the ratings. Right now, it's too over the top to be believable."

"Why you stupid, little—"

Euryale pulled the goddess back before she could cause a scene, even if she, too, was sick of the check-in girl. Though frustration was mounting inside and the gorgon worried she might lose control soon and wreck the terminal, she had an idea. "The truth of the matter is, I'm not here for her emotional support," Euryale said. "She's there for me, and that's a little embarrassing. She's my seeing-eye goddess."

"No, she's not," the girl said, sounding far less certain of herself then she had before.

"She is."

"It's illegal to pretend to have a disability for special treatment, you know. I'll have the fuzz on you."

Euryale lowered her hood, faced the woman directly, and pointed to her blindfold. "If you think I'm lying, take this off and see for yourself."

Chapter Mount Etna

Mount Etna dwarfed the Sicilian landscape. It stood nearly two miles high with a snowcapped peak and a wide base, thus making the infamous Mount Vesuvius a quaint site to visit for anyone who happened to be interested in minor eruptions. Nearby, mortals had built the city of Catania because local agriculture had bloomed for ages thanks to the rich, volcanic soil. Over the course of thousands of years, people had planted numerous orchards and vineyards, while at the same time developing the city into not only one of the largest in all of Italy, but into one of the most important cultural, artistic, and political centers to have ever existed.

Had the men and women of the area realized what was beneath that mountain, a seething monster with a hundred horrific heads and a twisted heart bent on seeing the world burn, Euryale was certain they'd have abandoned the island of Sicily long ago. Then again, she thought, perhaps deep down inside they'd always known the source of the constant tremors the volcano gave. That would explain all the wine they produced and consumed.

"Ready?" Aphrodite asked as the two stood near the top of a rising hill with the sea at their backs and the sounds of the Mediterranean filling their ears.

Euryale toyed with the sunglasses they'd picked up in town. "I think the real question is are you ready? You didn't want to try these earlier."

"That was before I realized spelunking with a blind gorgon might end in disaster, especially if Arachne is in there with her minions."

"Point taken," Euryale said. She traded the blindfold for the mirrored sunglasses and opened her eyes. Now that she could see again, the world looked as she'd always remembered it, though darker.

While Euryale was confident they'd work, Aphrodite wasn't taking chances. The goddess had her back turned. "Now or never," Euryale said.

Aphrodite sucked in a deep breath and slowly turned around. She spoke words of protection under her breath as she did, and peeked at Euryale with one eye. When that eye stayed fleshy, she opened the other.

Aphrodite remained soft, pink, and gorgeous. She sighed heavily with relief. "Thank the Moirae. They work."

"I told you they would," Euryale said.

"I admit it, you did," Aphrodite said. She then laughed as a new thought came to her. "Stupid Hera. I wish she could see how her precious spell was beaten by a cheap invention the mortals came up with."

"So do I." Euryale grinned and then surveyed the area. "Where's the bird you sent?"

"He ought to be back soon," she replied.

"Are you sure he can find what we need?"

"Don't worry. If there's a way into Mount Etna, he'll tell us."

A couple of minutes passed, and then a sparrow came chirping from behind and landed on Aphrodite's outstretched hand. The goddess brought it close and gave it a soft kiss on its head before speaking. "There you are, my cutie," she said. "Who's mommy's favorite bird? Who is?"

"I bet you say that to all the birds," Euryale said.

"Only to my sparrows," Aphrodite said. If the goddess took any offense to the quip, she didn't show it. After scratching the bird on the back of the neck with her fingers, she kissed it again before continuing. "Did you find anything out, love?"

The bird chirped excitedly.

"You did?"

The bird chirped longer this time and did a little hopping dance on Aphrodite's hand.

"What's that you say, Lady? Arachne and The Fox have been using a tunnel on the southwestern slope to carry Olympian artifacts deep inside the mountain and you overheard her saying she's ready to start up an ancient, long-forgotten forge in order to bring doom and destruction to all of Mount Olympus and we're the only ones who can stop her in time?"

Euryale's jaw dropped as the sparrow flew away. Furrows formed in her brow as she tried to wrap her mind around everything that Aphrodite had said. At some point, she spoke. "That bird gave you all of that?"

"Of course, you heard her," Aphrodite said. The goddess's flat expression, however, gave way to delight. "No, don't be silly. I made it all up."

Euryale shook her head playfully at herself. It felt good to have someone be so good-humored around her who wasn't her family. "So did she tell you anything?"

Aphrodite pointed to a small section of the volcano, about halfway up on the southern side. "She said there's a tunnel that some of the other birds saw a man and a woman come out of a few days ago—a man and a woman who looked an awful lot like Arachne and our fox friend, going by her description."

"That has to be it," Euryale said.

"Certainly no better place to start."

Off they went, and though Aphrodite had started the hike in a good mood, it didn't take long for her smile to dampen. "I don't suppose you have a plan. As fun as it is to feel clever for once in my life, I'm not sure I like marching into Typhon's final resting place with only my good looks and your semi-controlled rage at my side. Are you sure you don't want to get help?"

"I'm sure," Euryale said. "We need to strike before Arachne knows we're on to her."

"I hope you're right," Aphrodite replied but said no more.

The two worked their way toward and then up the southern side of Mount Etna, supposedly following the directions Aphrodite's sparrow had given. To Euryale's delight, they found a cave which turned into a burrowing tunnel not only halfway up the southern side, but they also found it in far less time than Euryale had imagined they would. Perhaps the Fates had decided to grant them a break or two.

Darkness blanketed the first couple hundred yards of the tunnel. Once the pair squeezed through a narrow crack, however, they found that on the other side, burning oil lamps had been set up and gave plenty of light.

"Do you hear that?" Aphrodite said after they had traveled a bit deeper. "It sounds like someone is working an anvil."

Euryale nodded. Though she had picked up on the soft, rhythmic sounds a couple of minutes ago, they weren't where her attention had been focused. "I hear it, but there's a foul taste in the air, too."

"From the forge?"

"No, I don't think so," Euryale said. "It tastes like…like…"

"Like what?"

Euryale's eyes glanced to the floor as she tried to pick out exactly what she was searching for. There were hints of a forge in the air, hints that reminded her of Hephaestus's abode, but behind those notes she could taste something else. Something that set her vipers on edge. "It tastes like old blood."

"Old blood? You mean dried?"

Euryale shook her head. "No. Old. Ancient. Powerful."

"You must be picking up on Typhon," Aphrodite said.

"Surely we aren't that deep yet," Euryale said.

"I don't know," Aphrodite said. "Father never said how far down he was buried. But if he's even a tenth as large as he's said to have been, I'm a little surprised you didn't notice him the moment we got off the plane."

The air thickened as they pressed on, and as its weight increased, so did Euryale's caution. More than once she wondered if the two of them weren't as clever as they believed themselves to be and Arachne was still several steps ahead of them. Perhaps what lay at the end of this tunnel was not her defeat but a carefully laid trap that would turn out to be far worse than any she could have laid before.

The gorgon stole a glance at Aphrodite and saw that the goddess had a similar expression of worry on her face. For one who was not used to open strife, Aphrodite was acting admirably as far as Euryale was concerned. Hopefully, her backbone would stay solid long enough for them to get to the bottom of this mystery.

The tunnel made a hairpin turn before rapidly descending in a spiral. It then dumped into a cavern large enough to make any dragon content enough to call it home, although it would need remodeling for it to be complete—the usual sorts of things: gold-lined floors, accents of precious gems, and a few cages to store fair maidens for entertainment, snacks, or both.

Though no immense fire-belching wyrm was there to greet them, five passageways leading out were. All were lit with the same oil lamps that had provided illumination thus far, and none seemed to stand out from any of the others. As such, Euryale and Aphrodite paused, unsure of where to go or what to do.

Euryale was about to ask if Aphrodite had any thoughts, when out of the middle passage a trio of humanoid creatures lumbered into the cave, clad in steel cuirasses with forearms that ended not in hands, but spike clubs. They each sported rotten faces that no mother could love, except for maybe Euryale, but even that was pushing it, since from their leathery skin wafted the odor of death. For a moment, the creatures held fast. What they were going to do, however, was up for debate.

Aphrodite gagged. "By the Fates, what are those things?"

"No idea," Euryale said. The gorgon coiled her tail and readied herself to spring forward or back as the near future would demand.

"What are you waiting for? Petrify them," Aphrodite said.

Euryale shook her head. "Not yet."

"If you haven't noticed, they're monsters. I promise you whatever they did to become like that, they deserved it," the goddess said.

A growl slipped from the gorgon's mouth before she redirected her attention to the now approaching trio. "Easy now," Euryale said, outstretching an open hand. As much as she hated Aphrodite's words, they weren't completely lost on her. She could feel her heart quicken and her senses heighten in anticipation of an attack. Moreover, she could feel the repercussions of all that as well, namely the slow but steady slip of control she had over herself.

The monsters paused a dozen paces away, bringing a bit of relief to Euryale. "We're not here to hurt you," she said.

Aphrodite coughed before covering her mouth with her free hand. "If we stay here much longer, I'm going to retch."

"Shh!"

Before Euryale could say or do another thing, the monsters lunged at them.

"Curse your mouth!" Euryale snarled as she surged forward to meet the attack. She managed to catch the arm of the lead monster before it could smash its club through her skull, but as she was tied to Aphrodite, Euryale was unable to defend herself from the second monster.

The creature swung, and its club connected with Euryale's midsection. The gorgon fell back against the blow and instantly relinquished her grip on the first. Another attack came that she managed to fend off with her arm, but the strike was enough to make her arm fall limp at her side.

Euryale howled, her legendary bellow being more than enough to stagger her attackers sideways. In the lull, Euryale lifted her head and leveled her gaze at them both. A torrent of feelings overtook her, but three were the most prominent: pity for what these creatures had become, anger for how they'd attacked, and most of all, hate for what they were now making her do.

Euryale clenched her jaw and lifted her sunglasses. In a split second, pressure built behind her eyes before her vision exploded in a flash of green.

Back to the land of shadows and demons Euryale went. There she fought her tormentors, striking with fang and claw at those who tore her skin or sought to break her bones. She pounced on one shadowy form, took its head in her hands and squeezed. She could feel its skull crack in her grip, but then it suddenly became as hard as stone.

Euryale shrugged off a strike from behind and whipped around in time to catch her attacker by the throat. Her claws sank into its flesh, and she relished the high-pitched scream the demon produced until it went silent. A third demon, near the second, tried to get away, but she grappled it with her tail, pulled it in, and ripped it to pieces.

Movement caught her eye, and the gorgon coiled herself around her final victim. This one struggled more than the others and felt stronger, too. Its grip on her arm felt nothing short of titanic, but Euryale didn't care. As long as it was within arm's reach, it was within striking distance.

Euryale drove her head forward, intent on sinking her fangs into the demon's neck along with every fang her vipers had as well. The demon, however, struck first. One hand firmly but gently held on to her forearm while the other pressed against the side of her face not hard enough to cause damage, but hard enough to keep contact. From that palm, a coolness radiated.

Euryale's heart slowed. Her temper faded, and for a brief second, she found herself looking at a terrified Aphrodite who was being held firmly in the gorgon's tail and had her head turned to the side to avoid her gaze.

Euryale instantly turned away and let go. "I'm sorry."

"Apology...accepted..." Aphrodite said between gulps of air.

"Thank you," the gorgon replied, not knowing what else to say. She looked around to see what other damage she'd caused. Two of the monsters who'd attacked her lay sprawled across the ground, gaping chunks ripped out of their flesh. The third stood upright nearby, frozen in time as a granite statue with its arms outstretched and face partially turned away. "We should get moving before more come."

Aphrodite took a few more deep breaths before brushing herself off. At that point, after Euryale had scooped up her fallen sunglasses and put them back on, the two headed down the passage on their right for no other reason than it wasn't the one where those monsters had come from, and it looked as good as any of the other options.

The tunnel ran through the mountain, constantly descending as it did. Several times they passed small alcoves and large rooms that had been cut out of the granite. In those areas were racks upon racks of weapons and armor. Once along the way, another group of monsters came by, but they were easily avoided. Their stench was potent, and thus Euryale and Aphrodite had ample time to duck into a side room and wait for them to pass.

"They're going to find those bodies soon," Aphrodite pointed out once the creatures had gone.

"I know," Euryale said. "Given all that we've seen in storage, I'm worried there might be an entire army down here."

"I hope there's another way out, too," Aphrodite replied.

Euryale nodded, and they resumed their descent. More twists. More branches. More dark tunnels and the ever-growing scent of old blood. But with that distinct smell, Euryale also tasted sweat...sweat and worry. The source became all but apparent when they rounded a corner and ended up in a branch where one passage was blocked off by an immense door with a small, barred gap at the top. Looking through that gap, Euryale saw a short passage that ended with yet another door, heavy and imposing, that had been secured by a heavy lock.

"What do you suppose is down there?" Aphrodite said, raising on her tiptoes as she peered in.

"A prison cell?" Euryale replied, giving the only answer that came to mind.

"Surely there would be guards, then," Aphrodite said.

"Unless they don't want whoever is behind that door to speak to them," Euryale noted. The gorgon glanced around, tasted the air with all of her vipers, and when she was certain no others were nearby, she called out, "Hello?"

Nothing.

"Hello?"

Still nothing.

Euryale looked to Aphrodite, who shrugged before she examined the lock on the door before them. The gorgon was far from a master locksmith, but when she peered inside, she swore at the complexity the tumblers had. "Gods," she said, shaking her head. "I bet this would take Hermes a week to pick."

"And then some," Aphrodite said, looking as well. She took the lock in hand and closed her other over it. "It has powerful enchantments, too."

"So we're not getting in," Euryale said.

"Not without a key."

Euryale had turned to go when Aphrodite pulled her back. The goddess put herself on her tiptoes again, sucked in a breath, and shouted. "Athena!"

The gorgon cringed, but before she could rebuke her, a faint, muffled voice could be heard. "Aphrodite? Is that you?"

"Athena!" Aphrodite shouted again, this time grabbing the door and yanking back as hard as she could. "We're here! Euryale and I."

"Quiet!" Euryale hissed. "You'll call them all to us!"

"Don't tell me—"

Aphrodite's objection was cut shut by Athena, who managed a decent yell from inside her cell. "She's right!" Athena said. "Get the key and get me out."

Aphrodite tensed and then blew out a puff of air. "Okay," she said. "We will. We'll be back. I promise."

Despite the goddess's words, Euryale had to practically pry Aphrodite off the door to get her to leave. Once they were moving, however, they raced through the tunnels with speed and purpose. They weren't simply exploring anymore. They were rescuing, and even though Aphrodite had been having spat after spat with her sister for eons, Euryale could tell none of that mattered now. The goddess was going to free Athena if it was the last thing she did.

It probably didn't hurt that if Aphrodite managed to free Athena, the Goddess of Love would finally have something she could hold over Athena.

Several minutes later, they reached an enormous chamber, easily a hundred yards across and twice that in length. The entire thing was bathed in the warm, orange glow of lava, which snaked its way from the opposite corner of the room to an exit channel nearby.

The floor was comprised of flat stone bricks, immaculately cut so that the seams between them were no bigger than a hairline, and in some cases couldn't be seen at all if it weren't for the slight difference in the pattern each brick had. Ornate columns rose from the ground and stretched fifty meters into the air where they supported a domed ceiling, while off to the side a large tree grew with several banners hanging from its limbs.

"Someone's been busy," Aphrodite said, taking it all in.

"Someone still is," Euryale replied. She pointed to their right, about twenty yards away, where the floor met a wide, short flight of stairs that went up to a circular platform in the middle of the chamber. In the center of that platform stood a large anvil with a rack of smithing tools and a table within arm's reach. Off to the side and straddling the lava channel was a forge made from a lustrous, grayish metal. At least, it was lustrous and gray where it wasn't covered in soot.

Aphrodite gasped and headed straight for the table. "Is that Athena's shield?"

"I think so," Euryale said as the two approached.

When they reached it, Athena's aegis was indeed there. For a brief second, Euryale stared at it in stunned silence. With all that had gone wrong for the past few days, months, or even year if she got down to it, on some level, she'd wondered if she'd ever find the thing, at least not without going on an odyssey that would span a few decades.

Did she still dare to think that by returning said shield to its owner, Euryale would be freed from her curse? Of course she dared. Not only did she dare to believe, but she also reveled in the thought.

"What's with those shavings?" Aphrodite asked, noticing a small pile of silvery flecks that filled a small vial.

Euryale picked up the glass tube and compared what was inside with the metal Athena's shield was made from. "Looks like adamantine?"

Aphrodite gave it a look. "Arachne must be scavenging every bit she can find. I wonder what she's making?"

"Something terrible, no doubt. Let's grab the shield and find that key so we can leave."

"Yes, let's."

Euryale glanced at Aphrodite.

Aphrodite glanced at Euryale.

The two lunged for the shield at the same time.

"It's mine!" Aphrodite yelled, managing to get a grip on the handle.

"You wouldn't even be here without me!" Euryale shouted. She snaked her tail around the goddess and tried to use it to pry her off the aegis, but Aphrodite grabbed her by the forearm with her free hand, and when she did, a soothing bliss washed over her, making her relax to the point where all she could do was put up enough of a fight that the shield didn't wind up completely in Aphrodite's hands. "It's not even your shield," Euryale said. "It's Athena's."

"And I'm her sister, which makes me next of kin," Aphrodite said. "Now hand it over!"

"No! I need it!"

"As if I don't? Let's remember who was cast out of Olympus!" Aphrodite shot back.

With that, Aphrodite yanked again, and the aegis nearly slipped from Euryale's hands. In that instant, Euryale, operating out of pure instinct, jumped on Aphrodite and sank her fangs into the goddess's neck. Her vipers followed suit and struck Aphrodite a half dozen times in less than a second.

Aphrodite cried out in pain as Euryale's venom ravaged her body. She relinquished her grip on the shield as she cast a spell to nullify the toxins. "You'll pay for that," she said, gritting her teeth in pain. Aphrodite grabbed a pair of tongs nearby and clocked Euryale across the face.

Euryale's head jerked to the side, and her sunglasses went flying in a twisted, broken mess. When she turned back around, her eyes met Aphrodite's, and the goddess shrieked in terror.

Her skin hardened, but not instantaneously. She managed to turn away and offer a counterspell as Hera had done. Euryale was about to press the attack when something slammed into the back of her head, and she fell forward.

Aphrodite caught her out of reflex, but Euryale's bulk was too much for the goddess. The gorgon slid down, ears ringing, vision fading. When she hit the ground, she dragged Aphrodite with her.

At that point, she became acutely aware of two things before she passed out.

One, blood was oozing from her head. Possibly brain matter, as well.

Two, Hephaestus, face full of sweat and soot, stood over them both, hammer in hand, and he looked like he wasn't finished cracking skulls.

CHAPTER REVELATION

Euryale groaned as her vision blurred. Thankfully, it eventually came back into focus, though the throbbing in her skull continued its relentless pounding. Aphrodite was still at her side, but that was only because they were still chained at the wrists. Euryale didn't doubt that it wasn't goodwill keeping the goddess at her side. That said, Aphrodite's focus was not directed at her, but rather at Hephaestus, who loomed over the both of them.

The God of Smiths and Fire mostly kept his eyes on Aphrodite, but he occasionally threw Euryale a glance as well, though it was obvious he kept his gaze far from the gorgon's eyes.

"Heph?" Aphrodite asked as if she didn't trust her own two eyes. "Is that you?"

"Who else would it be?" he replied. "Have you refused to look at us for that long you've forgotten what we look like?"

Aphrodite laughed nervously and shook her head. "No, sweetheart. I've been through so much. It's hard to believe the Fates have finally rid me of this cursed path they set me on," she said. The goddess then raised her arm to show off the chain that bound her to Euryale. "Can you help, dear? I tire of being stuck to this...thing."

Hephaestus motioned with his head to the forge at his side. "It will melt it with ease," he said. His gaze then fell on his wife, but there was no love in his eyes, only power and resentment.

Aphrodite tilted her head to the side. "Heph? What's wrong?"

The God of Smiths chuckled. "Now you feign interest in us? Your sweet tongue will have to craft something better than that to win us over."

"But—"

"Quiet," he said, cutting her off. "We will cut you free, but when we do, you will cease your affairs with others from this day on. You will be our devoted wife, more so than any other, no longer treating us as an outcast or something you can't stand to even think about."

Aphrodite didn't miss a beat. "Of course, my love. I know I've treated you...less than I should've, but—"

"We weren't finished," Hephaestus said. "You will swear to all of that by the River Styx."

The color drained from Aphrodite's face, and Euryale knew why. The goddess would never make such an oath, and even if she did, it was likely she could never fulfill it. Her heart did not belong to him, nor did she want it to. Then again, the gorgon thought, if the Fates considered such an oath made under duress, it would hold no meaning, and thus Aphrodite would not be bound to it. But would the goddess risk such a thing? Would anyone? If she broke the oath, her immortality would be as gone as Euryale's once fair looks.

"Heph, dear," Aphrodite said, clearly trying to stall for time. "Whatever is going on, whatever you think is happening, let's talk about this later. It's not safe here."

Hephaestus grunted and tossed his hammer onto the table. "Look around, wife," he said. "Do you honestly think we don't know where we are or what surrounds us? Do you think we work this forge against our will?"

"But...why?"

At this point, Euryale managed to coil her tail beneath her and rise. A tender touch to the back of the head told her that while the wound was painful and still bleeding, it was likely not as grievous as she had first imagined. Being the daughter of a god had its perks.

"He's working with her," Euryale filled in. Though her heart ripped in two at the betrayal, she knew the words were true. Hiding from them wouldn't change the facts.

"You're helping Arachne?" Aphrodite asked. Her face blanked as if she were trying to draw on a long-forgotten memory she had no hope of recovering.

"Why are you surprised?" he said. "For eons, all of you have shunned us, made fun of us. We've been nothing but a slave to Olympus, crafting the finest arms and armor without thanks or appreciation. All we've wanted was acceptance and we have been given none. This inevitable outcome is your own doing."

"You know, it doesn't matter," Aphrodite said. "Once Dad finds out, he'll dissolve our marriage with glee and then tear you apart. I can't wait to be rid of your repulsiveness."

To Euryale's surprise, Hephaestus took no affront to her words. He did, however, draw the corners of his mouth back into a wicked grin. "Zeus, yes, we would do best if we didn't count on him," he said. "He and the rest who oppose us will be cast low. Wait and see. For far too long they've treated us as the outsider, the lame god not worthy of their attention, but this outsider will no longer be treated so. They will fear us. Respect us."

"You'll never defeat them," Aphrodite retorted. "I don't care how many monsters you and Arachne have created."

Hephaestus held his grin as he took a few steps to the side. From a rack near the forge, he pulled a solitary item, a giant labrys that seemed as if it could fell an entire forest with a single stroke. Both heads on the axe looked worn, though there were new metallic additions to the sides as well as the handle—additions that were gold-and-adamantine inscriptions, bearers of powerful blessings that no doubt amplified the potency of the weapon. Tiny arcs of lightning jumped around the blades as Hephaestus held it, and the shaft glowed a fierce red as if the weapon embodied the rage the god had held for so long.

"We know what power Zeus wields," he said. "We're the ones who helped fashion his bolts so long ago. But you...you know nothing, as always. You know not what we've created out of the arms of others. Already this axe can strike down any Olympian with ease, and once I finish melting down Athena's aegis and adding its might, no one will dare stand against it."

"How many others thought the same? Even Typhon held to similar misguided beliefs, and look where he is now, imprisoned for eternity in this very rock, only fit to serve as a warning to others," Aphrodite said.

"We're not interested in what you think you know," Hephaestus replied. "All we want to know is whether or not you choose to be with us." His voice softened, and he extended an open hand. "Come, be our bride again. Together we can rule Olympus as husband and wife. Together we can wipe the smirks off the faces of those who whisper behind our backs, who think we're not fit for anything but to do their bidding and meet their needs."

"I'll never betray my father," Aphrodite said. "That is the only oath I'll make, and I make it gladly."

Hephaestus narrowed his eyes. "Then we'll lock you away for the rest of time."

Euryale inched back, gently tugging Aphrodite by the arm. "Hephaestus, it's not too late to stop all this," she said. "You were a great friend to Alex and me. I don't want any sort of fight with you."

"Yes, yes," Hephaestus said. "We would've hoped you join us, too, but that was before you attacked our wife."

Euryale swallowed hard. She could feel the tears welling in her eyes. How had her friend drifted so far away from her, from all of them, and she'd never noticed? How had Arachne turned him against her? "Please, Hephaestus, walk away," she begged. "I don't have a lot of friends. I don't want to lose you. We can make this right."

Hephaestus grunted. "Perhaps you should have thought of that before you turned our wife against us."

"Don't be stupid," Aphrodite scoffed. "She never turned me against you. I was never for you to begin with."

Hephaestus brought the axe up and rested it against his shoulder. "I won't ask again. Do you want to rule with us or live beneath us?"

Aphrodite didn't hesitate. "I'd sooner marry a gorgon."

"So be it," Hephaestus said, dropping the axe off his shoulder. "We take no pleasure in what we must do, but you've forced our hand."

Hephaestus snatched Athena's shield and spun. Using its highly reflective surface as a mirror, he guided his axe in a vicious backswing that almost took Euryale's head from her shoulders. She tried to stay upright after jumping back, but couldn't as the combination of Hephaestus's speed and Aphrodite's awkwardness did her in.

The flat part of the axe head connected with her side on the follow-up swing. It launched her through the air with a deafening thunderclap. Euryale and Aphrodite crashed down on the other side of the forge. They rolled across the hard stone surface and came to a rest near a sheer drop.

"Get up, gorgon," Aphrodite pleaded as she tried to pull Euryale off the floor. "He's coming."

The goddess's words barely reached Euryale's ears. The world spun around her, and she found it near impossible to right herself. Euryale had been hit before, but nothing like this. Eventually, she managed to steady herself in time to see Hephaestus closing the distance between them, still using the shield to avoid looking directly at her.

"Don't worry, Euryale," he said. "We'll not harm Alex. He has been a good friend to us, and we'll spare him knowing what the Fates have dealt you."

Euryale inched back. Her tail flipped over the edge of the dark pit behind them. Just the sight of the tremendous fall made her queasy, and her tail almost gave out. "This isn't over," she said, sounding far weaker than she'd have ever liked.

"It is for you," Hephaestus replied.

The God of Smiths marched toward Euryale and his wife. The gorgon took in a deep breath and slipped off the ledge, taking Aphrodite with her in the process.

Chapter An Unwanted Meeting

The pair fell for what felt like days, and given some of the pits in Hades, they might very well have. When they hit the granite floor, Euryale took the brunt of it with Aphrodite landing on top. Thankfully, it had a sharp slope to it so that their sudden stop ended up being more of a hard roll. The two tumbled even deeper underground, bouncing off each other and numerous rocky outcroppings in the process. Eventually, they slid to one side before making one final drop into a small cavern.

For hours, both the gorgon and the goddess lay still, never speaking, each simply trying to cope with the intense pain coursing through their bodies as their bones slowly knitted back together.

Eventually, Euryale managed to prop herself against a stone wall. She heard Aphrodite groan as she followed suit, and Euryale reached her good arm over to help. Well, good was relative. The arm tied to the goddess was dislocated and swollen.

Aphrodite conjured a ball of light. The goddess looked over herself and shook her head. Blood caked her skin, stained her torn dress, and covered her face to the point where she would've been better suited as the Goddess of the Macabre than the Goddess of Love, especially since portions of her cheeks, scalp, and hands still had gashes deep enough to expose bone.

"I can't believe Hephaestus did this," Aphrodite said with disgust.

"Why? You Olympians are always so damn self-serving."

Aphrodite scowled and spat out a tooth covered in red-tinged spit. "By the Fates, I must be hideous."

Euryale, too tired to care, gave a half grin. "You look just like I feel."

Whether Aphrodite took offense or even heard, the gorgon didn't know, but the goddess kept on with her rant. "Where does he get off, attacking me like that? Where does he get off, attacking any of us like that? Seriously, who does he think he is? Did the Fates suddenly strike him with pity? Madness is more like it. You'd have to be mad to think anyone would follow you if you're a disgusting cripple—"

Aphrodite suddenly cut herself off, and in that brief moment, Euryale sensed the goddess had had a moment of insight. "Sorry," Aphrodite said, shaking her head. "No offense. I'm a little pissed off."

"A little?"

"A lot." Aphrodite clenched her hand into a tiny fist and growled. "How did we miss his betrayal like that? It should've been so obvious."

Euryale shut her eyes and breathed deep. It still hurt to move, to talk, to even think, but at least she wasn't as broken as she'd been an hour ago. "I don't know," she said. "Perhaps if..."

Her voice trailed into nothing and silence lingered for a few beats before Aphrodite glanced at her. "Perhaps what?"

"Perhaps if we hadn't been so obsessed with hating each other, we might not have been caught off guard," Euryale said.

To the gorgon's surprise, Aphrodite's anger faded momentarily, and she nodded. "Perhaps," she said. "Believe it or not, this wouldn't be the first time getting caught up in emotion has led to disaster for me."

"I'm sorry I tried to keep the shield," Euryale said. "I know you only wanted it so you could avoid exile."

"Thanks."

Euryale grimaced as a new wave of pain washed over her, and when it was gone, she figured as long as she was confessing, she might as well do it all. "I'm also sorry for trying to petrify you. We were fighting. I was incensed, and the rest is history."

"I might have deserved it," she replied.

The apology shocked Euryale so much she was certain she'd misheard. "What?"

"I didn't need the shield," she admitted. "I wanted it. Hera never would've been able to banish me forever, especially when Dad woke up. I only wanted it so I could show up Athena for once in my life."

"Oh, I see."

"Honestly, I hope you don't," Aphrodite said. "It's pathetic how often she humiliates me." The goddess muttered a few curses and sighed heavily. "Why do I feel bad that she's locked up, then?"

"I think that's called being normal," Euryale said. "She is your sister, even if you two fight all the time."

"No, not bad," Aphrodite said, only half hearing the gorgon's reply. "Guilty…I should've helped her find her shield from the beginning. Maybe then she wouldn't have been caught, and none of this would've happened. Gah, I am terrible, aren't I?" The goddess paused to rub her temples. "Okay, that's enough of a pity party from me. How's your head?"

"Not bad, if you don't mind brains trying to leak out," Euryale said. "No worse than yours."

Aphrodite grimaced. "That bad?"

"I did say you look just like I feel," Euryale said. "Do you still have your phone?"

"I do," Aphrodite said as she took it out. Though it had miraculously stayed with her after the fall, it was of no use, something the goddess spent several seconds staring at the screen to come to terms with. "No reception? You've got to be kidding me. I get full bars even in the Underworld."

"Something has to be interfering with the signal," Euryale said. "Or someone."

"Typhon."

"He must be near," Euryale said, noting how incredibly hot the air was around them.

Slowly, painfully, she coiled her tail up next to her and flexed it a few different ways. Though it felt stiff and sore, and would likely stay that way for days if not weeks, she thought it could bear her weight. "Can you move?" she asked. "We have to warn the others."

With a great deal of effort, Aphrodite got to her feet. She did need to use Euryale's shoulder to help boost her up, and again to keep her steady, but at least the goddess was mobile. Well, mobile in the most basic definition of the word. "Where's Apollo or Asclepius when you need them?" Aphrodite asked with a pained laugh.

"Sleeping with the rest," Euryale replied, rising from her seated position.

"I know. I was bitching."

Euryale grinned. "You? Never. Anyway, it would probably take them both a week to tend our wounds."

"All the more reason we should be leaving." Aphrodite took a step forward but immediately froze in place after she did. "That really hurts."

"When we get back, we should get into Dionysus's private reserve," Euryale said. "I'd wager that wine would be strong enough to make us forget about all of this."

Aphrodite laughed, cringed, and then laughed again. "You have no idea," she said.

"I think after bringing Hephaestus's betrayal to light, I deserve an idea," Euryale replied, only half joking.

The goddess placed a hand on the wall to steady herself and took another step. This one came easier. "I'll think about it," she said as she moved forward yet again. "Provided you don't say or do anything to sour my mood."

Euryale pressed her lips together. Maybe it was the pain clouding her thoughts, but she felt that the goddess was being more serious than lighthearted with the remark. That said, Euryale chose not to dwell on it. She had to stay focused on getting out of there and warning the rest of the Olympians, if for no other reason than that the war Hephaestus was about to start would ravage the world. The God of Smiths might have lost his mind in choosing to try and usurp Zeus, but Hephaestus was far from stupid. The power he wielded with his new axe and the monsters he had at his command surely would give the gods a war they'd not soon forget.

"Do you suppose he's working alone?" Euryale asked as a new thought struck her.

"Aside from Arachne?"

Euryale nodded. "Perhaps he's getting more help elsewhere, too."

"Help from who? Mortals?"

Euryale shrugged. "I have a sinking feeling it might be more than that. Others...demigods. Gods, even."

"Olympians?" Aphrodite said, eyes full of both shock and insult. "How dare you even suggest such a thing."

Euryale held up one of her hands defensively. "Not Olympians, necessarily," she said. "But Hephaestus must have allies we don't know about. Even with that weapon of his, I don't think he's crazy enough to think that's enough. After all, you pointed out earlier there was a long list of beings out there who would love to see the Olympians gone. Zeus has made countless enemies throughout time."

The anger in Aphrodite's face faded. "He has," she admitted. "Hera's spies will ferret them out, though, now that we know who's behind all this, assuming Dad doesn't catch up to him first and tear him apart."

"I hope you're right."

"I am."

With that, the two began searching for a way out of the cavern they had fallen in. It didn't take them long to find a small tunnel at the far end. Its walls were narrow, and it was such a tight fit that more than once Euryale feared that they would both be forever wedged in its confines, but it soon opened up, much to her relief.

"We should go back for the axe," Euryale said.

Aphrodite snorted with disbelief. "Like this? We can barely walk."

"Yes, but if we can get it, everything changes," Euryale said. "Hephaestus and Arachne will be stopped, and Hera—along with anyone else who wants to treat us poorly—will be brought low."

"You're going to wield it against her?"

"If that's what it takes to finally be treated fairly, I absolutely will," Euryale said.

Aphrodite stared blankly, and when she didn't reply, Euryale let the matter drop. Together they kept moving, and the air grew more and more stifling. Its heat caused sweat to bead on Euryale's forehead and run down her face. Her throat became parched, and her head ached.

Soon, the passageway dumped them into a large cavern with a few exits scattered about. Euryale picked one at random and continued on. The passage twisted and turned, and more than once the pair had to scale a wall with great effort and even greater pain to continue. Despite the seemingly endless nature to the tunnels, Euryale did note that they had managed for the past hour to be making a gradual ascent. So if they could keep that up, eventually, she told herself, they'd reach the surface.

A deep roar, distant yet powerful, echoed down the passage, freezing the two in place.

"What was that?" Euryale whispered.

"I have no idea," Aphrodite said. She inched closer to the gorgon. "Should we backtrack and look for another way out?"

Euryale thought for a moment. "The last branch we took was probably an hour ago."

"Has it been that long?"

"If not longer."

Aphrodite wiped her forehead with her arm. "I don't think I can take that kind of setback."

"Neither can I."

Euryale sucked in a breath and started forward once more. At the very least, she told herself, since they had begun for the surface the pain stabbing through her body had lessened.

Her mind wandered back to Alex, specifically when he would recount the tale of his slaying of Mister Lion. The beast had been a descendant of the infamous Nemean Lion, and like his great-great-great-great (and so on) grandfather, Mister Lion had been impervious to almost every attack. As such, the creature easily "killed" and ate Alex on their first meeting. But since Alex sported a regenerating body courtesy of Hades, Alex was born each day anew, and thus the cycle would repeat until he finally managed to slay the thing by drowning it in a river. Thinking of that story, Euryale told herself if her Alex could get through such agony to see her again, then she, too, could make a little hike under a mountain with a broken body. After all, it wasn't as if she were getting multiple tours of a monster's digestive system.

The tunnel suddenly opened up into a cavern that could easily house half of Olympus. It was lit by scattered oil lamps that shone with unnatural brightness. The ground ran for a hundred yards before disappearing in the darkness. Walls rose high all around, only to be swallowed by more inky black. Ahead, six creatures like the ones Euryale and Aphrodite had fought when first coming to Mount Etna stood on a large rocky platform. Next to them was the shoulder of a gargantuan thing who was none other than Typhon.

The Father of Monsters lay on his back in a shallow dip, bound in giant chains that pinned his arms across his dirty chest and his leathery wings behind him. He had coils of serpents for legs, but from the waist up he was shaped like a man—sort of—if it weren't for his arms that ended in tentacles and the torso that sported a hundred heads. Of those heads, all were bestial, ranging from leopards to serpents to dragons to boars, but the one in the middle and on the shoulders, the largest of all, was like a man's, with eyes that burned like hot coals and pointed ears along with a matted beard covered in filth and reeking of death.

"Put out the light before they see," Euryale whispered, instinctively ducking back into the tunnel.

Her words were not needed. Aphrodite had extinguished the globe midsentence, and even though the goddess had heard of Typhon's appearance time and again from Zeus, being in the monster's presence took her breath away. His descriptions did him no justice. "I can't believe Dad managed to defeat him."

"Barely," Euryale said, not so much to argue, but to remind herself that even with Zeus leading an army of the gods, he had only claimed victory over Typhon by the skin of his teeth.

"What are they doing?" Aphrodite asked.

Euryale didn't answer but simply watched.

One of the creatures took a large, hollow spike and drove it into the side of Typhon's shoulder. The Father of Monsters shouted with such fury that Euryale felt as if her bones were about to crack. Viscous garnet-colored blood oozed and was quickly captured by the half dozen creatures in a slew of clay pitchers. Once the blood flow stopped, the monster up front wrenched the spike free before the rest of them turned and left. Thankfully, none of them were the wiser to Euryale's and Aphrodite's presence.

"They're bleeding him?" Aphrodite asked, her face a twisted ball of confusion. "Why?"

"That's how Hephaestus is creating his army," Euryale said. "I'll bet you a king's bounty that's the same blood Arachne used at my party to make those scorpions."

"It would have to be refined," Aphrodite said. "There are probably vats somewhere to do exactly that."

Euryale's voice reflected the angst in her voice. "There's no telling how many monsters Hephaestus has created."

"Enough that he thinks he can storm Olympus."

"So thousands? Ten thousand?"

"Hundreds, perhaps."

A somber look washed over the gorgon's face, but dread immediately replaced it when Typhon spoke.

"You can come out of the shadows, children," he said with a deep, rumbling voice. "I know you're there."

Chapter Wish Granting

Euryale and Aphrodite each sucked in a reflexive breath and froze. Typhon chuckled with such a dark, deep rumble, had the gorgon not been there firsthand, she would've sworn a storm unlike any that had been seen was rolling in. "I picked up your scent before you even came to this island," he said. "Do not insult me by thinking you can hide from my eyes. Now come. Let us talk."

Aphrodite shook her head, terror splashed across her face, but Euryale ultimately went against the goddess's protest and slithered forward.

"Much better," Typhon said once the pair had ascended to the top of the platform. His eyes darted between the two for a moment before an eye ridge dropped. "The two of you have seen better days, but I'm impressed you've managed to find me all the way down here."

"You know of him?" Euryale asked.

Again, Typhon laughed. The chains holding him rattled to such a degree it was a small wonder they didn't break free of their fastenings. "You think I don't know everything that happens in my mountain?"

Aphrodite tugged on Euryale's arm. "There's no time for this. We need to go."

"Goddess of Love, you speak when no one cares," Typhon said as he flashed a toothy grin with his dragon's head. "When I want your worthless opinion, I'll let you know."

"You boast a lot for someone chained like a dog," Aphrodite said.

Typhon let loose a gigantic gout of flame from his nostrils. Though the fires blasted the far wall, their searing heat was more than enough to cause both gorgon and goddess to retreat. "I could fill this entire cave with fire hotter than that if I wanted, goddess," he said. "So unless you want to be even uglier, I'd mind my manners if I were you."

"She'll turn you to stone if you don't mind yours."

Typhon laughed so hard the ground shook. "How you jest, silly child," he said. "Have you not seen me meet her gaze without a hint of fear? I assure you, I'm well protected against her growing power."

"What do you want?" Euryale asked.

"What else? For you to set me free."

Euryale tutted. "I'd sooner rip out my children's hearts."

To her surprise, Typhon showed neither offense nor surprise. "If I were in your position, I might say the same," he said. "But you and I are not so unalike."

"I've never waged war against the gods," Euryale said.

"Only because you couldn't," Typhon replied. "Tell me, gorgon, truthfully now, had you my power, would you not have led the charge against Olympus after what Athena did to your sister? Of course you would have. I can see it in your eyes. You despise her for having Perseus behead Medusa. Don't deny it."

The very mention of her sister and her fate raised the temperature in her blood a hundred degrees. She didn't even try to hide the anger. She did, however, point out something that Typhon had neglected to mention as he tried to draw a parallel between them. "I won't deny it, but I wouldn't have tried to devour the world at the same time, either."

"A minor detail," Typhon said.

"Which is precisely why I have no intentions of releasing you now, even if I could."

Typhon grinned. "Do you know why I came after them?"

"Does it matter?" Euryale replied.

"To you it might. As I said, you and I are not so dissimilar. I am a parent, too, you know. And those gods you protect threatened them all with imprisonment and slavery. So I did what any parent would do, what you would do. I defended my family to the bitter end."

Though Euryale hated to admit it, and though she had never been told the story in any detail, she couldn't deny there was an air of truth about his words. Had the Olympians gone after Typhon first? Had they threatened his family? She certainly wouldn't put it past them, and she could certainly relate. Still…

"Those are bold claims," she finally said.

Again, and to Euryale's surprise, Typhon remained calm and collected. "That they are. As you consider them, consider this: I will be free of this prison one day, gorgon. When I am, the list of those who helped me and those who hindered me will have long been burned in my mind."

"You're never escaping," Aphrodite said with a huff.

"So certain of that, are you? Even now I can feel these chains weaken. I might not be free today or tomorrow, or even in a thousand years, but what is an eon but a blink of an eye when you are immortal?"

"We're done," Euryale said, realizing there was no point to the conversation, and every minute they wasted here was another minute gone before they could get back to Olympus.

As she started for the other end of the cavern, however, Typhon spoke again, freezing her in place. "They threw you away on an island to be forgotten, the same way they threw me down here," he said. "Those gods you cower before, those gods who have you at their heels, don't hate you. No, child, what you mean to them is far, far worse."

Euryale turned. "And what would that be?"

"Nothing," he said flatly. "You mean absolutely nothing to them." When Euryale balked, Typhon grinned. "Free me, child. I assure you that if you do, you will forever have a special place in my heart."

"You have a heart?" Aphrodite scoffed. "Don't make me laugh."

"Says the one infamous for having affairs," Typhon replied.

Aphrodite narrowed her eyes. "If you knew half as much as you pretend, you'd know I never wanted anything to do with Hephaestus."

Typhon grunted and blew out a jet of flame from his nostrils. "Your point is a fair one, goddess," he said. "All the more reason you should let me go. It seems I have misjudged your usefulness."

"Why? Because you'll promise me vengeance on my ex?" Aphrodite replied.

"Among others."

"We're not interested," Euryale said.

Typhon flashed an array of teeth. "I doubt you're that certain."

Euryale tensed. She wasn't all that sure either. A dark part of her soul relished the thought of taking the power Typhon offered, taking whatever spot he'd grant her over the Olympians. A larger part of her, however, a stronger part, couldn't bear to let the world suffer for her selfish desires. "I'm certain enough," she finally said.

"You don't trust me."

"Why should I? You haven't even given oaths."

Typhon smirked. "Oaths? As if such things aren't constantly wrought to manipulate others. I'm beyond such pettiness."

"So you'll give none."

"I'll grant you something even better."

"Such as?"

"Your freedom from those bindings," he said. The dragon head of Typhon pulled back its lips and opened its mouth. There wasn't much space offered, but there was enough of a gap between his spear-sized teeth that the chains binding Euryale to Aphrodite could fit through.

"Don't," Aphrodite protested. "It's a trick."

"No trick, goddess," Typhon replied. "What would I have to gain?"

"Nothing," Euryale said.

"Exactly."

The gorgon spent a few seconds turning the situation over in her mind before approaching, half dragging Aphrodite in the process. Careful as to not stick any part of her hand or arm in Typhon's mouth, she placed some of the links between his teeth.

Typhon snapped his mouth shut, and with a loud crunch, the bindings broke with ease. The rest that were still attached to Euryale and Aphrodite's wrists fell away. "Do I have your attention now?" Typhon asked.

Euryale stepped back, but not near as quickly as Aphrodite did. The goddess darted away, and despite her grievous wounds, she moved far faster than Euryale would've guessed she could.

"Let's go," Aphrodite said, looking nervously about. "There's no reason to stay here."

"I would suggest otherwise," Typhon countered. "Perhaps another show of good faith?"

Euryale arched an eyebrow. "Such as?"

"I can sense the curse in you," he said. "It's stronger than it has ever been before, isn't it?"

Euryale nodded. "Thanks to Hera."

"Yes, thanks to Hera," he repeated, sounding as if he already knew. "It must be terrifying knowing that one stray look could petrify your husband—your children, for that matter."

A stab ran through Euryale's gut, and she tried not to let the thought get to her, but her imagination didn't allow it. All she could do was hope that somehow they'd find a way to fix things. How, she had no idea, but the alternative was far too torturous to entertain.

"You have thought about it," Typhon said. "Don't deny what's plainly obvious."

"I have, but there's nothing I can do about it now."

"Oh, but there is," he said. "Free me, and I promise that you'll never have to worry about hurting your family from this day forth."

"You'll remove the curse?" she asked. "Can you do that?"

"No, Euryale. He won't," Aphrodite said, pulling on her arm. "He's lying."

"I have no need to lie to her about such a thing. It would be my pleasure to help. Come close, and I'll give you a taste of what freedom could be."

"Don't listen to him," Aphrodite said, again trying to hold her back.

Euryale shrugged her off. She stepped closer, and at Typhon's request, she put a hand on his side. The Father of Monsters chanted in a deep, low voice. A tingling ran through her hand and up her arm before spreading through her entire body. Her vipers hissed softly, but soon relaxed as a warm, euphoric state enveloped every inch of her.

"There you go, gorgon," Typhon said.

Euryale glanced at her body. "I still look the same."

"A taste, I said, nothing more," he replied. "You look the same and will act the same, but as for the latter, only if you so choose."

"I don't follow."

"From here on out, you'll only petrify those you desire to," he said. "A much better way to live, don't you think?"

"It can't be that easy."

Typhon grinned. "Easy for some of us. See for yourself. There's a rat at your feet. If you're quick, you can catch it."

Euryale glanced down, and sure enough, nestled up against Typhon's body was a large rat who looked as if he'd made a nest next to the giant monster some time ago. He looked up at Euryale and squeaked happily, and the gorgon snatched him up. The rat squirmed in her grasp, and though she hated the thought of accidentally killing the little guy, she needed to know whether or not Typhon was telling the truth.

Euryale brought the rodent up so that her eyes locked with the rat's. Nothing happened. After a few more seconds of nothing, Euryale gently set the rat back on the ground and let it run off.

"As you can see, gorgon, I keep my word," he said.

Euryale shook her head, marveling at it all. If he could and would rid her of her gaze, or at least give her the ability to control it, would he honestly give her back her original form, too? "I don't know what to say," she replied, and she didn't.

"You could start with a thank you."

"Thank you," Euryale replied.

"There, was that so hard?"

Euryale shook her head. The simple act reminded her that deep down, she still felt ill at ease. Why, though? She began surveying the cavern for something—anything—that would help her sort everything out. "When did Hephaestus find you?"

"Does it matter?"

"Only to satisfy my idle curiosity," Euryale said.

"Come now, gorgon, do not insult my intelligence so," he said with a deep chuckle.

"Did it take you long to corrupt his mind?"

Typhon grinned with amusement. "You think I had a hand in turning him against Olympus? Is that what you need to tell yourself?"

"I tell myself only the truth."

"If you insist," Typhon replied. "But you know you're clutching at straws. Hephaestus's righteous anger has been burning for a long, long time. I've done nothing but watch it erupt."

Euryale shook her head. "I don't believe you. He wasn't like that."

"Trust me, gorgon, he was," Typhon said. "I know more about him than you will ever know, much the same way I know more about you than even your father does."

Euryale grimaced, though she wished she hadn't. Despite her wishes, she and her father had never had the close relationship she had always wanted. That said, she tried to hide her reaction as best she could. "If you do, then you should also know insults to my family won't win me over, either."

"I'm not insulting, merely observing," he countered. "Tell me, how much does Phorcys know you? Understand you? From what I've been told, he was sleeping for thousands of years before coming to your aid last year—and only then because your sister Stheno had been taken from you and your cries disturbed his slumber."

"That's not how it happened," she lied.

"How did it happen, then?" he said. "It would seem to me between Phorcys and myself, I've given you more conversation in the past five minutes than he has for the last thirty centuries."

"You know nothing."

Typhon's mouth pulled back into a knowing smile. "Neither of us believe that," he said. "Free me. Protect your children and your children's children for a thousand generations. Enjoy the control I've given you over your curse, and when you're ready, together we can create a world where your family is welcome and the creatures you save are not mercilessly hunted for sport."

Euryale shook her head at the deep, hypnotic quality Typhon's words had. Even though she understood their unnatural charm, she felt her defenses dropping and her willingness to hear his position grow tenfold. Or maybe it wasn't a charm. Maybe that was a convenient excuse for her to remain in a deluded fantasy where she, Alex, Aison and Cassandra could live in peace.

That's all she wanted. That's all she had ever wanted.

"Hephaestus is almost finished with the axe, gorgon," Typhon said. "When he's done, I can distract him long enough for you to steal it and cut me free. I promise I'll give you all that your heart desires and scatter your enemies."

"What makes you think I won't simply take the axe for myself?" Euryale asked. "Having it will go a long way in ensuring I get the justice I seek."

Typhon grinned broadly. "Try if you like. I'm sure I could do nothing to stop you."

Euryale mulled his words. His unspoken threat, she knew, was somehow not a bluff. That said, she also felt his promises to her weren't empty, either.

"Euryale, you're not seriously thinking about this, are you?" Aphrodite asked. "No matter how badly you feel we treated you, I promise, Typhon will be a thousand times worse. And not just to you; to the entire world."

"I know," she said. She then repeated it for her own sake. "I know."

"Then why are we still here?"

"Yes, gorgon, why?" Typhon asked.

Euryale set her mind back to its original task: looking for whatever it was about the situation that bothered her. Her eyes scanned the floor, wondering if there would be something to it, but there was nothing. It was bare and rough, with no signs of abnormal wear or anything left haphazardly. The walls, too, oil lamps aside, seemed unremarkable. When her eyes drifted over Typhon's body, however, or more specifically where the chains crossed over him, she realized her search had not been in vain.

Thin, silk sheets had been wedged in several places between the chains and Typhon's skin, and though the links themselves looked as strong as ever, she noticed flecks of metal sticking to the god's body. Furthermore, the blood that had been extracted from his shoulder hadn't been done in a hasty or brutish manner. The spot had been cleaned, and upon closer inspection, she noticed a semi-clear residue.

Euryale reached over, being careful not to lose her balance and tumble into the basin below, and ran a finger over the substance. It came back sticky, and the tips of her fingers began to tingle, and then her hand grew numb.

"What?" Aphrodite asked, clearly sensing Euryale was on to something.

The gorgon brought her finger up to her nose and inhaled slowly. A resinous aroma tantalized her senses. It was an aroma she knew and knew well.

Euryale took a quick step back. She tried to hide her surprise under a flat affect, but she doubted it was enough to slip past Typhon's watchful gaze. The ancient god's eyes brightened ever so slightly, confirming her worst suspicion.

"It's time to go," she said to Aphrodite.

As the two left, Typhon had one last set of parting words. "I'll see you soon, gorgon."

Chapter Desperate Plans

Euryale slithered out of the cavern as fast as she could, but between Aphrodite's wounds and her own, the moss on the granite floor probably grew faster. Up a rough, narrow tunnel they went, and after a few minutes of hurrying along in silence, Aphrodite pulled on the gorgon's arm.

"What is it?" she whispered.

Euryale put a finger over her mouth, certain that Typhon could still hear them. She looked around for a side passage or a cave or anything that might help mute their conversation but found none. In the end, however, Euryale decided it didn't matter. Typhon knew what she was thinking. "Hephaestus is going to free him," she said.

"No."

"Yes."

"No!"

Euryale shook her head, wishing she didn't have to argue the point, but she did. Truth did not yield to dreams, be they hopeful or delusional. "Your husband put padding between the chains for comfort."

"I didn't see anything," Aphrodite said. "And ex-husband at that. Besides, even if there was something, how do you know Hephaestus did it?"

"The silk used for the sheets was exceptional," she replied. "The only other silk I've ever seen with such quality is the silk that's been used for your dresses. Very few Olympians would have access to your wardrobe or bed set."

Aphrodite's look of denial waned. Creases of worry formed across her face. "Is that all?"

Again, Euryale shook her head, and again she wished that she didn't have to. Sheets in and of themselves could mean any number of things. What else she had seen, however, completed the dreadful picture. "The monsters collecting Typhon's blood used a special anesthetic. I found some of its residue nearby, the same residue we saw in Hephaestus's forge."

"Maybe it's to placate him so he doesn't thrash as much?"

"If only," Euryale said. "Did he look angry when they worked? No. He was willing, almost eager."

"But he roared when they stabbed him."

"That anesthetic is strong but topical. I'm sure it still hurt. Either that, or it was all for show," Euryale explained. "Also, think about when he torched the wall with his breath and threatened to incinerate us both. If he wanted to defend himself, he could have. He's clearly shown himself not to be helpless, despite the chains that bind him."

Aphrodite's face soured. She didn't speak her thoughts, but Euryale knew them all the same. The goddess was trying to reconcile everything and was failing miserably. "There's more, isn't there?"

"There are flecks of metal on Typhon's scales, near the chains. I imagine these are from Hephaestus's failed attempts at cutting through."

"What if it's not him?"

Euryale tentatively reached out with her hand, and when Aphrodite didn't shy away, she dropped it on the goddess's shoulder. Aphrodite had always been a sensual goddess, Euryale knew, touch being the primary way she found comfort and safety, and if Euryale were about to extinguish any and all doubt as to the traitorous nature of Aphrodite's husband, she wanted to be as gentle as she could. After all, wanting to get away from a soon-to-be ex was one thing. Learning he was going to bring about Armageddon was something entirely different. There's no couple's therapy for that.

"Zeus made those chains, so something incredibly powerful would be needed to cut through," Euryale said. "Hephaestus tried to break them, repeatedly, and each time he failed, he had to steal a new artifact, melt it down, and incorporate it into the weapon. That's why that weapon has parts that are worn and parts that are new."

"I can't believe he'd do this," she said.

"Neither can I," Euryale said. "But the most damning evidence is what Typhon offered."

"How's that?"

"He knows when Hephaestus will finish the axe, and I'm certain he could stop us from running off with it if we snuck in when your husband was 'conveniently' away," she explained. "Thus, if he could stop us, he could stop Hephaestus, too, from exploiting him. The only conclusion then is that Hephaestus, along with Arachne and The Fox, are all working for him. And what more certain way to topple Olympus than to free Typhon?"

Aphrodite wore a grave look upon her face, but her voice turned hard and strong. "We have to get that axe."

"We can't," Euryale said. "You heard Typhon. He dared me to take it for myself."

"So you think we'd walk into a trap?"

"Undoubtedly. The bait, if we took it and sided with him, would simply be a test of loyalty. I'm certain he doesn't need us to free him."

"Which probably means that axe will be done any day now," Aphrodite said. "We have to warn the others."

Euryale nodded. "Agreed."

"But surely he knows what we'd do if we escaped. Why would he let us go?"

"My only guess is he wants someone to herald his arrival so he can soak in everyone's fear."

Aphrodite sighed heavily and leaned against the wall with her shoulder. There she stood in deep contemplation, but unlike the previous time the goddess's thoughts had consumed her, Euryale didn't know what she was wrestling with as the expression on her face changed from panic to regret. "Why didn't you take his offer?"

Euryale's brow furrowed. "Typhon's?"

"Yes. You're siding with…well, some who haven't treated you well," she said.

"Because as you said, Typhon will treat the world worse than all of you have, no matter how true his promises are to me," Euryale explained. "I can't let that happen."

"I see," Aphrodite replied. She smoothed out her tattered dress and tried rubbing some of the dirt and blood off her arms, but it was clearly more of a nervous energy needing release than an actual attempt to be presentable. It was, after all, hard to look good, even for Aphrodite, when you looked like you'd just gotten done being Cerberus's chew toy. "There's something I should do, I guess, before we go on."

"What's that?"

Aphrodite didn't answer. She found a patch of dirt nearby and scraped it together before adding a bit of saliva. She cringed as she made the mixture and rubbed it together in the palm of her hands. "Could this make me more undignified?" she muttered with disgust.

Once done, Aphrodite went to slather the paste on Euryale, but the gorgon reflexively pulled away. "What are you doing?"

"Easing your curse," she said.

"I didn't think you could do anything."

"I never said that," she replied. "I might have...forgotten I could do something."

"Forgotten?"

Aphrodite's face soured. "Do you want some help or not? I'm about to rub this disgusting mess off my hand one way or another." When Euryale nodded, the Goddess of Love used one hand to close the gorgon's eyes and with the other, she smeared the paste over them.

Aphrodite spoke soft words as she did, and Euryale could feel a warmth build. It started in both eyes, but quickly spread across her cheeks and to the back of her head. A few seconds later, she felt Aphrodite start to wipe it all away. When she finished, Euryale felt...clearer. She still had a serpentine tail and a head full of vipers, but there was a peace to her soul that hadn't been there before.

"You're still potent," Aphrodite said. "In case you were wondering."

"What did you do?"

"Blessed your spirit so you won't go berserk during a fight," she explained. "It also made your eyes sparkle. They're very pretty now."

Euryale didn't know what to say. The gesture, even though small compared to her curse, felt monumental. Part of her even felt as if she'd imagined it all. "Why did you wait until now?"

"Because I don't hand my favors out to anyone," she said. "Certainly not you. Or at least, the old me helping the old you."

"The old me?"

"The old you as in how I saw you," she explained. "But if you're willing to stand up to Typhon on our behalf, after everything we've done, I owe you at least that much."

A smile crept across Euryale's face, and warmth enveloped her. "Thank you."

The two started down the tunnel again. Euryale strained her ears the entire time, trying to listen for any sign of Typhon's monstrous children. Twice she heard them coming in time for the pair to find a place to hide, which was much easier to do now that the pair weren't bound together. Two more times, she didn't hear them, but she could taste their foul presence in the air, like they were rotten fish under a blanket of thick sauce, and they avoided them easily enough.

It didn't take long before the tunnel's ascent became steeper and steeper. In several places, stairs had been carved, and iron ladders had been bolted into the walls. Even more spots saw the tunnel split into two, three, or even four directions. The maze-like nature gave Euryale flashbacks of her time spent in the labyrinth a year ago where she'd tried to kill Alex and Jessica. Those thoughts pained her deeply, and she distracted herself as best she could with any other thought that came to mind.

Eventually, they rounded a corner and ended up skirting along the top edge of a deep cavern where everything changed.

"By the Fates," Aphrodite whispered as she dropped low. "There must be tens of thousands of them. Hundreds, even."

"At least," Euryale whispered back.

A sea of creatures filled the cavern floor below, a cavern floor that easily stretched hundreds of yards in all directions. They sat on their haunches, curled forward, with arms wrapped around their legs, not moving in the slightest. Some looked like the ones they'd come across before. Others had wings. Some had tails that belonged to every manner of beast and monster out there—dragon, scorpion, viper, and so on. All had fangs and claws, however. All had been made for one purpose and one purpose only: to wage war.

Walking amongst this grotesque army were a dozen cyclopes clad in heavy armor. Some carried large swords or spears, but Euryale caught sight of a few wielding rifles and machine guns.

Hephaestus, it seemed, had taken lessons from Alex's triumph over Ares and was now outfitting his army with modern weapons. And if the God of Smiths had undertaken such a task, how terrible would those god-forged firearms be?

Worse, had Hephaestus created bigger guns for them as well? Alex had used artillery and tanks in his war against Ares, something that Hephaestus was well aware of. What sort of cannons could he craft?

Euryale shuddered at that question.

She then watched one of the one-eyed giants walk up and down the rows of creatures like an overseer inspecting his crop. What he was looking for, she didn't know. Her curiosity wanted her to stay longer, but the practical side of her knew she could not. Another thought struck her, one that caused her to lean back against the wall to keep herself steady.

"What?" Aphrodite whispered.

Euryale opened her mouth to explain, but chose not to. This wasn't the time. "I'll tell you when we're out."

The gorgon started to leave, but Aphrodite held fast. She whipped out her phone, and after snorting with disgust at still having no reception, she quietly took a dozen pictures of the army they were spying on. "Thought this might be helpful later," she explained.

"Absolutely," Euryale said, smiling. "Let's go."

Aphrodite put her phone away, and the pair carefully moved on. Twenty minutes later, the stench of the place no longer assaulted Euryale's nose. Ten minutes after that, she caught a freshness in the air she had wondered if she'd ever experience again.

Finally, Euryale and Aphrodite broke free of Mount Etna and collapsed under a starry night, relishing the air and their freedom.

Aphrodite rolled onto her back and stared at the sky. A small chuckle started inside of her and quickly grew into uncontrollable laughter. A half minute passed before she could recompose herself.

"I can't believe we made it," Aphrodite said. "Can you?"

Euryale, though grateful, did not share in her celebration. The severity of what they'd discovered weighed too heavily on her mind, especially when she thought about them getting a sneak peek at Hephaestus's grotesque army of creatures. "This was too easy," she said.

Aphrodite chuckled, but there was a nervous energy to it. "Easy? You call that easy? I've come across pigheaded slobs who would've had an easier time stealing my heart than what we went through."

Euryale pushed herself up, wincing as she did. Her wounds were healing, thankfully, but she was still a painful mess. "I'm not convinced anymore our only purpose was to tell the world he's coming. He wanted us to leave seeing his army. Why?"

Aphrodite's smile faded as she sat up. "So we'd leave in a panic?"

"Given we got a glimpse of his army, without a doubt," Euryale said.

"Then maybe us leaving has something to do with him getting free?"

Euryale tilted her head. "What do you mean?"

"I mean, my stupid soon-to-be ex hasn't managed to free Typhon yet, obviously, and the axe isn't as close to being finished as we were told. So that means Typhon is going to use us somehow to get whatever final piece is missing."

Euryale clasped her hands together and rested her chin on top of them. The goddess's insight seemed spot on. At the very least, it was the best guess they had. "What's our obvious move, then? We tell everyone what we've discovered, so what does that do?"

"Hera will raise an army and march on Mount Etna. Ares, Poseidon, and Artemis will join her on the field of battle."

"Which leaves the Cave of Nyx no longer guarded. Would Typhon dare wake Cronus?"

"Hera seemed to think Arachne would. Not sure I wouldn't put it past Typhon either."

"And if Hera doesn't bring them along, then what?" Euryale asked. "Hera attacks, but not as strongly as she could."

"He captured Athena when she was alone—or at least, Arachne did," Aphrodite said. "Does he want Hera, too?"

"Perhaps. She would have knowledge about Olympus few would."

"Then we don't say anything until we know for certain what he's up to," Aphrodite said.

Euryale shook her head. "No, our plan has to encompass more than that. Typhon knows there are a hundred different plays we'll consider and a thousand more we hadn't thought of. We have to assume he's still winning the game no matter what we do."

Aphrodite snorted. "That's it? Are we giving up, then? Or are you saying we're too dumb to figure this out?"

"Neither," Euryale replied. "I'm saying we need to stop playing his game. The only way we do that is by tossing the board and scattering all of his carefully lined up pieces."

Aphrodite nodded approvingly as she took to her feet. The goddess brushed herself off, all the while seeming to draw strength from Euryale's suggested course of action. "I like the sound of that, but it seems easier said than done."

"Probably. But what's the one thing we would never do?"

"Aside from groveling at Hephaestus's feet?"

Euryale cracked a grin. "Yes."

"Awaken Cronus," Aphrodite said.

"We might, if we were desperate," Euryale pointed out. "And if that's his overall strategy, it would make sense. From what I've heard, Cronus could rip apart Typhon's chains simply by thinking about it, and after that, maybe they'd join forces and tear us apart right after."

"For the love of all," Aphrodite muttered. "And here I thought we'd already dreamt up the worst case scenario."

"No kidding."

"If that's true, why would he tell you about the axe?"

"A test of loyalty, perhaps? A way of determining who he wants to keep around in his new kingdom?"

"Maybe..."

Euryale sighed heavily and then began to slither down the mountainside, motioning for Aphrodite to follow. "We might as well leave this place. Perhaps the trip back will help us think of something."

"Hopefully sooner rather than later," Aphrodite replied.

Euryale didn't reply. She was deep in thought about what their options were.

Would bringing the mortals into this help? Possibly. But then again, Typhon had certainly considered that. Even if he hadn't, or couldn't do anything about it, and even if humans had developed some of the most destructive weapons ever imaginable, from what Euryale had seen, they bickered and argued amongst themselves to an even greater degree than they had before. As such, Typhon would probably have conquered half the earth by the time any of them had settled on how to open whatever committee they'd formed to deal with his threat. After that, they'd probably be arguing on whether attacking Typhon was an attack on human rights or not attacking him was actually setting him up for defeat in some bizarre, 6-D chess match.

Thus, Euryale concluded, humans were out. Plus, Typhon could probably convince many of them to join his side.

What Euryale needed was a secret weapon. A weapon so unexpected, all Typhon's plans would fall apart. Or at least, he'd hesitate long enough so that Hephaestus could be stopped from freeing him.

"Think. Think. Think," she grumbled to herself.

"Of what?" Aphrodite asked.

Euryale paused halfway back to Catania. She opened her mouth to express her frustrations about being no nearer a solution than she'd been when they first started down the mountain when a thought struck her. "I think I have an idea," she said as a smile spread across her green face.

"How to defeat Typhon?"

"If only," the gorgon replied. "No, I mean something that may give him enough pause so we can regain the advantage."

Aphrodite tilted her head, and her brow wrinkled. "I'm not going to like this, am I?"

"No, but hear me out," Euryale said. "The natural move, in fact almost every move we consider, ultimately winds up with Hera leading us to Mount Etna, right? Whether we have all the mortals behind us or not, whether you decide to grant Hera's request and get Zeus's lightning or not, or anything else we think of, Hera will always be at the front, ready to see this finished. And let's face it, when she finds out Hephaestus is the one betraying us, there's no power strong enough in all of creation that will keep her away from being the first to bring him to his knees."

"I'd agree with that."

"So whatever Typhon needs, it has to revolve around her being there. The question then becomes, what is that?" Euryale asked. At this point, she paused, unsure which of two ways she wanted to continue down her thought process. She didn't want to lie, but any way she spun the possibilities of what was going on, she couldn't be certain of what would ultimately be the truth. In the end, she decided if Aphrodite took things at face value, all the better. Especially when she got to the part when she'd ask the goddess for a gigantic favor. "The answer to that question is simple."

"It is?"

"Yes. Hera has something that's needed to finish the axe, something she keeps on her at all times. Something The Fox can't simply steal as he did with everything else. Typhon wants her on the battlefield so someone, somehow, in all the chaos, can take what they need so that Hephaestus can finish the labrys and set Typhon free."

"Her polos," Aphrodite said, her voice almost a whisper. "She never takes that crown off. Not even to sleep."

Euryale smiled. "Exactly. Made from adamantine, imbued with power, it has to be the last thing they need."

"Even if they could steal it, how could they melt it down and make it part of the axe before we stormed the forge?"

Euryale shook her head. "That part, I don't know. But I'll bet a hundred years of servitude Typhon has that already figured out."

Aphrodite sighed and shook her head. "I bet you're right. So what do we do?"

"Like I said, something totally unexpected."

Aphrodite groaned. "This better not have anything to do with me pledging my undying love to Hephaestus."

Euryale drew the corners of her mouth back and shook her head, which seemed to put the goddess at ease a little. "No. Want I want you to do—what we need to do—is mass our army and put you out in front, commanding it all."

"What?" Aphrodite said, eyes wide. "No one will take that seriously. How does that do anything?"

"They'll take it seriously when you look like Hera, and she will look like you."

"Come again?"

"The two of you take on illusions to look like the other," Euryale said. "You will also wear a crown—a fake—that Hera can curse so that when it's melted down, it explodes and destroys everything."

Aphrodite bit her lip as she turned the idea over. "As much as I don't want to look like her, I still get the feeling that's not the worst of what you're asking of me."

"It's not," the gorgon replied. "To sell the illusion, you're going to have to be the one who wields Zeus's lightning."

Aphrodite's face went grave. "You want me to betray Zeus?"

Euryale nodded.

"You want me to steal his lightning?"

"Think of it as borrowing."

"Remember Prometheus? He only stole a little fire and had his liver repeatedly torn out for eons. Aside from Athena and impregnating every fair maiden that catches his eye, there's nothing Dad loves more than his lightning. What do you think he'll do to me?"

"He's sleeping. He'll never know."

"He'll know," Aphrodite said. "Especially when Hera demands I hand it over to her, which I'm assuming you don't want me to do."

Euryale nodded. "No. We can't do that. If anyone but 'Hera' is throwing bolts, they'll pick up on the ruse. You, Hera, have to be the only one using lightning, bravely taking the place of your beloved husband...well, maybe not beloved, but Hera has always had a sense of duty that's equally as strong as her sense of vengeance. If Hera, looking like you, hurls even a single bolt, it'll all be for nothing. No one will ever believe she'd let you wield her husband's power, especially in such a crucial battle."

Aphrodite crossed her arms and shook her head. Her eyes glistened, and it was painfully obvious she couldn't get out what she wanted to say. "I can't believe we've got to rely on a plan that reaffirms I'm the useless one. I'm the one that belongs anywhere but where things matter most. Should I let her borrow my mirror and comb, too? Maybe give her some tips on how to fix her hair in front of the troops?"

"I know I'm asking a lot—"

"No, you don't! You have no idea how much you're asking!"

"There's no other way."

"Really?" Aphrodite asked, inscensed. "Then what do I do after we win? Blow you a kiss goodbye? Because that's all I'll be good for when Zeus wakes up. Hera will march right up to him and tell him everything as payback for trying to usurp her position."

"Which is why you'll need to talk to her first," Euryale said. "You'll have to convince her our plan is sound."

"How about the seven of us, you, me, Alex, Ares, Poseidon, Artemis and Hera all charge in and take that stupid axe back once and for all?"

Euryale shook her head. "Our tactics can't be so simple a five-year-old child would see them coming." The gorgon winced the moment she finished that sentence. "Sorry, I didn't mean anything by it. I only meant Typhon has undoubtedly prepared for a frontal assault by the seven of us. Besides, it'll be a lot easier to sell a fake crown while a full-scale war rages at his doorstep."

Aphrodite cursed under her breath. "This won't work."

"It can, and it will. All we have to do is sell the illusion."

"And get Hera to cooperate. She hates us both already."

Euryale blew out a stress-filled puff of air. "I know. I was thinking, however, when you talk to her, maybe you could get her to think she came up with the idea. If you could do that, then she could claim the glory."

"All you've wanted to do was bring her down, and now you want to not only destroy the axe, but let her claim to be the victor in all of this?"

"I have to," Euryale said. "The needs of the world trump my own. That said, I'm tired of being everyone's doormat. If she treads on me again, I promise she'll regret it."

Aphrodite drew back a corner of her mouth. "Somehow I don't doubt that. So before I agree to this, is there anything else I should know?"

Euryale cringed.

"What?" Aphrodite said with a disbelieving laugh. "What could possibly make any of this worse?"

"You need to tell me how to get into the armory."

"Zeus's armory?"

The gorgon nodded.

"Why?"

"Because I'm not going with you to see Hera," she replied.

"Now you're not even coming with me?"

Euryale shook her head. "She's more likely to be receptive to your words if it's only you. I don't want to catch another curse because her anger is misplaced. Besides, if Hera won't listen to reason and she does something to you, we're going to need that lightning to defeat Typhon."

Aphrodite backed away, arms outstretched, and shook her head. "This is crazy. I'm not doing all this on my own, and I'm certainly not handing Father's prized possessions over to you. Even if I wanted to, you know I've given oaths. I've sworn I'd let no god or mortal in without Zeus's blessing."

Euryale took in a slow, deep breath, folded her hands together, and sighed. "I know I'm asking more than I should, but this is only a contingency plan, and you wouldn't be breaking any oaths."

"I don't see how."

"I am neither god nor mortal," she replied. "Your oaths do not apply to me."

Chapter So, Hera...

"I can't believe I let her talk me into this," Aphrodite muttered as she marched up the steps that led inside Hera's tower. If there were a silver lining to any of it, she'd at least been able to clean up and get a new dress (well, she'd helped herself to a black-and-gold one when they'd passed through Rome and she'd dropped in on Versace). All of that certainly helped her mood, and it certainly helped her manipulate Hera's guards. After all, it was hard to turn a man into a stuttering idiot if you looked like you'd been run over by a combine.

"You boys stand there and look pretty," she said, strutting between four armed men in black suits who had been posted outside the front doors.

"Excuse me—" one, and only one, started to say, but he was quickly silenced when Aphrodite threw him a wink.

"Shhh, love," she said. "I'll be back for you soon. I promise."

With that, the goddess entered the lobby. It felt ten times colder than the last time she'd been through it, and even the marble floor felt ten times harder as well. Her heels clacked loudly as she strode toward the elevators. A couple dozen security guards, most being satyrs, with two centaurs taking up space behind the security desk, immediately started for Aphrodite. Like the men she'd encountered outside, she demanded nothing but their complete obedience. Whether she'd get it was something else, she knew.

"You," one of the centaurs said. "Hera's—"

"Did I say you could talk to me?" Aphrodite asked, leveling her gaze.

"Hera—"

Aphrodite held up a finger. "I did not. And if you say another word, you'll regret it for the rest of your short, miserable life."

Her threats, thankfully, were enough to silence and freeze all of them in place. At least, they stayed that way long enough for Aphrodite to hop in the elevator and hit the button for the top floor. Up the building she shot, all the while watching the readout change as she zipped by floor after floor. At some point, she realized the guards below had no doubt alerted Hera to her presence. Shortly after that, she realized her hands were trembling. Worse, try as she might, she couldn't stop it from happening.

"Ares and Alex are coming," she whispered to herself. "All you have to do is get through this meeting."

Prior to her arrival at the tower, she and Euryale had also talked to Alex and Ares on the phone, and both had agreed to meet her at the vault. As nice as that was, however, she wished they could've made it here now. There was no telling how much fury the Queen of Olympus would heap upon her.

"Ares will come," she said one last time. The chant hardly turned her into a fearless warrior, but the reminder was enough that Aphrodite felt as if she could do it—as long as Hera held more contempt for the gorgon than for her, that is.

The elevator doors slid open, and when Aphrodite's eyes took in the scene before her, she felt her jaw drop. The entire floor had been remodeled. Most of the walls had been knocked out, leaving the area with a spacious floor plan. Directly in front of her was a sixty-foot walnut table with cross grain, a dark stain, and an intricate platinum overlay. Only two chairs sat at the massive piece of furniture, one at either end. Each one was made from ash-gray leather with a high back, fixed armrests, a gorgeous wood frame, and a price tag that likely rivaled any gift a lovestruck king had bestowed upon Aphrodite in ages long past. Set on the table in front of each chair stood a crystal wineglass with a matching decanter, and behind the chair at the far end stood Hera.

"Sit," she said, motioning to the chair opposite her.

Aphrodite hesitated, forgetting nearly everything she was supposed to say and do. "You were expecting me?"

"Yes," Hera replied. "Now, if you want to keep this cordial, sit."

Aphrodite quickly stepped forward and took her seat at the table. She threw a brief glance at the wine in the decanter, and that was all she needed to know where, or rather who, it had come from. Dionysus's special reserve could never be mistaken for anything else, which meant Hera was either looking to make amends—or at least, a peace treaty—or was giving Aphrodite a last meal before her execution. "When did you know I was coming?"

"From the moment the two of you left Rome," Hera replied, taking a seat at the table. She slowly poured herself a glass of wine and motioned for Aphrodite to do the same.

"I see," Aphrodite replied, not sure how else to respond. The Queen of Olympus had always been hard to read, but now she seemed downright impossible. Whatever that meant, Aphrodite guessed it couldn't be good.

"You're lucky you had a direct flight," Hera said. "Had I thought you were headed anywhere but back here, I'd have made it your last act of freedom."

"Of course I came back," Aphrodite said. "You need to know where we've been."

"Other than Sicily?"

Aphrodite sipped her wine to hide her discomfort. She knew once she started down this conversation, there was no going back, and if she didn't stay strong and hold her ground while at the same time somehow managing to keep Hera from obliterating her out of perceived insolence, all would be lost. "I know who Arachne is working with and what they're up to."

"Stop being vague and tell me."

Aphrodite nodded and nearly spilled her glass as she hurriedly put it back on the table. "Arachne and Hephaestus are working together," she said. "They've been stealing our artifacts to melt them down and forge an axe, an axe they intend to use to free Typhon."

"Impossible," Hera scoffed. "What makes you think such ridiculous things?"

"Because I was there," Aphrodite said. "Please, listen to what I'm saying. He's going to free Typhon if we don't stop him immediately."

Hera snorted. "You best have proof. Your previous wit and bravery is hardly something I can rely on. Nor can I merely take you on your word, which we all know serves you and you alone. How do I know you're not the traitor who's trying to pull my attention away from Cronus?"

Even though Aphrodite had expected such a reaction, she couldn't help but scowl. "I took pictures," she said, pulling out her phone and sliding it across the table. "I've also got scars on my body, too, if you'd like to see."

Hera hesitantly picked up the phone and spent a few moments flipping through the pictures Aphrodite had taken. When she finished, she set the phone down and looked unconvinced. "These are hardly conclusive. I don't know where these were taken, and I don't see your husband in any of them."

Aphrodite shook her head and muttered. Of course, Hera didn't believe her, as always. She could feel her eyes water, and as her throat tightened, so did her gut. At that point, frustration turned to anger. "Are you that spiteful you can't see what's plainly going on?" Aphrodite said, shooting out of her chair. "Would it be so terrible if I accomplished something the rest of you could not?"

Hera leaped to her feet. "Know your place!"

"And know yours!" Aphrodite shot back. "You are not some lofty, infallible thing that even the Fates won't challenge. And as long as we're entertaining the idea of traitors around here, maybe it's you."

"How dare you accuse me of such a thing," Hera said, her face an equal mix of shock and disgust.

"I'm being no more brazen than you are!" Aphrodite said. Though she knew she was teetering on the edge of disaster with Hera and the total loss of self-control, she loved the self-empowerment she now had. "Answer me! Why should I believe you? You haven't managed to come up with an antidote for whatever poison put the others to sleep, and you have yet to even catch a whiff of Arachne's trail on your own!"

Hera pursed her lips and growled softly. Her brow dropped, and the fire that burned in her eyes would've been enough to send Zeus and both of his brothers running for cover. But the goddess did not strike out. She exhaled through her nose before issuing her reply. "You are such an insolent child," she said. "That said, I'm hard-pressed to find a reason why other than you're telling the truth. Or at least, you think you are."

Tension in Aphrodite's neck and shoulders waned. "I am. By the River Styx, I am not lying to you. Please believe me. We have to get to Mount Etna before it's too late."

"There aren't many of us left. We will need to strike hard and fast."

"I know. That's why I'm here."

"Does this mean you're ready to open your father's vault?" Hera asked.

Aphrodite nodded. "I am. We need his lightning."

Hera's face softened, though Aphrodite knew it wouldn't last. "Good...good. Maybe you haven't completely lost your senses."

"But..."

"There's a but?"

"You can't have the bolts," Aphrodite said. Hera's face turned scarlet, and before she could sling a curse at Aphrodite, the Goddess of Love explained. "I'll take them. No one else, at least until Dad wakes up."

"You?" Hera said with a laugh. "You can't even throw a spear. What makes you think you'll do anything with that lighting other than char your face?"

Aphrodite swallowed, feeling the wind being stripped of her sails. She took a moment to relive the recent past where'd she had voice and authority, where she was not a useless goddess. "I'm to take your form, and you're to take mine."

"Oh, this is rich. Do tell."

"We'll craft a fake crown, one that looks like yours and one you can curse. When it's stolen on the battlefield and melted down, it'll explode."

"You think my crown is the missing piece?"

"They've stolen nearly everything else from us," Aphrodite said. She then went on to explain the rest of Euryale's reasoning. When she was done, to her surprise, Hera didn't laugh in her face. In fact, if Aphrodite didn't know better, she'd have sworn the Queen of Olympus was considering the plan. Hell, she almost swore that anyway.

"It's not the most terrible idea," she finally said. "I'll agree to it on one caveat."

"Which is?"

"If your plan fails, then you follow my orders without question. Understood?"

Aphrodite nodded. She didn't like the condition attached to Hera's participation, but with time being of the essence, she didn't feel like she could afford to negotiate, or was able to, for that matter. "Fine. I agree."

"Good," Hera replied. "Now let's get those bolts. You can fill me in on the details of everything else along the way."

Chapter The Vault

The double doors towered over them both, giving Aphrodite pause. Even Hera seemed to be wary of approaching them, and not without good reason.

Zeus had crafted the entrance to his armory using iron from the heart of a star. No walls were as heavy as those, nor were any other doors as strong. But the God of Thunder had not stopped at protecting his treasures simply with impenetrable barriers. The doors themselves crackled with energy, effusing the air with the smell of ozone, a caution to the would-be thief that powerful enchantments had been bestowed upon the entryway, enchantments that would turn trespassers into piles of ash should they not heed the warnings.

"We haven't time for you to gawk," Hera said. "Open the doors."

"I'm trying to remember how to do it correctly," Aphrodite replied. "Unless you want to go first, give me a moment to think."

Hera scowled but said nothing else, which was fine with Aphrodite. The Goddess of Love carefully went up the rest of the marble steps that lead to the armory's entrance, all the while wondering where Euryale had gone. Even though the gorgon was right in that her presence would no doubt enrage Hera, Aphrodite would've liked having her with her. The gorgon, apparently, had rubbed off.

When Aphrodite was standing in front of the doors, she examined them thoroughly. Each one had been purfled with gold and platinum, and silver had been used to fill hundreds of etchings across their surface—etchings that bound Zeus's enchantments to the entryway. Aphrodite couldn't read most of it. They were written in a language older than her, one that had been all but lost, and those who knew it now jealously kept those secrets.

On the door to the right, there was a large indentation of a powerful hand, the hand of Zeus himself. Beneath that were two smaller impressions. Each of those was lighter, full of grace and femininity. Though they were similar in size, they clearly were not for the same individual. One was meant for Athena, the other, Aphrodite.

The Goddess of Love sucked in a breath and placed her hand into her impression. Goosebumps raised across her skin and her hair stood on the back of her neck. Energy raced through her arm before spreading all across her body. It tickled at first, but soon every inch of her felt as if it were on pins and needles, and it took all of Aphrodite's self-control not to pull away.

At this point, she leaned in close and whispered so softly that her own mind barely picked up the words. "*Phylathion gryallaros ionine myrmonia otephone.*"

The energy flowing through her picked up. Her hand trembled, and the muscles in her arm and neck started to twitch. She hoped her words were true, but they'd been taught to her so long ago, she feared they might not be. It wasn't as if she practiced them daily, either. Maybe she should have, because that might have gone a long way in preventing her from having one of the worst hair days in all of history.

"*Dadenor tygros thekate aryx tagamemnon.*"

The doors rumbled as if they were the gatekeepers to a tempest that could blow away the world. Aphrodite retreated a few steps, and then twice that when Hera did as well. The two goddesses exchanged nervous looks, but they shared a laugh when the doors opened, revealing Zeus's armory.

"Nice to see I didn't forget anything," Aphrodite said.

"Agreed," Hera replied.

The two trotted up the steps and crossed the threshold to the armory. The room was circular, about sixty yards in diameter. A dome took up the majority of the ceiling, the latter being supported by a dozen evenly spaced columns. Throughout the armory were intricate friezes depicting hundreds, if not thousands of events throughout Zeus's reign. As far as Aphrodite could tell, every event of importance had been accounted for, events that ranged from Zeus's overthrowing of Cronus, to Athena being born from one of his headaches, to his involvement in the Trojan war and beyond.

In the center of the armory stood Zeus's specialized forge, complete with anvil, hammer, and a slew of tongs. Several small chests sat nearby, each containing the raw material needed to create the God of Thunder's mighty weapons.

A weapon rack made from heavy, charred oak stood at the far end of the armory. Giant bolts of energy were propped up in it, each as tall as a man and as thick as Aphrodite's arm. The air sizzled around them and crackled, putting Aphrodite on edge. Next to the weapon rack were a couple of barrels with smaller bolts stashed inside, though these had much more jagged bodies and instead of coming to a sharp point, they ended in forked heads.

That was hardly the end of Zeus's inventory of lightning, however. Scattered across a nearby table lay a half dozen smaller bolts, which Aphrodite recognized as stingers—the affectionate name Zeus gave those relatively low-powered pieces of lightning. Opposite them, hanging on the wall, were the largest and most powerful. Those were the ones Zeus would throw to level cities, or in Typhon's case, ginormous monsters. Each took a painstakingly long time to create, and each harnessed far more energy than Zeus could create on the fly.

"I had no idea he had so many," Aphrodite said, looking around the room in wonder, mouth agape, eyes wide. "Which should I use?"

Hera causally strode over to a chest near Zeus's anvil and smirked. "Still deluding yourself you can do such a thing?"

Aphrodite sighed. Would she ever be seen as anything but worthless in Hera's eyes? Maybe after the battle, she hoped. Not wanting to dwell on it anymore, she scanned the rest of the area. There wasn't much else, but there was a net hanging on the wall that she instantly recognized. "He has Hephaestus's net?" she said, more to herself than Hera.

"No. It's as unbreakable and inescapable as Hephaestus's, but it won't turn invisible," Hera said, shaking her head. "The net was a prototype that Hephaestus gave Zeus while trying to buy his way back into Olympus."

"Oh," Aphrodite said. She then turned her attention back to the large supply of lightning bolts that the armory held. "How many do you think we should bring? I'm tempted to say all."

Hera shrugged and opened the chest she was standing in front of. She sifted through its contents, seemingly unimpressed by most of it. "Junk. Junk. Junk...oh, now that's something."

"What's something?" Aphrodite asked.

"Essence of lightning, if I'm not mistaken," Hera replied. The goddess held a glass bottle with a rubber cork in the top. Faint clouds swirled around inside, while countless balls of energy bounced around, throwing tendrils of lightning in all direction. "It's what infuses his bolts with raw power, or anything else for that matter."

"Sounds potent."

"Very," Hera answered as she slipped the bottle into a leather satchel she carried. The goddess then made her way to a weapon rack. Slowly, she picked up a bolt of lightning. Her eyes stayed fixed on the weapon, and her face reflected a yearning for times long past. "You know, when Zeus and I were first together, he used to take me up to the tallest cloud we could find, and there he'd teach me how to throw these."

"He did?"

"Yes." Hera swallowed, and streaks of pain ran through her voice as she continued. "Those days were heavenly. Those were days where his whispers only found my ears, and days where he only sought my company. Days we used to spend lying around, wondering how best we could spend eternity."

"They sound like they were special," Aphrodite said. Despite Hera's vicious streak that was a mile wide, Aphrodite couldn't help but feel terrible for the goddess. Zeus's infidelity had taken a far greater toll than she'd imagined. She could hear it in her voice and see it in her face, and Aphrodite had empathy for Hera right up until she spoke again.

"Those days are gone and will never return," she said, sounding every bit as hard, cold, and cruel as she had ever been. "His reign is over. No longer will we suffer."

"We?" Aphrodite said. She backed away. Her hands reflexively started for a nearby stinger, but she froze when Hera raised the bolt she had in hand.

"Don't," she said. "I will take no pleasure in destroying you."

Aphrodite's mind reeled, and all she was able to do was laugh when she put it all together. "You orchestrated it all, didn't you?"

Hera bowed. "Everything from giving The Fox access to Olympus to making sure everyone drank from the wine I poisoned. Though that last part was messier than I'd have liked. Dionysus, predictable as always, insisted I finish the first goblet, so I had to bring along a little antidote. Other than that, I think it all went flawlessly, don't you?"

Aphrodite sighed with defeat. "Why would you do this to us?"

"Because I refuse to suffer any more of Zeus's empty promises," she said, her words holding more venom than all of Euryale's vipers combined.

"And because of that, you'd free Typhon and destroy the world?"

"I'm not freeing that monster. You saw what you were meant to see, nothing more. When I realized you and the gorgon were headed to Mount Etna, what better way to put you in a panic than to give you the full tour of the mountain?"

"Panic for what?"

Hera raised an eyebrow. "Are you truly that stupid?"

Aphrodite's face paled. "To get in here…"

"I knew you weren't that dumb," Hera said. "I can hardly reign with these available to anyone who wants them."

"You'll start a civil war," Aphrodite said.

Hera shook her head and she lowered the bolt. "Hephaestus will finish the axe, and he doesn't need my crown to do it. When that's mine, no one will be able to take the throne from me. Peace will reign, and that cheating bastard of a husband of mine won't even dare glance at another woman." Hera paused a moment as her anger faded. When she continued, her voice felt soft, almost motherly. "I have gone to great lengths to ensure no one was hurt, Zeus and Athena included. Well, at least not any more than could be helped. Join me, Aphrodite. Join us, and this will be over without further need of bloodshed."

"I'm no fool. I heard Typhon's words with my own ears," she said. "We saw the marks on his chains, the pieces of metal on his fur. He practically told us he'd be free by the end of today."

"And you believed him?" Hera asked. "He'll say anything to win servants, to find the weak and use them to set himself free. Trust me on this, Aphrodite. I'm the one who is in charge. No one else. Now do the smart thing and pledge your fidelity. We both know you're far too weak to stop me."

"Even if I am, Ares is not. Neither is Poseidon and Artemis. They'll never let you complete that axe."

"You might have a point if I hadn't managed to drug them both already," Hera said. "They'll wake when I want them to, when I can control the encounter to my desire."

Aphrodite had no retort, and all she could do was balk. Where was Euryale? Why hadn't the gorgon come like she'd said she would? How could she possibly stand up to Hera on her own? Those questions fostered a deluge of doubt in her soul, and though she felt herself wavering, Aphrodite refused to listen to Hera any further. "I'll never join you," she said, steeling herself for what was sure to come.

Hera raised the bolt of lightning. "Be sure of yourself, child. What you say next will determine whether I welcome you into my reign with open arms or I drag your charred body through my kingdom for all to see."

"I've made my decision. I will not betray Zeus."

"So be it."

With that, Hera attacked.

Chapter Stripped

Euryale shot forward.

The gorgon closed the distance between her hiding spot and Hera faster than any black mamba striking its prey. She'd hoped Alex would've already been here with Ares, but that was a luxury the Fates hadn't granted her. Before Hera could fully let go of the lightning bolt, Euryale slammed into her, wrapping one arm around the goddess's waist while the other caught the throwing arm around the elbow.

Hera's attack flew to the side, and the bolt of lightning carved a chunk out of one of the sandstone pillars. As it did, Euryale coiled herself around the Queen of Olympus, trying her damnedest to squeeze Hera into submission.

"You'll have to do better than that," Hera growled. With one hand, she clawed at Euryale's face and gouged her eyes, and with the other, she let fly a ball of dark magic at Aphrodite, who barely had the wit and reflexes to get out of the way.

"You traitor. You ought to be the one cursed a thousand times over," Euryale snarled. Her tail completed its fourth lap around Hera's midsection and legs, and she then threw herself backward to pull Hera off balance.

The move worked, exceedingly well, in fact. The two crashed down on the hard floor, and Euryale felt recent wounds split open. Her back and sides warmed as her skin grew sticky from blood.

"You should've stayed away, gorgon," Hera said. Her eyes narrowed as she started an incantation that no doubt was meant to wipe Euryale from existence.

The goddess didn't get but two words out before Euryale grabbed her head and forced her to look into the gorgon's eyes.

Hera grit her teeth, and as her skin began to harden, she snarled. "Your curse is mine. *Elepicus theokles hellisa!*"

Euryale's scales vanished. The vipers atop her head shrank into locks of golden-brown hair. Her tail disappeared, and a pair of slim, naked legs took its place.

"What's the matter, Euryale?" Hera asked with a cackle as she shoved her off. "Isn't this what you always wanted? To be 'normal' again?"

"I'll stop you just the same," Euryale said, though her voice wavered with each word.

She tried to strike Hera with a fist, but the goddess easily caught it, and with a simple twist, she locked Euryale's arm painfully against her side. "As old as you are, you're a stupid thing," Hera said. She threw a glance at Aphrodite, and just in time, too. The Goddess of Love had snatched one of Zeus's stingers and had it up and ready.

"Let her go!" Aphrodite yelled, launching the bolt.

The lightning crackled through the air. Hera twisted a split second faster than it came, and it passed harmlessly by.

"Pathetic," Hera said. "How you honestly thought you could take on Typhon is beyond me. I should've let you try so I didn't have to deal with you myself."

"Except you still haven't dealt with me," Euryale said.

Hera snapped her attention to the former gorgon. Euryale had plucked the lightning bottle from the goddess's satchel, and before Hera could react, she smashed it into the goddess's face.

With a thunderous boom, the room exploded in white. Euryale flew off of Hera and rolled until her body hit one of the weapon racks. Wisps of smoke rose from a dozen different places on her body, and her clothes were little more than charred tatters. Her skin was an array of Lichtenberg figures that spanned across her chest and ran down each limb and up her neck. The gorgon tried to push herself up, but between the weakness in her muscles and the pain coursing through her body, she could do little more than flop on to her side and twitch uncontrollably.

Hera groaned and staggered to her feet. The Queen of Olympus glared at Euryale and shot daggers of hate from her eyes. "Athena's wrath is nothing compared to mine."

Euryale's chest tightened to the point that it felt as if an elephant had brought a few friends and decided to use her as a park bench. Her head swam, and her vision blurred. Somewhere in the mess of color and forms, she saw Aphrodite come between her and her adversary.

"Surrender," Aphrodite said, lightning bolt firmly gripped in hand. Though Euryale had never seen it in the goddess before, Aphrodite seemed every bit as fierce as her sister, Athena, could be. This was something the former gorgon was ever grateful for.

"You think—" Hera started.

Aphrodite interrupted her by letting fly with the bolt. It sizzled through the air, striking Hera square in the heart. The goddess flew back and struck a pillar before collapsing in a smoldering heap.

What happened next, Euryale wasn't certain. Consciousness all but slipped from her. Curses flew in both directions. More lightning, too. When it was over, Euryale had the vague awareness that her lungs were barely moving the air around her, and her skin felt numb and distant.

Aphrodite appeared. The goddess pressed her fingers into Euryale's neck before leaning her ear close to the gorgon's face and lightly slapping her cheeks with panicked hands. "You're tougher than this," the goddess said. "Get up!"

Euryale managed to bat her hands away as Aphrodite tried to lift her. "Let me rest a moment."

"There's no time for that," Aphrodite said. "You're a mess."

Euryale's head cleared a touch, and she managed a feeble nod. "I know."

"No, you don't," Aphrodite said. "You're dying. You're not a monster anymore...not that you ever were."

Euryale managed a weak smile. Her eyes darted to each side, hoping that perhaps in her last few seconds, she might catch a glimpse of what she now looked like in a reflection somewhere. Her heart fluttered, and she realized the number of beats it had left could be counted on one hand. Summoning the last bit of strength she had, Euryale reached up and grabbed Aphrodite by the back of her head and pulled her close.

"Typhon's still coming," Euryale whispered. "It's a double cross. You've got to finish this."

"No," Aphrodite said, feeling her throat tighten. "We're finishing this together."

Euryale's grip weakened, and her hand fell.

Chapter Reunited with Alex

Aphrodite looked up at the sounds of approaching footsteps right as Alex and Ares bounded into the vault. Ares skidded to a stop, but Alex nearly fell over, clutching his heart when his eyes found his wife's body.

"Euryale!" Alex shouted, sprinting forward. He dropped to his wife's side, and with one arm around her back, he lifted her up to him. Her lifeless head flopped back, and vacant eyes stared at the far wall. Nothing he did changed any of it. Not the strokes to her cheeks or the tears falling from his face.

Shaking to the point where he barely had control, Alex set her down, fumbled to put his hands on her chest, and then started doing compressions. His palms drove down, fifteen times in all. Then he pinched her nose, put his mouth to hers, and blew air into her lungs.

The cycle repeated again. And again. And again.

Ribs cracked, and still he continued, a blubbering mess as he tried to count. "One...two...three...four..."

Aphrodite watched, speechless. Her heart broke for the man, and she didn't know what to say, didn't know what she could say. The only thing she knew for certain was that she couldn't help but feel partly responsible. Had she acted faster, fought smarter, this might have never happened.

"Alex," Aphrodite whispered.

Alex kept going, kept trying to save his wife. "You never gave up on me, damn you. I'm not giving up on you." But even as he spoke those words, his rhythm slowed and eventually stopped. "Euryale, come on," he whispered. "We've got to get home."

Alex picked up his wife's hand and brushed it against his cheek. "I need you. Aison and Cassandra need you. You can't leave us."

"I'm so sorry, Alex," Aphrodite said, but her words elicited no response.

Alex pawed at Euryale's hands and kissed the backs of them over and over before collapsing on her in a heap.

Aphrodite put a gentle hand on his back. "I want you to know—she would want you to know above all else—she loved you greatly."

Those last words broke Alex down to the core. No one said anything, nor moved a muscle, until Jessica burst in on the scene, out of breath, with Tickles by her side. Her jaw dropped at the sight of it all. "What happened?"

Aphrodite swallowed hard. "She happened," Aphrodite said with venom, pointing a finger at the knocked-out Hera. "She killed Euryale, drugged everyone, and backstabbed us all."

"Hera?" Jessica asked. "Why?"

Aphrodite recounted what had taken place. When she finished, Ares' face burned bright. He marched over to Hera, fists at his side. "Wake up!" he demanded. "Wake up so you can watch me cave in your skull!"

"No," Aphrodite said forcefully. "We don't have time for this. We have to stop Typhon from getting loose."

Ares' brow furrowed. "But you said she said—"

"I know what she said. That doesn't mean she wasn't lying, and it doesn't mean that Typhon still isn't orchestrating everything."

"You can't leave her here alone, that's for sure," Jessica said.

Aphrodite glanced across the room and pointed to the net that hung on the far wall. "Ares, stick her in that."

"Gladly," he said, doing as told. "We should toss her into the River Acheron. Let her suffer for the rest of eternity."

Aphrodite rose and took a deep breath. "No. Right now, we have to get that axe back. We can mourn and seek justice later."

Ares drove a fist into the palm of his hand. "Yes. War. That is what I need."

"Good, because that's exactly what you and Alex need to do," she said. "Go to Mount Etna and get that axe. Whatever army they throw at you, you make sure you throw one ten times bigger back."

"And what army do we have?" asked Ares.

"Alex," Aphrodite said as she tapped him on the shoulder to get his attention. "Did you get Hades' scepter?"

Alex cleared his eyes. His voice was weak and shaky, but at least he was answering. "Yeah. It's back in my chariot."

"Good, then use it," she said. "Make us the biggest army you can and storm that mountain."

Alex shook his head. "I...I don't think I can. I've got to find her. I've got to get her back."

Aphrodite took both sides of his face in her hands. "Listen to me, Alex," she said. "We have to stop Typhon. Euryale would want you to stop Typhon. Don't let her death be in vain."

"But maybe I can rescue her from the shores of Acheron before Kharon ferries her across...before she loses all her memories..."

Aphrodite dug her nails into his skin. Not hard enough to draw blood, but enough to get his attention. "You don't have that kind of sway with Kharon."

"I'm not leaving my wife!"

"Alex, your children's future depends on you and Ares going to Mount Etna. Do you understand?"

Alex started to argue, but he quickly cut himself off. "Yeah. I understand."

With a sigh of relief, Aphrodite let him go. As terrible as everything felt, as gut-wrenching as it was to see Alex still clinging to Euryale's body, a new, strange feeling took root in Aphrodite's soul—a good feeling. It took her a moment to figure out what it was. It was a feeling of importance and purpose.

"Is there truly nothing we can do for her?" asked Ares.

"We can do nothing, but that doesn't mean someone else can't," she replied.

"Who?"

"Cronus," Aphrodite replied. "I'll take her body to Nyx. With luck, she, in turn, will take her to Cronus. Even if he's sleeping, time bends to his will, and perhaps we can get him to bring her back."

"Cronus? Are you mad? If he wakes, he'll devour us all."

Aphrodite's gaze settled on the floor for a few moments as she carefully turned her plan over in her head. After a few beats, she exhaled slowly. "I know, but we need her. We're not enough to outsmart Typhon on our own, and her gaze may be the difference in victory or defeat."

Ares grumbled. "This is insane."

"Ares, I owe her. We owe her," she said. "She risked siding with us when Typhon offered her the world. I can't let such loyalty go unrewarded."

"We should work on waking the others, too," Jessica said.

"Do you know how?" Aphrodite asked.

Jessica shook her head. "No, but Hera has an antidote somewhere. Surely we can find it. Or at least recreate it."

Aphrodite drummed her fingers on her hips. The woman had a point, but whether or not the antidote was made already was far from a certainty. Still, finding it was worth a try.

"You have a point," Aphrodite said. "Scour her home and temple here in Olympus. Find that antidote or make it if you must. Once it's ours, wake the others, starting with Zeus. If I don't make it back with Euryale, Dad will be our only hope."

Chapter Nyx

"Things were so much easier when I hated you," Aphrodite grunted, doing her best to keep Euryale's corpse on the chariot as she flew. If there was a silver lining to recent events, however faint, it was that she'd managed to find one of Apollo's chariots on Olympus in short order, and the pair of Akhal-Tekes who pulled her along were ones who liked her.

As the goddess made for the Cave of Nyx, she glanced to the sky and realized her travels were taking far longer than she'd wished. With that thought, Aphrodite cracked the reins, driving her horses faster and faster.

The ocean beneath her gave way to a dark fog, and soon reality itself turned to gloom. The wind carried the scent of cherry blossoms and lavender, and she felt her mind numb, and her skin grow distant. Her vision started to blur, and a gentle, low-key hum filled her ears.

"Sweet love on a stick, I hate limbo," Aphrodite muttered. She took a moment to vigorously rub her shoulders to put some much-needed feeling and warmth back into them.

The Goddess of Love squinted. Off to the side and in the distance, she spied a long, mountainous island. Given the gloom of where she was, it appeared little more than a dark shade against a slightly different shade of dark. No mortal would ever have a hope of finding it, but thankfully, Aphrodite was no mortal.

A few minutes later, she landed the chariot atop a cliff overlooking the waters. Unseen waves crashed against the rocky shore, and Aphrodite quickly got out, created a floating ball of light so she could see what she was doing, and tried to pick Euryale up.

Instead of scooping the gorgon's body into her arms, Aphrodite lost her balance and fell back. She struck her head on a mossy rock, and Euryale crashed into her chest a moment later, knocking the wind from her.

"Would it have killed you to be a little lighter?" Aphrodite groaned as she pushed Euryale off. "Actually, don't answer that. Actually, do answer that. I need you to stop being dead."

"And to what do I owe the pleasure of your company, dear child?" said a quiet, refined voice from behind.

Aphrodite craned her head. Looming over her stood the island's keeper, Nyx. There was no mistaking this being of unparallel power and beauty. She had pearl-white skin that was wrapped in robes darker than any moonless night. Equally dark wings folded across her back, and Nyx regarded Aphrodite with eyes blacker than any demon's heart. Around the goddess's head floated an aureole of inky mist, and the aroma of dreams permeated the air about her.

Aphrodite scrambled to her feet, elated and terrified she'd found Nyx so quickly. However, when she was upright, she noticed she was no longer standing at the cliff top, but rather in the middle of a forest composed of wiry trees and cloaked in fog. Near her feet, a small fire crackled, the flames waning and the coals barely glowing.

"Where—"

"Are you?" Nyx finished. "You are at the edge of reality, child. Had you any sense, the very thought of coming here would have sent you fleeing in terror."

Aphrodite took in a breath and steadied herself as best she could. The world around her started to spin, and the ground beneath her feet shifted. She jumped with fright when she felt hands grasp her legs, but saw none when she looked down. Something flipped by her hair, and then she caught sight of something large, something sinister, coming at her from the corner of her eye. Again, Aphrodite spun, lashing out her hands in a feeble strike, only to be met with darkness and cold air.

"You flail like a madwoman," Nyx said. Her voice came from everywhere at once, yet the goddess was nowhere to be seen.

"Stop it," Aphrodite said, adopting a wider stance with her legs. "I will not be toyed with. I am the daughter of Zeus and Dione. You will bear their wrath if you keep this up."

"Adorable," said the voice. "The Olympian thinks she can threaten me."

Gale-force winds blasted Aphrodite's face, causing her to turn away and close her eyes. When they abated, she dared to look. Again, the scene had shifted, and now she was standing on the shore of a lake so calm, it might as well have been made of glass, even with the waterfall that poured into it from nearby. Aphrodite would've spent more time trying to work out the mechanics of such an oddity, had she not been on her knees inside a low cage made from bone and copper wire.

Nyx sat a few feet away, roasting a marshmallow on a bamboo spit over a cheery fire. "Would you like one?" she asked, offering the golden-brown delight.

"No, I want you—"

"Shh, little pet," Nyx said, raising a finger to her lips. "Wanting is noisy and rude." She then offered the marshmallow once again. "Take. It'll soothe that irritated psyche of yours. Bonding over desserts can do wonders for a relationship."

Aphrodite hesitated, but not seeing the harm, reached out from her cage and took it. The treat felt light and crispy in her fingers and tasted positively delicious in her mouth. Once she had swallowed, she dared to speak again as Nyx said and did nothing else. "Please, I don't have a lot of time," the goddess said as her desperation started to get the better of her. "I need your help. I need to see Cronus."

Nyx put another marshmallow on the spit. "Ah, so that's it. I wondered why you brought the corpse of a gorgon—well, a former gorgon. Even if she's much prettier now than when she had her snakes, her body isn't exactly a customary housewarming gift, is it?" Nyx cocked her head and shrugged. "Or maybe it is? It's been a while since I've played on Earth. Do the mortals give each other dead gorgons now? I suppose Perseus did start the trend. Perhaps it caught on."

"No, she died fighting Hera, which is why I need Cronus to bend time and make her whole again," Aphrodite said.

"Curse and all?"

Aphrodite nodded. "Especially the curse."

"So she's not a gift. Pity," Nyx replied with a shrug. "I think I might have come to like it if she were. Tell me, Goddess of Love, what's so important about such an ugly thing that you'd risk your very existence coming here? You may as well have tried storming the home of the Moirae. I hear the Fates grant a favor once in a while..."

"Hephaestus is about to usurp the throne," Aphrodite said. As the words left her mouth, anger boiled within. As she went on, her hands tightened around the bars of her cage. "Please, I need to stop him."

"And what of the other Olympians? If they cannot defend their house, I see no reason that they should keep it," Nyx replied. The goddess's eyes darkened, something Aphrodite would have never thought possible up until then. "Zeus has harried my children, and they did nothing to stop him," Nyx growled. "If anything, they should be glad I'm not the one who's come to put an end to their rule."

"The other Olympians are drugged, save Athena, who is imprisoned. I'll never wake them before Hephaestus seizes the throne."

Nyx stretched her wings before interlocking her fingers and stretching her arms in front of her. "Tell me, pet, why do you think so little of yourself?"

"I...I don't know what you mean."

"You come here to restore Euryale, sister of Medusa and Stheno, as if she's the one needed to stop Hephaestus. Surely between the two of you, she is the lesser."

Aphrodite shook her head and felt her throat tighten, and her eyes glisten. "She is only the lesser in the eyes of the foolish."

"Maybe. Maybe not. I do wonder, though, where your infamous hubris has gone. Or perhaps you've finally found loyalty outside of Ares?" Nyx popped a marshmallow into her mouth and smiled. "Mmmm. These are divine. It's a shame they took so long to invent."

Aphrodite, frustrated, groaned loudly. "Will you help or not? Surely you don't want to see the Earth in ruin."

"Honestly, I'm not that interested in it to begin with," she said. "Maybe it could use a little remodeling."

"This isn't a remodeling! And if Hephaestus frees Typhon, it will be even worse!"

Nyx smirked. "Is he still causing trouble? I swear, that's one child who never did grow up, or nephew as the case may be. Let Typhon have his fun if he likes. He knows better than to bother me, as you should have."

Aphrodite fell back against the cage, feeling utterly defeated. "Why don't you care?"

"Why should I? One little world matters not. You and your Olympians, so full of yourselves that you can't even begin to look beyond your myopic views and consider the grand cosmos that surrounds you all. The universe spans far greater than you will ever know. In it swirl places that you cannot dream, some a thousand times more beautiful than even you, others a thousand times more frightful than Typhon. They take eons to form and are swallowed by stars or ripped apart by forces you've never heard of in the blink of an eye. What happens for a moment on one of these worlds, even a very unique one, is of no interest to me. Though I suppose it has provided a little conversation and insight into the mind of a lesser goddess."

Nyx pulled another marshmallow and put it over the fire. "Would you like another?"

Aphrodite shook her head and sighed. She'd never felt smaller in all her life. At least she had always been able to pretend to be on equal footing with Athena. There was no pretending here. Zeus had always been wary of Nyx—fearful even, even if he'd never admit it—and now she knew why. Nyx's power was beyond her comprehension.

Minutes dragged on, then an hour or two. She couldn't tell. The passage of time was beyond her grasp in this realm.

"She's a mother, you know," Aphrodite said, hoping that might grant even the tiniest of empathetic responses.

"Is she?" Nyx paused. The marshmallow she'd been carefully turning over the fire browned on one end and then started to char.

"She is! Give her a chance to see her children again! Give them a chance to see her!"

Nyx let the bamboo spit dip, and in a flash, the marshmallow was consumed in fire. "That...is something unexpected."

"Please. I beg of you. Help us. Help her."

Nyx grinned. "Very well, pet, though you may soon wish otherwise. I will take you to Cronus, but know this: a favor from him will cost a terrible price on you all."

Chapter Cronus Stirs

Alex and Ares stood side by side, ready for battle, while Tickles stalked a butterfly behind them.

Well, Ares was ready. Alex, trying to keep his mind off his wife's fate, desperately wished they could've had a month or twelve to prepare, get NATO on board, and maybe field a few nukes, too, just in case. Alas, that was a luxury they would not be afforded, and no amount of wishing would change that.

Flanking Alex and Ares on both sides were nearly five thousand men Alex had created, courtesy of Hades' scepter. He hadn't made an army since he'd squared off with Ares over a year ago, but the one he'd made this time was done easily enough, and Alex was glad he hadn't lost his touch. Accompanying those men idled twenty M26 Pershing tanks, straight from World War II (as Alex still kept his resurrections and creations from the time period, as he was most familiar with them), as well as three dozen 155mm Long Toms.

"How long do you think it'll take to get inside?" asked Alex. He lifted a pair of binoculars that hung around his neck and surveyed the mountain. "For that matter, where do we get in?"

Ares grunted and squinted his eyes. It took him a few seconds to reply, but when he did, he pointed to a spot about three-quarters of the way up. "There."

"Where?" Alex asked, trying to find what Ares was looking at. "I can't see anything. Are you sure?"

"Very."

Alex nervously rubbed his hands together. "Do you think they know we're coming?"

A whistling hiss filled the air, and though Alex should've realized what it meant, the significance of the noise was lost on him until one of his men yelled. "Incoming!"

The world around him exploded. Rocks and debris flew everywhere. Alex, flat on his stomach, crawled into a crater. Ares, on the other hand, bounded forward with unbridled enthusiasm. "Yes, Alex," he called back. "I think they know we're here!"

The world dissolved.

Aphrodite shook her head and rubbed her eyes, feeling as if she had recently awakened from a long slumber. She stood in another cave, or perhaps it was the same cave, it was hard to tell. She didn't possess a geology degree, and one rock wall looked the same as any other. At least she was out of her cage. So that was nice.

Lying in front of her was an old man with stringy gray hair who was wrapped in nothing but a thin, black sheet. His skin sagged off a withered frame that was laden with warts, but despite its ancient look, it still hinted at untold power beneath. The man slept, snoring loudly, with his head on a blue satin pillow and his hands tightly clutching a long scythe.

Nyx knelt by Cronus's side and gently stroked his head. "This is your last chance to turn back, goddess," she said. "Who you see before you is the most foul, cruel and bad-tempered deity you've ever set eyes on."

"I know. Zeus loves to recount how he saved the family from Cronus's hungry stomach."

"You have no idea," she said with a devilish grin. "Cronus didn't try and eat them as babies simply because he feared being overthrown by Zeus. That was a convenient excuse to satisfy his near-insatiable hunger. The truth is, he has a malicious side larger than the heavens."

"I'll be careful."

"No, you'll be dead," Nyx said with a smile. "Not even your 'immortality' can save you from him. Time, goddess, will devour you all. It's only a matter of when."

Aphrodite took a moment to steel herself. She'd come this far already, and to turn away now would reinforce what everyone already thought of her. When it mattered most, she would be the first to run and save her pretty face. Perhaps that had been true before, but not anymore. If Euryale, an exiled gorgon, could take a stand against the Queen of Olympus, Aphrodite could at the very least whisper to a sleeping god. "If it's only a matter of when, then I'm hardly risking anything, am I?"

"All things in perspective, I suppose," Nyx replied with a short nod. "You're a clever pet. Does this mean you're ready?"

"I am," Aphrodite said.

Nyx's lips curled as she gently shook Cronus's shoulder. "Easy, dear," she said as the old god stirred. "There's someone here to see you."

"Mmmm...that's a lovely caterpillar you have," he said, shifting around. "Does he wear a hundred chitons or just one long one?"

"Nephew, listen to my voice," Nyx said softly into his ear. "Aphrodite is here. She's brought you a gorgon."

Cronus lurched upright. His eyes stayed closed, and he leaned heavily on his scythe to keep from falling over. "Who brought a what, what?"

Nyx glanced to Aphrodite. "This is as awake as I'll let him be. Speak, and speak fast."

Aphrodite stepped forward, reminded herself not to use Zeus's name, and tried to sound as strong as she could. "I, Aphrodite, Goddess of Love, daughter of Dione or the foam of the sea, depending on who you want to believe, have come to ask that you'd restore Euryale, sister of Medusa, daughter of Phorcys and Ceto, to life."

Cronus snorted. His head jerked left and right, and he smacked his lips. "A gorgon caterpillar? Now I've heard it all. Did someone squish it?"

"She was killed fighting Hera."

Cronus perked. His eyelids fluttered a fraction of an inch, but before they could fully open, Nyx rubbed his back and gave a soft shush in his ear. "Hera?" he repeated. Cronus stretched and yawned before settling back onto his rocky bed. "Euryale fought an Olympian? That would be funny if it happened again," he said with a soft chuckle. "Very funny."

Aphrodite didn't know what to say. It also seemed as if Nyx wasn't sure how to take his reaction either. "Why is that funny?" asked Aphrodite.

A mischievous grin formed on Cronus's face. "Imagine a gorgon seated on the throne of Olympus."

"She's not—" Aphrodite caught herself before arguing any further. "Will you help her, then?"

Cronus pawed the air. "Bring me the gorgon, and we shall ask what she wants. And tell the caterpillar I want more peanuts. But not the purple ones. They taste like sadness."

Alex and Ares had very different views on war. While Alex saw it as something one should only engage in as a last resort—especially when the gods were concerned—Ares thought of it as a pastime one should indulge in at every opportunity, no matter the reason.

Threat to Olympus? War. Threat to his love? War. It was Monday instead of Friday? War. Couldn't get the fitted sheet folded properly? That was worth at least two wars.

Even though Alex had always known and seen this stark contrast between the two, he was still amazed at the gleefulness Ares had while bounding over the terrain and rushing headlong into their enemy. Bullets nicked at his skin, and explosions pelted him with rock and shrapnel, yet the god took it all in stride. In the few short moments since Typhon's hidden army had started to shell Alex's men, Ares had sprinted nearly five hundred yards across open terrain to get to the good parts—the smashy, rippy parts, as Ares had described it. And in doing so, the god had drawn nearly all of the incoming fire, which Alex was now eternally grateful for.

Tickles, too, was having a much better time than Alex was. The chimera lazily circled the battlefield, patiently waiting for an opportunity to present itself. When it did, the monster would dive through the air, scoop up a helpless monster, sting another, and perhaps bite through the neck of a third, before rocketing up once more. There, what creature he happened to snag would either be devoured or simply dropped on whatever rocky outcropping happened to be six hundred feet below.

"Where's our counter artillery?" Alex asked into his radio, keeping his body flat on the ground.

"Firing for effect now," one of the artillerymen called back.

"Good," Alex replied. "I want whatever they're fielding utterly destroyed in the next minute. We're moving up."

"Copy."

Alex looked to his left where one of his company commanders lay. He was a muscular, hardened fellow with stubble hair all over his head and weathered, leathery skin that had baked in the sun for years. Had the man not been resurrected, Alex would've suggested the guy see a dermatologist to check for skin cancer and all. Then again, maybe he should anyway, after this was finished. The formerly dead still needed to be proactive in their after-afterlife, didn't they?

"Take alpha company up the left flank. I'll get bravo to hold them down here," he ordered. "Third and fourth battalions will move up the right."

"On it, mate," the man said. He then jumped up and sprinted away, hunched down the entire time as he relayed the orders to his platoons.

Alex leaped to his feet a moment later and charged forward. He turned over his shoulder as he did, and using his M1 Garand, he waved for his men to follow. "Come on, you devil dogs, do you want to live forever?"

Euryale, having waited for what felt like an eternity to get to the head of the line, squared off with Kharon, Ferryman of the Unseen, along the banks of the River Acheron. Behind her, a slew of shadowy forms waited patiently for their turn with the ferryman while countless others wandered the riverbank, skipping stones or meandering about.

None of them held Euryale's interest. She had one goal, and one goal only: to get home.

"I'm no mortal," she said. "Take me across."

Kharon scowled, further disfiguring his already disfigured face. "You know the rules," he said, slowly enunciating every syllable. "If you wish to cross the Acheron, it will be one obol."

"That fare is for the dead!"

"That fare is for the not alive. No exceptions," he replied. His hands tightened around the pole for his skiff.

"I am the daughter of Phorcys!"

"Minor correction, you are the not-alive daughter of Phorcys," he said. "Had you still been immortal, this would be a different conversation. But you're not. So we're having this one. In fact, you should be glad I'm not charging you three obols."

"Three?"

"Yes, three. Your husband is a liar and a robber and owes me two."

Euryale growled. She wondered what she could do to force her way across. But seeing how she was without a body, and her spirit form had reverted to her much less-snakelike figure with slender legs, luxurious hair (which was almost worth dying for, if she were being honest), and curves that Alex would no doubt go stupid over, it probably didn't pack much of a punch. And it certainly didn't pack near as much of a punch as her former gorgon self would have. "I will pay you a hundred times what you make in a day once I'm on the other side," she said. "Please, take me across. My children need me."

Kharon sighed heavily. "Look, this is very simple. You can't be hit with a billion volts of lightning and expect to live," he said. "And if you're not living, you don't get to cross without the proper fare. I won't repeat myself again. Pay or stand aside."

"I'm getting out of here."

"If you say."

"You'll see," she said, crossing her arms in defiance and trying to reassure herself of her fate. "I'll think of something."

"Only if that something means you'll come up with one obol."

"Yes," Euryale told herself. "A few moments from now, all of this will be over."

Kharon shrugged. "You'll be here awhile."

Euryale glared. She knew he was right. Worse, because he was right, she knew she'd never see her family again, and it wouldn't be long before her memories faded and she became like the other shades along the river, witless and clueless as to everything that happened about them.

"I'm done being nice," she said, approaching the ferryman.

Kharon took a step back and readied his pole as if he were about to go into combat with Ares himself, but before he could do anything else, his eyes grew large and the pole fell from his hands.

At first, Euryale didn't know what had elicited such a reaction. Confused, she glanced down in time to see what was left of her spiritual self blow away like chaff in the wind.

A voice boomed.

"You are a broken one."

Euryale opened her eyes and was shocked at what she saw. She stood on the peak of a snow-covered mountain. Stars more numerous than grains of sand on a beach twinkled above while dark clouds swirled beneath her on all sides. From those clouds rose a gargantuan, wild-looking and completely naked man with flowing gray hair and muscles that looked as if they could crack open a mountain. In one hand he held a scythe as large as he, and with his free hand, he scooped Euryale up and brought her close to his face.

"Cronus?" she asked, uttering the only name that seemed to fit.

"Yes, that is I," he said. "I wonder, gorgon, would you rather live or rather be fed?"

"Be fed? I don't follow," Euryale said, trying not to grimace too much at the god's horrid breath.

"To me!" he said with a hearty laugh. "My belly has room for you."

"In that case, as long as it's up to me, I'd rather not be eaten."

Cronus set her back on the mountain top and patted her head. "I thought as much. Your friend Aphrodite would like you to not be eaten as well. Did you bring my caterpillar?"

"Your—" Euryale stopped when she felt something crawl across the back of her neck. Gently, she plucked a bright green caterpillar with red and yellow spots off of her skin and presented it to him. "This caterpillar?"

Cronus beamed and scooped it up before setting it on his shoulder. "Yes. Funny little thing. Keeps changing back from being a butterfly. Can't make him stay that way. Likes eating leaves, I suppose."

"Are we...are we in your dreams?" Euryale asked, unable to think of any other explanation. After all, as far as she knew, Cronus was still sleeping soundly in Nyx's cave, and she'd heard tales of people and gods being sucked into the dreams of one another. Not to mention, the surreal nature to everything and the fact that Cronus wasn't out destroying all of creation led her to no other conclusion.

"Dreams? What are dreams?" he asked. "As if one reality is less than another."

Euryale nodded, thinking it neither wise nor fruitful to dispute the point. "You said Aphrodite wants me to live?"

"I did, and I can give you that gift if you like." Cronus paused as he started to chuckle, and it took him a moment to recompose himself as that chuckle grew into a full belly laugh. "In fact, gorgon, I would love to give you that gift—that gift among one other."

"What would that be?"

Cronus closed his eyes and breathed deep through his nose before gently placing his pointer finger on Euryale's head. A tingling sensation ran across her scalp before burrowing deep into her skull. Memories flashed by, and she soon felt as if she were watching a play detailing every moment of her life.

"Yes...yes..." he said as memories of recent events with Hera came to light. "You were strong. Possibly even stronger than they could handle, had Hera not reversed what she'd done. Your spirit, your strength, is precisely what I want and need."

"What does this have to do with you?"

Cronus pulled his finger away and leaned in close. His eyes were bright, and he wore a toddler's grin. "Me? No. Not me. You. I will restore you, gorgon, and bind your curse to your body so strongly that no Olympian can strip it for you. Once again, you will be able to petrify even the gods, and when you're seated over all of

Olympus, I shall laugh and laugh and laugh as Zeus, mighty Zeus, heels at the foot of a monster."

"I don't want to rule," Euryale said. "All I want to do is to stop Typhon and see my family again."

The lightness in Cronus's eyes faded, but he stayed close and held his grin. "I don't care what you want, gorgon. You can serve my will, or you can satiate my stomach."

Euryale tensed. She hated everything about this situation, but what choice did she have? She had to stop Typhon, and she had to hold her children and feel Alex's embrace again.

"You make a persuasive argument," she said, breathing deep and trying not to think about the potential consequences of this deal as much as she could. "I'll do as you wish."

"You bring joy to this old titan's face, gorgon. Thank you."

With that, Cronus placed a single finger in the middle of Euryale's chest, and in low tones, he spoke the deepest magic any being had ever said since the beginning of time.

Chapter Goatman

Jessica ran through the front doors of Hera's abode. The moment she crossed the threshold, she nearly tripped over her own two feet as she had the fleeting thought that she'd be turned into a two-legged cow that would be dropped into the middle of hungry wolves for trespassing.

Those thoughts, however, were washed away as the severity of what was happening drove her forward. She raced across the inner courtyard, darted around the five peacocks that strutted about, and bolted into the goddess's great room. If there was ever a place to start looking for the antidote, that's where it would be. She could only hope that her initial hunch was correct and that Hera had the antidote somewhere in her home.

Sadly, there wasn't a lot in the room that pointed to an antidote. Seated around a large, round golden table were four expertly crafted klismoi. The curved chairs, made from gold and silver, had elegant white pillows to sit on but appeared as if they'd never been used at all. The table, likewise, had not a thing on it, not even a mote of dust. And now that Jessica thought about it, nothing else around did, either. In fact, not only was there no dust, but there was nothing even remotely out of place.

The shelves had a few small sculptures on them, and each one was meticulously placed to take up the space available perfectly. The table had a single oil lamp in the center, and nothing more. The lamp, made from brass, had its oil filled to the top, and its wick had either been freshly replaced or carefully cut, as not one charred fiber could be seen at its top. At the other side of the room were dozens of shelves filled with bound scrolls, each carefully stacked on the other, and not one sticking up from the rest or pushed too far in. To her right, on a marble pedestal, stood a beautiful bust of Hera.

Hera, apparently, had a lot of time on her hands. Or at least demanded someone else keep her home to absolute perfection.

"Man, you've got one hell of a good maid," Jessica said, looking around and wondering where she should start tossing the place. A thought crossed her mind and she bit down on her lower lip as she gave it a few turns. "Or a resentful one."

Jessica spun around and darted back to the courtyard. She went left and then ended up going in the other direction when the door there yielded the kitchen and not the servant's quarters as she'd hoped. Two doors and a short hall later, she found exactly what she was looking for: a servant in the servant's quarters.

The quarters themselves were big enough to hold a small wooden bed filled with straw, a clay pot full of water, a small chest in the corner, and a satyr with curly brown hair and stubby horns sitting on a rickety chair.

"You! Goat man!" Jessica said, pointing an excited finger. "You take care of this place, right?"

The satyr jumped up. His brow raised and he spoke with a rushed, worried voice. "Who are you? You can't be here! You'll mess the house! The Fates only know how much dirt you've tracked in already!"

Jessica laughed. "I knew it!"

"Knew what?"

"You're Hera's slave."

The satyr looked away and shrugged. "That's an awfully strong word. It's not that bad."

"It isn't? Well, what would you call it?"

"A chance to prove my worth," he said, puffing out his chest. "Show the world what I'm capable of."

Jessica put her hands on her hips. "Right," she said, not believing one bit he was being sincere. "Look, I don't have a lot of time. I need to wake up Zeus. Show me where Hera's pet project was."

The satyr hesitated. "I don't know what you're talking about."

"Yes, you do."

"No, I don't."

"You know everything in this house."

"And? That's what a good servant is for."

"Or one worked to death," Jessica said, giving a half grin. "And if you haven't heard, she's in jail now—or where the gods toss each other after getting caught committing treason."

There was a faint twinkle of hope in the satyr's eyes, but as quick as it came, he straightened and blinked. "This is a test, isn't it?"

"It's not."

"I'm certain it is."

"Stop. It's not."

"That's precisely what you want me to think."

Jessica groaned. "Think this is a test? Okay. Follow me."

Jessica marched out of the room, paused to throw an I-dare-you-not-to-follow glare, and then went back to the great room. Once the satyr caught up, she leaned casually on Hera's bust. When it wobbled and the servant nearly had a heart attack racing over to keep it upright, she held up a finger. "Hang on a second," she said. "Is that dirt I see?"

The satyr's eyes went wide, and he spun around. "Dirt? Where?"

Jessica toppled the bust with her elbow. It struck the ground with a heavy thud, sending fragments and white powder in all direction. "Oops," she said. "I'm such a klutz sometimes."

"So this isn't a test?" he asked warily.

Summoning lessons learned from her brother when they were kids, Jessica launched the gooiest, most revolting, least ladylike wad of spit she could muster and had it land right on one of Hera's pristine white pillows. "Nope," she said, feeling both proud and revolted at herself. "So if you want to help me stick it to her, that would be great."

The satyr grinned. "I might know something..."

Euryale gasped.

She rolled on a cold, rock floor only to be grabbed forcefully by the shoulder.

"Careful, gorgon," said a dark, feminine voice. "A little closer and you'll wake him."

Euryale twisted to see Nyx kneeling at her side with a finger pointed at the god who slept less than a foot away. Though her body was close, her tail lay even closer. Not even a pinky could slip between its rattle and Cronus's foot.

Euryale had barely pushed herself up when Aphrodite mauled the gorgon with an enormous hug. "Thank the Fates," she said with a huge sigh of relief. "He brought you back."

Euryale returned the embrace, though not with as much enthusiasm as Aphrodite had given her. "He did."

Aphrodite pulled away. "Don't get too excited or thank me or anything."

"I'm sorry. It's only that...well, that was very risky."

"I know. I'm the one who had to do it," she replied.

"And brave," Euryale added. When Aphrodite smiled, the gorgon tacked on what she should have led with. "Thank you."

"You're welcome," Aphrodite said. "I figured I owed you. So now we're even. So don't expect me to do this again. And don't you dare run around telling everyone what you made me do for you."

Euryale grinned. "What I made you do?"

"Yes. Blasting yourself with lightning and forcing me to come all the way out here with your smoking corpse," Aphrodite said. "I can't be that mad, I suppose. You did help capture Hera. I only wish we'd known she was the traitor sooner."

"I had my suspicions," Euryale said. When Aphrodite's face turned sour, the gorgon explained. "She's one of few strong enough to break Arachne's curse, not to mention unpetrify The Fox," Euryale said. "Hephaestus, as pointed out earlier, couldn't have been working alone, and Hera was the only other Olympian not drugged who I couldn't rule out. Furthermore, when I saw her last, what sparkled in her hair wasn't glitter. They were flecks of adamantine, which I didn't put together until after we'd gone through the mountain."

Aphrodite trembled, and when she responded, her voice bordered on a shriek. "Why didn't you tell me? I can't believe you'd let me walk right into her trap!"

"I had to. I'm sorry," Euryale replied. "I couldn't risk Hera even getting a whiff of our suspicions."

"Some plan," Aphrodite said. "I mean, after all that precaution, you still managed to get yourself killed."

"I know. I didn't intend for that to happen."

Aphrodite crossed her arms over her chest and huffed. "I suppose the bit with the crown was a lie, too."

Euryale shook her head. "No, it was the only theory I had that made sense if Hera turned out to be innocent."

"Since she's not, what's Typhon up to?"

"That depends."

"On?"

"On whether or not Hera was really working with him," Euryale replied. "If she was, then he likely wanted the lightning for himself, or at least, in her hands so no one could use it against him."

"I don't think Hera is that stupid," Aphrodite said. "She'd never side with him, no matter how much she hates Zeus."

"Agreed. So that leaves only one other option. Hera honestly didn't know Arachne and Hephaestus were working with Typhon, and thus she had no idea that the axe was being made to cut his chains."

"Which means what?"

"It means Typhon didn't need her crown to have it finished. He only needed her anywhere but Mount Etna so she wouldn't interfere with his release. I imagine that her being caught by us was one less loose end for him to deal with."

"That's what you meant by the double cross."

"Yes. A well-timed one at that."

The color drained from Aphrodite's face. "Then we're almost out of time, aren't we?"

"I'm afraid so."

Chapter Return to the Mountain

"They're fighting already," Aphrodite said, leaning over the side of her chariot as a ferocious battle between man and monster raged below. "Can you tell who's winning?"

Euryale squinted. Though she could pick out the general flow of things, she was hardly Sun Tzu. It seemed Alex and his men were doing a fine job. One might even say they were slowly winning. Or Ares was, at least.

Euryale watched as the God of War jumped up on a large boulder with a 30mm rotary cannon that he'd ripped from something in hand. He opened fire with it, first on the general firing line of Typhon's monsters, ripping them to bits, and then on what remained of the artillery pieces the monstrous horde fielded.

"Ares is having a lot of fun," the gorgon said with a heavy sigh and a forced smile.

"Is that bad?"

"He'll probably stay out there until everyone is dead," Euryale answered. "Which means it'll just be you and me inside the mountain, since I don't think we can wait for him to finish."

Aphrodite pressed her lips together. She didn't share her thoughts, though Euryale had a good guess what they were. She was probably trying to decide whether or not they could get Ares to abandon his big fight to steal back the labrys. The answer to that, of course, was a resounding no. "Well, you and I went in alone the first time," the goddess said. "We can do it again."

"At least we're not tied together," Euryale added with a half grin.

Aphrodite laughed and brought her chariot down in a wide, sweeping turn, taking care not to get too close to the battle. As she came around to the other side of the mountain, she cursed loudly and pulled up. The entrance they had used before was heavily guarded. Three concrete bunkers had been built around it, and a heavy steel door had been installed at the tunnel entrance as well. To top things off, fifty monsters of various grotesqueness stood outside, armed to the teeth and tentacle.

"That's not going to be easy to get by," Euryale said. "And if we fight them, we're likely to draw more."

"Why couldn't they just be stupid and leave this place open?" Aphrodite asked with a huff. "Would it kill them to cooperate with our plans for once?"

"Maybe there's another way in," Euryale said, looking around. She didn't see any, sadly, but she also knew at this point any others would be guarded as well. "Any ideas?"

Aphrodite held up a finger and arched her eyebrows. "I have one."

The satyr pushed on a small, unremarkable brick on an unremarkable portion of wall inside an unremarkable side room in Hera's otherwise extravagant temple. It sank back a few inches before a large section of the wall swung in, revealing a descending spiral staircase.

"Here you go," he said, stepping to the side and waving Jessica onward.

"What's down there?" she asked.

The satyr shrugged. "Never was allowed to see. Only a fluke I discovered it and was allowed to remain whole."

"What did she say when she found out?"

"Nothing," he said. "I drank myself into a stupor that left me comatose for a week. Naturally, when she came back, she thought it was someone else who'd disturbed things."

"That seems a little drastic," Jessica said.

"Not if you know Hera."

"You really didn't peek at all, though?"

The satyr shook his head. "I'm half goat, not half crazy. If she's got something that secretive tucked away, there's a reason, and Fates help you if she catches your eyes on any of it."

"Point taken," Jessica said.

With that, she trotted down the stairs, but not before having to pull the satyr along. Even if Hera was bound and jailed at this point, her threats still carried nearly their full weight. Thankfully, thoughts of revenge seemed to weigh more on the satyr's mind, and he accompanied her down. Jessica slowed her pace considerably as the lighting was poor, even with the oil lamp she'd pulled off the wall near the start. The last thing she wanted to do lose her footing on the narrow steps and tumble down a hundred stories.

A smoky, sweet smell filled the air and became more pungent as they descended. Once they reached the bottom, the source of the aroma was apparent. They'd entered a small lab with a few tables in the center that hadn't seen a decent cleaning in ten years, and scattered across those filthy tables were a slew of chopped roots and herbs, various glassware with various amounts of sludge inside, dozens of measuring devices, and three unlit burners. Along the walls were more shelves crammed with reagents, scrolls, and what could only be described as miscellaneous crap that served no apparent purpose other than to take up space.

"What a pig," Jessica said, shaking her head. "Is she always this bad?"

"Worse," the satyr replied, not showing the least bit of surprise at the state the lab was in.

Jessica shuddered. "Cripes. She must work her servants to death."

"If only we were that lucky," the satyr replied.

Jessica shuddered again. "Okay, well, let's see what we can do in here," she said. "And we better be quick. I don't know how much longer we have."

"This isn't going to work," Euryale said, looking herself over. She wore a very Hera-like illusion, courtesy of Aphrodite. It wasn't that physically she didn't look exactly like the Queen of Olympus, because she did. What bothered her was the fact that there was no way she could carry Hera's attitude. Her heart simply wasn't spiteful enough.

"It'll work," Aphrodite said, backing up a few paces and smiling with pride. "You're a dead ringer."

"They'll never believe Hera would stride up like this with a battle raging," Euryale said.

"They'll believe whatever you tell them to believe," Aphrodite replied. "You're Hera. Your word is law."

"Then you be her. I'll be you."

Aphrodite shook her head. "I'm not that good of an illusionist, sorry. One is all I can keep up before they start to fall apart."

Euryale sighed and rolled her shoulders back. "Fine. Let's go before I think myself out of this."

Euryale took the lead with Aphrodite a step behind. The entire time they approached, the gorgon tried to hype herself up as much as she could with an aura of superiority and disdain. These *things* they approached served her. They bowed to her. They would open the door or Fates help them, they'd never have a second's worth of peace for the next ten thousand years.

They rounded a nearby boulder and stepped into view. Monstrous creations jumped in surprise. A few readied their rifles and spears, but even more swatted said weapons to the ground in a hasty attempt to not bring a mass curse to them all. Euryale smirked. So far, so good.

She said not a word as she marched between the bunkers, and she didn't bother to look a single monster in the eye. She caught whispers in her ears, whispers that held immense surprise and questions as to why she wasn't inside and why she'd brought Aphrodite along, especially as a few had pointed out that the Goddess of Love had recently fought with Hephaestus in the forge.

To all their questions, doubts, and wonderment, Euryale didn't offer a single reaction or explanation. They were not her equal, she reminded herself. They deserved nothing from her but scorn and the occasional mercy, should they obey without question.

When she and Aphrodite got to the steel door that barred entry into the mountain, the gorgon stopped, crossed her arms, and tutted. "Well?" she demanded. "Why is this still shut?"

A nearby guard, a monster made from part wolf, part crow, and part man, scampered to her side. "Arachne said the door wasn't to open for anyone," he stammered.

"I'm sorry, does Arachne speak for me?" Euryale said, taking a step back and feigning an overly exaggerated hurt. "Open the door, or I'll turn you into a newt!"

"And you won't get better," Aphrodite added.

The wolf-crow-man balked. "But—"

Euryale waved her hand and incanted a few words of nonsense, all of which were done to mask her powers flowing from her eyes. The obstinate guard dropped his shotgun as he tried to turn away, but it was too late. He let out a strangled wheeze as his flesh became stone.

At that point, Euryale whipped around to face the others. "Who else doesn't want to let me in?"

Half of the troops scrambled back. Half stayed rooted in place with fear splashed across their disfigured faces. A few even dropped the weapons. One fell over, possibly dead, but not from Euryale—or at least, not from being turned to stone. Her frightful performance, it seemed, was enough to make all the Muses proud.

"A moment," said a half man, half leopard. The creature clumsily ran up from the back ranks, nearly tripping as he did and barreling through two others as well. He held a large iron key on a thick ring, and with it, he worked the locks.

While they waited, Aphrodite casually picked up the petrified soldier's weapon and looked it over. "He won't be needing this."

No one protested, and two minutes later, Euryale and Aphrodite were making their way through the tunnels with smiles on their faces.

"Not bad," Aphrodite said. "Not bad at all."

"Thanks," Euryale said, feeling proud.

"One thing, though," Aphrodite tacked on. "If you're going to promise to turn someone into a newt, you better make sure you can. We're lucky they didn't wonder about that."

"Right," Euryale said. "Got a little caught up in the moment, is all."

Ten minutes later, Aphrodite heard the sounds of hammer on anvil up ahead. The strikes were powerful and fast, and though she and Euryale were far from winning the day, hearing Hephaestus work the forge bolstered her hope. The axe had yet to be finished.

After redoubling their pace through the tunnels, Aphrodite stepped into the forge with Euryale. As had been predicted, Hephaestus was at the anvil, but he no longer had his hammer in hand. Instead, he held the labrys, its head red-hot, and inspected his handiwork. Satisfaction played across his tired and sweaty face, and after a grunt of approval, he dropped the axe into a basin of water.

The waters hissed as thick steam rose into the air. Euryale nudged Aphrodite and whispered. "Is he finished?"

"I think so," she said, recognizing the look he wore. After all, even if she'd hated being around him, hated being married to him and had tried her best to avoid him, she had seen her husband work on more than one occasion, and there was no mistaking his affect when he completed a difficult task he'd set himself upon. The goddess glanced at her shotgun and double checked that the safety was indeed off. "Got a plan?"

Euryale crouched before throwing a half grin the goddess's way. "Of course. Well, half a plan. Might not work too well, but we'll see. Can you keep him talking?"

"Probably."

"Okay. Do that. I'll do the rest."

Aphrodite nodded, and the gorgon slipped off into the shadows. The Goddess of Love waited a few beats for Euryale to disappear and then cleared her throat. "Husband!" she called out. "It's over."

Startled, Hephaestus spun around, labrys in hand. He eyed his wife for a second before throwing a few glances to the shadows on both sides. "Husband? Do we honestly believe you've come to make amends?"

Aphrodite shook her head. "No. But I am here to try and reason with you one last time. Stop this madness. Your army crumbles. Don't destroy yourself."

Hephaestus stepped forward a few paces, his eyes continuously looking left and right as he moved. "Reason? What do you know of reason?" he scoffed. "Was it reason that saw you cheating on us time and again? Was it reason that kept your mouth shut when they banished me to my island because they couldn't stand the sight of a cripple walking amongst them?"

"They were wrong to do that," she admitted. Her voice lowered, and her head dipped. Sincere regret washed over her as those memories surfaced. "They should've let you live in Olympus.

I should have said something, too, but you shouldn't have kept me for your bride against my will, either."

"Are we still refusing to stay married to us, then?"

"You know I don't want to. Are you still insisting that I must?"

Hephaestus froze in place. He jerked his head around but caught sight of nothing but shadows and stone. "Where's the gorgon?" he asked, surveying the rest of the forge.

"Struck down by Hera," Aphrodite replied.

"One of your worst lies yet," Hephaestus sneered. "You still think so little of us, but you won't think that much longer."

"It's not a lie!"

"Then where is your proof?"

Aphrodite shook her head and felt her skin flush. "I don't have to prove a damn thing to you! And you know what else? Zeus is going to be here at any moment with the others. So unless you want to face his full wrath, drop the axe and surrender!"

Hephaestus's face paled. He backed with trembling steps. "Zeus? Awake? Impossible."

"Tell me, dear husband," Aphrodite said, marching toward him. "Does it sound like I'm lying now?"

The God of Smiths shook his head, more out of denial than argument. He pivoted on his heels and hurried for the exit on the far side of the forge. His twisted leg, however, made his attempt at an escape more pathetic than speedy, and when Euryale sprang from the shadows, he couldn't get away from her.

"You traitorous piece of filth," Euryale screamed, launching herself forward. "You were our friend! Our savior!"

Hephaestus managed to block her attack by putting the labrys between him and her. As they wrestled, he struck her with a quick jab from his left hand. "You're foolish to have returned."

Euryale coiled her tail around the god's waist and legs. She could feel her grip on his arms weakening and knew she could never outwrestle him. But she didn't have to. She only needed him to fall so she could force his gaze onto hers.

"Didn't you learn your lesson last time, gorgon?" Hephaestus asked with disdain. He jerked his arms toward his chest, drawing Euryale close. Before she could react, he smashed his forehead into Euryale's nose.

Predictably, Euryale fell back, disoriented, and relinquished her grip on the axe. Hephaestus sneered and rose the weapon high overhead and swung, at which point Aphrodite—who'd been patiently waiting for an opening—took her shot.

She squeezed the trigger, and her shotgun kicked like a mule against her shoulder. The blast struck Hephaestus in the hand, and the weapon went flying. The God of Smiths howled in pain, and Aphrodite fired twice more, doing her best not to hit Euryale in the process.

Hephaestus staggered into the table. Quickly, he snatched his hammer off it and tried to smash Euryale's head in, but the gorgon proved to be quicker. She dug her claws into the sides of his head and looked him directly in the eyes.

A half second later and with a heavy heart, Euryale uncoiled herself from the petrified god. "I'm sorry, friend," she said, eyes misting. "You left me no choice."

"Don't apologize. He deserved it," Aphrodite said, her voice upbeat and in sharp contrast to Euryale's mood. "Now let's get that axe and get out of here."

The goddess turned around, but instead of seeing the axe where it had flown, all she saw were the backs of Arachne and The Fox, each taking a separate passage out of the forge, each carrying a weapon in hand.

"Don't stand there! Get after them!" Euryale yelled, giving chase. "I'll get Arachne. You get The Fox."

"Me? He can't be caught!"

Euryale cursed and shook her head. "You can at least get the axe from him. It doesn't matter if he gets away."

Aphrodite nodded and started to run, but skidded to a stop a second later. "Hang on a second," she said. "I've got a better idea."

Chapter Foxes and Statues

The Fox slowed. He could still hear Aphrodite following, but he realized he was in the perfect spot to throw her completely off his trail. As such, he quickly double backed and popped into a side cavern. There wasn't much in it other than a low sloped ceiling and a few rocky outcroppings, but those would be enough to keep him concealed until she passed by.

He slipped behind the largest of the three and held his breath. Her footsteps grew louder as they drew near the entrance and then started to fade as she went by. But she didn't go far. He heard her return in short order, and though he wasn't worried about being caught, as he never could be, her actions were curious, and he wondered how much of a thorn in his side she would be.

"Come out, love," Aphrodite called out. "I know you're in there."

The Fox waited, not moving, but when she called out again, he sighed. Stepping out from his hiding spot, he glanced at the axe he carried, or rather, the former axe. The illusion had worn off and what he now had in his hands was a simple, long pole. He tossed it to the side. "Well, goddess, what now?" he asked. "We both know I'll escape."

"Aw, don't say that," Aphrodite said with a very alluring pout. "You'd leave me lonely?"

The Fox smirked and then, realizing there was no need to stay in his human form anymore, he reverted back to his true self. "You can't charm me into a net. That still counts as catching."

Aphrodite approached with her lips parted and hips swaying. "Don't you want to at least hear what I have to say?"

"No."

Her bottom lip quivered and her eyes glistened. "No?"

"No," he said again. With a yawn, he stretched into a long downward dog before moseying to the exit. His fox sense was at ease, and it was much more stylish to prance out of the room with his bushy tail held high than it was to turn and run.

"But, Fox, you amaze me to no end," she said.

"Nice try, but you're not my type."

"Oh, Fox, I'm everyone's type."

"You honestly believe that, don't you?"

Aphrodite nodded. "I know it. I could have you if I wanted."

"No, you can't."

"Really?"

"Really."

Aphrodite whetted her lips with a flick of her tongue. "Then look me in the eyes and say it."

The Fox laughed. "Gladly."

Aphrodite waited patiently for him to approach, which he did after spending a moment surveying his surroundings. When he drew his face close to hers, she grinned, and her eyes went from blue to gold. Her gorgeous locks faded and in their place was a nest of vipers.

"But—" was all The Fox managed to get out before his body turned to stone.

Euryale smirked as she stroked the top of his head. "But what? You haven't been caught. You've been petrified. Paused. It's a subtle, important difference."

Chapter Lava Baths

The chase was on.

Aphrodite pursued Arachne through the maze of tunnels with the vengeance of any Fury. Twice, Aphrodite had nearly caught up to The Spider Queen, only to have her efforts thwarted when she made a hairpin turn and ended up at a five-way intersection, where it took her a few beats to figure out which way the woman had fled.

Now, however, the Goddess of Love had Arachne's pattern figured out. In fact, she realized that the woman was about to cut through a lava-filled cavern up ahead after making a feint to the left. Even better, Aphrodite realized she could take a shortcut and head off Arachne instead of following in her footsteps. As such, at the next branch she hooked to the right and ran up a steep tunnel that dumped her directly into the cavern she wanted to be in, and not a moment too soon.

Arachne barreled into the area with her attention directed over her shoulder. She glanced forward right as Aphrodite raised her Benelli M1014 shotgun and squeezed the trigger, Arachne launched herself sideways while at the same time throwing the labrys. A rock directly behind where Arachne's head had been only an instant before blew apart, while the axe flew end over end before narrowly missing Aphrodite's chest. The weapon struck the wall and drove itself deep inside.

The Spider Queen shot out her hands. To her dismay, instead of a thick web slinging out of her hands, all that came forth was a weak spray, barely enough to catch a moth. Aphrodite smirked, coolly leveled the shotgun at Arachne's head, and pulled the trigger.

The hammer fell on an empty chamber with a loud click.

"Looks like we're both out of tricks," Arachne said with a chuckle. "Why don't you run back to your lover before you get any more dirt on that pretty little face of yours."

Aphrodite's eyes narrowed as she flipped the shotgun around and held it like a club. "If anyone should run, it's you."

Arachne charged, and Aphrodite swung for all she was worth. The Spider Queen slid, feet first, narrowly avoiding the blow. But instead of issuing a counterattack, Arachne kept with the momentum, scrambled to her feet, and ran for the embedded axe.

Aphrodite spun around and took off after the spider woman. Arachne beat her to the axe by at least a couple of seconds, but the weapon had buried itself so deeply into the rock, she was unable to get it free by the time Aphrodite caught up to her. "That's for kidnapping my sister," the goddess said, landing a wicked blow to Arachne's ribs.

Arachne stumbled sideways and nearly took a lava bath. Sadly, she recovered before falling in. "Even when I give my back to you, you're still not good enough," taunted Arachne, retreating a few more steps before adopting a fighting stance. "I'm going to enjoy burning your face off."

Aphrodite leaped forward in reply, swinging yet again for the woman's head. Again, Arachne came into the attack and ducked, but Aphrodite, anticipating such a maneuver, spun with her momentum, came fully around and brought the shotgun up in a wicked uppercut that caught Arachne right under the chin.

Arachne's head snapped back in a spray of blood. She reeled back a few steps before falling over. A large, silver key flew from the folds of her robe in the process and clinked loudly on the stone floor.

"Okay, that hurt," Arachne said. The woman gingerly touched under her split chin and winced. "Maybe you aren't as useless as I thought."

"I was never useless!" Aphrodite yelled.

The goddess approached methodically while adjusting her grip for one last blow, all the while Arachne scampered backward on her hands. "Do you honestly want to go back to how things were?" Arachne asked. "Back to living under the thumb of Zeus? Being mocked by all behind your back? Separated from the true love of your life for all eternity?"

"I've changed," Aphrodite growled.

"Exactly. You've changed," Arachne said. Her back suddenly found the wall, and her eyes went wide. Her voice wavered, and its tempo doubled. "You can rule, you know. With us. Typhon wants the strong, and you, Aphrodite, are one of the strongest I've ever seen. Strong. Tenacious. Smart."

Aphrodite's face hardened. "You forgot gorgeous."

The goddess stepped forward to finish the woman off, but in that split second, Arachne's face went from panic to pleasant shock. She shot out her hand and out flew a spray of web that entangled itself around Aphrodite's legs. The Goddess of Love lost her balance and came crashing down. Arachne hit her again with another web. It wasn't much this time, but it was enough. The web caught Aphrodite by the wrist and pinned her to the floor.

"Damnit," Arachne said, coming to her feet and looking at her palms. "I guess I'm drained again." She then turned to Aphrodite and kicked the shotgun out of her hands. It sailed through the air before disappearing into the river of molten rock. "I told you to run when you had the chance."

Aphrodite struggled against the bindings. She could feel them give and could tell they wouldn't be able to hold forever. Given time, she could break free. Given time...

"Still trying to get away," Arachne said with a chuckle. "I suppose we'll have to put an end to that, yes?"

The woman turned her back to Aphrodite and casually made her way to the labrys. At that moment, the goddess knew she had one opportunity to act. Sadly, there was nothing in arm's reach to help. Nothing but a river of molten rock which was anything but helpful.

"Do you have a preference which limb I cut off first?" Arachne asked, throwing Aphrodite a glance over her shoulder.

Aphrodite growled, and the moment Arachne turned back around, she sprang into action. She rolled to her left, and with her free hand, she scooped out a glob of molten rock. The pain the lava brought nearly caused her to pass out, and it was only by some strange intervention of the Fates that she didn't scream. Before the lava could burn through her hand, she dumped it on her wrist and legs. The bindings on both melted in a flash.

Arachne spun around, hearing the sizzle. "What—"

That was all she got out. Aphrodite, with a second glob of lava in hand, launched the molten missile. Her aim was true, and she nailed Arachne directly in the face. The woman screeched like a banshee. With one arm she flailed around, while the other desperately sought to claw the lava from her skin.

"Die, you bitch," Aphrodite yelled, closing the distance between the two. She punched Arachne in the throat and spun her around. She then gave her a shove while sticking one foot between her two.

Arachne tripped, landing face first into the lava. Any other would have succumbed to such a fate instantly, but the spider woman fought on. "You'll never win! Typhon will feast on every last one of you!"

"Maybe, but you'll not be around to see it," Aphrodite said. The goddess pounced on Arachne's back. Using her good hand, which was relative at this point, she grabbed Arachne by the back of the head and shoved her under.

The woman thrashed wildly, and the immeasurable pain that raced through Aphrodite's body only fueled her wild strength even further. As Arachne flailed, her hands sent bits of lava flying in all directions. Most went far and wide, though some globs found Aphrodite's neck and chest. A few even seared her face, but the goddess did not relent.

Finally, Arachne ceased her struggle. Aphrodite took to her feet. Her left hand had been charred to the bone, and the flesh of a rotted corpse looked better than what was up to her elbow. She had little doubt these wounds would take a long, long time to heal. Years, maybe. Centuries? The molten rock had been far hotter than she'd ever imagined.

"I told you, I'm not useless," Aphrodite spat before kicking Arachne's body in. She watched Arachne sink before picking up the fallen prison key. When she looked up, she found that she wasn't alone.

Near the axe stood a cyclops who grabbed the labrys and yanked it free.

A split second later, it turned tail and ran, disappearing down a tunnel.

CHAPTER THAT CAN'T BE GOOD

Euryale heard the screams.

They were far, and since they bounced off the tunnel walls from seemingly every direction, it was hard to tell where they were coming from. One thing, however, was certain: Aphrodite was in an intense fight with Arachne. Who was winning, Euryale didn't know. She certainly hoped it was the Goddess of Love, but if recent events had taught her anything, it was that Arachne should never be underestimated.

Euryale followed a passage to her left, thinking the sounds of battle were coming from there. She redoubled her pace as they grew stronger, but ended up having to backtrack twice when she realized she'd gone the wrong way. At an intersection, she stopped and listened. A loud screech blasted down the corridor on her right, after which all was silent.

"Oh no," the gorgon whispered, fearing the worst. She raced down the passage with such blinding speed that when she rounded a corner, she didn't have time to react as she ran straight into a trio of cyclopes.

She hit the first one square in the chest, and the two became entangled. The second came to his comrade's aid, while the third, armed with the labrys, seemed unsure of what to do.

"*Gormph nrag ar prumf!*" the first yelled.

Euryale, never having been one to bother with studying the intricate language of the cyclopes, couldn't give an accurate translation, but the intent was clear. The armed cyclops raced forward, axe held high.

"You picked the wrong fight," Euryale growled. In a flash, she untangled herself from the two she was fighting and sprang forward, using every bit of strength she had in her tail.

She hit her attacker so hard he fell on his back and relinquished his grip on the axe. His head struck the ground with a wet thud. Euryale pounced and turned him to stone before he had a chance to even think about looking away.

A heavy fist struck her in the back of the head. Euryale fell forward but caught herself before striking the ground. She twisted, and as the second cyclops jumped on top of her, she coiled her tail around his waist and used the anchor point to hoist herself up.

Unlike her first victim, this cyclops had a few more bits of wit—assuming one ignored the fact that he'd picked a fight with an enraged gorgon. The one-eyed giant kept his eye shut and swung blindly with his fists, hoping to connect. Euryale dodged the first two, but ended up getting struck in the shoulder and then the chest.

The blows, though hard-hitting, weren't enough to knock her down. Euryale deflected one last strike before sinking her fangs deep into the monster's bicep. Her vipers struck a split second later, each one finding exposed flesh to pump their deadly venom into.

Euryale bit him two more times as the cyclops writhed and screamed in pain. When he still refused to open his eye, she bit once more, this time on the side of his neck. The monster's eye shot open, and the last thing he saw was Euryale driving his face into hers.

The gorgon uncoiled from the statue, intent on finishing the last of the three. She came around in time to see the cyclops scoop up the fallen axe and sprint down the tunnel as fast as his giant legs would carry him.

"Run, coward!" she yelled as she gave pursuit. In reality, she couldn't blame the poor guy for not sticking around, but she had hoped the jeers would be enough to slow him, or better, have him turn around.

They were not.

She pursued the cyclops relentlessly through a dozen tunnels and branches until she ran straight into a heavy, barred iron door. She struck it with her shoulder, but it remained standing. So Euryale did what any good, pissed off, and determined demigod would do. She hit it again and again. And again. With each strike, she could hear the rock around it crumble, which helped her to redouble her efforts.

"I swear, when I get a hold of you," she muttered, ramming the door yet again. This time, it caved a foot and a half while also partially ripping free of the rock. Euryale smiled. "It's about time."

The gorgon backed a few feet and crashed into the door one final time. The door blew apart in an explosion of metal and rock. Bits of shrapnel and debris cut into Euryale's shoulders and sides, but she barely noticed. She had a labrys to retrieve and a Father of Monsters to keep in prison.

Off the gorgon went. Thankfully, despite the sizable delay she'd experienced, the tunnel branched no more. Instead, after a few hundred yards, it dumped her into the middle of Typhon's chamber.

"Oh damn," she said, sliding to a stop, eyes wide, mouth refusing to do anything but hang open.

The cyclops she'd been pursuing stood next to Typhon, holding the axe high over his head. *"Ker ag nephra!"*

With that, he brought the axe down. The blade bit into the chains. Thunder clapped. Lightning shot out in all directions, and the chain shattered.

Aphrodite clutched the iron prison key as she stumbled through the tunnels. Her vision blurred, and what was left of her right arm was the source of an immeasurable amount of agony. But she didn't let that get to her. The old her would have succumbed long ago to the pain and run home.

But she was not the old Aphrodite. She was going to be the Goddess of Love, the true Goddess of Love. The goddess who came to the aid of family, friend, and even quarrelsome sister, no matter what state she was in. That thought bolstered her strength, kept her legs moving, and gave her courage so that every time she turned the corner, she would be ready to face down whatever minions Typhon and Arachne still had roaming around.

However, by the time she reached the large iron door that led to the prison, she had encountered no one, which she certainly wasn't complaining about. With a shaky hand, Aphrodite put the key in the lock and gave it a turn. It took a little bit of wiggling to get the tumblers to cooperate, but after a few seconds, she opened the door.

Quickly, she ran down the short stint of tunnel that led to the prison door at the other end. At that final door, she raised on her tiptoes to peek through the tiny, open window up top. A roughly twelve by twelve prison cell was on the other side. A shadowy figure lay curled on the floor, hands and legs chained to the wall.

"Athena?" Aphrodite called out.

"Aphrodite?" her sister replied. "You got the key?"

"I did." Aphrodite fumbled as she unlocked the door. Once it was open, she burst through.

Athena recoiled at the sight of her sister. "By the Fates..."

"I'm hideous. I know," she said as she knelt by Athena and took care of the lock.

"No," Athena replied. "You're the most beautiful sight I've seen in a long, long time. Where's Arachne?"

"Dead," Aphrodite said.

"Are you sure?"

"Seeing how I'm the one who held her under the lava, yes," Aphrodite said as she helped her sister to her feet.

"I'm impressed," Athena replied with sincerity. "Where are the others?"

"Alex and Ares fight outside, and Euryale is chasing a cyclops, trying to stop him from freeing Typhon."

Athena cursed as she rolled her shoulders. Whereas moments ago, she'd looked tired and weak, now her strength was returning. Aphrodite could only guess what sort of curses Hera had put on those chains. "There's more you should know. Hera betrayed us all. Hephaestus, too."

"Hera?" Athena echoed, looking shocked. "I had Hephaestus figured, sadly too late...but Hera?"

Aphrodite nodded. "She orchestrated it all. I'd fill you in on everything, but we haven't much time. We need to help Euryale before Typhon is freed."

A massive earthquake followed by a bellowing roar shook the cell.

Athena's face turned grim. "I think we've failed in that regard."

Chapter A Crash Course in Alchemy

The volcano exploded.

A few seconds before it did, a deep rumble ran through the battlefield, and Alex threw himself to the ground, half expecting to see a jet of lava shoot into the sky a mile high. Sadly, what came out was much, much worse.

Typhon, Father of Monsters, sailed through the air on leathery wings that looked like they could shade a dozen football stadiums with room to spare. He landed near the base of the mountain, sucked in a deep breath, and spewed massive torrents of lava that charred a half-mile stretch of the landscape. Sure, he roasted large amounts of his own spawn, but he also fried as many of Alex's men. Maybe more. Who knew? With everything and everyone reduced to cinders, it was hard to get an exact count.

"Jesus H. Christ!" Alex yelled, scampering behind a large boulder as a second blast of molten rock engulfed his world. He fumbled with his radio and did the only thing he could think of. He called for artillery. "Blast him! Blast him with everything you've got!"

"Say again?" the radioman on the other end replied. "Everything?"

"EVERYTHING!"

"Copy that. Send us the grid or a polar plot."

"I don't have any bloody grids! Everyone is wiped!" Alex said. He leaned around the rock and immediately jerked back when his hands inadvertently touched the smoldering face and got burned. Minor wound aside, at the very least Typhon had his attention directed somewhere else. "Shoot at the big monster thing! How hard is it to see that?"

"Copy, but you'll need to help us walk the shots in," the radioman said. He sounded so calm that Alex wondered if he truly appreciated what the hell they were now fighting. Probably not, because if he had, no doubt the lot of them would have run. "Firing for range. Stand by."

Off in the distance, Alex heard the distinct boom of an artillery piece firing. He tensed, waiting to see where the shot would land. When it did, he couldn't have been happier. The shell slammed into the ground and exploded not too far from Typhon. "You're maybe a hundred yards short and a quarter of that to the right!" Alex said. "Just send it all at him, now!"

"Copy, adjusting," the radioman replied. A few moments later. "Firing for effect. Standby."

Tickles landed next to Alex and dropped half the body of a dead monster at his feet. The chimera looked at Alex with bright, shiny eyes and nudged the corpse toward him.

"What?" Alex asked, stupefied as to what was taking place.

Tickles let loose a meowing chirp and nudged the body again before sitting on his haunches and straightening, tall and proud.

Alex rolled his eyes. "Oh geez," he said, sighing. "Yes. Great present. Thank you. Go find Euryale!"

Tickles cocked his head and chirped again.

"Euryale!" he said, pointing to the mountain that had lost its top. "Find her!"

Tickles meowed one last time and took flight. A second later, dozens of booms filled the air as the entire complement of artillery that Alex had created answered the call. Right before the shells impacted, Typhon turned around to face the incoming shots. Half of them hit the ground near his many tails, while the rest impacted on his chest, shoulders, and arms. One even struck him on the left temple. Not one caused him to flinch, let alone drew blood.

"You've come a long way from catapults and ballistae, little mortals," Typhon said as he sped across the battlefield. "But I'm afraid nowhere near far enough."

"Eye of newt? Are you sure?" Jessica asked as she rifled through the shelves for the fifth time.

"That's what it says, don't blame me," the satyr replied, double checking the scroll he had in hand. "At least, I think that's what it says. It might say yellow cold. Her handwriting is worse than her personality."

Jessica groaned and rubbed her temples. "Where do you get that anyway, eBay? She might not have any here."

"From a newt, of course."

"Do you have one on hand?"

The satyr looked around and shrugged. "Is that a trick question?"

Jessica sighed. "If only." Her brow furrowed and she drummed her fingers on the table as her eyes fixated on the nearly prepared brew they'd made. It sat inside a crystal flask, swirling with reds, blues, greens, and yellows, all the while lightly smoking out the top. The entire thing screamed magic potion, but according to Hera's notes, it was not. "You guys don't have a spell component emporium up here?"

"A what?"

Jessica shook head. "Never mind. You sure we can't skip it?"

The satyr shrugged again. "Like I should know. All I do around here is dust and tidy. Want to know the best way to draw dirt out of a tapestry? I'm your goatman. Need to polish a thousand pieces of silverware in an hour? Look no further. Desperate to reproduce a secret formula with missing ingredients before Typhon eats us all? Not exactly my skill set."

"Well, we've got to do something," Jessica said. A flashback to her bartending days during grad school popped into mind, and she hoped that this wasn't too dissimilar from mixing drinks. After all, it looked like a drink..."Can we substitute it? I mean, what does eye of newt do, anyway?"

The satyr skimmed over the scroll, muttering to himself as he went over the ancient Greek. "Catalyst," he finally said, dropping his finger on a line Jessica couldn't read.

"That shouldn't be too hard to recreate, then," she replied. "We could heat it up a little first, right?"

"I think it'll take more than some fire," he replied. "It needs a lot of energy."

Jessica's mouth twisted to the side as she tried to come up with a new plan, and when one hit her, her face lit up. "I've got the perfect idea."

Without explanation, she grabbed the flask after putting in the stopper and beelined out of Hera's abode. Ultimately, she was going to head for Zeus's temple where the ruler of Olympus slept, but along the way, she made a detour that took her to the god's armory and procured herself a two-foot-long bolt of lightning. The weapon tingled in her hands, and she wasn't exactly sure how it worked, but she did have the vague idea that once it was thrown, it would change into what she needed—at least, that's what she figured going by all the artwork she'd seen. And how wrong could they be?

She tried not to think about that last part.

Once in Zeus's temple, she ran up to the sleeping god and poured the elixir into his mouth, doing her best not to spill a drop. She had no idea how much was needed, but she decided that erring on too much was far better than too little. Worst case, she hoped, it would act like a super jolt of caffeine, and he'd be jittery for a few days. Or maybe months. Who knew? Who cared, really? As long as he'd be there to help bring down Typhon, she didn't give two licks how many late-night jumping jacks he'd be doing.

"Are you sure about this?" the satyr asked as Jessica took a few steps back.

"No," she admitted with a half grin.

"Well, do it fast," he replied, covering his eyes and turning away.

Jessica nodded. She held her breath, adjusted her grip on the lightning bolt, and gave it a hurl before she could think herself out of it.

Thunder clapped through the temple as the bolt streaked through the air. It took a jagged path, but it struck Zeus squarely in the cheek.

"I've never seen her before in my life!" Zeus yelled, shooting upright with eyes wide. He then shook his head vigorously while blowing a giant raspberry before he spied Jessica and the satyr nearby. His brow furrowed, and his face reflected a monumental amount of confusion. "What's going on?"

"Long story," Jessica said. "I'll give you the short version. No, check that. That's too long, too. Here's the short, short version: Typhon's loose."

Euryale groaned as she woke from her dreams of cupcakes.

She didn't appreciate being ripped from her fantasy and would've liked to indulge in the mountains of chocolate and vanilla delights for a lot longer, and she certainly didn't like that being ripped from said dream meant she found herself back in Typhon's cave, buried under rock with a bloodied face and ears ringing. In fact, she hated it so much, she was certain that she could've gone her entire immortal life without having experienced such a thing and been just fine.

As her vision came back into focus, she surveyed her surroundings. Heaps of rock pinned her to the floor. Dust filled the air, and a hazy light filtered in from a gigantic tunnel in the ceiling where Typhon had burst free. Though her hearing felt muted and her head was foggy, sounds of combat drifted to her ears and made her acutely aware of two things: First, Alex was out there, fighting that nightmarish monster, and second, unless she did something soon, Typhon would crush them all. What she could do, she had no idea. Especially with the rock pressing down on her back and tail.

"Come on. Get free, damn it," Euryale said to herself as she tried to wiggle out. She did manage to shift her right arm about half an inch, but as it was trapped under her stomach, in the end, it didn't do much other than offer her a slight bit of extra comfort—which of course, was completely relative at this point.

The sound of a large blast echoed in from outside, spurring the gorgon into action. She traded her careful movements for a more random thrashing, but its accomplishments numbered in the ones. Or more precisely, numbered one. Her tail developed a strain near the midpoint.

A series of explosions filtered in seconds later, followed by a deafening roar which could've silenced a thousand dragons. Euryale's imagination filled in the details, and while she watched the mental picture of Typhon finishing off whoever was left, she felt her body slump and despair take over. "This can't be it," she said, eyes watering.

"It's not. Now get up."

Euryale jerked at the sound of Athena's voice. She craned her head over her right shoulder and saw the goddess standing a foot away as she started to clear the rocks with her bare hands. She might not have had Ares' bulk, but the Goddess of Wisdom's strength was on full display as she effortlessly tossed boulder after boulder. Within seconds, Athena offered Euryale a hand and pulled her free. "Aphrodite says you're more potent now," she said. "Is this true?"

"Yes," Euryale replied. "Thank Hera and Cronus for that."

"Good," Athena said giving a nod as determination set in her face. "Get up there and make Typhon your best statue yet. Ordinary weapons will not stop him, but if we can get a hold of that axe, perhaps we can weaken him enough for you to turn him to stone."

"The exit is so far," Euryale said. "Do you know of a faster way out?"

A smile grew on the goddess's face. She pointed to the giant hole in the ceiling right as Tickles came swooping in. "I believe your mount has arrived."

The chimera landed next to the gorgon and nudged her with his lion head.

"You want me to fly?" Euryale asked.

"I want your pet to fly. I want you to hold on."

Euryale's stomach formed violent knots at the thought of having to be airborne. Flying in an airplane was bad enough, but hanging on to a flying monster? Sadly, there were no other options. The fates of Alex and her children were riding on her stopping Typhon. Oh, and that little detail about stopping the end of the world, too.

"What are you going to do?"

"I'm going to get my shield," Athena answered. "We're going to need it."

"Then I guess I'll see you outside," Euryale said as she climbed on Tickles's back as best she could. Since she still had a tail instead of legs and there wasn't a proper saddle, it was more of her lying between the chimera's wings and wrapping her arms around one neck with her tail coiled around his torso. "Any suggestions?"

"Yes. One. Don't get eaten." Athena swatted Tickles on a hind quarter, and the chimera leaped into the air.

Up they spiraled. Euryale instinctively tightened her arms and kept her eyes clenched shut. When they broke free of the mountain, she felt the fresh air on her face and opened her eyes. Below, Typhon was batting around men and tanks like a giant cat toying with mice. Dozens of craters filled with twisted metal and remains of tanks and artillery smoldered across the battlefield. Where Alex was in all of the mess, Euryale couldn't tell, but seeing the carnage galvanized her nerves to where her only thoughts centered around stopping Typhon.

"Get in front of his face!" she yelled. "I need to see into his eyes!"

Tickles roared in response. The chimera folded his wings and entered a steep dive. He tore through the air like a peregrine falcon before leveling out, but as he'd come in with so much speed, he ended up having to make circles around Typhon in order to slow down. As he whipped around the god, Euryale caught sight of the labrys Hephaestus had forged. It was clutched tightly in one of his tentacles and held close to his chest.

"Alex! Your wife lives and has come to join the fun!" Ares bellowed.

Euryale scanned the battlefield a couple of times before she found the God of War. He was covered in dirt and blood, wielding a giant hunk of metal—a ripped-off tank barrel, from what she could tell—and was gleefully swatting his way through hordes of minions.

"Ares!" she yelled. Somehow, in all the chaos, he heard her and stopped his swatting to listen. "Get that axe!" she said, pointing to where it was on Typhon. "It's what—"

Tickles banked and then rolled in the opposite direction so hard that she was nearly thrown. If she hadn't anchored her tail around his hips, she surely would've gotten a crash course in battlefield skydiving. Before she could orient herself to what was happening, mainly because she and Tickles were tumbling far more than flying, Typhon snatched her from the air and easily ripped her free of the chimera.

"You have such a tenacious spirit," he said, bringing her up to his face. "I love it."

"There's a lot of me to love," she replied. Her eyes widened, and her curse flowed free.

Typhon, with one set of eyes still fixed on hers, grinned and patted her head. "Not today, gorgon. Not today." Holding her by one wrist, he brought her so close to his face, any of her vipers could have reached out and tasted his nose. "Do you see how futile this is?" he asked. He then turned her so she could have a better view of the mountain. From one side, a dozen more streams of monstrous creatures poured out. "Their numbers are legion."

"We'll still stop you," Euryale growled.

"Last chance to join me, gorgon. I do love how strong you are."

"I'll never join you."

"Then let's see what kind of snack you make."

Chapter Bolts of Lightning

Zeus climbed to the top of a thunderhead the size of Nebraska. One hand kept a grip on the cart he'd been pulling, a cart laden with lightning bolts that ranged in size from javelins to blue whales, and the other hand toyed with his beard as he surveyed the battle below. Though Jessica couldn't see it, the look on the Olympian's face told her all she needed to know. Things were dire.

"Things are not dire," he said, throwing her a glance over his shoulder with a bright grin.

Jessica blinked. "Say again?"

"Things are not dire."

"But Typhon...?"

"Is still weak," he finished. "We have a chance at defeating him before he regains his strength."

"How much of a chance are we talking?"

"Less than certain, but better than none."

Jessica rubbed her hands together and bit a knuckle, not liking the god's tone. "Maybe you ought to let me help. I bet I could zap some baddies."

"Let a mortal touch my lightning?" Zeus asked, sounding caught somewhere between comedic disbelief and utter outrage.

"A mortal who did come up with the idea on how to wake you," she pointed out. "And managed to make that happen, too."

Zeus continued stroking his beard. "Perhaps I could trust you with the little ones," he said. "It would be funny, once I have Typhon back in chains, to mock him with your presence, to let him know a woman of thirty-some years scattered his army and brought him down."

Jessica gave an excited eep. Her heart raced and both excitement and dread filled every fiber of her being. Was she actually going to be taught the finer points of hurling lightning by Zeus himself? Her request had only been halfhearted, for she'd never expected it to be granted. That said, however, it seemed it was about to be. But how would she even see her target?

As if reading her mind, Zeus waved his hand over her head and spoke in deep tones. Instantly, her vision sharpened a thousandfold. She stumbled backward as her world took on a surreal nature due to the crispness of everything. She could see the deep valleys that made up her fingerprints as well as bits of moisture that clung to the inside of Zeus's nostrils (the sight of which, no doubt, would need to be worked out in therapy for several months). Had there been a penny on the moon, she thought she'd be able to read its inscription as well.

"Better?" Zeus asked with a laugh. "You have my eagle's eyes. Aim well."

"Oh. My. God!" she exclaimed looking around. She ran over to the edge of the thunderhead and peered down.

The battle raged in gruesome detail. Men and monsters were locked into both an intense firefight as well as brutal hand-to-hand combat. She held her breath as she scoured the area for Alex. She found him inside a crater, repeatedly firing with his rifle. For every foe he shot, three more drew closer. She could see the dirt smeared across his face as well as the numerous cuts he'd received on his arms and legs. Worst of all, she could see the worried look on his face, and her heart pained for him.

"Hang in there, Alex," she whispered.

Zeus handed her a bolt the size of a hefty spear. "Go ahead. Have the first throw."

Jessica nodded, and keeping her eyes on the swarm of monsters rushing Alex's position, she hurled the weapon. As before, the moment the bolt left her hand it changed into a sizzling blast of lighting that clapped through the air with a thunderous roar. It struck not even ten feet from Alex, instantly obliterating the crab-like monstrosity that had nearly managed to get to him. Once the lightning struck, it branched out and leaped to four others, and then four more for each of those four. By the time it finished jumping, three scores of Typhon's minions had been reduced to ash.

Jessica squealed and jumped up and down several times before she managed to recompose herself. She shot Zeus a sheepish grin. "I know we're supposed to be serious right now, but that was amazing."

Zeus handed her another and then took one for himself. "When this is over, you and I should celebrate your inborn talent over the course of many nights," he said. Before Jessica could wrap her mind around his blatant pass at her in what had to be the most inappropriate time, he added, "Now keep throwing and don't miss. I'm still not convinced we have enough to put an end to all this."

Euryale, arms pinned against her side, bit down on Typhon's tentacle as hard as she could. Though Cronus had blessed her with an unmatched gaze, he'd neglected to improve her jaw strength. He also hadn't sharpened her teeth to where they'd cut diamond. Thus, instead of sinking her fangs into flesh, her teeth did nothing but protest—painfully at that—when they couldn't pierce Typhon's skin.

"Fighting to the end," Typhon said, chuckling.

His laughter cut short as a bolt of lightning struck him on the nose. Electricity jumped in all directions, a couple of arcs even hitting the tentacle he gripped Euryale with. The Father of Monsters shook his head and growled, but when he regained his composure, Euryale struck again. Not with fang, but with curse.

Her eyes locked with his and out flowed her power. Typhon's eyes widened as his skin turned gray, but it didn't last. The Father of Monsters uttered his counterspells, deep and low, from a dozen of his heads, and his flesh returned where the stone had formed.

"That's it," he said. "I've had my fun."

Another blast of lightning ripped into the monster, this one ten times bigger and ten times louder than the previous. It left Euryale's ears ringing and her vision blurred, but it also sent Typhon stumbling. Smoke rose from a large patch of black skin on his shoulder, and the god faltered. A smaller bolt, similar to the first, hit him yet again. His tentacle spasmed, and the gorgon was thrown from its grasp in the process.

"Euryale!"

The gorgon, flat on her back and out of breath, rolled over and saw Alex calling out to her, fifty yards away. With his rifle shouldered, he relentlessly fired into the hordes of nearby monsters that still came from all sides.

"Alex! Get out of here!" she yelled, fear of her husband's demise driving her into action.

Typhon jumped back, dodging a blast of lightning. The force of his landing caused the entire island to shake and the ground to split for a hundred yards in multiple directions. "Enough!" he yelled.

He sucked in a deep breath and was about to incinerate both the gorgon and her husband when Ares popped up on the far side, a giant artillery shell in hand. Like a hall-of-fame quarterback in the last seconds of the Super Bowl, he hurled the shell for all he was worth, putting a wicked spin that saw it fly straight and true.

The tip of the warhead nailed Typhon directly in the eye. The explosion, though not enough to cause any real damage, was enough to deflect Typhon's attention so that when he bathed the area in lava, it wasn't sent at Euryale and Alex, but Ares.

The God of War laughed as his powerful legs drove him clear of the attack. The only things that were cremated were a few patches of grass and another dozen of Typhon's minions that happened to be nearby.

While Ares sailed through the air, another bolt of lightning struck Typhon, and then many more came in rapid succession, decimating his monstrous army that was still on the field. Whereas the Father of Monsters could weather the blows, his minions could not. At first, the creatures tried to push through the relentless storm, but their will was not as strong as Typhon's hide. Morale failed, and as the survivors decided that the only fate that awaited them was a charred one should they stay, be it either by Zeus's lightning or Typhon's indiscriminate fiery breath, they fled.

"I don't need those cowards to finish you," Typhon growled, squaring off with Euryale before charging.

He came blindingly fast, and if he hadn't picked up a slight limp, courtesy of the bolts he'd already suffered, Euryale probably would've never managed to slip away before being trampled.

Another bolt struck him square in the back, this one sending him to the ground and the axe flying from his grasp.

"Alex! Get the axe!" Euryale said as she darted forward. If they could keep hitting him on the ground, keep him weakened, maybe she could climb up to his face and petrify the god once and for all.

"On it!" Alex said, bolting forward while his men began to pepper Typhon's face with rifle fire.

Typhon looked up and snarled before spitting a ball of lava at Alex. The glob hit a few feet away and exploded. A small amount spattered on his legs and side, but it wasn't enough to stop him.

"Don't let him get it!" Euryale yelled. She jumped up and started climbing one of Typhon's lame tentacles. She'd barely gotten two feet off the ground when Typhon turned and charged for the axe.

Before the god could scoop it up, however, Athena was there, shield in hand. She snatched the weapon off the ground. The moment it was hers, Typhon reared back and sent a full blast of fiery breath at her.

Athena crouched behind her shield as the molten rock struck dead on. Euryale nearly lost her grip as she gasped, thinking there was no way the goddess could have survived such a devastating attack. But when the torrent of lava stopped, Athena stood proud, smiling, and determined, with not a single hair singed.

"Impossible," Typhon said, and for the first time since Euryale had met him, he sounded worried.

"And that is why you lose," Athena replied.

The Goddess of Wisdom leaped through the air and swung. The axe struck Typhon in the side, carving a deep gash in his body and sending bolts of lightning everywhere.

Ares, too, joined the brawl while Typhon lashed in every direction. He found a section of armor plating that had separated on one of the god's lower appendages and ripped it off. Seeing soft flesh exposed, Ares drove his fist inside and tore out tissue with glee.

Typhon roared and then rolled, throwing Ares off and nearly crushing Euryale. When he righted, Athena charged back in and called out to the gorgon. "Get up there and finish him!"

Euryale set her jaw and redoubled her effort. Up she climbed, fast and determined. The god's constant fighting, however, made things almost impossible, but at least his focus was on the others now and not her.

She was almost to his midsection when Typhon's dragon head dropped into view. It narrowed its eyes and hissed.

"Bah," Typhon said, swatting her off.

Euryale hit the ground, her vision exploding in a colorful array of starburst lights. She struggled to get up and regain her focus. A few seconds later, her senses returned in time to see Typhon dodge another bolt of lightning before knocking Ares and Athena to the side and taking to the air.

"Relish this minor victory while you can, Olympians," he called back. "It will be the last one you ever have."

CHAPTER INTO THE DEPTHS

"Stop him!" Athena said. "He can't get away!"

The goddess threw the labrys at the back of Typhon's head. It struck him below his left horn, taking a huge chunk out of it when it hit. The Father of Monsters faltered but did not fall from the sky.

"Do something!" she shouted.

Alex, armed only with his rifle, took shots, but he might as well have made mud pies.

Ares, with nothing to throw, stood and shrugged. "I have nothing."

Euryale's mind raced and her spirit refused to give up. She seized the one stupid idea she could come up with within a split second. She jumped in front of Ares and said, "Throw me."

"What?"

"Throw me, damn it!" she shouted.

Ares grinned and hoisted her up. She straightened as best she could so she fit more into his hand like an oversized javelin than a battered gorgon, and before she could have a second thought, the God of War launched her into the air.

Euryale hurled toward Typhon as if she'd been strapped to a solid rocket booster. That said, the amount of grace she had while flying bordered on zero. Some might even say she was in the negatives, if such a thing could be measured, especially since Ares had seen fit to practice his quarterback skills one last time and put her into a tight spiral. The g's she underwent caused her arms and snakes to fly wide, which then turned to her flopping through the air like a hooked tuna right up until she impacted with Typhon's body.

While she wasn't about to win any awards at the Olympics for her landing, at least the monster's thick, matted fur gave her a little padding, and at least she had the wherewithal to hold tight instead of bouncing off and plummeting to her doom.

Euryale adjusted her grip and ended up digging her claws into Typhon's skin a few yards above his waist. The Father of Monsters roared, bleated, and hissed from a dozen of his heads in response. As she started to climb, a goat head near the shoulders turned and looked at her while one of many dragon heads, this one covered in mud-brown scales, lowered itself so that it and Euryale were face to face.

"Oh damn," she said.

"You're a troublesome thing, aren't you?" Typhon growled.

A small bolt of lightning shot between the two, and for the moment, Typhon was distracted. He banked hard to the left, nearly throwing Euryale in the process. A sudden roll to the right almost did the same. When he looked for the gorgon with both goat and dragon heads again, not only had she not fallen, but she'd even managed to crawl up his side a few more feet.

Typhon slapped at her with a trio of gargantuan snakes. The blow was enough to knock the wind out of Euryale, but still she held on. Even when he hit her again and again, she held on. Had she not had divine blood, her body no doubt would've been crushed into a bloodied pulp.

"Do you plan on hanging there until I shatter all your bones?" Typhon asked with an amused smile.

"I plan on hanging here until you're a pretty statue outside my home," Euryale countered.

Typhon laughed, deep and strong. The rumble coming from deep inside his chest sounded like a volcano about to blow its top. That laughing, however, was cut short as a bolt from the heavens struck him square between the shoulder blades. He roared with defiance, but it did little to keep them in the air. As the lightning raced through his body, his wings froze, and he started to plummet.

Euryale summoned what was left of her strength and raced up his back, clenching fists of fur as she pulled herself up. By the time Typhon had regained control of his body and pulled out of his downward spiral, they were skimming the Mediterranean Sea not even a hundred feet above the water.

The first head to spot the gorgon's new position was the goat. It bleated and spat, sending a spray of thick, foul-smelling goo all over her. Typhon tried to grab her again, but a hit from another lightning bolt kept her out of his grasp.

Sensing an opportunity, Euryale let her curse flow. The world flared its brilliant green, and when all returned to normal, Typhon's bellows filled her ears—bellows that came from everywhere but the goat. Instead of bleating or watching her every move, it was now nothing more than a giant bust—a bust that not only weighed several tons but a bust that completely threw Typhon off balance.

"Impossible!" he roared.

"You should've stayed chained in that mountain, Typhon. I told you we'd be your undoing."

The Father of Monsters tried again and again to knock her off, to swat his tiny adversary, but the dead weight of his petrified goat head was making flying difficult and dodging the continued blasts of Zeus even more so. Not to mention, now that he was carrying around a useless head, he had a large blind spot the gorgon was taking advantage of.

"Swear by the River Styx and the Fates you'll stop this pointless war forever, and I'll let you go," Euryale called out, taking a moment to hide under the stone chin of the goat. "This doesn't have to end like this."

"The only end that is coming is yours," Typhon said as he went into a violent barrel roll.

"You can't win!"

"I've already won! Every second you struggle barely delays the inevitable," he shot back.

Euryale shook her head. Even with all that had happened, she didn't want to destroy him outright. She hoped, even if it was a fool's hope, he could be redeemed. Even monsters deserved that chance. But as she knew all too well, wants and needs seldom lined up perfectly. And in this case, they turned out to be polar opposites.

"Have it your way," she muttered. Euryale took a few steady breaths to prepare herself for the last sprint up to Typhon's head. When he made a sharp right turn to dodge some more lightning, she made her move.

"Holy snort, this is fun," Jessica said as she grabbed another mini-lightning bolt out of her barrel. She squinted and aimed at Typhon, but before she threw, she looked sheepishly at Zeus. "Maybe I should be more serious, given we're trying to stop the end of the world."

Zeus shot her a brilliant grin. "No, Jessica, this is fun. Never apologize for indulging in something that brings you great joy, especially when that joy is smiting something as foul as Typhon."

"If you insist," Jessica said. She was about to throw when she noticed that while Zeus had in hand the biggest bolt she'd ever seen, the granddaddy of all lightning, one that could likely split apart the moon, it was the god's last one. The cart was empty. Their supply, save a couple of stingers she still had left, was depleted.

"Don't worry," Zeus said. "We will triumph."

"I hope you're right."

"So do I," he said. "Now put one across his face so we can do the rest."

"We?"

"Euryale and I."

Jessica nodded. She watched Typhon fly for a few seconds to anticipate where he'd be and then threw the mini-bolt of lightning as if the world depended on it—which it did.

Lightning cracked in front of Typhon's face. Like many others, it was hardly a life-threatening event for the Father of Monsters, but he'd been singed enough by now that he'd grown jumpy at even the slightest bit of electricity. After all, even if you happened to be a grotesque colossus who snacked on countries and considered devouring an entire species as a decent hors d'oeuvre, you could only get hit so many times before it became downright annoying.

Typhon jolted to the left. Euryale continued to hang on, and by now, she'd managed to reach the back of his neck.

A black dragon head rose from his shoulder and stared Euryale down. "Game's up, gorgon," Typhon growled. He turned his gaze away from Euryale before she could try and curse him again, and despite this, he managed to pluck her from his body.

Euryale squirmed in the crushing grip of Typhon's serpentine hands. Her bones started to crack, and the air was driven from her lungs, and all the while pain raced through her body.

A second later, the largest crack of lightning anyone had seen or heard in thousands of years drilled Typhon at the base of his skull. The Father of Monsters spasmed, and he relinquished his grip on Euryale and fell from the sky once more. Down they went, but while Typhon was out of control, Euryale was anything but. She held on to one of his flailing tendrils and used it to fling herself toward Typhon's face. She hit him square on the cheek, and within seconds, she'd clawed her way up so she could look him directly in the eye.

"I gave you a chance," she said. "And now it ends."

Her powers flowed out of her like water from a bursting dam. She pulled on everything she had and threw it at her adversary. Typhon's eyes widened. His cries thundered from a hundred mouths, only to have them silenced a moment later as his flesh turned to stone.

A second before he became completely petrified and they both hit the water, a devilish grin formed on his face. He attacked Euryale with one last serpentine arm and wrapped it around her body.

"If I go, so do you," he sneered.

Euryale tried to break free, but between his sheer strength and the literal rock-hard grip he possessed, there was nothing she could do but suck in a breath as they hit the water and sank.

Chapter Fin

Darkness.

For some unfathomable amount of time, that was Euryale's life. Darkness coupled with the crushing weight of an entire sea above and the insatiable burning in her chest as her lungs starved for air. She might have been immortal, but that didn't mean she was free of endless suffering.

She'd hit bottom long ago, and no amount of struggle saw her free of Typhon's grasp. All she could do was try to retreat into the warm memories her mind had, warm memories of days spent courting Alex, days spent chasing both Aison and Cassandra out of fun or frustration. Days spent when she never thought she'd ever be isolated again.

Sadly, that's exactly what her fate now was.

An eternity passed.

Pressure lessened on her tail.

Her eyes opened.

Darkness still greeted her, but so did a current that flowed down her face. No, it wasn't a current. She was rising, shooting up through the water at tremendous speed. Euryale straightened, and she hoped and prayed that she wasn't delirious and that she was truly heading for the surface.

Soon, she spied a tiny light above, and the black around her faded into a dark blue. Not long after that, she found herself rocketing through the last bit of ocean that remained overhead. She broke free of the water's surface, gasping and sputtering. It took a few seconds of laughing, sobbing, laughing, and sobbing again before she got her bearings. She was treading water far off the coast of Sicily, and judging by Mount Etna's location on the horizon, there were probably fifty miles of Mediterranean Sea between her and it.

"Damn, that's going to be a long swim," Euryale muttered to herself.

"Only if you want it to be," said a voice from behind.

Euryale twisted. A few feet away floated a feminine figure in a swan-drawn chariot with Ares at her side. The woman wore a veil over her head that completely shrouded her face, a long-sleeved gown, and gloves that ran up nearly the entire length of her forearms. Despite the obscurity, there was no mistaking Aphrodite's voice.

"You found me?"

"Of course we found you," she said, sounding insulted. "We haven't stopped looking for you since you went under…five days ago."

"Five days?"

"Give or take a few minutes."

Ares offered the gorgon a hand and hoisted her into the chariot. "Your bravery and skill in battle will give your little ones much to look up to as they grow."

Euryale smiled at the compliment, even if she didn't want her children to have to go through an ounce of what she had, let alone look forward to it. That said, she knew Ares' praise in such matters did not come lightly, and she took his words in stride. "Where's Alex?"

"In Olympus," Aphrodite said as she steered toward the divine city.

"He's not out looking for me?"

Aphrodite laughed. "He went crazy looking for you, as in absolutely bonkers. He tore up the shore, swam the oceans, and didn't stop until he passed out from exhaustion not even an hour ago. What happened to Typhon?"

"I—I don't know," Euryale admitted. She glanced behind at the dark waters and shuddered.

"He didn't turn to stone?" Aphrodite asked.

Euryale shook her head. "He did. But..."

"But?"

"He had me in his grasp when I petrified him, and then he dragged me under," she explained.

"How did you get yourself free?"

"I didn't," Euryale admitted as she tried to replay everything that had happened, desperate to come up with a solid answer. Had her curse on Typhon failed? Or had Cronus intervened somehow from the world of dreams and cut her loose, so she could do his bidding? The implications of both were equally terrifying, and to either, she could only say one last thing. "All I can say is, this battle may be won, but our war is only beginning."

Ares put an arm around Euryale and squeezed. "That, gorgon, is the best news I've heard all day."

Trumpets sounded.

They filled the air with majestic tones and were soon joined by a myriad of other horns and drums. Euryale, who waited a few steps outside the Great Hall in Olympus, shifted back and forth on her tail while fidgeting with her peplos. The gown, made from white Olympian silk, clung to her body gracefully, a gift to the gorgon by none other than Aphrodite herself.

"Nervous?" Alex whispered, squeezing her hand.

"No," she lied.

"Your dress looks nice, at least, even with the tail," he said. "Not that I mind it, but I would've thought you'd have shifted back to the legged version of yourself by now."

"I thought I would've, too, but it seems when Cronus said he'd bind my curse, he meant all of it. I suppose we should be lucky he let me keep my wits."

"I still love you," he said, squeezing her hand again. "Tail and all."

Euryale smiled. "Love you, too."

The massive double doors swung open before they could continue, and the music intensified. Having mentally rehearsed the ceremony a thousand times in her head since learning of it, Euryale entered the hall with her head held high, shoulders rolled back, and husband in step at her side.

Creatures, heroes, and demigods filled the hall on both sides. As she snaked down the blue carpet, she tried to keep her eyes focused ahead, to where Zeus, flanked by the other Olympians, stood waiting. Halfway down, however, she caught the eyes of both Heracles and Odysseus, who gave approving nods, and she couldn't help but smile.

When she reached the end, she stopped, bowed, and waited to be acknowledged.

Zeus stepped forward, his eyes filled with electricity. "Euryale, daughter of Phorcys, wife to Alexander, mother of Aison and Cassandra," he said. "It is with tremendous pleasure and gratitude that we honor you today for your commitment to Olympus, and for your hand in defeating Typhon, Father of Monsters."

"It is only by the Fates' will I've done what I have," she said, executing her line flawlessly with another bow. "May they continue to bless your rule."

"Many would heap treasures upon you for your efforts. Others would have your name written in the stars for all generations to see for the rest of time. Some have even suggested we forge an artifact for you."

Again, Euryale bowed, following the script perfectly and without hesitation. "Whatever gifts you bestow upon me in your wisdom, I will forever cherish."

"That is why, Euryale, we will give you none of them."

Euryale straightened, even more than she already was. Her heart skipped, and she blinked. Had she heard right? She would receive nothing at all?

"All such gifts require a unanimous agreement," he said. Though his words were confusing, she couldn't help but note the gleam still in his eye. "At the request of one and the approval of all, we offer you something else."

Euryale's mouth dried and her mind blanked as she tried to keep up with what was going on.

Zeus twisted in place as a satyr came from the side. In his hands was a white pillow with a crown made of gold and purfled with adamantine. "With everyone in our Great Hall as witnesses, we hereby offer you a seat in our throne room. What say you?"

Words failed her. Her heart almost did as well. Her eyes darted around and caught the looks of expectant Olympians. At that moment, she realized how this was even possible. There were twelve thrones for ten gods. Hera and Hephaestus no longer sat.

Zeus leaned forward and whispered with a wry grin. "This is the part where you say yes."

"Yes," Euryale said, snapping back into the moment. She laughed, buried her face in her hands, and spent a few seconds recomposing herself. "I would be honored."

The ruler of Olympus beamed with approval. He gently lifted the crown off the pillow, and once Euryale had dipped her head, he placed it upon her. "From this day forth, Euryale, daughter of Phorcys, wife of Alex, mother of Aison and Cassandra, you will forever be known as the Goddess of Stone. Come, take your place among us."

The crowd erupted in cheers, and the rest was a whirlwind of activity. Dionysus, tired of formalities, had his best wine reserves ushered in by his servants while satyrs entered with gold trays laden with cheese and fruits. Dancers came with colorful ribbons and naked bodies to join the celebration, and music flowed freely for hours.

A full day passed before things came to an end. Slowly, the crowd dissipated, leaving Euryale in the Great Hall with Alex, her children, and a few others. Happy and exhausted, Euryale plopped down in her new throne, which, of course, was made of stone. Across its back and sides were reliefs depicting Euryale throughout various stages of her life, the most prominent and notable scenes being her marriage to Alex, her raising her children, and her battle with Typhon.

"How does it feel to be a goddess?" Alex asked.

Before Euryale could answer, Aison and Cassandra jumped in her lap, knocking the wind out of her.

"She said I got to sit here first!" Cassandra said, shoving her brother.

"Liar!" Aison said, shoving back.

"Python poop!"

"Typhon tit!"

"Demon di—"

"Hey!" Euryale said, grabbing the two by the arms and pulling them apart. "We do *not* talk that way."

The two slinked off her lap and ran away, while Alex shook his head and laughed. "Some things will never change," he said. "Even if now you're an Olympian."

"True enough, Alex," she replied.

"You never did answer that question."

"How it feels?"

Alex nodded.

Euryale settled back into her throne. How did it feel? Fantastic. Not because of the power she had, or her position in the cosmos, but because she finally felt accepted for who she was—

what she was. "I could get used to it," she said. "I hear the benefits are nice. There was something about good dental for the kids, too."

"Seems you've won the respect of the others, as well."

"That helps," she said.

"Don't suppose you know what happened with Aphrodite and Hephaestus?" Alex asked. "I mean, now that he's a statue, did Zeus give her an annulment?"

"I think so," she replied. "I haven't talked to her much yet, but that's what others have been saying in quiet whispers—that and Athena gave back Divineder. Most of the gossip, however, has been guessing at what Hera's fate will be."

"Where is she?"

"No one knows," she admitted. "Zeus has her locked away somewhere, but he hasn't told anyone the specifics."

Alex's face scrunched with confusion. "Really? I wonder why."

"He's probably leery there are more spies and saboteurs still around. Doesn't want her to be freed." Euryale's voice trailed as her thoughts went back to Cronus, and more specifically, the deal she'd made with him. The titan wanted her seated over them all, and that little caveat to her resurrection was known only by her. Not even Alex knew of it. She wondered if—no, when—the other Olympians would question her on how and why Cronus had brought her back. When they did, would she tell them the truth or would she have to lie? If she opted for the former, would they even believe she didn't want to usurp Zeus's reign, or would they see her as they now saw Hera, a traitor to them all?

Euryale didn't have an inkling to any of that. Thankfully, Alex cut into her thoughts and redirected them...somewhat.

"That makes sense," Alex said. "I wonder what he's going to do with her."

"I shudder to think," Euryale admitted. "I'm sure we'll find out soon enough."

She furrowed her brow, and her eyes darted around the room. "You know, I never did ask...well, I guess it doesn't matter. Might be rude, regardless."

"Ask what?"

"Who proposed I should be elevated to this position," she said. "Do you think it was Athena? We did rescue her, after all. Or maybe Zeus?"

"I'm insulted you even have to ask," said a new voice.

Euryale turned to find Aphrodite standing a few feet away. Her injuries had far from healed. Clumps of her hair were gone. Her skin was shiny and leathery from countless burns, and the digits on both hands were either stubs or missing altogether. Up until now, Euryale hadn't appreciated how hot the lava had been—so hot that not even Apollo was going to be able to heal her injuries without copious amounts of time. Still, despite her grievous wounds, she had a smile on her disfigured face and Ares at her side with his arm around her waist.

"I didn't want to presume," Euryale said, stammering. "I'm sorry, I—"

Aphrodite held up a hand and gave a stern look. "Euryale, if you're going to be one of us, there are two things you must absolutely remember."

Euryale nodded. "Go on."

"First, we don't apologize," she said with a playful grin. "And second, we're never, ever wrong."

Euryale laughed. "I'll keep that in mind."

"See that you do." With that, Aphrodite turned and led Ares away. She went a few paces before turning back around. "Oh, Euryale, one last thing."

"Yes?"

"Athena would like to see you when you get a chance," she said. "Something about finding one of her missing heroes...Perseus, I think. Anyway, I'm sure the two of you will get that sorted out in no time."

A Storm of Blood and Stone
Myths of Stone Book III

What she wanted was to reunite with her exiled sister.

What she got was a betrayal that left her with a broken body and a shattered family.

Euryale had always tried to live her life in peace, but clearly that was a mistake. Now, the gorgon is determined to rise from the ashes, save those she loves, and lay waste to all who wronged her.

And if that means making pacts with the darkest, most powerful beings in all of creation to burn Olympus to the ground, so be it.

Acknowledgements

I have to thank all the fans of *The Gorgon Bride* for giving it a shot and making it such a hit. Without all of you, this book would never have been created.

I also sincerely appreciate everyone—fan and critic alike—who expected, wanted, and even demanded more Euryale. I hope I've met those expectations and done her justice. She's great fun to write, and I love her as the lead.

Natasha, you will forever have a special place in my writing heart for breathing such wonderous life into all of these characters.

Crystal, as always, you are nothing short of a spectacular editor, and along that front, Katrina Roets, you did a wonderful job going over the copy one last time so I could keep my sanity.

Last, and never least, I have to thank the Mrs. and the kids for putting up with me when I obsess over daily word counts and drive myself into a frenzy trying to get things "just right."

Now I need a drink so I can get myself ready to turn out book three and hopefully make it worthy of the gods.

About the Author

When not writing, Galen Surlak-Ramsey has been known to throw himself out of an airplane, teach others how to throw themselves out of an airplane, take pictures of the deep space, and wrangle his four children somewhere in Southwest Florida.

He also manages to pay the bills as a chaplain for a local hospice.

Drop by his website https://galensurlak.com/ to see what other books he has out, what's coming soon, check out the newsletter (well, sign up for the newsletter and get access to awesome goodies, contests, exclusive content, etc.)